DRY YOUR SMILE

DRY YOUR SMILE

SMILE *a novel*

❋ Robin Morgan

Doubleday & Company, Inc.
Garden City, New York
1987

This is a work of fiction. Any resemblance to
actual events, locales, or persons, living or dead,
is not intended and is purely coincidental.

Library of Congress Cataloging-in-Publication Data

Morgan, Robin.
  Dry your smile.

  I. Title.
PS3563.087148D7   1987   813'.54   86–32972
ISBN 0-385-23226-8

For Lois Kahaner Sasson

"Of course you appropriated me—but too much."
—Wolfgang Amadeus Mozart
in a letter to his father, Leopold

Contents

DRY YOUR SMILE

EXPRESSIONS OF LOVE ✻ A Novel

"When a woman loves a woman,
it is the blood of the mothers speaking."
—Caribbean proverb

PART ONE

September, 1980

Momma's funeral service failed to reassure me.

For one thing, it was being held at the Church of the Resurrection. In the Performing Arts Chapel. For another, there was no body—a combination of events which conspired to make me feel as if the real action were taking place somewhere else, offstage. I don't mean offstage at the cremation, that imagined twilight-zone affair of smoke pots and dry ice, or even offstage behind the altar of the church, where the Channel 2 remote news team huddled, hissing curses at one another because their mobile generator had gone dead and they had to plug into the sacristy. No, I mean offstage in her cluttered co-op on Sutton Place, where at that moment she had slammed down the phone on her stockbroker and given herself up to the loud pleasure of sucking marrow from the chicken bone she had been splintering with her teeth, for emphasis, during her conversation with Trackill, Trackill, Bray, Greenbach, and Jones.

Momma's funeral service was proof only that no matter how many times you buried her, she rose and walked again, unanswerably shrewd folk sayings rich on her tongue and merciless love for you watering in her eyes.

So there was nothing to do but proceed through the charade of a service, trying to fix one's expression to attentiveness as various aging American actors each adopted individual ver-

sions of British accents in their procession to the pulpit to
eulogize her. Then it was my turn. The only member of the
"Family" company left alive—unless you considered it possible
to remain alive in Los Angeles, where my erstwhile onscreen-
and-in-living-color father and older brother now lived, still
trying to survive in what has come to be called the television
industry. I hadn't wanted to come to the memorial service to
speak "on behalf of the cast"—had dreaded it, actually—but
the temptation to bury her proved, as always, too strong. So I in
my turn ascended the pulpit and lugubriously intoned from
my notes how Elizabeth Clement had been a great actress to
the world and really a second mother to me, how I had had the
good fortune to grow up under her influence and to work with
her for almost a decade, an unheard-of privilege for a child
actor.

I scrupulously avoided any mention of how her temperamental scenes had embarrassed me, since even at age six I was
not indulged in such tantrums. Or of how imperiously she had
treated her maid, an elderly black woman called only "Rose,"
who taught me how much a single look at someone's turned
back can mean. Or of how in sympathy Clement had been with
the red-baiting blacklist against leftist actors during the Joe
McCarthy years. I spoke, instead, about her love of fine things
—flower arrangements, music, the theater, vintage wines. I
spoke of her generosity, and the annual party she used to
throw for the "Family" company at her country house—a lavish ritual we all, and myself as a child especially, looked forward to each year, a ritual over which she presided in the
grand manner of hospitality. I spoke about the grace with
which she had made the transition from her decades of "legiti-
mate" stage work to the small-screen intimacy of a television
series. I neglected mentioning that this transition seemed to
have caused her as much personal discomfort as did the notorious migraines she attributed to it, convinced to her dying day
at age eighty-seven that despite the wealth the series had
brought her, she was somehow slumming to have become a
household word. I eulogized properly. I euphemized. I lied.
Which turned out to be excellent preparation for the Actors'
League memorial reception scheduled for immediately after
the service.

There, assembled over drinks surprisingly stiff considering

that we were gathered in the Parish House, we drank her a toast, at least half the room silently wishing for her a flowering stake in the heart. Maybe it was the overstrong vodka and tonic after only coffee for breakfast, but the naïve theatricality of the toast touched me: the gesture was sufficiently blatant to lend itself innocence—the way Kabuki theater defies an audience to notice its visible stagehands. So when the tall, chic woman with frosted hair approached me, dressed-for-success in her business suit, her familiar double martini in hand, I was tipsily reconciled to being sentimental.

"My *god,*" she declaimed. "It's The Baby!"

"The very one, Paulie," I smiled back gamely, "Forty next year, escaped from the business, a writer, married: The Baby."

We brushed cheeks. She still wore Tigress. I hadn't smelled it in years.

"Well, of course I knew you'd left the business long ago, and I'd heard you'd become some sort of book writer—I mean not for TV—and got married." She banged her glass against mine in what I took to be congratulations. "Never could understand," she went on. "You had real talent. Christ, you were a fucking *star.*"

"I don't know whether to say thank you or offer an apology."

"Well. So," she sighed, "any best sellers yet? Or are you a mother? Ever thought of writing scripts? Still married?"—managing to register rapid-fire disappointment and insult under the cover of interest.

"No to the first three questions, I'm afraid. I write poetry, and my prose books are about women, political stuff. I doubt I could ever write a TV script. So I work as a free-lance editor, too. But yes to the fourth question. At least I was still married when I left the house two hours ago. The same man, almost twenty years."

"Sweet Judas! I don't see how *any*body can live with *any*body for twenty years! It's psychotic." She drained her martini and reached for another from a tray offered by the passing caterer.

"Well, maybe you have a point. But there it is." Then, trying to parry her thrust, "What about you, Paulie? You hardly look a day older than you did when I was seven. Didn't I read somewhere you'd left writing nighttime sit-com shows behind and

gone on to writing soap operas? Aren't you famous now? Paola
Luchino, the Suds Queen?"

"Well, I'm a long way from the wop ghetto in Brooklyn,
dearie, where *I* grew up. And we call them daytime dramas,
sweetie-pie," she purred. "I know you women's libbers are
down on all that, but we believe we're providing a vital service
—romance, excitement, glamour—to all those dreary housewives. An escape. You know, from Dullsville."

This was dangerous. I could feel my canines lengthening and
fur sprouting on my palms.

"Actually, Paulie," I began, in my tight surely-we-can-be-
rational voice, "the women's movement is saying that home-
makers don't lead such contemptuous lives, after all. That they
deserve respect as much as women with paying jobs—"

"—that they take *pride* in their truly *invaluable* work. Yes,
sweets, we all know the feminist jargon. You gals need better
scriptwriters. If you're one of 'em, you ought to go back to the
drawing board—or the typewriter. Me, I use a word proces-
sor."

It felt oddly the same as when she used to riffle my bangs and
coo, "Our Baby Bernhardt is growing too fast. We're going to
have to put bricks on her head to keep her television's favorite
wee girl." She made me feel simultaneously malicious and
powerless.

"It may sound like jargon, Paulie, but it happens to be true.
Housewives *are* proud of what they do, believe it or not." I
sounded defensive to myself, and I knew I was spouting rhetoric, but I couldn't stop. Then, all at once, I understood where I
was going and discovered, after so many years, the weapon
with which to counterattack. I sipped my drink and smiled.
"There's a, well, a whole new pride lots of women are feeling.
Like, for instance, younger lesbian women being proud of who
they are and refusing to cower all their lives in the closet, the
way so many older women were forced to."

I had hit my mark. Her face fractured along tiny fissures of
seasoned pain—and I felt instantly rotten. *You are a heel,* I told
myself, *you are not only Politically Incorrect, you are also an
idiot who has let yourself be reduced to saying something
nasty you wanted to say to Paulie for totally other reasons
when you were eight years old but only now have the adult
capacities—of perception and viciousness—to articulate.*

"Oh hell, Paulie, I'm sorry. What I really meant was—" But my attempt to make amends was smothered in the bear-hug of a round, bald, beaming little man who abruptly precipitated himself into our conversation.

"It's the *Trooper!* Julian!" he yelped, and only when I had extricated myself from his embrace could I recognize Abe Gold, the show's former assistant director who had taught me how to play a mean game of poker during rehearsal breaks. I greeted him with genuine pleasure and refrained from blurting out how he seemed to have been the victim of a trade leaving him with more flesh and less hair. Abe dutifully shook hands with Paola, but when she murmured something about having to dash to an ad-agency meeting, he and I exchanged a glance of mixed relief and guilt.

"Say, you were sure good at the service, Julian. Classy. Too bad about Miss Clement, huh? Still, she lived to a ripe old age, didn't she? But how's your real mom, kid? She okay?" It was classic Abe, showing the same solicitude and directness that used to get him into chronic trouble—like the day he had actually dared ask Elizabeth, "Jeez, Miss Clement, you paying Rose enough, I hope? She sure works her ass off for you."

"Hope? Hope's not so good, Abe," I answered, hearing the Paola-brittleness drain from my tone. "She has an awful disease, in fact. One that affects the nervous system."

"Aww, kid, that's too bad. Funny, she always talked about her nerves, too, ya know?"

"Oh yes, I know. Growing up, I used to think 'nerves' was a disease in itself."

"I mean, there you'd be, whoopin' around, doin' kid things on some five-minute break, and there Hope would be, saying 'Don't do that, honey, quiet down. Remember my nerves.'" He looked suddenly apologetic. "Oh, hey, I don't mean you goofed off a lot or anything like that. You were a real pro."

"Thanks, Abe. It's nice to hear that, especially from you."

"Yeah, a pro. So much so, you scared the shit out of me sometimes."

I couldn't help laughing. No wonder I'd liked him.

"Look, kid, I didn't mean any offense—"

"No, no, I didn't misunderstand you. Don't worry, Abe, you were always great. You never patronized me, always treated

me as if I were a person. You treated everyone decently, in
fact."

"Well, I dunno about all that . . . but what *is* it with Hope,
anyway? This time it's serious?"

"Very serious, I'm afraid. Not just 'nerves.' It's something
called Parkinson's disease. There's no cure for it, just medication to slow the degeneration. Sometimes there are temporary
remissions, but eventually . . ."

"Aww, kid. Damn. I'm real sorry. What a shame. But she's a
strong lady, isn't she? Comes from Ashkenazic stock, Polish-
Russian Jews, just like me. Don't I remember right? She never
liked to talk much about that, though," he trailed off, mourn-
fully.

"You have a gift for understatement. She changed all her
names. Hokhmah to Hope. Broitbaum to Baker and—then to
Travis. How more Anglo can you get? No, claiming her roots
was never Momma's favorite hobby. On the contrary, she
reinvented them all the time. Still does, god love her."

"Oh well," Abe continued, never one to be dislodged from a
nonjudgmental stance, "my father shortened Goldenblatt to
Gold."

"Abe, dear Abe. There's a difference between the half-
hearted disguise and the outright disavowal, you know."

"Huh? Well, anyhow, I sure am sorry, kid," he summed up,
about everything or nothing in particular. "So, look, give her
my love when you see her? Tell her Abe Gold remembers her
and says hello and that she should get well real soon." It was
hard to tell whether Abe's flat-out rejection of tragedy made
him a simpleton or a saint.

"I'm going over to her apartment right after this, in fact, and
I'll tell her," I reassured him.

"Right after *this?* Whew. Heavy day, kid."

So he was no simpleton. We embraced again and he drifted
off. It was another half-hour—of small talk, gossip about the
threatened Actor's Equity strike, reminiscences about Elizabeth Clement that were lovingly etched with acid, and never-
to-be-used telephone numbers exchanged with promises to
"get together for lunch soon"—before I was able to make my
way out of the fake Romanesque building and into the light
drizzle falling on West Forty-eighth Street.

Walking felt good despite the cold, no cab was in sight anyway, and procrastinating a visit to Momma was always in order. Besides, talking to Abe had reminded me of some of the good times, and I wanted to savor them, go over them like a litany, the way I used to in my twenties when I would catch friends regarding my childhood with horror and pity, as if it had been a latter-day version of some Judy Garland–Hollywood scandal: drugs, orgies, and depravity.

"Look," I would patiently explain to my captive listener and myself, "I was spared the rejection experience of lots of child actors, those endless routings in and out of casting offices. No matter what other parts I played—more dramatic, more creative, more satisfying—this job remained steady for seven years, the heart of my childhood, playing the daughter in a not too badly written series about a Swedish immigrant family. Most of the time, the scripts managed to avoid mere wholesomeness. Some of the time they actually grappled with issues of poverty and ethnic discrimination. Some of the time, too, the company really did serve as a surrogate family for an only child like me, raised in an all-female world of a single mother and aunts." Friends would nod sympathetically.

It was raining harder now, and I began to walk faster, searching in earnest for a taxi. *Look at it this way,* I muttered to myself in a familiar personal mantra, because all thought-roads seemed to lead back to Her, *the series earned you quite a bit of money before you even turned fourteen, money which, though never at your own disposal, nonetheless kept Momma more than comfortable in her Sutton Place co-op. Moral: you don't have to support an elderly parent now, because you unwittingly provided for that by age fifteen. Besides, you know by this time that holding firm to a sense of irony may yet save you from the cliché bitterness of the ex-child star, godforbid.* These self-lectures usually had a bracing effect, and today a further positive reinforcement against self-pity pulled up in the shape of a free taxi.

The doorman of Momma's building eyed me with disdain as I passed by him. I might be dressed up on *this* occasion, but he had seen me too often in jeans and navy pea jacket to be fooled. Even as I moved across the lobby, sinking into the plush carpet at each step, the old hit of anxiety, dread, and longing began to seep through my veins like some addictive drug. Rising in the elevator, I wondered when I might learn that I would never get through to her, when I would ever be at peace with that knowledge.

"Just a minute! I'm on the phone! Use your key!" she shouted in answer to the doorbell chime. It was a small point of contention among so many others—that I should use the key she'd given me. I claimed I didn't want to use it except in emergencies; that it was an invasion of her privacy, even when she knew in advance that I'd be coming, like today. She claimed it was for her convenience, so she wouldn't have to get up and answer the door. The subtext was that her doctor had said she *should* try to move about, that exercise was crucial to stave off muscle atrophy. The *sub*-subtext was that she wanted to believe I still lived there and used the key as if it were to my home—while I wanted to assert that I was a visitor, even a stranger, on her premises. First skirmish lost. I found her key in my purse and let myself in.

"Anaconda Copper is down *what?*" she was saying sharply over the phone. I peeled off my coat and took advantage of her preoccupation with her broker to adjust myself yet again to the astonishment that was her apartment.

Here, on the twelfth floor of one of Manhattan's best buildings, Momma had managed to create a high-baroque slum. Pink marble lamps in the shape of cherubs shed their glow through shades festooned with torn, dust-gray lace. The faded champagne-brocade sofa was piled with papers—stock-market proxies, canceled checks, past issues of *The Wall Street Journal,* months-old undone "To Do" lists scribbled on yellow legal-pad sheets. The television blared a "daytime drama." Along the walls, ladies billowed their skirts from summer garden swings in Fragonard-type prints hanging crookedly amid a tapestry of framed photographs. The Baby in front of a microphone at age four, anchoring her very own radio show. The Baby in tutu, on point. The Baby tap-dancing at a charity benefit for paraplegic children. The Baby selling U. S. Savings Bonds. Even as a teenager, The Baby was always smiling. I turned away, and spied a cockroach ambling across a corner of the once-splendid Bokhara carpet. Stomping on it brought relief.

"Sit down," she barked, half covering the phone receiver with one hand. "I'll get rid of this schmuck in a second. Eat something," gesturing toward the open box of stale canoles on the cardtable that still served as her desk. Then back into the phone at high decibel, *"No,* dammit. I said *sell* the Marietta Mining and *buy* more of the AT&T!"

The chairs had succumbed to the same fate as the sofa. There was nowhere to sit except on her bed, now plonked in the middle of the livingroom, and she was already on it. I chose to walk around. But the apartment was an emotional minefield.

Bric-a-brac, furry with dust. More cherubs and cupids. Porcelain rabbits from the Danube Valley. A demitasse in a wooden stand. An open-box-displayed fake turquoise and silver bracelet. And an occasional eclectic intruder into this Kitsch City—a carved ivory buddha, a genuine Sèvres plate, a lone teakwood chess queen, a gold-plated tea strainer. It was a collection to no purpose and of no consistency. Some of the pieces she had been told were "valuable," some actually were, some she had bought because they were "cute," some were gifts, some she had kept out of sentiment or superstition. Most of all she hated to throw anything away.

I turned to the bookshelves, the safest spot in the room. There *they* were, also dusty, leaning drunkenly this way and that, but their power still intact—the magic that had sustained me. My childhood books, which she'd refused to let me take with me, were jealously guarded here: the *Alice,* the *Enchanted Garden,* the *Arabian Nights,* the Dickens and Stevenson and *Oxford Collection of Children's Poetry.* And the later treasures: my *Complete Stories and Parables of Kafka,* which she herself had once loved. And here, Blake's *Songs of Innocence* and *Songs of Experience,* which she'd also cherished. And my first copy of Lao Tzu, which she'd given me, with her own inscription, "Let emptiness fill your life, and you will never be prey to greed."

I knew tears were on their way to stinging my eyes even before I felt them. What could you do to heal such a life, without going under in sacrificing your own again? Hundreds of women—strangers—you could help, but not this one woman. *Shit!* I whispered fiercely to myself, brushing at my eyes as I heard her bang down the phone.

"So where have you been?" she started in briskly. "I could have died."

"I was here just day before yesterday, as usual. You look fine. *Hello,* Momma," I said, moving to where she sat, a wasted buddha plumped on her pillows. *Control and restraint,* I told myself, that's the key.

I reached over to kiss her and was struck by the slightly sour smell of her flesh. Her housecoat was stained with food drips. Control and restraint.

"Momma, you've really got to let me do something about the state of this apartment. Let me do a laundry, a big cleaning. Have the place repainted, even. Get the carpets cleaned and some exterminators in. Maybe even get you to see a new doctor? The works." It came out in a rush, too brightly, lacking authority.

"Leave it!" she snapped, as I stooped to pick up a used Kleenex by the side of the bed. "I know where everything is. I like it just this way. The last time I came home from the hospital and you'd done one of your 'the works' I couldn't find anything for weeks. As it is, that woman you got to come in and fluff up pillows and bring groceries every day drives me crazy."

Long-suffering Mrs. Dudinsky. How she pitied Momma, but also how many pleadings, on the average of twice a month, it took from me to get her to continue, in the face of Momma's abuse.

"All right, *all right,*" I mumbled, my voice already taking on the vintage tone of pacification. "At least let me turn down the TV."

"Turn it off," she commanded, "I never watch the thing anyway."

I switched off one of Paola Luchino's soap heroines in mid-anguish, removed the bathrobe and the Annual Report of IBM dumped on a wobbly French Provincial chair, added these two items to the precarious paper Alps on the sofa, and lowered myself carefully to a seat.

"You didn't call today, Julian honey." She settled in, feeling things were normal at last.

"Momma. I call every day and come up every other day. You know that. Don't you remember yesterday I said on the phone I'd be by as always today but I wouldn't call this morning at the usual time because I had to go to Elizabeth Clement's funeral?"

"Oh yeah," she mumbled with disinterest. Then, "You wore pants to a funeral?"

"These are silk slacks, Momma. With a silk shirt. This is the way I dress up. These are in dark blue, even. Respect for the dead and all that. Nobody minded." Not exactly the truth, since the president of the Actors' League had raised his eyebrows at my forked legs and the Episcopal minister appeared to have mild indigestion as I mounted his pulpit.

"Well," she shrugged, "your life is your own."

"Yes. It is."

"Ruin it as you choose."

Evasive action was called for.

"Abe Gold was at the service, Momma. Remember him? The A.D. who was always so nice? He asked after you and sent you his love. You wouldn't recognize him. He's gone bald—completely, like Yul Brynner!"

"So? I don't know what you're talking about. Everybody goes bald. Or dies. Even that bitch Elizabeth Clement."

"Channel 2 was there, covering the service." Sly boots, I knew how to pique her interest.

"You're kidding! Will it make the six o'clock news, d'ya think? Oh God, and you in *pants.*"

"I doubt it'll make the news, Momma. They were having some sort of equipment trouble." Lift her up, drop her. Were most conversations between grown children and their parents war games?

We paused for a breather. Then she was into the field again.

"So. And how is *he* these days?"

"Laurence is fine, Momma. Everything's fine." Why tell her we'd been up until three, crying together again over whether we should separate? Why tell her if it would only bring her pleasure?

"You're still living *there?* And you say 'everything's fine'?"

"If you mean my home, Momma, yes, I'm still living where I lived day before yesterday, and for almost twenty years before that. And it still happens to be the Chelsea area. Oh come *on,* darling. You ought to be used to it by now! They say it'll even be fashionable in a few years."

"I'll never get used to it! Why should I? You live in a slum!"

I glanced at the Collier brothers surroundings she had accrued in the middle of Sutton Place and thought of my polished wide-plank wood floors at home, the sunny loft windows, the Franklin stove crackling away with real logs, the whitewashed walls and exposed brick, the books neatly lining their shelves, the green masses of plants, the understatement and order.

"Well, then, learn to laugh about it," I answered instead. "Don't you think it's funny that every big financier talks about how he worked his way up from a poor neighborhood to Sutton Place—while I chose to work my way in the other direction?"

She snorted. "I'm dying from amusement. 'When the Tsar plays peasant, the peasants should watch out.' "

"Well, let's see . . . *I* know. Here's something that *will* please you. I'm giving a poetry reading in Boston next week and they called yesterday to say five hundred tickets had been sold. In advance! How about *that?*" I wound up with a triumphant flourish.

"How much are you getting paid?"

"Well, actually, I'm not. It's a benefit, Momma. For a feminist newspaper up there. But it's a really good cause. See, these newspapers mean a lot to, well, just hundreds of women who depend—"

"I'm not hundreds of women. I'm *me.* I'm your mother. 'What's done for free always costs.' I don't like people taking advantage of you. I don't like it how that husband of yours doesn't have a job, either."

"That's not *true*, Momma. Laurence works free-lance, just like I do . . . Oh, and Momma, I might have an article accepted by *Harper's?* And I finished correcting galleys on my new book yesterday?" She had managed to reduce my statements to questions, as always.

"Oh," she answered, "that's nice." Her eyes glazed over with boredom, then came to life again as the telephone rang. Saved by the bell, I lit a cigarette, went and rummaged up a saucer from the kitchen for an ashtray, stomped another cockroach en route, and sat down again to watch her as she talked, animatedly now, on the phone.

Once, she had been so beautiful. A delicately boned face with features exquisitely chiseled, huge dark-brown eyes, what I'd come to call her Nefertiti neck, and that incredible alabaster skin—her flesh so pale and fine-pored as to seem translucent. She'd always been overweight, of course, ricocheting from merely plump to quite fat, perpetually on one diet or another. Growing up, I knew when a lot of eggs appeared that we were going on The Mayo, when steaks filled the freezer that we were Doing Protein, when bowls of bananas sat on every table that we were embarking on The Bland. Still, she *had* been beautiful, and not only to a child's perception. Even now, I could look at old photographs of her with adult objectivity but admiration. That luminous skin, those fawnlike eyes. The perfect teeth in a radiant smile. No matter what happened, her smile, when beamed full on its fortunate recipient, descended like a blessing.

Now only the eyes were left—still large, black, clear. Her features had slid almost imperceptibly sideways since the minor stroke. Years of being overweight left sacs of loose flesh on her body, as she grew thinner from loss of appetite, lack of muscle tone, nerve degeneration. Bat-wings of skin swung from her underarms, the color of the flesh a light sepia, the texture like clotted cream. Worst of all were the tremors, because of what they did to her pride. The youngest daughter of immigrants—a former rabbi and his peasant wife, the girl with a lovely voice who had dreamed of becoming an opera singer until told that performing publicly was lower than prostitution, the woman who had been afraid all her youth of poverty and ignominy until a shining precocious daughter came into her life—all that woman ever had was her pride.

Could she, then, have died of a heart attack—quick, clean? No, she had been cursed with a lingering degenerative disease that could take up to a quarter-century to run its course, one for whom the hallucination-inducing, blood-clot-provoking medication was almost as dangerous as the malady. None of this she acknowledged. She simply tremored. But the pride wouldn't let her tremble in public—a coffee cup clattering uncontrollably as she set it down in a restaurant, an occasional dribble down the chin, the terrifying unmaneuverability of a street curb. Not quite a recluse yet, she nonetheless had made it clear, unspoken, that she was choosing this path, and when those huge eyes seemed to plead *I can suffer pain but not humiliation,* I committed myself to respecting her decision. For six years, she had consistently refused to accept the identical diagnoses of three separate doctors. And she still ignored medication. The shoebox kept under her bed brimmed with unfilled prescription slips.

Now she was flirting by phone with her broker of over three

decades. Surely he must know . . . or was this a reliable, compassionate game between them?

"Well, handsome, before I go out for dinner with you, I'd
have to buy something new and *very* special to wear, no?" She
winked at me. Oh those eyes. I couldn't help winking back.
"And I'd need some better dividends for that, don't you think?
So look, you just be a lamb and do what I say, like always. I
don't care what boom *might* happen if Reagan gets elected in
two months. I want *blue chips,* not those goddamned money
markets, you understand? Don't give me trouble. Don't make
me nervous."

Still the manipulator with the eyes of God. And I, a grown
woman with a messed-up life of my own, still afraid of her, still
afraid *for* her, still strung taut as a violin string with pity for
her, still loving her hopelessly.

I was grateful for the phone-call interruptions. Little atolls in
a pacific of grief, they made these meetings bearable. In another hour I could go. Home to Laurence where nothing was
resolved. Abe Gold was right: heavy day, kid. I got up and
began to wander around again, as if the room might this time
yield a secret exit I'd overlooked for years.

But I didn't want to go into the bedroom, where she and I
had slept in twin beds right up through my adolescence until I
finally left, penniless, but with a secretarial job and at least with
a walk-up room of one's own in Yorkville. No, the bedroom had
been turned into some Luis Buñuel version of a shrine: hideous
calf-length full skirts of the 1950's, pastel Capezio shoes, pill-
box hats, a dyed-blond beaver coat, a white mink capelet. The
dresser boasted my Honor Student citation framed in rose
velvet matting, the New York State piano competition medal
for first prize (third-year students), two acting awards, a ballet
competition trophy, the Golden Record earned by sales of my
one and only recording, and the "Ideal American Girl" special
citation from the American Federation of Women's Auxiliaries.
The doll collection was arranged on what had been my bed, all
their glass and plastic and painted eyes still wide with unblink-
ing wonder, their legs stiffly spread for balance, their arms
rigid and outstretched. No, enduring the clutter of the livingroom was preferable to entering the bedroom.

She hung up the phone. But I knew I was safe when she
began to talk about the market. I had long ago ceased to de-

claim, "But Momma! The rights of labor! Deforestation, strip mining, multinationals!" I had quite given that conversation up by the time I was twenty-three, exhausted. It was ceded terrain now, all hers. In that sense, safe for me. Now she was off on the bastard at Trackill *et al.* not having informed her in time about a hot new issue, and how she dropped a bundle on that one but was going to make a killing this time.

"Make some tea, Baby," she finished cheerfully, not waiting for my response. "You shouldn't smoke. I have to call my other broker. 'Never hide all the silver in one hole.' Then we'll have a nice cup of tea."

Washing the kettle, the pot, the cups and saucers and spoons before using—all this bought more time. I could hear her chattering cozily away on her life line, content that I was simply here. How long had it taken to learn such an obvious thing? That it was my mere physical presence she required, not *who* I was, most especially not who I had become. But the *what* of me still delighted her. She alone could see baby teeth in my adult smile, child-star long blond curls in my short brown hair, fear and love still fighting each other for supremacy in every glance I paid her. Danger to *talk* about anything, anyway: politics, religion, sex—all the subjects forbidden for polite dinner conversation in 1890—were still off limits with her in 1980. But so was her health. So was my writing. So were her friends (almost all turned away now from pride), my friends ("hippies and bohemians"), her liaison with my father, and my marriage to Laurence. The weather was a safe subject. Also Old Times— although less safe for me. Danger to think she'd ever be proud of anything I'd accomplished since Old Times. Danger to try to show her my writing. Whether she was afraid she couldn't understand it or afraid she could, she would transform the shy gift of a manuscript into a bedtable coaster for her water glass; I could watch it lie there, gathering dust and accumulating glass-rings, pages beginning to curl, until I would by unspoken agreement quietly remove it when she wasn't looking. A published book, on the other hand, would be propped up on the paper-strewn cardtable as if on display for friends who rarely were allowed to visit. A published book would at least be examined in my presence, the jacket criticized ("They could've printed your name bigger; you still have fans out there, you know, who might buy books"). A published book laid as an offering before the bedclothes of the throne would at least elicit a kiss, a "Congratulations, dear," and momentarily misty eyes—though whether misty with pride or loss one couldn't tell—before the advance copy was handed back.

"But it's yours, Momma. This copy is for you. See? I inscribed it for you, and—"

"That's lovely, Julian, that's nice. Put it on the cardtable, Baby. I'll look at it later."

Which would close the subject.

Maybe standing in the kitchen and watching the kettle come slowly to a boil did it, the water gathering heat so that its molecules whirled faster and began to break surface in small and then larger bubbles—like the circular-conversation battle with Larry the previous night, the duel with Paulie that morning, the millionth non-encounter exchange here with Hope. I began to get angry. A healthy, "empowering" emotion, all the shrinks said, but an emotion that somehow felt self-indulgent and counterproductive, one small step on the well-intentioned path toward nuclear warfare. Still, the kettle lid began to hiccup with contained pressure, and I decided Okay, Julian, Let's Get Angry Constructively. Let's go in there and say . . . what? Momma, you've got to see a doctor again. Momma, you have Parkinson's, face it. Momma, one defense against getting sicker faster is to move about, try to live life as usual, hard as that is. Momma, you have to let me clean up this place and get somebody to help keep it decent. Momma, life is not just the Dow Jones Index and the constant television you claim not to watch. *To hell with restraint and control,* I told myself. *You are a grown woman, Julian. How about firm?*

She was lying back on her pillows, eyes closed, when I brought the tea in and cleared away proxy notices from the cardtable in order to put the tray down. Then poured two cups and brought her one, with extra sugar, just as she liked it. I cleared my throat, nervous because I was sure what her reaction would be (no difficulty in expressing anger, not her), and because I was equally *un*sure of what actors always call "the motivation." Elements of loving concern, common sense, and sadism were woven through any decision of mine to talk to her about The Illness. An especially treacherous ethical ground when one knew one could pull off an act of revenge via a gesture of ostensible *caritas.* Truth as a bludgeon. How expert Laurence and I now were at using that against each other.

"Hope," I began.

"You know I don't like that," she said wearily, her eyes still closed. "I'm your mother, not a name."

"Momma, then. Look, we really—"

"You remember that story? Way back from some book? I was thinking about that story. Something about a mole making tunnels. He was scared a fox or whatever would get into one of his tunnels. He kept on making more and more of them but then he had to keep the ones he'd already made from crumbling and be sure the entrances were kept unblocked for air but still kept small enough so no bigger animal could get in but he could get out if he had to. And he kept running around to all his tunnels all the time, checking and fixing them up and rechecking. Remember? What story was that?"

I set the cup down gently in a small diamond of space on her bedside table, and stood there feeling the rug being whisked from under my feet. Where had this come from? Beyond pain, beyond fury, beyond fear or love or even renewable amazement, the *awe* of her struck me again. An unerring virtuoso at coincidence, a maestro of emotional derring-do, of the disarming statement, the shocking insight that threw all one's tactical troops, however well marshaled, into disarray.

She opened her eyes and looked at me, mildly accusing, as if she'd caught me not knowing my next line in answer to the cue she'd just fed me.

"What story was that, Baby?"

I cleared my throat again. "It was 'The Burrow,' Momma. One of Kafka's greatest parable stories." Could it be pushed further? "It's—it's about terror and denial and hoarding—"

"Yeah, yeah. Poor little animal." She sighed.

"What made you think about that, Momma?"

She wheeled in her tunnel and glared at me.

"Nothing. I just happened to remember it, that's all. I have to give reasons?"

That entrance blocked. No numbskull fox was going to get in that way.

"I saw the Kafka stories on the bookshelf just now. Want me to get it for you? Would you like to reread it?"

"You know reading gives me a headache."

"Well, you read those bloody stock reports all the time without complaining. But . . . if you like, I'll read it aloud to you . . ." Already on my way to the bookcase, self-righteously mature, in control, bliss in the heart at a possibility of spending the remainder of our time together *reading*, and *Kafka*, to boot.

"Forget it," she said flatly. "Maybe some other time. We'll see."

"Momma, 'we'll see' are the two words a child of any age most dreads hearing from a parent. Come on, honest-to-god—"

"I don't want to. Please. Just sit down and have your tea." Her voice had gone plaintive now, too fatigued to bully me, resorting to a wheedle. For how long had our meetings been an exchange of weariness, a surrealistic tennis match? The ball of exhaustion is now in your court, dear, oops here it comes back to me with one whack of your devastating backhand.

I sank into the chair and swallowed some tepid tea. Silence filtered in along with the afternoon autumn light and lay on the floor in stripes cast by her half-closed blinds. Finally I put my cup down.

"I have to call Laurence now, Momma. And I have to go soon." Almost in a whisper, in case she was—as we both knew she wasn't—asleep.

"So? Call. Who's stopping you?" She wouldn't open her eyes.

Her pink Princess telephone was the same model she had wanted to get me for my sixteenth birthday, when I had crossed her by preferring a plain black regular telephone but *not* an extension, a line of my very own. We had compromised on a plain black instrument to fit in an extension jack, of course.

Laurence sounded barely awake. It was two in the afternoon. "Larry? You okay?"

"Uh, oh, Jule. Oh sure. I was just, uh, taking a nap. Where are you?" Did that mean he hadn't yet got up at all?

"I'm at Hope's. But leaving soon. I had the Clement memorial service this morning, remember? You were still asleep when I left."

"Oh that's right. I forgot. Yeah . . . I guess we should talk when you get home, huh?"

"All right. I mean . . . well, let's see how we feel. It's been a bitch of a day."

"Watch your mouth," my mother mumbled, in unconscious alliance with my feminist sisters.

"Yeah, well, I had a rough day too, you know."

"Look, I only meant—"

"Sure, sure," he finished listlessly. "See you later."

"Right. G'bye." Princess receiver into Princess cradle. Sorry, Sleeping Beauty. No prince, slender-limbed and fierce-eyed, on the way to rescue. Prince already arrived, long ago. Prince fallen asleep under the same spell. Prince snoring.

"Well, Momma," I announced, trying to establish the pre-liminaries-to-leaving atmosphere.

"You're going. So go."

"No, I'll clear away the tea first. Look, you haven't even touched yours. Would you like me to warm it up or make fresh?"

No answer. The pre-departure sulk.

"Then I'll take these into the kitchen. Mrs. Dudinsky is coming around six, isn't she? So she'll bring you your dinner and visit for a while and tidy up."

She gave her pillow a feeble punch and heaved her bulk sideways in reply.

Back in the kitchen again, washing out the cups and the teapot again, another Zen exercise in meaninglessness. Bone china, Haviland—but with fine cracks webbing the surface, chips serrating the edges. *Stupid idiot*, I thought, *stupid grown woman to stand here at this sink clasping a cup and crying. Stupid idiot to remind yourself of that favorite photograph of her, taken when she was seventeen in Mexico City, the single vacation of her life. The one free time and space she would ever know, on a prize trip as a student, when she could see the burnt-orange murals of Orozco, the Kahlo alizarine-splashed canvases, when she could break away from the Victorian shadows of the rabbinical home and stand in a bleach of lemon sunlight surrounded by trumpets of crimson hibiscus and toss back her hair and laugh into the camera lens.* Faded and cracked now, that life, like the ambering photograph, like the cup. Doomed. *Oh Momma.* If I'm the only one who remembers that long-ago-dead seventeen-year-old, the sole repository of an existence you've forgotten, so are you the only testament to some long-ago-dead image of me, smiling and curtsying, Baby Bernhardt, television's darling. Each of us haunted by the girlhood of the other. Each of us denying her own.

If only I could ever really write about it. Then I might come to understand it, forgive it. Not as some sophomoric catharsis; she would be with me past her own death and unto mine. Not as another act of vengeance against her; I alone bled from those. Not even as an expression of love; all the poems of anger or of longing I had written her, dared not show her, then dared show her, then dared surviving her indifference about—expressions of love all, they hadn't managed it. Not for her, then, and not even for me. This time, simply, to comprehend the secret—what I'd never written, though I'd sworn I had; what I'd never said, though I thought I had; what I'd never claimed as mine, though I believed I did. Had I ever committed an act pure of her? Had I ever loved anyone who wasn't her? This time, *this* time to *really* write about it, her wardrobe of faces and the faces she bequeathed me, lies appliquéd with the skill of a needleworker, possession and terror and hunger so interthreaded and unacknowledged as to become inseparable from the fabric of living itself. *Fool, you'd have to dare become her even more than you fear you already have. You'd have to burrow behind the lies she lavished on you deep to some truth you've never known. You'd have to invent her truths—the way she herself did. And could you avoid the perils of yet another tale about childhood sorrow? Could you risk tracking her ghost through every path it stalks for you, Julian? How many masks—hers, yours—would you have to peel off or layer on before finding the mask of your own? Do you dare really write it, Julian, all of it? Isn't it easier to stand at her kitchen sink and cry? And who are you crying for, anyway?*

Dry your smile, she'd always say, whenever I got teary with an attack of stage-fright (rare as time went on) or got scared being mobbed at one of those hellish personal appearances. Do not get drawn in. Cups in drainboard. Do not get sucked into scouring the kitchen. The more you clean up one thing—the greasy rotisserie, say—the more you will notice the stove-top is crusted. Control and restraint. *You call yourself an existentialist. Stop looking for miracles, then. Don't try to call her by her name.*

I got my coat from the rack by the door and crept back to

her bedside, hoping she was asleep by now. But as I bent over, she half opened her eyes and murmured,

"Poor frightened little animal. I don't understand it." She laughed drowsily. I tried to laugh, too. But all I could answer was,

"I'll let myself out. I'll use the key."

"Good girl. Call me tomorrow." Eyes already closed again.

"I love you," I whispered.

And went and locked the door quietly behind me, glancing at the mazuzaleh nailed to the doorjamb, that small gold tube containing the Hebrew writing for the sacred unpronounceable name of what they always wrote in English as "G-D." You knew what it was, and you knew everyone else knew what it was, too, but no one dared articulate it or entrust it to parchment. Like anything sacred: unnameable. As if, were it actually spoken aloud or attempted in letters of fire, the living presence would appear, manifest in terrible majesty—or else, once and for all, a hollow echo would confirm that there never had been anything there at all. And none of us knew which of the two possibilities was to be feared most.

PART TWO

October, 1941

"God! I'm dying, God! This baby's murdering me!"

"Stop with the screaming, Hokhmah. Dying you're not. Nobody's murdering nobody."

"How would *you* know?" her sister wept softly. "You can't know till you go through it! They never tell you it'll be like this —ten hours, fifteen hours, eighteen hours—"

"So it's a long labor. The world should end?" Yetta rested her knitting in her lap and looked at her younger sister. "Don't make a production. You're making it worse than it is."

"It couldn't *be* worse! It's—it's like some kind of devil inside me. It's like being—being drawn and quartered when the pain starts up. What do you know about it, Yetta?" She tried to shift position in the narrow hospital bed, but every part of her felt raw. Raw in the spine from arching and twisting, raw in the crotch from being hammered at inside, raw in the throat from screaming.

"I know you got yourself into this, that's what I know." Yetta shrugged and picked up her knitting again. "You made your bed, you lie in it." She nodded for emphasis.

"*He* was the big-shot doctor, I was the virgin, *what* was I supposed to know? Momma never told us nothing about that, and you and Essie never—"

"Don't start with the blaming everybody else, Hokhmah. It's your fault and your burden."

She peered at Yetta through the bars of the bed, her sight blurred with exhaustion and tears. The heavy-set woman sat there implacably, thighs and arms like hams, hair already going gray, her glasses slipping down her nose. Not to become like her, not to be like them. They never heard you, they refused to understand.

"Yetta," she began again, almost in a whimper, "you know I didn't want it once he said he didn't want it. What else could I do? Didn't know how to get rid of it—"

Her sister looked up sharply. "God forgive you for saying that!"

"—and nobody I could ask. God doesn't need to forgive me, God already knows I trusted Him to take it, to kill it!" She turned her face, wet with tears and sweat, to the ceiling. Plaster cracks, puke-green paint curling off, a huge flat expression with a hundred mocking grins. "It's not too late, God," she cried out, "this is punishment enough, *please* let it die and let me live. Don't let it murder me this way! Don't let it be born and kill me all my life through, either, like Momma said!"

"Momma never said nothing about killing, Momma wouldn't never—"

"She did. That's what she said to me. She stood there in that housedress, the one with the daisies blotched all over it. Her face was—like a savage."

"God *forgive* you for speaking so disrespectful of the dead! I won't let you—"

"I tried to tell her. 'Momma, please,' I said, 'Momma, I'm so sorry, please.' But you could never make Momma hear you, never."

Yetta heaved her bulk out of the chair and stood, hands on her hips, trailing yarn behind her. "How dare you, Hokhmah! *Me* she never heard. *Esther* she never heard. But *you* she always—"

"She didn't, she *didn't*. She said I was a whore. She said in the old village they'd have flogged me in public and then run me out. She kept saying 'How could you do this to me? My youngest daughter!' and then her face would shrivel up and she'd moan and wave her head from side to side. She said I deserved pain. She said if I didn't die giving birth to my curse, then I'd have to live with it all my life. One way or the other, she said, it'd destroy me, like I'd destroyed her."

"You *did* destroy her! You killed your own mother!" Yetta's jowls quivered with grief and rage.

The young woman half rose in the bed, appealing to the older who loomed above. "I didn't! You and Essie keep *saying* that, saying I killed her! That's a horrible thing to say! You only say it 'cause you know she loved me best!" She dropped back against the pillows again. "Oh, Yetta, why couldn't she forgive me? 'I turn my face from you,' she yelled. 'I never want to see you again as long as I live.' *Why?*"

"Momma dropped dead of a heart attack less than a month after you told her, Hokhmah. So? You don't think that's the same as you killing her?"

"Momma had a bad heart for years!"

"Still? The shame you brought on her, on all of us? God forgive me, but it's a blessing Poppa's dead five years, God rest his soul, so at least *he* was spared—" Yetta saw her sister's face contort suddenly. She threw her knitting to the floor and moved swiftly to the bed.

"Oh God, ohhh it's starting again. I can't stay still, can't sit can't lie on my back or side can't breathe can't bear it! It's like my bowels bursting, like something's . . . chewing at all my bones and muscles oh *God!*"

Yetta tried to grab the flailing arms.

"Hokhmah, wait, don't. Here, Hokheleh, here little one, hold on to me, hold on." She grasped her sister's fists. They spasmed open and closed again around her own in a vise.

"Yetta, oh Yetta . . . why's it *hurt* so much? It's not supposed to, nobody'd go through it if it was! There must be something wrong!"

Yetta rocked back and forth in rhythm with her sister's writhing, old enmities and judgments suspended, drowned out by the animal cries of the woman before her.

"Can't you get them to give me something? Yetta? *Oh!* Gotta be *some*thing . . . they can give me! It's 1941, not the middle ages . . . gotta be some shot or— *Oh God!*"

Her sister spoke rapidly, the pace between them accelerated by pain. "There's nothing, lovey. Nothing to give for this. Hold on. Bear it. Just hold on. A little bit more." But the other was being consumed before her eyes, a body curling and twisting like a shred of paper in flame, the breath coming in sharp grunts.

"Must be . . . *something* . . . hell burning inside me . . . oh *please* dear God . . ."

The claw-like grip on Yetta's hands ached up through her wristbones. "Hush, lovey, hush. Just a few seconds more." Then the talons began to relax slightly, the breathing came in slower gusts.

"Oh, there . . . it's letting up . . . Oh thank you, God, thank you."

Yetta eased Hokhmah back against the pillows and extricated her hands, flexing her numb fingers. She dipped a washcloth in the enamel basin by the bed, wrung it out, and bent to wipe the sweat-soaked head that was now crying soundlessly.

"Ach, Gott. Look at you. Poor little one, poor Hokheleh."

"So . . . *ashamed,*" came the whisper. "So . . . *scared.*"

It brought forth a fierce protectiveness in the older sister. "What? Why for? It's *his* shame, not yours. You got nothing to be ashamed. I didn't mean it, what I said before. Momma didn't mean nothing neither. Where's the shame? Nobody *knows.* Essie loans you the money to come here, out of state. I'm with you so you're not alone. None of Momma's friends or neighbors know, so it's no shame on her memory, see?" But the silent weeping continued. "Anyhow, you're right, Momma always loved you best, so how could she mean what she said? The firstborn in the New Country, the first real American in the family, she'd always call you, remember? For you special she'd make *kreplach* in chicken soup, and koogle, and every day when you came home from school—the first one to go from the start to an American school—she'd spread a slice of black bread with *schmaltz* for you and we'd all sit at the kitchen table and you'd tell what the education was like. Remember?"

A small smile played on the weary face below her. "Yeah. She loved me then, didn't she? She loved to hear me singing around the house while I helped with the chores." Hokhmah's tone changed. "Only later did she hate my voice."

Yetta seemed to regain her severity the moment her sister regained her pride. "That was after that highschool teacher put it into your head to be 'a real singer.' That was the start of all the trouble." She flung the cloth into the basin and stalked back to her chair.

Hokhmah ran her fingers through her matted hair and let out a bitter laugh.

"The start of all the trouble. Everything I was going to become, be, do." She laughed again, but the laugh was part sob. "Me, here in this dump of a small-town hospital. Me, who was going to sing Tosca and Marguerite on all the European stages. I was going to be beautiful and loved and rich and famous, with a God-given talent pouring out of me that would make the packed houses weep. The only thing that's going to pour out of me is blood and mucus. And a bastard."

"Momma was right to forbid it. You weren't just anybody, you were the firstborn American, the daughter of a rabbi. You should parade yourself on the stage in front of strangers? You might as well have walked the streets. God forbid. You, who won a real scholarship? Who was educated all the way through one year college even? Who got to go on a foreign-country trip?" Yetta angrily yanked a length of yarn from her ball.

"So what good did it do me? To have a door opened and then sealed shut in my face again? What good? I'm lying here like—like a whore giving birth under the bridge in the Tsar's old Kiev, instead of . . . instead of the way I imagined it: a pink room filled with flowers, my own handsome doctor husband bending over me, everything spotless and modern and . . ." The tears started again. "Not this—this *cell,* this stink of Lysol and my own sweat that turns the sheets grey. All I can taste is salt, from crying . . . When all the trouble started, you say? If Momma wanted me to suffer, she sure is having her revenge."

"Momma only wanted the best for you. That you catch a good man and give her the first real American grandchildren."

"Well, I did and I am, but not like she expected," Hokhmah muttered.

"You know I don't mean like that!" Yetta snapped. "But at least you'll be a mother, the greatest thing that can happen to a woman. Not like poor Esther, a widow already with only stillborn twins to show for it. Not like—not like me, who couldn't even get pregnant."

"I bet that's not your fault," her sister said, looking at the broad-hipped thick body in the chair. "I bet it's that goodfornothing husband of yours, that weakling from the Old Country only fit for working in the hardware store with Poppa. I bet—"

"Shut your mouth, Hokhmah. I heard enough about that already from Momma. I didn't want him in the first place. But the *oldest* daughter," she sneered, "doesn't get asked her opinion, you know. She marries who she's told to marry in the Old Country. *You* were Momma's big hope. *You* were going to be the one who would bring the whole family up, maybe marry a man rich enough to move us all to a big city where Poppa might find a temple congregation, be a real rabbi again. So Momma could be the rabbi's wife again, like back in the village."

Hokhmah unconsciously twisted and retwisted the damp bedsheet. "I *did* everything Momma said to. I quit college to help Poppa in the store. I helped her in the house. I helped Essie and you. I watched Avraham get sent *all* the way through college, and him only half so smart as me."

"Hokhmah, you crazy or what?" Yetta chided. "Avraham would need to support a family in time. You know that."

"And when Poppa died I took care of her. Other women my age had children already. That's how she'd taunt me. Never a word of thanks I stayed with her instead. All those years, singing only to myself in my room but quiet, *quiet,* so she wouldn't hear and have her heart wounded by my voice . . ."

Yetta sighed and wiped her glasses on her skirt hem. "So? Who knows? You think anybody else gets to do what they want? Life takes and does on you how it likes."

But her sister rambled on, caught up in an eerie energy of bitterness. "I saved up my pennies scrimped from household money, and I bought the music and learned them in secret—all the arias I might have sung. All of them still there, fragments of melody inside my head, snatches never coming together whole—"

"Ach, you don't even know what you're saying anymore, Hokheleh, you're so tired—"

"Never one full coming-together American meal at home. Always the day-old bread, the cheapest cuts, always either dairy or meat, always the kosher kitchen even after Momma got sick and I had to keep it, her sharp eyes spying out when I tried to sneak and not wash everything separately—dishes, silverware, pots, pans."

Yetta stared at her in amazement. "Now there's something wrong with keeping kosher? God's own Law isn't good enough

for you? Like Broitbaum wasn't a good enough name for you?
You always gotta be different?"

Hokhmah shut her eyes. "Oh, you don't know," she said
listlessly, "you don't even know what an aria *is*. What's the use
of trying to make you understand?"

"It's *him* put that into your head," Yetta grumbled. "Like
Momma said, he might as well have come from *goyim*, your
precious David. Not a religious man, not—"

"He's not Orthodox. He's an *educated* man, Yetta. And he
did always fast on Yom Kippur."

"I should give him a medal?"

"I bet him and Poppa would've liked each other, though.
Educated men, I mean—"

"Poppa knew the Talmud like a genius. Your fancy David
ain't good enough to clean Poppa's boots."

Hokhmah buried her face in the pillow. Not to have to hear
it anymore. Was that one of the reasons she had loved David?
Because he taught her that she could eat ham and lobster and
laugh about it and not be struck dead by Jehovah? Because he
recognized what she was singing when she sang? She heard
her sister rise and move about the small room, arguing with
herself.

"Empty he was, your David, behind the eyes. I saw that. I
saw it when I went with you to meet him and the other refugees at the dock. Momma knew. 'We don't got troubles enough
of our own?' she said to me. 'Now Hokhmah has to play big-
shot Miss Millionaire? She has to volunteer to sponsor some
high-class snob who just discovered pogroms exist? Some pretend *goy* who wouldn't lower himself to speak to the likes of us
in the old days?' *Nu?* Momma was wrong? Time proves."
Hokhmah could hear her busily rearranging the few items on
the bedtable. "Momma saw the emptiness, when she met
him."

"I saw it, too, Yetta," came the muffled reply, "but I knew it
was there from—from loss. Not from what Momma said—'a
soul full of scorn.' Momma kept hissing any man who could
slice cold steel through warm flesh somehow wasn't right."
Hokhmah lifted her face from the pillow. "So much for his
being a surgeon, the divine doctor I thought would please her.
The tall, light-brown-haired—almost blond even—professional
man. The German Jew, the pick of the crop, not Polish-Russian

border like us, pogrom-peasants. From Vienna yet, speaking four languages, and with the devil's cleft of a dimple in his chin."

Yetta paused in her ministrations and nervously tucked a strand of her hair back into its bun. "I never knew what to say around him," she shrugged, a gesture at indifference.

"You had plenty to say behind his back. I was reaching above my station, wasn't that it? Essie kept saying what would he want *me* for? You all thought he only wanted me for to be sponsored for citizenship. But I'd already done that, through the Jewish Refugee Committee. I knew he wanted me for—for something about *me.*"

Made uneasy by the longing in her sister's voice, Yetta retreated to her chair and lowered herself into it with a short groan. "So maybe," she offered awkwardly, "we was all just jealous." But Hokhmah, oblivious of both the offering and its cost, was helplessly tracing memories of her own loss.

"Merciful God, how I loved him! Everything about him—his immaculate hands with their clipped fingernails, the way he could order in French at a restaurant, how he took me to chamber-music concerts—even though he said the performances were 'lamentably inferior' to those in Vienna. His English was so elegant, wasn't it, Yetta? So much better than mine, and I'd grown up speaking it, even. You know my heart would just stop, for pride, when I was with him? Because he said I was pretty. And with him I was. My skin, my eyes, I could *feel* them glow. With him I always held my head high, because he said I had the throat of a woman in a Klimt painting he'd show me someday. In some museum in Vienna, that I never got to see." Yetta sat listening, an expression of spellbound wonderment on her face, like a child hearing a fairy-tale. "I *loved* him, don't you see? I loved the way he moved—crisp, never a gesture wasted. I loved even his suffering. The only one left of his whole family. Thirty-seven relatives swallowed up by the concentration camps and belched out in oven-smoke. His whole world gone. The Bechstein piano he'd learned to play Beethoven sonatas on, the fancy Biedermeier glass, the Augarten china. Skiing in Switzerland on school holidays, the Salzburg Festival every summer. Not for him the Judengasse section of Vienna. Did you know that one of his third cousins had married a Rothschilde? One of his great-uncles even converted . . ." She turned to her sister, who sat staring at her with an awestruck glimmer of comprehension. "Oh, what's the *use?*" she added in despair, "You can't possibly understand."

Stung, Yetta threw back, "I understand. I understand he *used* you. He needed to be supported in comfort while he studied to take the American medical examinations. You gotta face it, Hokhmah, *face* it!"

"You understand *noth*—" Hokhmah's fierce gaze went blank, her sight wrenched inward as if listening for where the stabbing would puncture next. "Here it comes oh God God God here it comes again . . ."

This time the pain hit as a great wave, jagged edges of agony bobbing in its sweep like shards of glass that only a thousand years of tidal ebb and flow might smooth. She went under, surfaced, gasped for air, was pulled under again. She was distantly aware of her sister moving, shouting to her, trying to hold on to her against the convulsive pull and roar. Had she once been alive? Was that it? Was that what he'd loved her for? That she'd brought him life after all that death? "You have the pulse of life in you, my dear," he'd said. She dove and swam in the hurt, a whole wide deep-sea underwater landscape of pain where she cried aloud in voiceless bubbles of oxygen *I loved him.* For having survived. For having realized what was happening to his beautiful rotting Europe. For having escaped and faked papers and crawled through sewers and worked with those surgeon's hands as a manual laborer. For moving on again and sleeping in railway stations and conning police and border officials with his perfect accents in French and Italian. For finally connecting to the Dutch underground and making it to England and to freedom . . . She floated free now, free and at home in the anguish. She was somebody else. *Est-ce toi, Marguérite, Est-ce toi?*

Somebody was calling to her. She called back to him. I was so sure I could do it, David. Triumph over the death camps, the goose-stepping armies, the neighbors who looted your family home. My singing could drown out every sound you'd been forced to hear between the last notes of a Beethoven sonata struck on your Bechstein until the evening your face showed such surprise that I could sing "Vissi d'Arte." My body, "the Rubens nude with the Klimt throat" you call it, this body that's not marked by tattooed blue numbers, this body can wipe out the silhouettes of walking human skeletons. These eyes, "dark as the Donau flowing through the Wienerwald," you say, my eyes can drown whole firmaments of yellow stars. *Il m'aime, il ne m'aime pas . . .*

Dimly, she felt a hand on her forehead and opened her eyes. But it was Yetta, not him. It was a dry flat world, alien as the cavernous deeps of pain once had been.

"I didn't know about her," she mumbled plaintively to her sister, "I didn't even know there was a 'her.' " She couldn't stop babbling through these lips so cracked they must belong to somebody else, not the lips he'd kissed. But she had to make Yetta understand. "Somebody meant for him, pledged to him by family ties. Somebody of his own class and education who'd already got out of Vienna and was waiting in London for him to settle here and then bring her as his bride. I didn't *know*," she repeated. "It never occurred to me . . ."

Yetta tried to cover her concern with a familiar harangue of harsh love. "Ach, little one, always you were arrogant. Always wearing blinders to what you didn't want to see."

She felt her eyes fill again. Was this all they could ever do, accuse?

"I thought—I thought the letters with King George's face on the stamps were from friends who'd helped him in England. I thought he wanted to marry me, that we'd spend our whole lives together and die in each other's arms. I thought someday Momma'd have to admit I'd been right to defy her. I thought he just needed—time. To feel alive again."

"You thought!" Yetta snorted. "Who are you to think? *Face* it, I tell you. You were a meal-ticket." Exasperated at her younger sister, she tried to change the subject. "You want some water? You want to smell the nice flowers I got you? See? Whachama-callits."

"Chrysanthemums." Hokhmah turned her head away again, and heard Yetta withdraw to the chair. The click of knitting needles maybe meant that her sister would leave her in peace. How could you ever make anybody like Yetta understand? But then, she herself couldn't understand. Her mind kept circling round and round what even now she couldn't believe. He'd never *said*. He'd never said a word. Not until she'd told him she was pregnant. *Colla mia! O Scarpia, avanti a Dio!* Maybe she'd still have chosen to give and do for him and feel alive in doing it. That crooked, sad smile of his that ripped her heart with pity. Like she used to rip open a garment, seam by seam, to redo it. Working as a seamstress in the custom dress shop to support him. Oh yes, for him she'd dared to leave Momma, and quickly, break with everything, start in a new place, a real city, find a tiny apartment. Work in the shop all day, get groceries, cook, clean. Endure Momma's phone calls of hatred. Quiz him for his oral exams half the night and make love with him the other half. Hold him tight and sing to him when the Nazi nightmares came haunting. Then get up and do it all over again the next day. Maybe she could have fought for him, if only she'd known what she was up against. His parents' plans for him. His loyalty to them still rising in him like a plume of smoke from the crematoria. His clinging to the one person left who shared those childhood memories of the Bechstein and the Danube, the woman he'd already become engaged to at a banquet in the Hotel Sacher right in the teeth of war rumors. If only . . .

As if she'd been eavesdropping on her sister's thoughts, Yetta interrupted them. "Stop *thinking* about him, Hokhmah. Mooning over him won't change facts. You're no baby. You're a twenty-nine-year-old woman and you're gonna have a child. We gotta think what to do. You better make up your mind, you come live with me and Jake or you go to Essie. Maybe in time you find a *decent* man to marry you and be a father to your baby. Maybe one of Jake's friends. That Shlomo, he always fancied you. In the meantime, soon as the baby's big enough, you get a job, maybe at the dress factory . . ."

Yetta's voice droned on, bleakly outlining an intolerable future that roused every cell of her sister's brain and body to resistance. Maybe it wasn't too late. Maybe she could still fight that sick old world of his, those ghosts. With her peasant energy, her Klimt throat and Rubens body, her arias. She didn't have to wind up like Yetta and Essie . . .

Hokhmah cut through her sister's plans in a furious voice. *"No.* You'll never *never* understand. I'm not *like* you! I can't *live* like you do!"

Yetta's face grew ugly with an old envy and a still older fear. "You and your fancy education, Hokhmah! How *dare* you look down on your own family? *I'm* not the one lying there pregnant by some scum who abandoned me!" She lumbered up out of the chair again and stalked over to the bed. *"Grateful* you should be, down on your *knees* with thanks to Essie and me for standing by you! You got nobody else, you hear me? *Nobody else* in the whole world!"

"I've got *me!* And I've got my baby! What makes you think when his son is born he won't change his mind and realize he wanted to marry me all along?"

"Dreamer! Crazy stupid fool! Blinders again you're wearing! You're *nothing* to him! You were an affair, a stopping-off place! You were his *whore!"*

Hokhmah struggled to sit up in bed, rage and will lifting her above the wrench of bone and muscle.

"That's what *you* say, Yetta. But I know better. *You* can't *have* any kids. But I'm going to have a son. You've never known what it's like to feel—real passion. Well, I *have.* I always wanted to feel what none of you'd ever felt, and I *have*—a sweet wild loving you'd never talk about, a—a joy in the body you always whispered didn't happen for a woman, something beyond what Momma always said was bearing it and the reward being children and then—*what?* Getting fatter, getting older, fighting with each other in Yiddish, dying?"

Yetta struck her hard, in the face. She could feel her cracked lip begin to bleed, but she wore it in triumph, like a heroic wound. Yetta was screaming at her, the way Momma had, the only way they knew how to live. She reached out and grabbed the chrysanthemums from their vase and threw them in Yetta's face.

"Get out!" she yelled. "You're coarse and vulgar and ignorant! You'll never in a million years know who I am! I don't need any of you! *Get out!"*

To her amazement, Yetta obeyed. She watched her older sister, livid with insult, gather up her belongings and huff to the door.

"Momma was right to curse you, Hokhmah! You're a crazy woman, a—a *snake,* an ungrateful—"

"And *stay* out! Forever!"

She went. She actually went.

Alone in the room, Hokhmah felt an exhilaration of freedom thrill through her. Then the fear struck, harder than Yetta's hand against her face. And with it came the next sweep of pain, drawing her down into herself, into a dark world lit only by flares rupturing along every nerve, a world where now only her own consciousness, her own voice, could keep her from going mad.

Oh . . . It's fading again, thank God.

Oh *no* . . . oh *somebody help,* I peed all over myself in that last one, didn't even know it, couldn't even feel it.

God this is so *humiliating!*

Where in hell is that—

"Nurse!"

Why me? *Perché me rimunari cosi?* Why did this have to happen to me? Just because I wanted something different from them? Things they never even *knew* about me . . . In Mexico, that time . . . for Momma and all of them I left him. Strange beautiful man. Wanted to make love to me. Sent me flowers. They never even knew what I *could* have done, didn't, for their sake. And for Your sake, damn You, God. *Te amo,* he kept whispering to me, sitting there in that sidewalk café with those little mosaic tables and the candlewax dripping down the bottle. I didn't know what to say back to him. I could feel myself getting wet and I thought how funny I must've got my period early or something so I got up and went to the ladies' room but there wasn't anything except me being wet. What in hell did I know? I was seventeen. I wanted him to love me and I didn't want to lose him or make him mad at me. So romantic he was. It was like fire, like a brand, where he touched my elbow, steering me through the crowds. His handprint on my elbow, under my short sleeve . . . But I didn't. I remembered how I'd hurt her about the singing and so I didn't. He never even got mad at me, just such a pitiful smile when I told him I couldn't. I cried. He kissed my hand, gently. His lips were like moths. That's when he gave it to me, the turquoise bracelet. He took it out of his pocket, wrapped in bright red tissue paper. Wrists like a Mayan princess, that's what he said. These wrists, swollen like my ankles have been for months. These wrists.

How funny, there's tiny crescents, half moons in a row where the fortune tellers say the life line is. What *are* those, in my palms?

Oh, I know.

Just where I've been digging my nails in, making fists without knowing it, I guess, when the pain peaks.

That's why you've got to grip the bedrails . . .

There was a young crescent moon that other night. *He* was the *right* one, I thought. Not some half-Indian with a smile like . . . slow lava. But when *he* touched me with his surgeon's fingers and reached for me in the night like I was life itself, he could make my breath catch and hold and explode like—

Oh Momma, here comes the pain again!

Momma, Momma . . .

Linda, the other one said *linda* it means beautiful but I never did it no I was the best daughter . . .

Momma make it *stop!*

Ah . . . it's dying down.

Finally, ah . . .

My *hands,* so cramped, never dared let go of the bedrails . . .

"Nurse, goddammit, come *give* me something!"

Nobody hears, nobody comes. Maybe nobody remembers I'm in here. Maybe—

But the door—

"Who are *you?*"

Stands in the doorway, staring. A *schwarze* in a bathrobe, just like that, out of nowhere.

"Who in hell are you?"

"Don't flap your wings at *me,* honey. We're just two gals in the same boat." She grins. "I could hear you from way down the hall, yellin' blue murder. Came by to say hello, see if I could help . . ."

I'm in the same hospital with a colored woman. A *schwarze* who says we're in the same boat, yet.

"No, I—I'm fine. I don't need any help."

She shrugs.

"Sure sounded different to me. Sounded to me like you was one big talkin' bruise in here. And lonely like nobody but a gal in labor can get."

"I need the nurse, that's all. I just need—"

"Pain pill? Don't hold your breath. That lady hoards them pills like they were goin' outta season. Probably pops 'em herself for ear-ache with the likes of us around all the time."

Why does she keep comparing her and me? Her belly's not big. She's not pregnant.

"Yeah, well, I dropped mine yesterday. One of the worst. Now I'm just wadin' around. Don't believe 'em when they tell you it gets easier each time."

"You— How many—"

"Four. This one's the fifth. And the last, no matter what I gotta do to be sure of *that.*"

Five times she's gone through this. My God, she must be nuts. How does she do it? Why does anybody do it once they know what it's like?

"I'll *never* have another one, never. Not me."

"That's what we all say. Probably see you back here next year. Your man, he'll want more kids. They all do. *They* don't have to have 'em. *Or* raise 'em."

My man. It goes through me like a knife. Even she has a man, the *schwarze.*

"Please . . . just leave me alone. If you want to help, go ask the nurse to come in. But just . . . leave me alone, will you?"

She shrugs again.

"Whatever you say. You pantin' like a racehorse. Just thought you might be lonely. Everybody's got a right. But whatever you say." She turns in the doorway, then says soft, over her shoulder, "Yell your heart out, honey, if that's what you wanna' do. Least the sound of your own voice keeps you knowing you're still alive. You change your mind, want company, you yell out 'Vi!' That's me, Violet. I'll hear ya." She shuts the door behind her.

Everything quiet again. The room comes back. The smell comes back, the silence. Why did I make her go, oh . . .

No oh *no,* oh this is going to be a real bad one!

"Help, Nurse! I'm being torn in pieces!"

The little *demon,* I want it to *die. I hate you, God.* I want to hurt you the way this baby's hurting me!

Dear vicious God, God of my mother and my sisters, God David never believed in, God who let Cossacks and Prussians trample us under their horses' hooves and Nazis churn our filth into soap for their tidy Lysol-smelling unkosher kitchens, God who made me love David and try to fill his nothingness, *Your* nothingness, *pace pace, mio Dio,* God *it hurts it hurts it hurts*

Hitler's inside my body testing how to make every nerve-end scream in pain!

Then *let* me die! Let both of us die. Wipe us out, God. If I die, oh if I die and it lives, then what? Who'll take it? Yetta or Esther? Over my dead body. But that's what it'd be, big joke. Him and his thin-blooded Viennese fiancée? Then he'd be sorry. Dear Führer, let me and the baby both die?

Oh, you are good to ease the pain a little.

Oh yes, *yes*.

Thank you mighty Tsar, bless You, bless Yourself.

I'm so tired . . .

I never thought anybody could be this tired and still live.

So sleepy . . .

The smiles of all the Cossack host of angels there above me . . .

Too tired to keep climbing this staircase. It never ends. Step after step, and this sack like lead on my back, hauling it up and up and up. Wait. No. Yes. There's a landing. I can get there. I can do it. See? This door, opening . . . all this light streaming through it, where is this place? Who are they all in there, a vast room filled with old people, sitting, rocking, standing in groups, talking quietly. *Anges radieux* . . . Such light, golden . . . the light actually *sings*. Momma, is that you, walking toward me through the light, smiling? You always *knew* I was different, I wasn't a whore, Momma you did love me after all! Let me come in, Momma, please? Let me put down this burden and come into the room? But you put out your hand to stop me. Arm straight, palm up, your fingers radiating crescent moons. "No, my Hokhmah, you can't come in yet. It's not time yet, my daughter. You have more flights to climb. And you must carry your burden with you."

"Mercy, have mercy. Listen to me. Momma, I'm saying Kaddish for you: *Yis-ga-dal ve-yis-ka-dash she-moi ra-ba be-al-ma* . . . I'm saying Kaddish for myself, Momma. Let me in? Let me enter the light?"

"Go away, Hokhmah, it's not time. Turn and pick up the bundle again and go on."

"Don't push me out, Momma. Look how I remember, see, I can say it: *I am abashed and ashamed of the wicked deeds and sins I have committed. Please accept my pain,* dear Momma, *please accept my suffering,* mein Führer, *as atonement, and forgive my wrongdoing, for against You alone I have sinned."*

But she stands with her hand against my entering. She stands with her hand set against me, only her rain of crescents, like the holy *yods* Poppa would tell us about, falling on me.

"Klayne libe, klayne Hokheleh, uber itst du gayn. Itst. Now. *Meina tokhter, zeit gazunt, meina tokhter."*

So I turn. You can never make Momma hear you, never. I turn from her radiant crescents and her Yiddish farewell. I hoist it up, the bundle, and sling it back over my shoulder. My face is slick with tears and my body is slick with sweat and I turn and place my right foot on the first step of the next flight. And I look ahead and the stairs wind up and up and I can't see any landing or ending or place to rest, ever. And the left foot goes up. And then the right again. Shelter me in the shadow of Your wings: *Ve-i-me-ru* Amen. And I leave the singing light behind me and rise up into the dark.

"Miss Baker? Miss Baker? There now. Goodness, I almost thought we'd lost you. You can't give in like that, dear."

Who is this woman? Why is she all in white? Is she one of Them, from the room that glows and sings?

"Who are you, Lady? Can I come in?"

"You *are* in, dear. You must have dozed off and had a dream. It's good to rest between contractions, but you overdid it. Lost consciousness for a few minutes. Gave me quite a fright when I looked in. You were out like a light."

Out like a light.

The green walls.

The mocking ceiling.

The spark of hurt, catching and smoldering back toward a blaze of pain.

"Now you mustn't cry, dear. Oh my, we've soiled the sheets a little. Here, we'll just fix you up a bit. Where's your sister gone? Out for some coffee? Aw, you're having a hard time of it, I know. Doctor will check on you in a while."

"It's *been* a while. It's been a hundred whiles. Can't you give me a pill? Or a shot? *Anything* to put me out or dull the pain?"

"Miss Baker, you know I can't do that without Doctor ordering it. Let's not pity ourselves, dear. Millions of women have gone through what you're going through, and even worse."

"I'm not millions of women, damn you, I'm *me*. This baby is murdering me, can't you see that?"

The chippie, all she can do is stuff towels under me and straighten the sheets.

Eva Braun herself, she must enjoy this.

"Look, Miss Baker, honest, I'd give you something but I don't dare to without his permission. And he's gone to dinner. You'll be all right, just hang on. You're not going to die. You'll have a fine baby, I'm sure. Grip the bedrails when it gets too bad, like I showed you, and try to think about other things, happy pleasant things . . . Oh you poor— Look, I'm really sorry. I know this is a bad one."

And the chippie spins on her squeaky rubber soles and leaves.

Just like that.

Eyes teary, the hypocrite. Who does she think she is, Eleanor Roosevelt?

You won't die, she says—her personal guarantee.

The guarantee of a hypocrite who just said "We almost lost you for a while."

A fine baby, little miss crisp starched white predicts. Then she goes off.

All right. Go ahead. Leave me alone. I can do it. I'll show all of you. I'm special and always will be. Meant for something great and shining, like—

Oh there it goes again, coiling around my bowels and slicing up through my spine—

—think of something else something *oh* pleasant—

Virtuoso pain, coloratura pain sustaining it *oh* high note nothing in the world but that sound *demon* Hitler Goebbels extracting me from myself teeth bone hair skin with his light shading through it, a whole choir of pain melting me down and spilling me out over the packed house of all my cells *God David Momma!*

There . . .

There. Bring it down. Slowly, pull it back in the throat lovely throat he said Klimt and wrists like a Mayan princess *linda* not a whore the good daughter a real American soft now like Momma's lap after school, *pianissimo*. There.

I'll make it through. His firstborn son, his one hope for the future of his family name. Then he'll change his mind.

Avraham graduated college, became an accountant. Gold-glinted hair he'll have, like you, David, and hazel eyes. I'll save this baby. I'll bring you into the world, little jewel burning in the casket of my body. I'll show you, Momma. He'll love me more than I ever loved you. More than I ever loved *you,* David. You hear, both of you?

Oh God God *God* there it goes again so fast now let me die *let the baby die* and I *promise* I'll love him, this golden creature all my very own *see?* Doctor if he wants to be—

—think of happy things—

—yes, yes, a great surgeon, a genius in the operating room, they'll whisper. Or the finest tenor or baritone of the century. How they'll weep at his Cavaradossi, scream for his Don Giovanni! Or a world-famous artist maybe, yes, beyond your feeble Klimt and Rubens. In the finest museums, all the different portraits of his mother. Followed by women everywhere and traveling the world but always returning to the one woman he knows understands every particle of his being. He'll love me better than anyone has loved me. And I'll deserve it because I'll be the best mother the world has ever seen, you hear that Momma?

Hold on hold on grip the rails think about—

Then David will beg me to marry him, mother of his first-born son. But I'll make him wait, make him crawl through the sewers before I accept. Then Essie and Yetta will be lovey-dovey to their baby sister the doctor's wife, mother of the prodigy. No no no *I hate it* I want it to *die let me live free* no yes I have to do it together you and me. Us against the world. How they'll envy us with the God-given talent pouring out of you like light spilling from some secret room filled with radiant angels watching only over you and me—

Yis-ga-dal ve-yis-ka-dash she-moi ra-ba

—you will be my aria, my masterpiece, *vissi d'arte, ve-i-me-ru* I hate you, tsar nazi devil glittering in my bowels, fiend *I'd kill you if I could.* God of my fathers, decree that I shall die of this affliction grant me Thy perfect healing—Rot in hell—*Heilige Führer take them all into Your fiery bosom—consume them in Your ovens* Momma David Poppa who rocked and stared and mumbled his wisdom *weak* never aloud *coward* never saved us dragged himself left foot right foot from the *shul* to the hardware store and Yetta and Essie and Madam

Betrothed Vienna—*cleanse me of their filth, take them,* they're Yours. *I don't need any of you.* I'm creating my own miracle. Full American he'll be, peasant strength and aristocrat's elegance blending in his tiny veins. Someone who *belongs* to me. My son, to seize the whole world in his little fist! And I'll love him. Damn you all *I want this baby now.* Do you hear, Momma? Do you understand, David? Waltzing together through that room washed with light, *you're dead*—one of you dead inside and the other dead everywhere. But *I'm alive* and I'll live in spite of you! Up and up through the darkness, carrying my own light inside me, my casket of jewels, my little Mayan prince, my tiny Cossack to crush them underfoot and avenge his mother. My son, my life, my voice, my secret shining self, my future, my weapon! *Mine.* See? Even the Tsar has come to offer his respects to us. See how he beams down at me from under his high pearl-encrusted crown? White, so white! So tall! He wants me to marry him now, my little princeling, see? The Tsar himself has come to ask forgiveness, to pay homage! The Tsar . . .

"It's all over now, Miss Baker. You had a very difficult labor, Nurse says. And I can certainly tell you it wasn't an easy delivery. High forceps. Frankly, you almost lost the baby and we almost lost you. But you'll be all right now. And congratulations. You've given birth to a fine baby girl."

PART THREE

May, 1981

But how could Julian write about herself? Julian is only a figment of her own imagination—or of mine—she thought, reclining in an armchair forty thousand feet above land. Julian is only a character, an illusion. God knows who Julian really is. Hope was another matter. She knew Hope better than she did herself. Hope was as large as life. Larger. She was in a lifelong obsessive affair with Hope even when, perhaps especially when, she was able to forget her.

But what could she say about some mythical Julian-self on an evening in May, sitting in a plane after more than a decade of sitting in planes, on the way home from a speech after more than a decade of speeches, marches, demonstrations, meetings, and press interviews, a decade of trying to reach women like the one who sat next to her now? Her sister passenger.

Peculiar, how often that word "sister" felt contrived, even after years of public usage. Because of residual convent or labor-union-solidarity associations? Or because such a word grazed against internal wounds, provoking an anxiety of recognition which, no matter how proselytized, trivialized, or denied, did vibrate between women? A recognition that could still annunciate itself as shock or terror, anger or humor or even hope—another maddening word for which there was no precise synonym, so Julian could never avoid using it, despite its being *her* name.

Nonetheless, she thought with a sidewards glance, a true-to-life sister passenger this seatmate was, a woman she knew as well as herself: a white woman in her mid-fifties, nondescript in careful home-permanent hairdo, brown polyester pantsuit, yellow blouse, a woman immersed in reading the airline copy of *Good Housekeeping*. Her sister, Polly Esther incarnate, who was happily married and had been for years, a full-time home-maker and mother, the kind of woman who resolutely tried out all the recipes *Good Housekeeping* fed her, went to church every Sunday, had voted for Ronald Reagan. The kind of woman who deferred to her husband—even if she did some-times find herself crying into her pillow soundlessly in the middle of the night without knowing why.

Polly Esther, unscathed by any "women's revolution," tak-ing a plane ride as a big occasion, maybe to visit her own mother in some other city, or to see her grown children off now at college. Polly Esther, buckled into an aisle seat next to a Julian Travis who once would have deftly engaged her in con-versation, moving from the casual through the personal to the political, so that by the time they landed in New York at least a flicker of feminist interest would have been kindled. Nor would it have been one-way, either. Polly Esther would have touched something in herself and Julian would have retouched something in herself—and retouched Hope.

Was that old organizer now just a character, too? Julian won-dered. Yet she could still get inside that character so deeply the adrenaline coursed in her veins as she and other women as-sembled for a march, or as the energy hit her fingertips in the parry-and-thrust of a question-answer period after a speech. She still loved to throw herself, an emotional ventriloquist, through the façades of other women, into motivations familiar, articulable, more moving than her own. Yet they were her own. Who, then, was the ventriloquist?

Julian poured the second half of the miniature in-flight vodka bottle into the remains of her Bloody Mary, swirling it with a plastic stirrer and watching the clear liquor cloud and then vanish, absorbed by tomato juice. Her own motivations? What were they? Once, they had such clarity, such intoxicating certainty. Now everything felt muddled. Where had they gone, those convictions earned the hard way—by trying to question everything?

She glanced surreptitiously at her seatmate again, then looked away, out the window. The certainty had been there a decade earlier, in the old group—one of the first consciousness-raising groups—when she and nine other women met once a week, to sit in a circle on the floor in one or another of their apartments. Those women *had* tried to question everything, had dared peel off each of their masks in turn, with exquisite care. The skins of an onion, yes, through to what core? But "sisters," yes. It was in that group Julian finally had been able to whisper—bringing forth the sin with the mortification of one who had surely invented it—that she had at times faked orgasms with her husband. It was in that group Iliana had leaned across the circle and replied merrily, "Oh, you too?" It was there that Julian felt one whole fronted self crack like a plaster cast and drop from her body while the room broke into a laughter giddy with mutual relief. Recognition. Innocence. Freedom. Momentary, but a glimpse . . . Yet even there, in the halcyon days of honeymoon "sisterhood," Julian had not spoken of her childhood or of Hope. Even there, when they delicately probed in that direction, she had stopped them. They needn't know behind-the-scenes details. They needn't further know she nursed a secret grievance that they hadn't persisted, had settled instead for respecting her privacy.

Privacy. Julian sipped her drink and smiled to herself. Such moments as these, she thought, in airplanes, motel rooms, taxi-cabs, were the only privacy she now knew, maybe had ever known, except for those few months in that tiny walk-up apartment of her own before moving in to live with Laurence. But hadn't she chosen a mode of living-in-public through her writing? "The personal is political" had been a Julian Travis phrase, and she felt required to live by it, as if to prove its validity. "Living out loud" had been her phrase, too, a deliberately opted-for vulnerability to the women she wanted to reach, at no small costs to the Julian-self and to those close to her who might not have chosen quite such an on-stage existence had they been consulted first.

"Celebrity Diet Tips" headlined an article in Polly Esther's magazine. The hunger to be perceived. Wasn't that a basic human hunger, not merely the neurotic tic of an ex-child star?

But being perceived and being looked at weren't necessarily the same. Julian suspected that she felt visible only when looked at. Didn't that mean she couldn't look back at, much less perceive, others accurately? "But Momma, how can I see who's out there when the footlights are so bright?" she'd complained to Hope after her first appearance in proscenium theater. "They're here to see *you*, darling; you don't have to see *them*. Trust me." Curiosity sacrificed to self-consciousness— but self-consciousness lacking a self, which in turn meant finding something external to reflect. Maybe, she shrugged to herself, that's why I play witness, watching other women's suffering and transformations to learn some of the shapes of my own —then putting it down in code, marks on paper. If so, then politics at least had reshaped pretense into an eerie Moebius strip—a consciousness curling back on itself, like Iliana's "Oh, you too?"

Julian tossed down the last of her Bloody Mary and crunched a chip of ice between her teeth in unconscious imitation of Hope. I've changed somewhere along the way, she realized, I've grown greedy about what privacy I do have, moments like this—so I'm not up to initiating a one-on-one mini-CR session with my seatmate. It didn't occur to Julian that the woman beside her might also not feel like talking. She knew her Polly Esthers too well. Is this what they call burn-out, she wondered, this lack of energy, this floating anger—at whom? Hope? Larry? Myself for being so damned sure I know what the conversation with Polly Esther would involve that I just can't begin it? If only she could sleep . . .

But she knew the answer. The women's movement had become a personal Hope Travis of her adulthood, the creature Julian felt had birthed her, saved her life, given her language. The women's movement was the creature she loved passionately and seriously, believing it to be the last best nurturant hope for humanity. It was also the creature she served and sang and danced for, performed for, donated part of her earnings to, felt guilty about not doing enough for. It was the creature whose approval she desperately sought. It was the creature who had given her what Hope had never permitted: a mask of one's own.

The words she spoke and wrote this time might be forged in a million disparate experiences of other women, but when

Julian spoke them, they were her own. The issues might be shared or alien, slack with imprecision, macrame in correct-line thinking or taut with insight, but when she wove them, they had a Travis stitch. So all the old skills she had come to regard as superficial and treacherously addictive, the ones employed whenever she mounted a podium or handled an interviewer or faced into a camera, were this time put to a purpose larger than her own—and through that crucible the skills themselves were somehow cleansed.

Was that how it worked? she brooded: you started out thinking you were doing something for others, to find you were doing it for yourself—or the reverse? And was that a good thing or not? Certainly it had been a good thing in the old group, which she had joined claiming it was not for her own needs but to bring "those feminist women" some sobering political analysis from the Marxian New Left. Fortunately, "those feminist women" asked questions of themselves and of her that not only encompassed her missionary message but revealed it as puerile; they got to her before she got to them. Thank god for that, Julian almost muttered out loud, remembering the first time Maggie had asked her, "And, uh, where do housewives fit into your economic analysis, then?"

If the women's movement had come to function in her life as another stage mother, at least its early years had bathed her with support the way she remembered those other early years when Hope had been plain Momma. Never had Julian laughed so hard as in the old group: the night Judy mimicked each of the male bosses at the architecture firm where she worked as a secretary, taking them on one by one with devastatingly vivid gestures and in different accents of pomposity; or the night Ivy demanded to know why scientists able to send ships up into space were unable to invent a diaphragm that could be inserted without making a woman engage in a solitary bathroom game of (greased) frisbee; or the night Andrea wondered why she had to be born female *and* Jewish *and* a Scorpio *and* be right in the middle of her Saturn cycle, *and aware* of all those burdens—only to have Miki top her, chuckling, "Try being all of that—well, at least *half* Jewish—*and* black *and* a lesbian. That's me, kiddo. Isn't that cheery?"

We came to love each other, it was that simple, Julian thought. And somewhere in the process, we came to like ourselves a little. Never had she cried so unselfconsciously as in the old group. Never, before or since, had she looked forward to a meeting. Never had she been so happily exhausted before, during, and after demonstrations: up straight through the previous night at the mimeograph machine cranking out leaflets, or arguing hoarsely over slogans to be magic-markered on pieces of cardboard strewn around the floor in a tangle of blue-jeaned sprawling women, or consuming cup after cup of black coffee in order to stay awake and do more of the same. Never, in the earlier years of the anti-war movement or the civil-rights movement, had she so felt as if she had a real people of her own.

The seatmate finished *Good Housekeeping*, neatly slid it into the seat-pocket in front of her, and immediately opened a copy of *Family Circle*.

But the old group did even more. They taught Julian new dimensions of intimacy. She learned that sometimes disloyalty wasn't even disloyal, as when she confessed that she must be a prude because her husband's unabashed belches and farts dismayed her—only to hear the reliable chorus of "Oh, you too?" from five other women in the group. She learned that she didn't need to prefix an insight with "I must be crazy, but I wonder . . ." She learned that exposing a long-dead self could lure that self up into existence. And like every new convert to a belief in resurrection, she had longed to pass that message on. The irony was that in the passing-on process, a public self—a new one—got reconstructed.

She rubbed her eyelids, thinking dully that she should take out her contact lenses; the recirculating cabin air always dried out your eyes. I never should have given in to them about the media, she thought, resting her head against the seatback and closing her eyes. As the movement began to surface in the press, she had refused to be any kind of spokeswoman. Yet her whole group knew about her childhood even if no one spoke of it, and finally they tactfully admitted their awe of someone who wouldn't be intimidated by a microphone. She countered by setting up women's media workshops:

"Look, it's really just building a repertoire of gimmicks. Afraid of speaking to a group of people? Well, imagine them all sitting out there not on chairs but on rows and rows of toilets, their pants down around their ankles. Who could be intimidated by that? Afraid an interviewer might lead you astray with a tricky question? Well, just side-step it, say something like 'Interesting you should ask that, and I'll get back to it in a minute, but what I really think is relevant is . . .' Afraid of a camera? Well, look right into the lens and *through* it, to the woman who's watching the program while doing her ironing or the woman seeing the picture in her morning newspaper on the bus as she rides to work, *that's* who you're really looking at."

But it hadn't succeeded. Her protegées still trembled with stage-fright, fell silent before a perfect-cue question, managed to be sick or busy when the moment came. So, kicking and screaming, Julian went. Kicking and screaming but with the blasé pride of the old pro, Julian went. She had sat in audiences and stood offstage too many times by then, wringing her hands with frustration over a missed chance to make a point, over a tone that lacked conviction though she knew its speaker had the conviction. She had endured the frustration of the teacher unable to correct or cover up the nervous mistakes of prize pupils. She had glimpsed the helplessness of the stage mother. At last, when they repeated that they needed her, she sprang to the call with an exultation that warmed her sisters and chilled her soul.

Then, suddenly, it was too late. There was a new persona: Julian Travis, the feminist. The exposure that shone on *that* face was unsettlingly familiar—and antithetical to the other exposure, the hunger to be perceived.

Privacy, she mused. And so, in an act of insanity, she was now thinking of *writing* about it? She shook her head violently against the seatback. The gesture of an exhibitionist, she admonished herself, not someone seeking privacy! What kind of madwoman would try to bring the behind-the-scenes—of a childhood, a marriage, a political movement—center-stage, as if reality were a rehearsal for art?

But even to pose that rhetorical question was to activate an internal dialogue between two familiar voices, resident character-actors in her own private repertory company:

"*Why* would you write it? To justify yourself? Poor beleaguered Jule, beset by evil nonstepmother and then by wicked nonprince and finally by starving masses of enthralled women? Come *on.*"

"Well, to justify *them*, then? The other characters? To kill them off, free them from their long-term contracts in a series gone stale? How about that one?"

"That's a more interesting one, I'll grant."

"And—to understand something more about it, beyond stereotype of child star, rhetoric of politics, erosion of marriage, pretense of truth. To find something . . . universal in a life so peculiar? Recognize something that . . . recognizes itself as real?"

Julian loosened the seatbelt and fumbled at her feet for her overnight bag, fishing the writing pad from its depths. Like a neophyte possessed by her first visitation, she hurried to locate a pencil, grope for the overhead lightswitch, unhook the tray-table.

The white sheet of paper. The world before her, hers to choose.

She'd have to do it as a novel. Hadn't Mary McCarthy once said somewhere, "Only in fiction can I tell the truth"?

But if she did it as a novel, then it would be too close to life—autobiographical, *roman à clef,* or godforbid "confessional." Or else it would violate life: it would disguise. Which was the problem and always had been. The masks beneath the masks. The nested Chinese boxes. And all the while famished for the core, for one thing simply true.

She wrote at the top of the lined pad:

"A Mask of One's Own"
Notes for a Novel:

But *how* could she do it? She'd *been* Julian, all the Julians. Now she wanted to see Julian in the third person. Change her name; something else, also genderless: Ashley or Leigh? Lesley. Shawn? Blair. No, not right, any of those. Never mind, she could keep her as Julian for now, change the names later. Write it with the real ones, fiddle the details afterward. She could try to go behind the scenes of the writing of a novel itself. Behind the proscenium, the set, the frame. Behind the Stand By We're On The Air sign. Behind the script. Yet the opening line of the book should be in the first person. Yes, she reasoned, but I don't want to get trapped in Julian's first person. I've been her and *been* her.

She drew in a sharp breath, as if the realization were a

sudden paper-cut along the skin: *I don't want to be her anymore.*

"Excuse me . . . I'm sorry to interrupt you, but aren't you Julian Travis?" the stewardess smiled above her.

Polly Esther on the aisle side looked up at the flight attendant, then over at Julian.

"I—uh, yes. I am."

"Oh I thought so," Cindy-from-her-lapel-name-marker chimed back. "I just knew it. I saw you on television last week, that talk show, what was it—"

"Mel Chester."

"Mel Chester! Yes, that was it. You were talking about—uh, not equal pay for equal work but, uh—"

"Equal pay for comparable—"

"Yes, that's it! Comparable. And you said schoolteachers and flight attendants get paid less than truckdrivers or, uh—"

"Parking-lot attendants—"

"Right! Parking-lot attendants. Because we're mostly women."

"Yes, well, it's true. I—"

"And you said after all what should a society value most? Its safety and its education, or trucks and cars? I *loved* it."

Julian couldn't help but grin back at her. "Thank you. I'm glad it sounded good." Stand By We're On The Air.

"Well, I really didn't want to disturb you. But I just . . . and there's another thing, too. But I must be crazy . . ."

"No, really, it's quite all right. I'm sure, whatever it is, you're not crazy. What were you going to say?"

"I wondered about this before, when I saw your picture in some magazine. Is it possible? I mean, what I'm trying to say is, when I was growing up, every week just like a ritual I used to watch this TV show called 'Family.'" Cindy began to giggle. "You couldn't be. Could you possibly be the same little Julian Travis who was on that program?"

Julian adjusted her smile. Try to relieve this woman's embarrassment. Remember that the idiot box can reduce us all to idiots. Remember that this woman is capable of directing the evacuation of a 747 in three minutes flat.

"Yes," Julian nodded, "the same person." At least try to use it constructively, then. "How nice that all this time later we're both in the women's movement."

"Well, I'll be . . . Oh I'm not really *in* . . . Well, yes, it's nice. Oh and that wonderful Elizabeth Clement. Does she still—"

"She died, I'm afraid. Last year."

"Oh what a pity . . . Well, anyway, sorry again if I disturbed you. It was great talking to you. Now you just buzz if I can get you anything, okay?"

Julian smiled her thanks and turned back to her tray-table, sensing the curious gaze of Polly Esther fix on her profile.

Notes for a Novel, the paper demanded.

It wasn't even discomfiting anymore, hadn't been since—when? Age four? It was neither embarrassing nor thrilling, not a violation or an ego-lift. It was "normal." There was only one unsettling aspect to it, against which Julian's reactions had gritted for years, trying to pearlize some matter lodged inside her shell exterior: the admiration or hostility accompanying recognition always landed just off-tilt, for the wrong reason or at the wrong time or for the wrong Julian—for the spotlit persona she followed like a shadow, the doppelgänger who had usurped her life, whose movements and convictions were more convincing than her own. Only some obscure Julian knew what she had accomplished that genuinely merited praise or warranted criticism; the heights of her secret worth, the depths of her hidden evil. And how does anyone believe in the validity of their own vantage point? Megalomaniac! she chided herself. Who are you not to be misunderstood? Every actor knows that a drunk scene, or one involving hysterics or "madness," can be counted on to bring down the house—just as every actor knows that melodrama is child's play and that comedy is what requires seraphic technique: nuance, timing, understatement.

Still, beyond her longing for the dross to be seen as dross and the gold gold lay her lust for "the real." And beyond that lay the painfully gained insight that most attempts to live the real appeared to invite cries of "Fake!" What doubts she might have entertained about that had been put definitively to rest by a vulgar little man named Harry Clayburn.

He worked in the first agency she registered with to apply for any kind of basic office job, so she could get her own place and support herself free of Hope and free of Hope's withholding of the childhood earnings.

"I know this name," he said, looking up from her filled-in card and peering at her over smudgy bifocals.

"Uh. You do?"

"You were a child star. TV kid. Big stuff."

"Well, that was a while ago. Look, I realize I have no office skills and no experience, but I'm willing to take whatever—"

"So, Miss Big Stuff, why's a millionaire who got rich from doing nothing but being cute want a secretarial job, anyway?"

The old ignorance, the old envy, she had thought. Don't get smart with him. Play humble. The Little Match Girl.

"Because I need the job, sir, that's why."

"How come? Spent all your money on caviar lollypops? What are you really up to, huh? Doing research for some role on being a schmuck of a secretary? Ya know, there's broads *really* need these jobs, cutie."

"I know. And I know they have the skills, too. But *I* also really need this job. Now, could we please discuss any openings you might be willing to send me on?"

"Nope."

"Nope?"

"That's right, nope. No go. Forget it."

"Because I have no skills?"

"Nope. Because you're you. I won't play the patsy for whatever ploy you're up to, cutie. Try somebody dumber at some other agency."

So, shaking with humiliation, Julian had done that. After three weeks of pavement pounding, being told she should go to secretarial school or "get experience first" *(how?)*, and after three weeks of having nursed a festering desire to get back at Clayburn, she had learned more than any secretarial course could have taught her. So she returned to the seedy Placement Perfect offices on West Forty-second street, filled out a new card, and sat again in front of his desk.

But this time her own skills were being practiced. Clayburn glanced at a card which listed her accomplishments as typing sixty words per minute, rapid-write shorthand, fluent French and German, previous experience three years in executive assistant positions with convincing-sounding small businessess abroad. The signature at the bottom of the card was in an ornate scrawl, but might be deciphered with difficulty to look something like "Janie Purvis." Clayburn looked up from the

card, impressed despite himself. The young woman he saw
wore glasses, earrings, and a deep shade of lipstick. A russet
scarf wound in a turban covered her hair. She smiled win-
ningly at him. Clayburn never stood a chance, especially when
she began to respond to his questions in her boarding-school
voice with the faint British pitch—acquired from years of
working abroad. He began to comb his files for something "of
her class." Together they chose a distinguished literary agency,
the post of executive assistant to the head of the periodicals
department. He told her who to call and how to approach
them. He wished her the best of luck and in a fatherly way
assured her that if this didn't work out she should come right
back to him and he'd be darned if he wouldn't find something
worthy of her sooner or later. It was only after she'd thanked
him effusively and was turning to go, job address and person-
nel contact's name secure in her purse beyond reclamation,
that he glanced again at her signature and called,

"What's your name again, baby? Janie? Junie?"

—permitting her the supreme moment of turning, whip-
ping off her glasses and scarf, and smiling, "Julian. Julian
Travis. And don't call me cutie. And *never* call me baby,"
before she stalked out of the office.

She had not yet learned that such a triumph warms the
victor with a gaudy temporary satisfaction only to smolder in a
long-fuse doubt that one has not only failed to educate the
person one was trying to impress but has confirmed his preju-
dices. Nevertheless, that time Julian learned part of the lesson.

And that time she got the job.

Her gamble had been correct: Clayburn was too embarrassed to call and denounce as an imposter someone he would
have to admit he himself had sent over. Nor did cautious Julian
cite him as a reference. She said that she'd heard about the job
as a favor from a (nameless) friend at another placement
agency, thus saving both the new boss and herself paying commissions. It had been astonishingly simple. She had called for
an appointment and gone looking like herself but lying about
her office skills and experience, which she'd scripted this time
in a literary direction. Her references weren't checked. Instead, she was asked if she could start on Monday.

It had been, Julian remembered, what the New Left mili-
tants would later call "Another whoops radicalizing experi-

ence." Now she wondered wryly how many radicalizing experiences it took to bring you round full circle into becoming
reactionary.

"A Mask of One's Own," *Notes for a Novel,* stared up at her.

But Sister Passenger, who had disappeared off toward the
lavatory, could be seen weaving her way down the aisle back to
her seat. Julian, afraid the flight attendant's revelation might
inspire a conversation, snapped off her light and settled
quickly into a pillow, turning toward the window.

Hypocrite. Playing at sleep. Just as you once played at being
a child playing the part of a child. Deliberately played to Laurence, when he appeared miraculously, an honest presence
moving crude as a bull through the bric-a-brac china-shop of
Sutton Place. Knew somehow that the simplest brown wool
sweater should be dug out of the bottom of the drawer, that
this was not the time for the pale cashmeres Hope liked to see
you in. Knew which was the best facial angle to present to him
during long intense talks about art, knew how to sit (cross-
legged, not demurely), knew how to pepper your speech with
a few four-letter words. All the while longing for him to see
through to whomever was looking out of you, desperately
wanting what he represented.

Julian saw the reflection of her own smile twisted on the
night-backed plane window, as she remembered how with a
single gesture—loving Laurence—she had managed both to
get away from Hope and to get back at her on every level. To
love anyone but Hope at all. To love a man. To love a man
twelve years her senior. A man from a working-class background, a man who was born a Christian—and, worse, became
an atheist. A man who would never be wealthy.

Age, class, religion, style—Julian had touched almost all the
bases. Laurence had been a bargain. Not all Hope's tears, her
screams of betrayal, collapses, threats, warnings, and curses,
could halt the inevitable. Laurence had been freedom on every level Julian could conceive. Loving him was the act of
Persephone uprooting the aconite so Hades could roar through
the split maw of earthcrust and sweep her away to an alien
landscape where the beauty of growing things lay not in petaled preciosity but in thick-braided furry roots. Laurence was
the region where all rivers began, where the fickle weather of
Demeter—her fog, her noon blaze, her sheet lightning—could

never prevail. Life with Laurence would be privacy, peace. And it would be defiance.

Beyond the plane window, a fragile membrane stretched against forces of enormous pressure, Julian could see a drift of midwest plains and farmlands. Wide patches of darkness were punctuated by clusters and then larger constellations of lights, as the megalopolis that now stretched from Kansas City to St. Louis distantly approached. Towns spreading into cities, roads widening to streets to avenues to highways to superhighways. The night retained its starless indifference if one looked up, but every downward glance encountered more displaced brightness exhibiting itself: streetlights, roadlights, car head-lights, small yellow-lit houses swelling into white-lit buildings. None of the lonely autonomy of stars here, winking at one another across absolute space and silence. No, these dots of brilliance below were proudly artificial, signals of a human vigil, beacons of people clinging together, brittle and brave, risking the appearance of being flashy in their insistence on becoming visible, in their denial of the power of night.

Like Laurence and Julian, she thought: with my rebellion I thee worship, he might have vowed; and with all my worldly resistance I thee endow, she might have responded. A mutual, interlocking defiance. Laurence and Julian, in a conspiracy like that between aircraft and air, an utterly mismatched couple in league against the logic of gravity.

Julian's reverie was broken by the voice of Cindy, chirping through the plane's intercom that the movie was about to start and the sound could be located on channel five of your ear-phones. Julian stirred and glanced at her seatmate. Polly Esther remained immersed in her magazine, unruffled by the announcement.

I've got to try, I've got to at least try, Julian thought, if not about *her* then at least about *him.* Switching her own light back on, she took a fresh piece of paper and began to write:

It had been a year of barely touching, of talking passion-ately about art, of meetings in secret and delicious conversa-tions in which he lost contempt for my childhood and came to have compassion for it, in which I lost admiration for his childhood and came to commiserate with it. Each loved each for the dangers each had passed, and each loved each that each did pity them.

I would sneak off to his Chelsea loft to sip instant coffee in a cracked mug without a handle, and watch him work. I loved the simplicity of the loft: light streaming through uncurtained windows, the clean expanse of unstained, unvarnished, uncarpeted wood floor, the double mattress covered with an India print in earth colors, pushed against one wall. There were two rickety chairs, rescued from a street-discard pile, and a paint-spattered stool. On one of these three I always sat, or on the floor itself, avoiding the mattress where he often sprawled and where I fantasized sprawling with him.

Most of all, I loved his sculptures that populated the loft. They were to me classical, romantic, modern—all at once. In those years Laurence had already been forced to sacrifice working in marble, partly because it was too expensive but mostly because no gallery would touch his marbles: too neo-classical, outré. Some of them still stood in corners—nude male torsos twisted in strenuous effort, as if leaping or lifting or straining in orgasm. But through the muscle tension gleamed a lyricism, something of the indomitable human spirit, that took my breath away. He loathed the avant-garde, the rise of Warholism and cynicism. He would say, "If it's going right, the work sings."

His current style, a compromise between his private vision and survival in the art world, managed to be arresting, yet to sing. For me, it gave back to my eyes and touch what no external objects had: my own interior landscape.

Because Laurence worked with masks and mirrors.

The masks weren't derivative of African or Eastern or Native American art; they were wood or plaster faces of ordinary people—subway riders, salespersons, people at checkout counters—but the expressions were stretched in a torsion of extremity, joy or anguish. The eyes were sometimes mirrored, sometimes blank, but always open. Tiny shards of mirror would appear unexpectedly—in the corner of a smile or grimace, or the ears would be totally mirrored, or the lips. In one unforgettable mask of a child's face, a sharp icicle of mirror was plunged straight down through the top of the head. My favorite was a double mask, a work in layers, where the grinning top face was totally covered with a mirror mosaic except for the blank holes of eyes; this layer was hinged to the face beneath and, when raised, disclosed a bare plaster face, expres-

sionless, with glittering mirror eyes and one mirror teardrop on the left cheek. His gallery had derided this one as "corny," but that single work pierced my loneliness with what seemed a perception as penetrating as a spear in the childmask brain.

I was impaled. I loved him.

With this person, I decided, I could dare rid myself of my virginity. And I could be proud that I would not merely be receiving some god-knew-what concept of womanhood from him but would at the same moment be bestowing on him some god-knew-what concept of manhood, because, although he had had his share of affairs, he had never bedded a virgin.

And so, after months of agitated plotting and playing to him on my part, we became lovers. It was after a party at his loft, after the poets and choreographers and painters had drifted off, happily drunk and stoned. I stayed behind to help clean up. He put Dvořák's "New World Symphony" on his tinny phonograph and began dancing to it, a broom as his partner. I cut in. And then I was at last on the mattress and our clothes were coming off and the ghostly audience of faces dangling from the ceiling gleamed with mirror-flecks of guttering candlelight.

Afterward, he said I had screamed as he felt the hymen break. But I had no memory of that scream. I felt only the triumph of my own rite of passage, which something in me observed as dispassionately as if I too looked down from the loft ceiling. He whispered,

"Did you come?"

"No," I smiled to the darkness, wanting to reassure him, "but I didn't expect to, the first time."

So are all lovers saved from a knowledge that they exchange cliché dialogue by some deeper knowledge that they communicate archetypal messages.

And we entered the affair. It was a physical communication at first innocently unconcerned with its awkwardness, its (surely temporary) lack of a satisfaction I had known with no one anyway. Besides, where brain, spirit, and heart were so engaged, could flesh be far behind?

I didn't tell Hope for months, until after I'd got my own apartment. We'd been in a state of open warfare anyway, because she disapproved intensely of my working in an office job, knowing it was so I could save money to make the move. We inflicted hideous screaming fights on one another almost every evening. But the crisis came sooner than I'd planned, the day she demanded half of my weekly salary (take-home sixty-two dollars and twenty-seven cents) for "room and board" at Sutton Place. Within forty-eight hours I had found a place of my own—a gloriously squalid six-flight-walkup studio apartment in Yorkville—and moved. Two suitcases, two shopping bags, one carton of books: it could be managed in a single taxi. It was all she'd let me take of my own things. Still, I was free. Loving Laurence had freed me.

I didn't intend to marry him, nor he me. But neither of us counted on the emotional tide of that summer, the way events in our two lives kept breaking epiphanies over us, drawing us closer to what would be that fateful walk over the Brooklyn Bridge. And neither of us counted on the murderous intensity of Hope's rage, when I finally did tell her that Laurence and I were lovers. At least we had not expected that the rage would be bent toward such a surprising end: her insistence that he must marry me.

At first Laurence and I laughed about it. It was so Victorian a reaction. Even when she threatened to file a complaint and have him arrested "for impairing the morals of a minor," it seemed absurd, melodramatic, hilarious.

"But Momma," I would say, "this is 1961! I just got my own apartment. I want to live in it."

"How do you know that goddamned pervert didn't get you pregnant?" she would snarl.

"Because I'm not, that's how. Because I went and got myself a diaphragm and learned how to use it. That's how."

"And what about the first time? It can take a while to notice, you know. Some women go on having periods and don't even realize that—"

"Because. I was lucky, I guess. But that's beside the point. Neither of us want to be mar—"

"Lucky," she spat out bitterly. "Always you've been lucky, you don't know how much. Always you've been loved, you don't know how much. The golden girl. Oh God help me what did I do to have this happen to me? Why did you do this to me, Julian, why?"

"Jesus, Momma, I didn't do it to you! Can't you imagine one action I might ever take that isn't in reaction to you? I did it for

me, do you understand? For me. And because I love Laurence. I love his life. What he stands for. His work."

"What in hell do you know about love? I'll tell you about love! I loved you more than anything in the world. I gave up my whole life for you. Everything was for you. So you could live and breathe and burst on the world like a flaming meteor. So you could be rich and famous and do whatever you damned wanted. It's the only way out for a woman, the only way to independence. If you were some little black boy in Harlem maybe you'd have to make it through boxing or something like that. But you're not. You're a girl and white and lovely and smart as a whip. You'd never have to marry if you didn't want to. Or if you wanted to marry you could've had anyone. A millionaire. A prince. They always want beautiful actresses. Anyone you wanted. So what do you find yourself? A bohemian. A bastard who can barely make a living because he's too busy chipping away at pieces of stone. A weakling. He's weak, Julian, you'll find that out. A con-man who knows a good thing when he sees it, who thinks he'll get his hands on your money!"

"What money, Momma? I don't have any of my money! I live in a one-room walk-up and work every day as a secretary because you won't let me have any of my so-called fortune for myself! All I have left from having worked nonstop since I was two years old is a bunch of scrapbooks you won't even let me have, and a trained memory that lets me fake not having shorthand by writing down just a few clue words. You wouldn't even give me money for secretarial school! Christ! My fortune!"

"You wouldn't know how to handle all that money. Besides, you could move back here tomorrow, give up that ridiculous job—"

"But I don't want to move back here, Momma. That's the point. I want my own life. So why are you bent on my marrying Laurence if you hate his guts? He's not stopping me from living my life, Momma. You are!"

She had never, in all our years of fights, struck me. But now she reached for the nearest thing she could use as a weapon, and her fingers closed round the brass desk clock that sat incongruously on her cardtable. The face she turned toward me was one I had never seen before, the face of a woman maniacly transfixed by hatred. The clock came flying at my head, and I ducked just in time. It hit the doorjamb behind me and took a chunk of wood out as it flew through. I ran from the apartment, but her voice pursued me through the hall and into the elevator:

"He'll marry you, Julian! By god, he'll marry you, or I'll see him dead! I swear to you that you'll be married to this man!"

She was right—though not because of the reasons she thought. Or perhaps because of them, although it would take years for Laurence or me to suspect that. All we knew then was the sense of promise he said I brought him, the sense of freedom I said he brought me, the adventure.

We came to stand, one rainy autumn evening, before a maverick all-denominational minister who would accept less payment than the two judges we had approached for a civil ceremony. We stood in a small side chapel of the People's Community Church, decorated only by four candles burning on an otherwise stripped altar. I wore a five-year-old black velvet dress. Larry wore his good suit, which was brown. And so we were married.

Later that night, I lay awake beside his slow breathing and thought, this is freedom. What I'm feeling now—a confusion of fear and safety—this must be real. I'm truly experiencing these moments. I'm cut loose from Hope at last. It was she who snapped the thread by refusing, despite all my pleas, to come to the wedding she herself had demanded. I'm a married woman. Not playing adult. Being it.

I had done it at last—I was wed to everything I believed in, locked by choice into it so I could never desert it: a world where people felt authentic emotions, truly said what they truly thought, forged genuine art, suffered for being nonconformist or poor or homosexual or dark-skinned. People who drank jug wine indifferent to vintages while they argued into dawn about politics and poetry, rejected plastic artifacts and attitudes, were blithely unconcerned about appearances or other people's approval. Laurence was real as the sleeping stranger beside me, frighteningly real as his sculptures that bore witness around us, blessedly real as the stranger I could now become. Under the burning-glass of his ferocious truth, I could learn to feel, think, and act without plotting how each emotion, thought, or gesture would be viewed. This was all onstage and there was no possible rehearsal for it. Like his sculptures, this was the nude torso of life itself, uncostumed. As for the fear—I would love him enough, and that would make everything possible.

Not quite everything.

Not the flaw at dead center.

Not the lie that was to become—

Julian stopped writing. She re-read the pages just scribbled, then sat back, spent. The in-flight movie screen glowed with a series of soundless tableaux: a woman and a man were arguing; the woman's body language betrayed whatever vituperation the channel five earphones might be verbalizing; she was crying through a face distorted with anger, her outstretched hands open in a plea from which the man turned away.

Julian looked at the last page she had written.

Not the flaw at dead center.

Not the lie that was to become—

Slowly and deliberately, she tore all of the written pages, first in half, then in quarters, then again and again until a small pile of paper flakes lay on her tray-table. She carefully stuffed them into the empty Bloody Mary glass for handing to the next flight attendant who passed. Aware that Polly Esther actually had been distracted from her family homilies by this display, Julian coolly switched off her overhead light again, plumped her pillow, and settled sideways, her back to her seatmate. She glanced out the pressure-resistant window. Below, the East Coast USA already advanced, spreading its urban tentacles like seams of light in all directions until the sequins studding the dark would gradually densify into one blaze solid as a closely beaded fabric.

The flaw at dead center, the lie, she thought. For almost twenty years—half of her life—a dogged endeavor to love and live with each other had held out against every pressure. In fact, at the first hint of pressure cessation, either Laurence or Julian in an unspoken bargain could be relied upon to seek out more pressure, as if each sensed that without relentless forces battering against the membrane of their life together, the pressurized cabin within would be unnecessary, even dangerous for permanent habitation.

But inside the cabin, what hijackings to unplanned destinations? What had they done to one another, beyond what Hope could have done to them? Julian stared at her dim reflection in the window.

For how many years had Larry's sculptures borne mute evidence to that pressure? Long ago gone into storage his gleaming marble torsos, his masks and mirrors. A sole block of Carrara remained in a corner of his studio, unchiseled, a rosetta stone he would never decode. For how many years now had he built "dwarf environments" consisting of bent iron bars, blackened and rusting like dollhouse prison cells abandoned by even the most sadistic of authorities as unfit housing for the most violent of criminals? For how many years had Julian herself been writing in cipher, with the justification that "struggle" in a marriage could be a useful subject for the women's movement if universalized into generalization, anecdotal at times but still safe from offscreen specifics? For how many years had their relationship, and their work which had held the relationship together, been barren—as Laurence believed she was?

The flaw at the core, the lie: that they could have no child. She winced to remember all the early arguments about it, his eagerness, her insistence on postponement, his disappointment again and again, her irritation. Until one day it just seemed easier to tell him she'd seen a doctor and learned she couldn't have a child, ever.

Did I fear then that he'd leave me? she silently asked the window-woman. Did I secretly hope so? Did I just as intensely hope he'd see through me? But he never did—and whatever he sensed or wished for, he never raised the issue of adoption.

Only Julian knew the truth. Only Julian would have been capable of such complex and intimate deception for years: the humiliation of a wretched abortion in secret; the caution that made sure the pill prescription was at a pharmacy across town, different from the one they both used; hiding the pills in a bottle labeled for menstrual cramps; the continual alert, the guilt, resolve, fear, self-disgust. So much for honesty, for the revelations of Julian Travis the writer, the fiery self-determination of Julian Travis the feminist. A *real* feminist would have laid it on the line: I never intend to have a child, that's it, take it or leave it, take *me* or leave *me;* it's my body and my decision and those are my terms. A feminist wouldn't have skulked, connived, shuffled. Only a Julian would have been capable of decades-long double-agent contrivance—all the while waiting for Laurence to name, at whatever cost, the truth.

Lights went on in the cabin and Julian turned to see that the screen had gone blank. The pilot's microphoned voice informed his passengers of the impending landing in New York. The seatmate glanced up, then over at Julian, then back to absorption in her trash.

Time to re-enter the present, Julian told herself, shifting her seatback to an upright position. Baggage carousel, taxi stand. Then the ride into the city—the fast-food drive-ins, factory smokestacks, giant oil drums and warehouses and cemeteries of the outer city sliding past the cab windows. Approaching the inner city, the expressway would break out in more and more billboards, SpecialOneTimeOnly neon shopping-mall marquees. How was love between two human beings, simple, frail, to survive in a country where cheer and joy were detergents, where awe and behold had slid from the King James Version to the furniture-polish shelf? *Toys "R" Us!* a sign would proclaim in alternating shudders of red and blue. *Xmas All Yr Round!* still another would wink. Even the official road-signs ached for a copy editor's firm hand: *Thruway, X Entry, Detour (King Konstruction Co.).* When language becomes meaningless, when communication becomes Communications, when the mystery of a once holy Logos is cheapened to Madison Avenue slogans, academic jargon, diplomatic doubletalk, political rhetoric—how can love, a subtle and barely nameable mystery, hope to survive?

Cindy came on the intercom again, alerting the passengers that "We are in a holding pattern above New York's La Guardia airport because of heavy air traffic, but will be landing shortly."

Julian stretched, feeling the ache of familiar kinks in her back and neck after a long flight. *Flight,* hell yes. But how could you flee from it? How could she possibly be fair to Larry, if she were to write about this? Not deal with him at all? Disguise him, too? Change him from a sculptor to—what? Put him into one of his own long-lost beautiful mirror masks? How much can you torture one human being?

Christ, a voice screamed inside her, *we've loved each other for twenty years! Doesn't that count for something?* Where does it go—the fire, the possibility, the sweetness? How does it dwindle into dailiness? And why couldn't we have been born in some future age when women and men speak the same language?

Meanwhile—replied a Mercutio voice from the internal rep company—meanwhile, dearie, there's a real Laurence waiting, and what mood will he be in tonight? Welcoming or sullen, hopeful or withdrawn, angry, distant, depressed? Will the concern you're suddenly feeling for him appear sentimental, hypocritical—the world-traveler conquering heroine returning to the faithful spouse who's been tending the home fires?

Julian glanced down at her writing pad. The original page lay on top. Under the words *Notes for a Novel* she scribbled:

(Need for Disguises)

Then she slid the pad onto her lap and clicked her tray-table back up into position.

The Sister Passenger suddenly turned toward her.

Here it comes. Places, please. Lights to full. Five seconds to airtime.

"Excuse me," Polly Esther said, "I didn't want to disturb you before. It looked like you were writing, or . . . thinking."

Smile, Julian. There's a close-up coming.

"I couldn't help overhearing the stewardess earlier, about your being Julian Travis." Her voice deepened, warmed, the pale eyes intensifying their blue. "I know what you must be thinking. But you see, the odd thing is that if the stewardess hadn't said all that nonsense, then I'd never have known. I don't have a television. Never have. Can't bear it. So I would never have recognized your face or voice."

"I—I'm sorry, I don't quite understand . . ."

"I read. Addicted to it. Somehow lost my book in the airport without realizing it and so," gesturing toward the *McCall's*, "had to settle for this. Even this though, it's better than watching the movie. To me, at least."

"I still don't—"

"I've read every book of yours, Ms. Travis, even the poems. Always wanted to write poetry but know I can't. Always wanted to be politically involved, whatever that means, but have to settle for fighting my local fundamentalists about what books we carry in our small-town library. I run the library. I *read,*" she repeated, gently, urgently, as if to a child.

The lurch Julian felt was surely more than that of plane wheels touching down on tarmac. But Polly Esther gathered up her raincoat, ready to spring from her seat the moment the taxiing stopped.

"That's all I wanted to say, really, Ms. Travis. Don't feel you have to respond or gush or anything like that. It can't be easy, being you. Please, don't say anything. I want nothing of you, no favor, no autograph. Oh, I do want to add one more thing. The writing you've done about your marriage—loving and hating all mixed up in some kind of commitment, well, I want you to know that I was in a marriage like that. For thirty years. Often I just . . . gave up. I think we would have got divorced, but he died suddenly, two years ago. Still, your marriage—and your honesty in writing about it—gave me courage. That's all."

She was out of her seat and down the aisle before Julian could answer, and the other passengers blocked her from sight. There was nothing for Julian to do but pull herself together for the disembarking.

There it lay in her lap, staring back at her.

"A Mask of One's Own"
Notes for a Novel:
(Need for Disguises)

The rest of the page was blank.

A MASK OF ONE'S OWN

❊ A Novel

"Paradox: All Cretans are liars."
—Epimenides the Cretan

CHAPTER ONE
1950–1951

Dear Diary,

These will be the first words I'll ever write in a diary of my very own. Momma gave you to me, and I think you were the best of all the presents she gave me on yesterday, my eighth birthday. I will never ever have another eighth birthday in my life. I also got a new pair of barrettes for my hair and three more dolls for the collection and a pair of white kid gloves and Momma and I had lunch at the Plaza Hotel and last night we went to the opera to see Carmen who had a rose between her teeth and got killed. It was very interesting. But you are the best of all, Dear Diary, because I wanted a diary and Momma knew that and here you are. I love your shiny blue leather cover with the strip that has a lock in it and the tiny golden key that can shut you. Momma is going to keep the key because she says I'll just lose it and also she wants to check and be sure I write in you every single day and also so she can correct my spelling mistakes. Because she says you never know who else might look. I'm a pretty good speller and I think nobody would look if I had the key but then you never know and they could always just cut the strip I guess anyway. So I'll be careful what I write in you I mean about the spelling.

It is a wonderful feeling to write in you because your paper is smooth and slippery and the color of the cream I lick off the milk bottle's round cardboard top. You are very important to me even if anybody else can look into you because you never know.

Your friend, with love,
Julian Travis

Dear Diary,
Momma says she is glad that yesterday I wrote down all the good things we did on my birthday and how special it was. She says it will be a treasure for me to look back on when I grow up and remember how happy these years were. I'm sure Momma is right because otherwise a person might forget these things when they get old.

Today was pretty normal so there's not much to tell you about. I know it's funny to call you "you" dear diary but you seem real to me. Anyway, today Momma and I got up and had breakfast. Momma always has coffee and a muffin which is also one of her names for me. Muffin I mean not coffee. So our joke is that Momma always has coffee and me for breakfast. I had cereal which I always hate especially the raisins which I know you're supposed to like because most people eat the cereal only for the raisins. But the raisins don't help me because I hate both. Anyway, so then we got dressed and I wore the pink organdy with white butterflies aplikayed (spelling? Help Momma!) on it that Momma sewed for me (Momma makes all my clothes, dear diary, and she's wonderful at it) and my white maryjane shoes with the straps that I hate but today I didn't have to use shoe polish to clean them because they were still clean from yesterday when I wore the black patent leather ones instead.

Then we took the train into New York City to rehearsal (we live in Yonkers, dear diary, which is called a suburb) and went to rehearsal and then I had an interview which is why the pink organdy today and then we took the train back. Then there was school and ballet and tap class and then I did my homework and practiced piano and studied my lines for tomorrow's rehearsal. I should tell you more I guess but I'm too sleepy right now. I almost didn't want to write in you tonight but I want to every single night so I did.

Your friend, with love,
Julian Travis

Dear Diary,

Momma says I should put the date on every time I write in you so that years later when I am grown up I will know the exact time of my happy memories. Today was October 10, 1950. I should tell you who I am, dear diary.

My name is Julian Travis and I am an actress. I'll tell you about me the way I'm supposed to in an interview. I had my own radio program but that was when I was younger and also I was on "The Whiz Kids" for two years which is a show they put you on if you're smart when you're little or at least can say funny things that sound smart. But now I'm on a television show every week in "Family" (that's the name of the program) and I'm Ingrid (that's the little girl I play). It is very popular and I am famous I think. But I am not just famous. I am a serious actress. I can become anything anyone wants me to be. Anyway, I live with my mother, whose name is Hope Travis— and it fits her because she always says she is full of hope! We live in apartment 3-A, which is on the third floor (we don't have an elevator but Momma thinks someday soon when I make enough money we might move into the city itself and live in a fancy elevator building). Our apartment building is only one block from the railroad station which is good because we go into the city for rehearsals and the shows and stuff every day except on weekends and sometimes I do a fashion show even on a weekend day (I'm also a model, diary). What is not so good about our apartment house is that it is right next door to a place everybody says they should tear down and make into something clean like a parking lot because it has lots of little funny wooden buildings on it, sort of leaning as if they could fall down. A lot of Negro people live there and some of the houses don't have electric light and everybody says they are a fire hazard. They are a fire hazard because the Negro people have to use candles to see by and have wood stoves everybody says. But I don't know how you're supposed to see in the dark or keep warm if you don't have electric plugs. They are very poor, Momma says, and always on Thanksgiving and sometimes on other holidays (but not on Jewish holidays because Momma says none of the Negro people would ever be Jewish) Momma and I go over to the houses with shopping bags. We bring cans of food we buy on special at the A&P and lots of oranges you can get in sort of wiry bags. And we put some of my clothes I get too big for to give in the shopping bags. But we never put the organdies in there even when I get too big for them. Because Momma thinks we should save them so I can treasure them when I grow up and also she says where would the little girls next door wear such things?

There is one little girl next door who is just the same age as me and her name is Jewell which is sort of like Julian and I think she would look beautiful in one of the organdy dresses because she has a nice smile and is very friendly but Momma told me it would be an insult to give her one of the organdy dresses and I would never want to insult Jewell. I'd like to go play with her sometimes but Momma and I talked about that. She explained to me that everybody was exactly the same and Negroes were just as good as white people and poor people were just the same as rich ones. But life wasn't perfect, Momma said, and you had to face facts. Facts was that if Jewell came to 3-A to play she would only get jealous of all the dolls and pretty dresses and how lucky I was. And if I went over to Jewell's house to play first it was too small and we would have to play outside and we shouldn't play outside because that was dangerous the ground over there has broken glass and bottle tops and rusty metal things and I might fall and hurt myself or even bust up my face. And Momma also explained that wanting to play with Jewell was a wonderful idea but it wouldn't work because Jewell and I had nothing in common and Jewell knew that even if I didn't. I don't think Jewell knows that. Even if she did we would have a lot more in common if she had one of the dolls and an organdy dress. Besides, they don't have television sets over there next door because no plugs which means that Jewell doesn't even know I'm on television. So she might think I'm just a little girl like her. She always smiles a nice smile at me.

If we went to the same school maybe we would have something in common and would be allowed to become friends and play. But I don't know where Jewell goes to school. I go to a private school and there are only fifty pupils in the whole school and nobody looks like Jewell. I mean not only that nobody is a Negro person but also nobody smiles a nice smile at me. At school everybody knows I'm on television every week so they act like we have nothing in common. Also I'm pretty smart in school and a good reader and have what Mr. Pierce (he's the director of our show) calls "a fast memory." That helps with learning my lines and also in school. But being good in school doesn't help me have more in common with the other kids there. I think they think I stink and am a rotten stuck-up pig (Doris said that) but Momma says I should ignore it and trust her and that they're just jealous. I think Jewell would have a lot more to be jealous of me about if she wanted to because she has only one doll which is a Raggedy Ann and no organdy dress but she seems to like me. But since we have nothing in common I guess we can't be real friends. Momma says we can be friends of course, and I should always smile back and be polite and greet *all* our neighbors (in the building and even next door) when I see them. But that's not being real friends. I will understand all this when I'm old, Momma says, I should trust her and besides the world will change and people won't be poor anymore and she is full of hope. I believe her because she's the best Momma in the world and she is giving her whole life to me. I love her more than anything else and I hope I die before she does because I wouldn't want to live without Momma.

I'm too tired to write more now so I'll tell you more about myself another time, maybe tomorrow. Good night.

Your friend, with love,
Julian

Dear Diary,
This time I really will tell you about myself. I am eight years old, but you already know that because you were born on my eighth birthday (which means we have the same birthday, Oct. 7!) and I have brown eyes and blonde hair. When I was young my hair was very blonde. You can see it in the pictures of me when I did the baby food ads and the toddler clothes ads. But last year it began to get dark and become what Mr. Pierce called "dirty blonde" even though we wash my hair every night and Momma sets it in curls with bobbypins and hairset while I sit on the toilet seat and study my lines. Anyway, Mr. Pierce and even Miss Unger (she's our show's Executive Producer) were getting worried, and so they had a talk with Momma about my hair and now since January we go every three weeks to Charles of the Ritz to keep my hair blonde. I

like Charles of the Ritz, because it means I miss half an afternoon of school even if I do have to do makeup homework. Charles of the Ritz is named after a great hairdresser who is either dead or anyway never there. It is in the city and very expensive Momma says so I always sit still and don't waste time. I like the shiny white marble floor and the pink silk coat they put on you and the big soft chair you climb into that turns in every direction and walls and walls and even the ceiling of mirrors. You can see millions of yourselves turning in all directions. The rest I hate. Miss Frances is very nice to me and always talks about how I am a little princess but then she puts this stuff on my head and it stinks awfully and the smell makes me sick in my stomach. Momma and Miss Frances say to hold my nose and breathe through my mouth but the smell even stings in my throat like it does on my head and it goes on and on because they leave it on your head and go away while you do your homework or study your lines or something. You have to be very *very* careful not to let it drip down your forehead into your eyes if you bend your head down because you could go blind. So I always hold my head straight ahead of me and lift my homework or my lines to up there which makes my arms tired. After a while, Miss Frances comes back and then it gets better because we have a shampoo which gets the stuff out and then conditioner she says and a set and then I sit under the dryer like all the women in their silk coats. And then we do comb out and it all is silky golden curls and Miss Frances and Momma and Miss Unger and everybody is happy. Your head stays stinging for two or three days and hot water especially on it hurts when your hair is getting washed even at home but then the sting goes away until the next time you have to go to Charles of the Ritz. I wish I hadn't become a dirty blonde.

Dear Diary, I'm very sorry and I apologize because I always mean to tell you about myself but always get too tired. Today I had rehearsal in the morning and then school and then the lesson with my drama coach in foreign accents. We did French and British today. Tomorrow I have piano after school so I had to do extra practice tonight after homework because I was falling behind. So now I'm too sleepy to write more. I apologize dear diary.

Oh and I almost forgot. I'm not going to sign what I write in you like I have been, I mean "your friend with love, Julian" anymore. Because way back that is what we decided I should write on the fan pictures I autograph (we are very honest about this and I sign them all myself for real even if other television stars use a rubber stamp because Momma says we have a duty to our fans). But you are not a fan and I don't want to sign this like that. Even if you feel like a real friend and I feel like I really do love you, those words got used up somewhere else. But I don't know what else to sign this with. I would never want to insult you. I apologize.

Julian

Dear Diary,

Today is October 12th and I don't see why I have to always tell you what day it is because I've been writing something in you every single day since Momma gave you to me on your and my birthday so if anybody reads this because you never know they can always count up. Momma did read you last night after I was asleep but I guess you know that. This morning on the train she explained to me that it was a waste of time and of you with your blue leather cover and creamy paper to fill you up with drivel she said about things like Jewell and Charles of the Ritz. She said a person should be positive and write happy things in a diary or else if anybody looked at it you never know they would get the wrong impression and think life was nothing but miserable. My life is not at all miserable and I know that I am very very lucky to be beautiful and have a fast memory and be a television star and have hundreds of loyal fans and go to a private school and have organdy dresses and a doll collection and wonderful privileges like music and dancing lessons and the best mother in the whole world. I apologize, dear diary, if I gave you the wrong impression. Momma explained that even if nobody ever read what I wrote in you still when I was old and read you myself I might get the wrong impression and besides who wants to remember bad things an old person wants to remember the good times. I have never been old yet so I believe what Momma says. I certainly would not want to give me the wrong impression.

I'm very tired tonight so I guess I will stop now and I'm sorry I didn't write in you much today.

Julian

Dear Diary,
This is October 13th and it was Show Day. A Show Day is always special. I don't go to school at all on Show Day (I do full school makeup work at home on Saturdays) not even for a half-day as usual because we start rehearsal at ten in the morning right in the studio itself and do a runthrough and then a lunch break and then a full dress rehearsal and then dinner break and then get our makeup put on and there's The Show itself. We don't get out of the studio until ten o'clock at night! And so even though I'm tired I'm going to write in you right now on the train going home (I apologize that's why my writing is so bumpy) because I know that when we get home Momma always puts me down right away even if I'm excited because she says she knows I'm tired and also there's the Saturday makeup schoolwork tomorrow and a new script to start learning. And I have my singing lessons on Saturdays, too.

Anyway, today was *Friday the 13th!!* And Miss Clement and everybody else in the cast went around very nervous because it was Show Day and we do our show live and not on tape beforehand which means anything could go wrong you never know. But doing our show live is what gives it its magic Miss Unger says. I wasn't nervous even though I had a big part in this one which was about Ingrid, who is the little girl I play, remember? getting in trouble for being a tomboy until she wins a baseball game for the neighbor kids by hitting a home run. I wasn't a bit nervous because in secret (except for Momma, who knows *all* my secrets) I know that 13 is my lucky number. So even though I could have been nervous because I'm not a tomboy and I don't even know how to throw a ball right or catch one I still wasn't nervous. In rehearsal Mr. Pierce had said he "despaired" of me. "Julie," he said, "I despair of you." I hate hate hate it when anybody calls me Julie. I don't mind Jule so much but I hate hate hate Julie. But you can't say that to Mr. Pierce, no matter how politely. I asked Momma to tell him but she said she didn't dare to either and besides everybody else called me something different from Julie anyway like Elfin and Sweetie and Princess and whenever they talk about me between themselves they call me The Baby which Momma says I should understand because after all I am the youngest member of the cast and why be fussy? I hate hate

hate The Baby, too. But anyway dear diary I want to be positive and Mr. Pierce is really very nice to me and says I am brilliant and a trooper and professional and precocious (spelling? Help, Momma!) and his little Sarah Burnheart (who was the greatest actress who ever lived and died a long time ago). But he despaired of me this time and swore bad words and yelled why can't this kid even catch a ball. I couldn't help it. I kept shutting my eyes tight and sort of ducking down when it came flying at me. You never know, it could bust up your face. Momma talked to me and I tried I really tried to keep my eyes open but then my hands went up in front of my face instead. I don't think it's so silly to duck when somebody throws something at you and it wasn't so silly that time when the crazy man threw a rock on the last personal appearance tour. It was good I ducked that time or Momma said I could have got a scar or lost an eye or something horrible. They took the crazy man away to an insane place and he was crying and everything and I felt sorry for him but I sure wasn't sorry I ducked. Jewell next door can throw a ball and catch it perfect every time. I've watched her do it. After Mr. Pierce despaired of me in rehearsal I thought it would be a wonderful idea if Jewell could teach me how she did it after all it was for my part and she could rehearse me all week on my ball stuff after school just like Momma rehearses me my lines and cues after homework. But Momma said that was not practical and so Momma and Mr. Pierce and Miss Luchino (she writes the scripts for the show) all had a conference because nobody wanted to bother Miss Unger and they solved the whole thing by hiring a double to catch and throw (that's called a stunt) and they would shoot that scene in a long-shot. It felt funny to see another little girl wearing my costume with her hair done up just like mine. It felt funny to see her being *me*, except for in the close-ups. They called her the stunt kid and I never even got to know her name. She knew just how to do it, too. I don't know how she learned to throw and catch like that but Momma said which would you rather know how to do, throw a ball or be a star, catch a ball or get A's in school, and I told Momma I'd rather be who I am and we laughed together at it. I love Momma because she didn't want me to feel bad and so she told me to dry my smile and remember that anybody could play ball but only me could be loved by thousands of people I've never even met.

The train is getting close to Yonkers so I will stop writing this now. But Friday the 13th was my lucky day and I wasn't nervous at all. Thousands of people will love me even more because they won't have any idea it was my double in the long-shot. They'll think I am the best child star in the world and can also throw and catch good as Babe Ruth. Like Momma says, it was a triumph.

Julian

Dear Diary,
Today I have been eight for a whole week! And you are one week old! This was a wonderful week. It started with my birthday but you know about that. Then I got First in class doing multiplication (spelling? Momma?) tables by memory. Doris stuck her tongue out at me and Teacher saw her and she got caught and had to write I WILL NOT BE RUDE in her notebook 20 times and was I glad. She is just as good as me in arithmetic but does not have a fast memory ha ha. Also Teacher said my vocabulary (spell?) is remarkable (spell?). But that's not all. Mr. Jonas (he's my piano teacher) gave me a postcard with Beethoven on it because he said I was "coming along so well" and had real talent. Momma says she isn't surprised and that I am a walking talent factory! Today Mrs. Douglas who is my singing teacher said even if I couldn't hardly carry a tune (and Momma thinks she's crazy wrong about that it's just I'm too little yet) still I can talk-sing Mrs. Douglas said with "such charm" it didn't matter and Shirley Temple couldn't carry a tune either. (It matters to Momma, who wants only the best for me in everything, but it doesn't matter to me because Shirley Temple was sort of musical comedy and I am a serious actress and so don't need to sing anyway.)

Then there was my triumph about the double girl last night and how no one will know I can't throw or catch a ball as if I cared. Momma rolled her eyes at me and whispered how we should hope hope hope Miss Luchino never writes a show where Ingrid will have to roller skate or ride a bike or do something else silly or even dangerous! We crossed our fingers together and giggled, Momma and me. A person doesn't need friends in school when she has a mother like Momma! (I don't care even if Miss Luchino does write a show like that because now I know they can always hire the little girl who can do these silly things to be me and nobody will even know.) It's more important (and even Mr. Pierce says this) that I am such a professional and never complain (which reminds me of the best thing of all but I'll tell you after I tell you this) and that I have a fast memory and am so d——n (Mr. Pierce uses bad words a lot) smart and also can cry real tears any time the script says Ingrid cries. (I can, too. Even better than Margaret O'Brien. They said she always had to wait and think of something sad first. But I can just cry whenever they need me to. I don't know how I do it.)

But Pay Attention as Mr. Pierce always says if I talk too much. Pay Attention, diary, to the best part of all this week. I didn't tell you this before because I was too scared I wouldn't be able to finish it perfectly. See, every year on my birthday I always give Momma a present, too. Because, like she says, she was there when I was born. She almost died, too, diary. I never want to have a baby and almost die. Every night I pray thank you to God she didn't die and leave me an orphan. So when I was a tiny baby for my birthdays she would always get herself a little present too, along with the presents for me. Because she didn't die. But when I was four and already a big girl *I* started to give her her present on my birthday instead of her giving herself one. I only started getting an allowance last year (a whole quarter a week!) so until last year I drew a picture for Momma or wrote her a poem for her present. Last year I saved up my quarters *all year* and when Aunt Essie came up to New York I got to go shopping with her and I bought Momma pearl earrings. (They weren't real pearl but almost.) Momma loved them! But this year Aunt Essie never came because Momma and her had a fight last year and she hurt Momma's feelings and was just jealous of us. Aunt Yetta didn't come either. So how was I going to buy Momma her present without anybody to take me? (Never mind Momma if you see this ha ha I'll keep saving it up for *your* birthday, if I can find somebody to take me by then). Anyway so what was I going to do this year for Momma's present on *my* birthday? I didn't want to give her another poem or draw another picture. But then I thought of the perfect thing!

Well, diary, this is what I did. Before my birthday, I mean for a while before, maybe a month, I had been being a very diffi- cult (spelling?) child. I didn't mean to, but I guess I was. I had talked back and had a sharp tongue and left my white shoes not polished so I couldn't wear them one day when they were supposed to be ready. And also I acted phony because when Momma let me go to the library for Saturday afternoon story hour all by myself (because the library is right on the other side of our apartment building, and Momma can watch me from the window) I went but then snuck out and ran back across to see if maybe Jewell would like to teach me about the ball thing. But Momma was still at the window and yelled out and so I had to come in and I missed even story hour by being a phony. There were more things I did like that but I don't want to remember the bad things I'd like to be positive. I was very very sorry to have made Momma so miserable during that bad time. So I thought of the perfect birthday present for her! It was to *promise* for a whole *year* not to ever make her miserable. I drew a chart and everything. At the top it has the days of the week. On the side it has a list of things I do that give her nerves or hurt her, and not to do them to hurt her, the dearest Momma in the whole wide world! This is the list I made.

> To Obey
> Not to Argue
> Not to be Lazy
> Not to Complain
> Not to Talk So Much
> Not to be Selfish
> Not to be a Phony

That is the list. Then I gave Momma the chart and a little box of gold stars I had that you can paste on things. And I told her that each week all year we would make up a new chart and I'd try for perfect for the whole year until I was nine. Momma laughed and hugged me. Then she said what was going to happen after I turned nine? So we both giggled and she said my grandpa who I never knew always would say "Left foot right foot" so Momma said let's just try it a week at a time okay?

So dear diary we did just that!

And now I can tell you on *every single day* of this last week there is a *gold star* beside every single thing on the list!!! I didn't make Momma miserable or give her nerves *all week long!* Momma says it already is the best present she's ever had in her whole life!

I am going to stop writing now because I wrote a lot whew and my hand is tired. Tomorrow Momma is getting me a surprise privilege because I'm the best child anybody could ever have. But I can't tell you what because I don't know yet. Be in suspense like me, diary! Good night. I love you.

Julian

Dear Diary,
We slept till nine o'clock! And then Momma made lots of bacon and toast for breakfast! And then we made peanut butter cookies together. I made the crisscross designs to flatten the cookies with a fork after we rolled the dough (spell?) into balls on the cookie sheet. Then we took a bubble bath together. Then we played tickle after the bath without our clothes on and I got her and she got me and we laughed so hard we almost cried. Then we got dressed and went for a walk to the park and fed the ducks in the pond. They were so cute and there was a Momma duck with the baby ducks right behind her in a row (just like Momma and me!). I would love to have a pet but they can give you diseases Momma says. But I'm sure glad I *don't* have any brothers or sisters like those ducks. I wouldn't want to share Momma so I'm glad it's just the two of us against the world like Momma says. And *then* we went and had dinner out and I had chicken and mashed potatoes with gravy and *peach!!!* ice cream! Momma had shrimp salad because she's on a diet. And then we walked home and looked in the store windows on Franklin Street and I told Momma I'd like to be able to buy her a mink coat and anything else she wanted. And we decided that our career was going wonderfully and if Mr. Ehrenreich (he's my agent) could get me that salary raise (I don't know how much money I make but I guess it's not enough yet) then we would just *do* it! We'd move into New York City (that's Manhattan, diary) into a fancy building with an elevator! Momma would love that, and I would too. Because I don't like the smell in the hall of our building. It's like somebody spilled grease on the floor and it got old but then you tried to clean it up with strong cleaning stuff but both smells stuck together.

And we only have one bedroom here anyway, so Momma and I have twin beds but maybe when we move I can have my very own room!! Also like Momma says, there is just almost *no* closet space in this apartment so that's why we have to hang things on the back of all the doors but there's so much hanging there that it sticks out all big and puffy with the sleeves like arms and if you wake up in the middle of the night it makes scary shapes that you don't want to move in bed for fear they might notice and come down from hanging there and get you with their flappy arms. And then maybe I can do extra parts in other shows if Mr. Ehrenreich can get Miss Unger to not have me in an exclusive contract. After all, I can pretend to be anybody they want me to be. I'd like to play other parts too because sometimes I get sick of Ingrid all the time but still I'm lucky because the cast is like having a second family, with another Momma who's Miss Clement and a brother and even a father and everything. (Oh diary I forgot to tell you that my father died before I was born. He loved Momma more than anything else in the whole world but he had to go into the war. He was a doctor and so he became a doctor in the army and cured soldiers and never killed anybody but he got killed anyhow. I maybe will be a doctor when I grow up, like my father.)

Anyway Pay Attention! So we could get out of this apartment and the smell in the hall and Hazel the woman next door who talks to herself on the stairs and Momma says stay away from and Mr. Tompkins the super who drinks too much and says worse words even than Mr. Pierce and never fixes *any-*thing. There's plaster coming off the wall which Momma says she hates hates hates just behind the storage trunk that's covered with the big Mexican blanket. But Momma also says it doesn't matter that Mr. Tompkins won't ever paint because we'll probably move from here soon anyway and besides who wants to take down the pictures from the walls? There's lots of them, diary, *lots.* They're almost all of me (Momma says I am the most photographed child in history!) in different show costumes or in my ballet tutu (that's a very short dress and is puffy and one of them that looks scary on the back of the door) and modeling and on a horse once (that was for publicity and I got *right* off!) and other stuff. So you see it's just as well we don't get painted by Mr. Tompkins after all. But still, there's this long orange face in the sink from the drips all the time. And there's a green snake in the tub from the drips there. Also sometimes there are bugs in the kitchen and *I* hate hate hate *that.* That's not our fault we're clean and spotless it's Mr. Tompkin's fault and the other people in this building. Or maybe the fault of the

Negroes to the side of us because Momma always makes me scrub hard in the tub after we bring them baskets? I don't think it could be the fault of the library because the library is *really* spotless and very very quiet. I love the library. And I'm a good reader (I could read even before I started school!) so I try to go there every time I can (except that time I was phony and snuck off to Jewell and gave Momma nerves).

The library has a *huge* round ceiling inside and on every single wall there are just books books books. Also on stands right in the middle of the room. Also in glass cases. Also on little carts. You could never read so many books in all your life even if you didn't have rehearsal and school and singing and piano and tap and ballet and everything else. But I would like to try. I would like to live in the library. It's spotless there for real and so quiet that Miss Quentin says Shhhh! if anybody makes noise to disturb you or give you nerves. You can learn about *every*thing *any*where in there. I never thought of it before but I bet you could even learn about balls and bikes and roller skates and surprise everybody by just knowing how to do it! (If you ever get a surprise like that, Momma, if you're reading this, you'll know what I was doing in the library!)

But really now Pay Attention!! So Momma and I came home after the walk and we talked about our Future and how even if it is just us against the world we're special enough to triumph. I don't care if it's just us, I'm glad. I'd hate a real brother or sister and I'm glad I don't have a daddy even if that is a terrible thing to say and even if sometimes I miss him but like Momma says how can I miss him when I never even met him? And besides, I have Lansing Harris, who plays my television father and is so nice that I call him Papa even off the set and he likes it. I'd hate to have a wicked stepfather.

So I really have everything and I'm glad Momma and me have each other just to ourselves. She says what do we need with a husband *I'm* like her tiny husband because my acting brings home the bacon, she says, and it will take us far. I want to do that for Momma, more than anything in the world. She's my dearest little Momma and I can take care of her better than any old husband could. She's so good to me, she never punishes me, even if I give her nerves. If I'm bad, I just get my privileges taken away, like going to the library that time, or being taken to the movies, or watching Milton Berle on TV or playing cards with Abe on the set in the breaks. Stuff like that. But privileges are bonuses anyway, like extras, so I shouldn't miss them, having them taken away that's not really punishments like other kids get.

Most of all, there isn't a little girl in America who wouldn't want to be me. Everybody says that. Momma says if we keep on this way I'll be a rich woman all my life even if I decide to stop acting someday and do something else (like be a doctor) but that it would be a shame to leave our career when I was already a star and going to be an even bigger star. I don't care about being a rich woman all my life but I would like to be a little bit rich and make Momma very rich so she can have all the things she wants like a mink coat. She says the way up for us is just what we're doing and every little girl dreams of getting up there by being a star. And last year when I was only seven I got a big scroll we have up on the wall from these people the American Federation of Women's Auxiliaries and they named me the Ideal American Girl. So it must be true.

Well diary I have to go study my lines now because Momma and me we played all day so she says we better do *some* work before our beauty sleep. And Momma is working on her stocks which are also going to help make us rich. It was a wonderful day and I wish it wasn't going to be tomorrow soon.

Goodnight, diary,
Julian

Dear Diary,
Today was October 22nd. I haven't written in you for a whole week. I apologize, diary. But it wasn't my fault. Well, in a way it was, but not because I didn't care about you or writing in you. I really love writing in you even if somebody else will read it because you never know. I didn't just not pay attention to you for a whole week because I don't care about you. I couldn't find you.

You see, I did a terrible thing or at least it turned out terrible and I should have known better. So I had a big privilege taken away and that was you. I couldn't write in you for a whole week. A whole week missed out of my life that you'll never know about because I can't remember all of it even though I'll try.

It started with the terrible thing, right at the start. On Monday, because it's an easy day and I don't have any special lessons after school so there's only homework and the script Momma let me go to the library for a half hour. And I really did go. I am reading Lamb's Tales of Shakespear because in only a few years I will be old enough to play Juliet in Romeo and Juliet she was really only fourteen did you know that, diary? I didn't. That's what reading gets you. And I asked Miss Quentin to please come and tell me when half an hour was up because even though there's a big clock in the library I'm not so perfect at telling time yet. (I'm okay on the hours but I sometimes get mixed up on the quarters and halfs and anything in between.) And so she did and I left right when I was supposed to leave. I was trying for my second Perfect Week with stars but now I've gone and ruined everything for the whole year. Even if every single other week is perfect the whole year won't be because of this week and the terrible thing I should have known better.

So I was walking all by myself (I love that part) next door to our building. And then I saw just ahead up the block by our building this awful thing. It was a fight. It was Benjy and Roger who are these two boys from upstairs in 4-A and Benjy is also eight and Roger is ten and their father is not dead but him and their mother are divorced. That means they don't live together anymore and probably hate each other. Miss Clement has been divorced three times and is on her fourth husband and she says when will she ever learn and that must mean a lot of hating. Anyway, sometimes Momma and Liz from 4-A have coffee together and talk either upstairs or down here and when they do the kid or kids in whichever place is sent up or down to the other place. Us kids are supposed to play together whichever place we are. But I hate hate hate Benjy and even more Roger who is a bully. If we play up in 4-A they have only airplanes and guns and boring stuff and never want to play house or doctor or Hamlet. (I read Hamlet in Lamb's Tales I told you about and I thought we could act a play on it, with the ghost and everything.) They are very very stupid dumb boys. If we play down here in 3-A Roger likes to twist my dolls' arms around and once he broke one. They do not even know how to play poker and you can't teach them anything they are too dumb. Benjy likes to bang on the piano and I hate that. He can't even play Chopsticks and I tried to teach him it was no use. I despair of both of them. So we just watch TV but I think the cartoons are boring because I've seen how they do them on these big drawing boards and now it's never the same. But there's nothing else to do with these boys. The only good thing is when it's my turn to go upstairs I can have a Coke because they always have lots of Coke in the icebox. Liz says Honey (she calls everybody Honey) I'm from Mississippi (spell? spell?) and we just all *live* on Coke and cigarettes! I'm not allowed Coke except on special occassions (spell?) and we never have it in our icebox because Momma says it will rot my teeth and give me *huge* cavities. But I can have a Coke when I go upstairs and that's the only good thing I can think of about Benjy or Roger. And it's no good saying what can you expect from kids who don't have a father around (Hazel says this to herself whenever she passes them on the steps) because after all look at me I'm not dumb and a bully. I know I'm lucky to be me and not everybody especially not boys can be me but still they could be better than they are.

Well, diary, on that day they were specially horrible. Because it was Roger I saw up ahead on the street, and he was hitting and kicking at Jewell. Benjy was helping him and dancing around them and singing yaa yaa niggerbaby and terrible words like that that Momma and I never never use. And Jewell she was fighting and hitting back and shouting words like Mr. Tompkins uses but I was proud of her because she would have licked Roger right out except it was just not fair because there was Benjy to help hit her when Roger went down so they took turns but she never got to rest in between. And there were two of them and one of her and that's just not fair. So before I could think about it and I know now I should have known better I ran right up and I hit Roger hard on the back of his head with the Lamb's Tales of Shakespear Miss Quentin had let me take out now that I have my junior library card and then when he turned around (and was he surprised, dear diary!) I kicked him in the shins.

Benjy just stood there. But it gave Jewell time enough to reach out and sock Roger biff bam wham like in the comic books right on the side of his turned around surprised face. Roger hit me and pushed me and I fell down in the gutter where it's all dirty and my dress (which wasn't one of the organdy ones thank you Dear God) I heard it rip and then Roger jumped on me with his knees and he was very heavy because by this time Jewell had jumped on his back and was strangling him around the neck but the two of them together were *very* heavy on my stomach. And so I reached up to get Roger off of me because there was murder in his eyes (I read that somewhere maybe about Othello who really did kill someone or maybe about Macbeth who killed lots of people) so I was worried. Maybe his eyes were just bulging because Jewell was holding on so tight from behind his neck but I didn't want to take any chances and besides the two of them were making me not breathe almost. So I started to bang and bang at Roger's face with my book and his nose started to bleed and the cover got bloody and then once I missed Roger and hit Jewell by mistake and then Jewell got thrown off him which I didn't like because then she fell but at least it wasn't so heavy because I was beginning to worry that Benjy would jump on Jewell who was on Roger who was on me at the bottom in the dirty gutter and I'd get squashed flat and die.

Anyway, so then Benjy started to cry like a baby when he saw Roger's nosebleed and I bet Roger got extra mad because not only was he getting beaten but Benjy was there and seeing it. So he picked up this dumb stupid part of one of his airplanes he must have dropped in the fight that was laying on the ground beside me in the gutter and he started to hit me in the face with it like I had hit him with the book. And then there was yelling and grownups around and I heard Momma screaming My God Where Where and her voice was coming closer and then Roger was getting pulled off of me and Benjy was crying louder and the snot running down out of his stupid nose and the blood running down out of his brother's stupid nose and Momma was screaming and bending over me and Liz was yelling at Jewell and I turned my head and I saw the front of my dress torn bad and also bloody. But I didn't know if that was Roger bleeding onto me or me bleeding onto me because what I really paid attention to was Jewell running away. She was running like the wind, faster than Atalanta in my big Greek myths book and she was getting smaller and smaller and she ran even past the Negro houses and kept on running and disappeared around the corner down by the railroad tracks where kids sometimes hid or played you could see them when you were waiting for the train to rehearsal.

And I started to cry, too, then. Because all of a sudden I

wasn't sure if Jewell had thought I was joining in with Benjy and Roger against her or if she knew that the two of us, her and me, were on the same side. How could she be sure, because after all she always smiled at me but I never asked her to play and she never got one of my organdy dresses, and maybe she knew that I did play with Roger and Benjy even though I hated to but how could she know that? I thought as she got smaller and smaller like the wind and then disappeared that now I'd never get to learn how she was so good at throwing and catching balls. Maybe she just wasn't scared when things got thrown at her and so she threw them back. But she was scared of the grownups and none of the grownups were Negro people. They were Momma and Liz and even Miss Quentin ran out and she took back the book before I could say I apologize about the blood on it. And there was Hazel out of nowhere talking to herself and Mr. Tompkins saying These people It's just not right This used to be a good block.

But most of all Momma was crying and crying and because she was screaming "Your face! Your face! My God My God" I knew it wasn't Roger's nose on my ripped front then and finally I got scared too.

Well, diary, Momma carried me upstairs and everybody was crying and the doctor came and it was just a long scratch from under my eye down to my jaw and the doctor said it wouldn't leave a scar. I wonder if they called a doctor for Jewell, or if she needed one. And after Momma stopped saying Thank God over and over and hugging me she got mad. I had done a terrible thing that could have ruined our whole Future and she had a bad bad case of nerves.

So I had my bath and my dress was "hopeless" Momma said and she threw it out because she was "disgusted" with me she said. I had been fighting in the street right in the gutter and I was the Ideal American Girl and it just made her disgusted. And then I had to go to bed early and she took you away and there went my privilege of writing in you for a whole week she said.

I tried to explain about two against one and not fair because Momma says always how important it is to be fair but she said she didn't want to hear it. So that was that.

And the rest of the week sort of just got worse. Mr. Pierce swore at Momma when he saw my face next day at rehearsal, and Miss Luchino said she thought she'd have a heart attack. They called up Miss Unger so you knew it was really bad. She came down to rehearsal wearing the sun-glasses she always has on so you can never see her eyes even in the dark studio before the lights get turned on, and it was only after she said like some sort of wise judge or king in a play deciding something while everybody waited around, she said "I think our magician Pietro can fix it with makeup by Friday." And then everyone sort of breathed and laughed and said that's what they thought of course themselves. Mr. Pierce and Miss Luchino said they were sorry to have to call her down to rehearsal like that but they wanted to be sure it wasn't an emergency.

So then I knew Mr. Pierce and Miss Luchino were in trouble with Miss Unger and Momma was in trouble with Mr. Pierce and Miss Luchino and I was in trouble with Momma and everybody else.

Things didn't get better and by Friday Mr. Pierce said this was the worst week of his directing career d———n all of you meaning the whole cast. Miss Clement had three migraines (spell?) in one week and Mr. Pierce said I'd probably brought that on because Miss Clement hated violence of any sort (after four husbands and all that hate you can understand why). Then Ricky (that's Rick McPherson who plays my teenage brother even though he's 23 but looks younger) lost lots of money at the track (which is where they race horses and bet money on them) and wanted his salary in advance but Mr. Pierce said No that had happened once too often. I thought poor Ricky he was once a child actor like me and sometimes he makes me laugh about things but Momma says he never was a real star like me so what does he know and we have nothing in common even though I should always be polite. But I like him a lot anyway because he can't ride a bike even now at 23 years old. But I don't want to grow up like Ricky and lose all our Future at the track. I heard Miss Luchino say to Mr. Pierce that it was an addiction (spell?) like booze (which is getting drunk). Which reminds me that to make everything worse, Papa (that's not my real father you remember diary he's dead but this is Lance Harris who I call Papa because he acts it) well Papa came to rehearsal "drunk as a loon" Miss Clement said right out loud. I don't know what a loon is but it must be drunk, because Papa was very happy and lifted me up and kept throwing me in the air and I loved him even if his breath did smell a little like our apartment building hall. And then he threw his arms around Mr. Pierce and called him "Sid darling" and Miss Luchino said sharp to Momma Get that kid off the set.

So you see it was a very terrible week, diary, even if we are really a happy family on our show. Momma says it's a miracle we got through it. But we did. And there's no more time to tell you about school or anything else which was all the same as usual anyway.

You see why I apologize to you for paying you no attention all this time but I couldn't get to you. And now there's never going to be a Perfect Record of writing in you every single day ever again because that's been ruined for all time and this terrible week has ruined my Perfect Chart for all year.

I really really had wanted to write in you every single day for the rest of my whole life, and now I'll never be able to do that. I'm really sad about that. I'm so very sorry, diary. Forgive me and please try to understand.

Apologetically (spell?)
Julian

Dear Diary,
I know this time I missed two days but at least it's not a whole week even if I did skip all by my own fault and not from losing a privilege. But it's just not the same now that I can't say I've never missed a day because I had to miss that whole week. It's not perfect anymore. But I still love you diary don't think I don't. If I was allowed to I would even show you to Jewell because then she could see from the earlier stuff I wrote in you that I had liked her all along for real and she wouldn't think I had joined in to help Benjy and Roger. But I'm not allowed to do that and I've "butted in enough" like Momma says. Besides, I haven't seen Jewell down by the tracks or playing in front of her little wood house since that day, and I don't know if she's hiding or moved away or maybe even died from being beat up by those dumb stupid idiot bullies upstairs I still hate them and always will. Momma and Liz go on having coffee together but us kids don't go up or down to play together while they do it. So something good came out of the terrible week anyway. But I hope Jewell's not dead or hurt bad and Momma says I have a tender heart but I should know better than to butt in and she

says trust her she's sure Jewell is fine because nobody could run like that and be hurt. But Hamlet gets a mortal wound (which is the kind you die from) and goes on and fights more and even kills a few people and gives a long speech to the audience all between the time he gets hurt and the time he finally dies and while all this is happening he knows he's dying. It's very very sad and it makes me worried about Jewell no matter what Momma says. If her family moved away like Liz told Momma they should, then I'll never even know if Roger and Benjy gave Jewell a mortal wound or not. But Momma says there's nothing I can do. And she's right, because I'm not allowed to.

I don't want to write in you anymore right now, dear diary, and I hope that doesn't hurt your feelings. Sometimes after Momma has worked a long time at the stocks that are going to make us rich she gets that deep line in her forehead that she likes me to smooth out for her but not at those times because she says it's nothing really she's just "depressed" (sp?). That means sort of sad like you sometimes get after the show is over or when you go to an audition but they say they're looking for somebody younger or older or not so blonde or different. You sort of know what it is you're sad about but the sadness is bigger than one thing and spreads over lots of things. So that's why I don't want to write anymore for now, I think. It must be I'm depressed.

I apologize, diary,
Julian

Dear Diary,

I know I skipped again, four days this time. But Momma says I have a busy schedule and there are more important things to pay attention to and if I don't write in you every single day she says it's alright. I hope you think so, too.

There's no big news that's happened anyway. It's been warm for this late in October which is nice because I like to put off wearing my leggings as long as possible. I hate hate hate them but I'm not old enough to wear tights and we can't afford to have me catch a cold, not after the way I already got us into trouble even up to calling in Miss Unger about my face.

The scratch is disappearing, which makes Pietro glad and also Momma and everybody else too. But I'm sort of sorry because it reminded me every time I looked at myself in the mirror how I gave Roger a bloody nose and how Jewell and me fought like the Amazons in the Greek myth book even if Jewell might not ever know I was fighting on her side or might be dead by now of a mortal wound. Roger and Benjy just walk around free when I think Roger at least should go to jail because he might have murdered Jewell you never know. I won't speak to him or Benjy anymore and Momma says that's okay even if it does make her life difficult with Liz.

So the only big news I guess is that we had the cast party for a whole day out at Miss Clement's country house in Connecticut (I know that's right because I looked it up. If I use the dictionary for words I'm not sure about then maybe Momma won't have to check in here for spelling mistakes). We have the cast party every year but it's always in the summer so we can all go swimming in Miss Clement's pool. But this summer we never had it because Miss Clement's fourth husband was sick with something. (I think maybe she poisons them like Gertrude did her husband in Hamlet because they always seem to disappear. But Momma says No they just get divorced although she says she wouldn't put it past Miss Clement to poison a person). Momma doesn't like Miss Clement. But she's always very polite to her because after all Miss Clement is the Star of our show even if I am more popular with our hundreds and hundreds of viewers and get the most fan mail of anybody, Miss Luchino says.

So this year we couldn't have the cast party until now and nobody could swim in the pool which was alright with me because I don't know how to swim anyway and you never know you could drown like Ophelia did.

But there still was water in the pool because Miss Clement likes to swim for her constitution (looked it up!) which means not the Declaration of Independence, diary, but her health, and so she swam right into early October when it was warm and the pool still hadn't been drained out yet. Miss Clement is a magnificent (looked it up) actress and it's no wonder she's famous and has been on the stage on Broadway and in London too because she sort of acts all the time even out there at her country house where she says she "lets her hair down." (Not really, diary, she keeps it pinned in a bun on top of her head like always, that's a saying that means she doesn't have to act at the country house, but I think she does at least when anybody else is there I bet even all the husbands.) So Miss Clement stood there in her hostess gown and when Mr. Pierce had so much booze he fell into the pool she wasn't even worried about Ophelia (he can swim) but just stood there with her right hand up to her throat and her big blue eyes open very wide and sort of sang out (Miss Clement can carry a tune and has perfect pitch and used to sing with Noel Coward who was very famous and is old now and maybe dead) anyway she sort of sang out "*Sid*ney! I am ap*pall*ed!" But everybody laughed and he climbed out and Rose (that's Miss Clement's maid who is a Negro lady) got a big towel for him and then he even had another drink.

Ricky played pool (not the water kind but a game with sticks and balls on a table) all day inside with Abe who is our assistant (spell? No, l.i.u!) director and who I love. He always calls me Hey Kid or Trooper or just Julian but never The Baby because he says that years don't count and I'm the oldest one on the set. Which is very nice because I get tired of always being the youngest everywhere. Miss Luchino sat in a deck chair by the pool and kept shouting inside to Ricky that if he was losing his next week's salary he could go to hell before she'd plead for him again with Darlene. (Darlene is Miss Unger's first name but *nobody* not even Mr. Pierce calls her that except only Miss Luchino and Miss Clement and the men from The Sponsors when they visit the control room on Show Day.)

Everybody was having a good time and Momma sat off to one side like she's always careful to do because you don't want anyone to think you're one of those awful stage mothers like other kids in the business have. She drank lots of coffee and talked with Betty who's our script-girl lady and Helga who's the wardrobe lady. Helga comes from Hungary and got out before the communists (l.i.u!) came, by the skin of her teeth she says. And Momma even said I could go for a walk along the forest path all by myself (Miss Clement told her it was "perfectly safe" and not to be "overprotective" (l.i.u.) so what else could Momma do but let me go. I whispered to her that I'd wear my sweater and my muffler and only go a little way and come right back, and I'd gone that path a year ago together on a walk with Momma at the last party so she knew it really was okay and not in woods or anything jungley (?) but just a sort of field with trees back of the house and the pool.

And so diary I had a whole walk in the country all by myself! It was *magnificent*. I saw a skunk! (But I didn't scare it I stood perfectly still until it went away so it didn't put out its smell.) I saw a brown rabbit for just a minute. I wanted to pick a flower but I didn't because you never know there could be poison ivy or something and then I'd get us all into trouble again. So I stuck to the path and looked up at the red and yellow leaves, and when I squeezed my eyes almost shut the sun made sparkles (l.i.u.) like the air was a green color. There were lots of birds but you couldn't see them, only hear them. I stood like a statue and didn't move a muscle like you have to do when being fitted for a costume or if you're posing for a picture where they use a long exposure. But here I stood still just because I didn't want to scare off the birds or the forest or anything. I pretended to myself I was part of the forest, a tree or a wild creature (l.i.u.) just being there. It felt real and I loved doing it. And except for the birds singing and the leaves sort of Shhhing when they fell in the green color air it was so *quiet,* as quiet as the library. Even if Mr. Pierce does despair of me because he says I'm such a hopeless city child (he grew up in Montana which is mostly not cities) Momma always tells him not to worry about me I'm doing just fine and as usual Momma is right because I sure was doing fine all by myself on my first walk alone through the country.

So I kept to the path and remembered my promise to Momma and turned around after a while and came back. Well, to tell the truth, diary, I would have gone on a little more, but I saw something funny through the trees up ahead and I knew better than to butt in. Pietro was there. He is our makeup man who fixed my scratch remember? He really grew up in Brooklyn but is called Pietro instead of Pete because it fits a makeup man better and besides he lived in Rome for three whole years. He is nice and very funny and makes me laugh and calls me his little Garbo. (She is a famous actress who doesn't talk too much, not like me!, in fact she hardly talks at all but is very famous and not dead yet). Pietro was there up ahead through the trees with Lee, who is Miss Clement's house-boy which means he takes care of her house like Rose takes care of her. I like Lee (who isn't a boy but old, about 25 or even more and who always sneaks me Cokes) and of course I really like Pietro a lot and I was going to run up and say Hi to them but I didn't. It was funny. Not funny ha ha but funny strange. Pietro was on his knees in front of Lee and Lee's pants were down around his ankles even his underpants. You could see Lee's bare bottom white in the sun against the brown tree stems or whatever they're called. Lee's head was sort of thrown back and he made sounds like he was in pain. So then right away I knew Lee had been bitten by a snake or some other poisonous thing and Pietro was trying to save his life by sucking out the venom (l.i.u.) like they tell you in first aid books and on TV. I knew Pietro would be very brave about saving somebody's life because he is gentle and tall and handsome. But I hoped he would remember you had to spit out the poison and not swallow any or you could die after you saved the other person.

Anyway, I knew better than to butt in. Besides if there were snakes in that part of the woods I sure didn't want them to bite me and they might too because I am shorter than Pietro and nearer to the ground. When Momma and I play tickle she sometimes acts like a giant and she says in a loud voice "Ho! Tender baby flesh! Yum yum!" and of course I know Momma is just playing so I laugh but I sure didn't want the snakes to think I was tender baby flesh because the snakes would not be playing. Also I didn't know if a person could suck out the poison from two people one right after the other or die themselves and so Pietro might not be able to save me if I did get bitten and then what would I do? I might die of snake poison or ruin the cast party and get Momma and me into trouble again.

So I just turned around very very quiet like in the library and pretended I was an Indian walking through the woods in my moccasins (l.i.u.) without cracking a twig. And I made it all the way back to the house and the pool without a sound.

It was a magnificent walk and Momma said she was proud of me. But when I whispered to her about the snake bite and maybe we should tell the others and call for the ambulance because Pietro might not have got out all the poison you never know Momma said very fast No and not to mention it to anybody that she would take care of it and I should forget I'd ever seen Pietro and Lee in the woods at all. I tried to explain to her how important it was but then I'm trying to get back at least to *near* Perfect on the chart so I stopped because one of the things on the chart list is Not to Argue. So that was that.

Momma was right as always and I should have known better.

Because sure enough a little while later Lee and Pietro came up to the pool but not together and since people were coming and going in and out of the house nobody even asked where they'd been or wondered if they'd been dead or alive (which Lee almost was, dead I mean, if Pietro hadn't saved him). Lee didn't mention the snake bite and he looked okay. Pietro didn't mention it either, and I knew that was because Pietro would never brag and I guess he made Lee not tell everybody how brave Pietro had been too. I think Pietro is a good man. He took me to a ballet once on a Saturday afternoon because he knows a lot of the dancers.

Anyway so that's the big news. And Momma and me went back early by train even though we had drove out in one of the cars along with Helga and Betty. But the grownups were staying later and I felt sorry that Momma couldn't stay with them because after all she is a grownup even if she is my Momma. But I had to be got back home early and somebody had to take me and so of course it was poor Momma. She said she didn't mind a bit and she would rather be with me than anybody in the whole world anyway.

We had a nice long train ride which I love because Momma reads the newspaper or a magazine and I can just look out the window at things going by and think. You can't think very much at home because there's always homework or the script or something to do or else you should be sleeping your beauty sleep. But there's not much you can do on a train because it bounces too much to write your homework clearly. You can always be running your lines over in your head to save time but sometimes you can just stop and think a little. So I looked out the window and thought a little and then I guess I fell asleep because I woke up with my head on the windowsill which was all dirty and Momma said I was a filthy-faced muffin and what was she going to do with me? But I knew she wasn't mad or anything, so I didn't complain when she took out a hankie and spit on it and rubbed my face clean. I always hate hate hate when somebody even Momma does this to me and I wish they'd at least let me spit my own spit on the hankie if there has to be spit on the hankie at all when there's no water around. That way I would be smelling my own spit on my face while it dries instead of somebody else's spit at least. But I was too sleepy to care much so then we got home and went to sleep.

That was the only big news which is not very big unless you think Pietro saving Lee's life and being too much of a hero to tell anybody is big news. Which I do. But Momma says we'll keep Pietro's secret, just her and me and not tell a soul.

So I only told you, diary, because you're not a soul.

I love you diary.

Julian the country kid

Dear Diary,

You are a soul, I guess. I have to be careful what I write in you. Momma was checking for my spelling mistakes even though I told her that I promise to look up any hard words myself to save her from having to correct them. Momma says I haven't got the hang of writing in you yet and if I don't get it soon she will hide you away until I'm older.

You see, I should not be putting in these things all the time that really don't have anything to do with me. Like Jewell, because Jewell and I had nothing in common. Like Miss Clement and the husbands and her being an actress even when she lets her hair down. Like Ricky and the track and Mr. Pierce and the booze and the pool. Especially like Pietro saving Lee's life.

I can understand about everything but Pietro because you could sort of say the other things are not positive and might give me the wrong impression when I grow up and read you, diary. But it seems to me that Pietro's being such a hero and so modest about it is *very* positive and something I will want to remember as a happy time of my childhood, to read about when I'm old. And I would never ever show you to anybody else now that Jewell is gone forever. So Momma would be the only person to read you, and then me when I'm old, and both Momma and me already *know* about Pietro saving Lee's life so I don't see what was so wrong about writing that in you.

But I don't want to be difficult all over again and Momma almost had nerves over it so I'll just obey which will give me another star on the chart at least.

I'm sorry, diary. But that's the way it is. You never know.

Still your friend anyway,
Julian

Dear Diary,
There are lots of things I'd like to write in you tonight but I don't think they're in the hang of it so I just better say Hello and I love you. Besides, I'm tired and sort of depressed, I guess.

Julian

Dear Diary,
Today is November 18th. Thanksgiving is coming soon. I'm going to be Queen of the Macy's Thanksgiving Day Parade and wear a crown and the tutu and ride on a float!! Also soon Momma and me will give the food and old clothes to the poor Negroes next door. I wonder if we'll see anybody special. Today was okay. Rehearsal, a tunafish sandwich and milk at Grand Central Station before catching the train back to Yonkers, school, ballet and modern dance class one after the other, homework, piano practice, the script, supper, and to bed for the beauty sleep.
   My Momma is the most wonderful Momma in the whole wide world. I love her so!!!

Julian

Dear Diary,
Today was Thanksgiving Day. I have so much to be thankful for. The Parade was nice but I was cold. Still, I was a trooper and am the luckiest little girl in the world. We ate turkey and mashed potatoes and gravy and cranberry sauce in a restaurant. It was very traditional (sp? Help Momma!).

Happy Thanksgiving!
Julian

P.S. We gave food and clothes to the poor Negroes next door and they were thankful. The only little girls over there now are all bigger than me so there wouldn't be anybody to give an organdy dress to anyway, even if it would be an insult which Momma and me would never ever make. Nobody else was there.

Dear Diary,
Soon it will be Christmas and no school and a whole week with no other lessons either. But we still do the show. And there are

presents. And we celebrate Hannukah too (sp?) and that's more presents. I am so lucky.

> Merry Christmas and Happy Hannukah,
> Julian

Dear Diary,

Well it's the New Year which is 1951. Happy New Year! It still feels funny to be living in the 1950's, even if we already did that for a whole year. That's because I've spent almost my whole life in the 1940's, Momma says. What is even more funny is to think way ahead to things like the 1960's and 1970's and even 1980's. They don't seem real, sort of like science fiction, and it's a strange feeling to think that unless I suddenly die or there's a war and they drop the atomic bomb and I can't get to duck and cover under a desk or table in time like we're taught to do in school, then I'll actually be a grownup and have my own room or maybe even my own apartment or house and not be living with Momma anymore. Of course I would miss her very much but probably I'd see her every day so it would be alright. I think about that a lot, especially around my birthday and like now, New Year's.

I didn't make it through 1950 perfect on the chart and now there's all of 1951 ahead of me until October to try and get perfect again and stay that way. I don't know why but that makes me depressed.

But I'm going to be positive and full of hope, like Momma!

Yesterday Momma and me went out to dinner and she showed me how to eat a lobster with the claws and all. You get a big bib just like a baby which I hated but they give you these nutcracker things which I liked. Also I liked that you're supposed to get as messy as you want, the waiter said (he recognized me and so we gave him an autograph for his little girl who watches me all the time).

> Happy New Year!
> Julian

P.S. I'm reading Fairy Tales from the Brothers Grim now and I love it.

Dear Diary,

I know it's almost Easter and Pesach (spell?) together and I haven't paid you much attention. I apologize. I've been very busy doing important things but I still love you.

Mr. Ehrenreich got me out of the exclusive contract with Miss Unger so now I can play Ingrid and other parts too if they don't have a "time conflict" because playing Ingrid has to come first it's steady. And we had to give up the raise in salary to get the contract different. But I got to play Alice in Wonderland on a TV special!! So I'm very busy, you have to understand and not complain, dear diary. I just finished reading The Snow Queen by Hans Christian Andersen and it is my favorite now of all stories in the world. I love love love the Little Robber Girl. I love Little Gerda too. I even think the Snow Queen herself isn't so scary. I think she's beautiful, in fact.

Your friend,
Julian

Dear Diary,
Momma says we're going to give me special private swimming lessons at some club soon so I'll never die like Ophelia did. I'm scared of learning but I know it's important not to drown.

If I die in the first lesson, remember that I loved you, dear diary.

With love, for real,
Julian

Dear Diary,
No news. My swimming teacher, Hank, says I have a terrific (sp?) backstroke and he could train me to be in the Olympics but Momma says I should just learn how not to drown. She says there I go again, her little talent factory!

Esther Williams
(no, really Julian)

Dear Diary,
Momma says I'm hopeless and I've been forgetting to tell you when I write in you. I apologize. Today was June 11th, 1951. Mr. Jonas wants to enter me in the New York State piano competition in the third year student group. He thinks I can win. Momma says now *that* would be something, not like being

in the Olympics. It gives me nerves so I am practicing hard and won't have much time to write in you.

Arthur Rubinstein
(no ha ha Julian)

Dear Diary,
Like Momma says, how time does fly!

Here it is September already again (the 6th) and school starts soon. I meant to write more in you over the summer but I was very busy and did a lot of extra shows. I must be making more money but we're still in 3-A and can't be in an elevator building with my own room yet. Momma gets depressed with her stocks but we're being positive and we have hope. Maybe next year.

Julian

Dear Diary,
Life is very busy so you still have to not complain that I write so little or with such long times in between. I stay awake in bed sometimes and think about what I would write in you. If I wasn't too tired to write it down, I mean. I made up an imaginary *(looked it up, Momma!)* friend named Bunker who is half-girl and half-boy and goes with me everywhere. Momma doesn't mind and says that shows imagination *(l.i.u.M!)* but it shouldn't go too far and carry me away. Bunker is only a kid too and not strong enough to lift me or carry me, so I don't worry about it. Anyway, at night I tell Bunker things I would write in you. If I wasn't so tired, I mean. I hope that doesn't insult you or make you jealous, diary.

Please understand.

Still your friend,
Julian

Dear Diary,
It's the night before my ninth birthday and I'm excited to see what all my presents will be. I can tell you what I got Momma because she won't read you until tomorrow and by then she'll have it so it won't ruin the surprise. I gave all the saved up money (because there still was nobody to take me shopping on *her* birthday in July so back then I made her an ashtray out of modeling clay because even though Momma doesn't smoke

cigarettes you never know there could be a guest come over who does), anyway, I gave the saved up money to *Papa* in secret at rehearsal and told him what to get and he got her a *magnificent* pink silk stole (that's like a big scarf) from Saks 5th Avenue, all wrapped and perfect and will she be surprised! I've made it through to tonight pretty perfect on the chart with a few slip up no star days but all in all Momma says very good. But I didn't want to repeat myself this year by doing the chart all over again because you should never repeat yourself or you get typecast (which is why it's so good I'm doing other parts and not just Ingrid all the time) and it is *death* Mr. Ehrenreich says for an actor to get typecast.

So I don't think I'll do the chart ever again.

Tomorrow will be my last birthday ever in a single number. The one after that will already be my tenth birthday and I'll be in two numbers then and stay that way for the rest of my whole life, unless I live to be 100 years old. Momma would be dead by then, which is hard to imagine. It's hard to imagine the rest of my life. But I guess it will really happen.

Happy Birthday to you dear diary, you're almost one year old. I apologize that I'm so busy I hardly tell you things anymore. You understand. That's how it is. I loved you anyway. For real.

Your friend, with love,
Julian Travis.

CHAPTER TWO

Autumn, 1981

Laurence Millman stood at the stove and thought about Tillie Olsen. All those readers. All those hands turning the pages of her now famous piece that began "I stand here ironing." All those people who had bought her book *Silences,* about the erasure of women. All those women who had touched their own anger and wept; those few men, himself included, who had wept to touch their own guilt. All those people.

"I stand here sautéing onions," he said aloud to the empty kitchen. Ridiculous. The rhythm was wrong, as lacking in dignity as he seemed to himself—a fifty-two-year-old political organizer who had made no impact on society. Not a dent, not a scratch in over a decade, because he had been too busy wielding this revolutionary weapon of a wooden spoon, too preoccupied believing such an act was vital for men, too active rebelling against the male stereotype by being passively obedient. Just his luck, to have been born male and white at this point in history. What rotten timing. Then he had to go and become a pro-feminist man. Exchange all of the privileges and power for all of the consciousness and guilt. Never again now to see the world solely through his own eyes.

"I stand here irony-ing," he tried aloud. Less ridiculous, but too arch. Neither good theory nor good practice, which should be effortlessly married. Did he still believe that? Even when

this politics—*her* politics—had convinced him that for a man
the spatula was mightier than the sword?

"Never really believed it," he proclaimed aloud, lifting the
colander of rinsed tomatoes from the sink and beginning to
slice them into thick rounds. But hadn't he? Hadn't he wanted
some force, sudden and beautiful as the mountain blizzards of
his Colorado boyhood, to bear down upon him and swallow
him up, a force savage as history, that would put his talents to
use against suffering? Who would have expected such a force
to wear the face of a seventeen-year-old girl?

She had indeed engulfed him. Everything got drawn toward
Julian's gravity, a gravity she herself couldn't perceive or acknowledge, so obsessed was she in trying to tear herself loose in
turn from the magnetic pull of Hope.

Laurence combined the onions and tomatoes with the already boiled and drained pasta and peas, and began to grate
cheese over the concoction. It was the best thing he cooked.
"Laurence's Baked Dish," he called it—an aromatic conglom-
eration of noodles, onions and garlic, melted cheese, and assorted vegetables. Julian was definitely not a vegetarian. Julian
was a carnivore. Although she had, he granted, made every
effort to like the casserole (pretentious East Coast term). What
she hated was that he always made it in large quantities.
"When I see the Baked Dish," she would tease him, "I know
that fourteen people are coming to dinner or else that two
people will be consuming the same fare for a week."

"Well, *I* really *love* it, dammit," he muttered to the shred-
ding curls of cheese. If he had his own way, he'd be a total
vegetarian, not just settle for the compromise of chicken or fish
they agreed on most of the time. If he had his way. I once had a
way, a personality, he thought. Who was it? Where did it go?

Into Julian. His ideas, skills, energy—sucked toward Julian.
And Julian's life still sucked toward Hope. Everything devouring and being devoured in turn, everything distorting at the
speed of light as it ran its course toward Hope, all matter and
energy disappearing into that voracious Black Hole wheeling
through the universe.

"I once had an identity," he announced without conviction,
as he closed the oven door on the Baked Dish. 'One of the most
promising political minds in America,' the *National Progressive* had called him. He knew parts of that article by heart. Just

as well, since the clipping had disappeared into one of Julian's files and the *Progressive* had long ago folded. Student organizer of the first campus strike in the country, when he was only twenty. Brilliant tactician, dynamic activist, even right through the Death Valley days of the 1950's. A speaker so charismatic he could turn a rally into a march, a sit-in into a building seizure. Architect of the grassroots protest that had driven strip-mining out of a whole region of Colorado—and kept it out. A tireless coalition builder who could talk to the press, U.S. senators, minority communities, and back-country farmers with equal persuasiveness. A young Lenin, they had called him. One of those who had laid the foundation for the 1960's.

"Ha," he snorted. He poured himself a glass of jug wine and went into the livingroom to wait for her. She was late, of course. Not her fault: the plane delayed, or the meeting running longer than expected, or the necessity of going for coffee with the local women after her speech . . . she was always apologetic, but it never changed. She'd eventually totter in exhausted, despite her maddening ability to fall asleep the second she got on a plane. He looked up at the advance copy of her latest book on the Franklin stove pseudo-fireplace mantel they'd built together. There had been a time when they were introduced as "Laurence Millman—and-his-wife." Not that this had given him pleasure. On the contrary. Hadn't he taken pride in building her politics, nurturing her tactical instincts, feeding the hunger that raged through her for tools and skills with which to forge change? He shook his head more in confirmation than in denial.

All of his friends had warned against it. In those days, Julian had no friends, of course. But Hope was against it—and Hope was a sufficient barrier to whatever she chose to block. He watched a brief downdraft stir the ashes in the Franklin. What more challenging inspiration could two lovers have had than unanimous opposition to their love?

"You wanted me for the very qualities you've crushed in me," he murmured to an invisible Julian, as if she sat on the mantel next to her new book.

God, but he'd been defiant in those days! Defiant against everything he'd fled from: the alcoholic, battering father, broken by a life in the mines, the mother who never made a sound

when she cried, the poverty of experience that left him perpetually intimidated by shopkeepers and train conductors and
headwaiters.

He drifted back to the kitchen, checked the oven, started to
pour another glass of wine, then switched to a diet cola.

"I had defiance to spare, then," he told the jug, pushing it
aside. Defiance against everything he had fled *to:* ivy-covered
academic walls that turned out to house more departmental
jockeying than educational riches; state politics that he discovered had settled for becoming yet another establishment; the
great Eastern city that promised such power but extracted as
payment his feeling insecure as a country cousin.

And then there she was—a strange, fey child with shrewd
eyes. An anomaly, reading Camus's philosophy, Marvell's poetry, Hegel's theory, smack in the middle of that hilarious
apartment of her mother's where even the toilet bowl was
pink and you expected after you shat to find little pink turds
floating around in it. She stood in the midst of that static
barococco paradise like a young rebel angel, blazing for the
chance to join Lucifer and fall into freedom, a current of promise swirling around her like a storm warning in the airless
room. Young enough not to be confused with any of the other
women he'd loved, and free of their bourgeois pretensions. But
old enough, given her peculiar context, to move through the
world's maze of shopkeepers and headwaiters with just the
right touch of cordial haughtiness. Unformed enough for him
to shape; sophisticated enough for him to feel blessedly pro-
tected. Perfect for stereotype-smashing. Defiance, oh yes.

He wandered back toward the livingroom. The table was
set, with flowers and candles. He glanced at his watch again. It
seemed he now spent most of his life waiting. Not only for
Julian—though that, yes, a lot of the time. For her to appear,
for her to decide . . . whatever. For her to notice. This was
what they meant, women, about lives spent in waiting. He
raised his glass to the air.

"Take that, Tillie. The 'feminist prince' is a male spy in the
harem. He's learned what it is you suffer. He's had waiting and
watching and shutting-up and putting-someone-else's-needs-
first engraved on his skin like Kafka's penal colony prisoner
under the needles of the Harrow. To you and me, Tillie. To us."

Dimly, he could remember a time when he had acted, not

reacted, initiated, not waited. The lovely lustful years with Joyce, seizing that supple dancer's body with eyes and hands and mouth. Finding the Chelsea loft. Daring to juxtapose culture and politics long before the hippies—his spiritual offspring—brought that juxtaposition into mainstream consciousness. Christ, how he had loved the Sixties. Excitement. Possibility. Rock music in everybody's rhythms, a mellow sharing of grass everywhere you went, the crazy funny colorful way people dressed themselves up—every meeting or march a carnival. Costumes. Beads and headbands and dashikis. India-print jackets and tie-dyed pants, Nehru and Mao coats, motorcycle helmets plastered with slogans. A walking gallery of refusal and celebration. All those people sharing the same vision of rebellion, the same summer of love. All those people . . .

"I'm coming I'm *coming* forchrissake," he yelled to the telephone's tyrannical summons, but his irritation couldn't cover the itch of fear he felt whenever she was late and the phone rang, an unmentionable fear because it might seem the protectionism of a fuddy-duddy hubby.

"Yes? Hello?"

"Hello. Uh, is Julian Travis there?"

Laurence automatically reached for the pencil and pad religiously kept by the phone.

"No, I'm sorry, she's not in at the moment. May I take a message?"

"Who's this?"

What the hell business is it of yours, buddy, he wanted to spit back; this is her secretary-housekeeper-male-nanny. This is the Best Supporting Actor here.

"This is Laurence Millman, her husband. May I take a message?"

"Larry! I'll be damned!" the voice boomed, "Haven't heard that infamous baritone in years! Hey, Larry, this is Tim. Tim Monahan." Inconceivable to Tim Monahan that anyone wouldn't remember *him*.

"Tim. Oh yeah. It sure has been a long time. Not since the Media Watch Committee fell apart—"

"Back in the Year One, by god. Well I'll be damned," Tim repeated. Still the same fatuous clod. "So, Larry, what are you—"

"How're you these days, Tim?" Laurence interrupted.

"Terrific, just doing terrific. Once I decided to trade in the torn Levi's for the three-piece suit and join the media instead of monitoring it, I did terrific. Infiltration and all that, you know." Tim offered a hearty laugh.

"Yeah, I can imagine. Infiltration."

"Right. Right. I mean, times change and we've gotta be able to move with 'em, Larry, gotta survive. Can't just sit out the Big R Revolution on the radical sidelines, ya know. A few years, a few maneuvres, time to learn the lingo, the way things get done, yeah okay so a few compromises maybe. But the upshot is that little Timmy here is the producer of the most watched public affairs show on network telly, boy. Not that *any* public affairs show has what you'd call a mass audience. But we do okay, we do okay. Quality show, good ratings, make an impact. Your old comrade here can't complain. Own a co-op and a beach shack out in the Hamptons, a Porsche, a terrific wife, two terrific kids. You gotta make the Big R Rev for yourself *while* you change the world, comrade." Laurence closed his eyes and swallowed. "So. What are *you* doing these days? What's the ol' Red Menace up to in the Eighties?"

There it was.

"Fine, fine. Doing great, too."

"Yeah? Doing what?" So Tim was still unable to resist the baiting tone he had once used to taunt cops during supposedly non-violent protests. There always was a Tim, ready to provoke a bust.

"I'm, uh, into radio stuff, actually. I figure you reach more people that way. I mean, TV's wonderful but, well, there still are folks who can't afford one, believe it or not. And then all the captive radio audience in cars and with headsets. So I—"

"Well, that's terrific, Larry, terrific," Tim cut in. It was not an act of mercy; it was boredom with inconsequential details. "Thing is, Larry, I'm a little rushed right now. Maybe we can get together sometime and talk about the old days, huh? Thing is, I was calling—"

"—for Julian. I know."

"Right. Right. Terrific how she turned out, isn't it? You're some Pygmalion, Larry. Must be real proud of her."

"I am. Would you like to leave a message for her?"

"Right. Thing is, we're planning a show around the last gasps of the Equal Rights Amendment. Everybody knows it'll croak next year. I'd like Julian on the panel. I've got a green light from Phyllis Schlafly, we'll pull in one of the women congressmen, get some average Mrs. Mom type for mainstream, and then maybe one of the Establishment libbers. But we need Julian for some flash and fire, ya' know? Some sexy radical pizzazz on ERA. Ya know?"

"Sure, Tim. The Big R Rev."

"Right. You got it. Terrific. So have her call me at the office tomorrow. She knows the number, she just did the show a few months ago—that special on the bombings of abortion clinics? She was terrific, nice and bitchy, lotta flash and fire, called it 'Reagan-sanctioned terrorism.' Brought in a lotta mail on that one."

The oven began to sizzle ominously. Laurence was desperate to get off the phone, but Tim Monahan was not somebody to whom you could plead that your baked dish might be burning.

"Well, Tim, I'll pass it along to Julian and she'll probably give you a call."

"Thanks, you old hellion. Terrific talking to you. Might do a show one of these days on whatever happened to liberated couples, an update. Anyway, we'll get together—"

"Sure Tim sure. Look, I've got to run. I'm late for an appointment."

"Right. So you tell Julian I called, okay?"

"I'll tell her. Goodbye, Tim."

He hung up the phone with the trace of a slam and hurried to the kitchen. The Baked Dish was only bubbling. He turned down the oven and poured himself a glass of wine.

"Don't let it get to you, ol' Larry comrade hellion," he whispered between clenched teeth. "You've been *living* the Big R Rev in ways costlier than the Tim Monahans can wrap their tattered brains around." Loving flash-and-fire Julian for all these years has been a front-line Big R act of courage. From the very start. He took a deep breath to exhale the anger, then deliberately steered himself back toward the livingroom, away from the kitchen.

Front-line all the way. Daring to take that virginal plump body in his arms. To seek her through all her terrors, lies, carefully dropped clues. To fight off Hope, her shadow beating its huge wings over them. To haul Julian out in the middle of a blizzard—a plain snowstorm by Colorado standards—and roll in the snow of the park and teach her how you could lie there and carve snow angels by waving your arms along the ground as if you were flying, then take her for hot chocolate and watch her face glow with excitement and cold and reborn heat. His Julian. Now she belonged to everybody; when you belonged to everybody you belonged to nobody.

"My child," he whispered to himself. "The first, last, and only child I ever got to love." The child he had brought to womanhood. The child who now swept rapidly through airports and meetingrooms and podiums and this loft in a honed-down body, lean as a predatory bird. The child now in total control.

She'd never really liked the Sixties. Hairy beards and sandaled dirty feet, she'd complain. Well, the music, okay—until rock lyrics became certified as a sexist no-no. The silly wonderful costume-clothes? Not on her; a stripped-down-for-the-revolution blue jeans, boots, and sweater kid, her. Always the pro. No long hair—a cop could drag you off by it. No earrings—the same. No— but there had been no excuse for her taking off her wedding ring. Just like the one he still wore, the one he now twisted aimlessly. She had said it was "an act of solidarity with single women, and with married women too poor to afford rings, and with prostitutes, and with" . . . That was already later, when she took off the ring. That was feminism. And then, the ring got lost somewhere. That had made her sad. She looked and looked for it. But it . . . got lost.

"Like me," he muttered. "Lost. Like the child she used to be." The child who now earned more money than he did. The child about whom people now said, in introductions, "This is Julian Travis—and-her-husband." She suffered at that, he knew, feeling her pain feeling his feeling hers in a sympathetic circular agony of guilt. Trapped.

But at least a new challenge had been discovered against which both of them could gamely brace themselves: *"They"* may think we're hurt by "role reversal," but *"We"* know otherwise. *We're* the vanguard of revolutionary relationships between women and men. We defy, therefore we are.

Are we? he wondered. He was getting on. As his uneducated wacky deceased mother would have said, he was no spring chicken. Fifty years and more—and for once he wasn't thinking about how long it took to pass women's suffrage. Definitely gray now, all those distinguished silver swatches at the temples. They colonized the whole head of once carroty hair that had, along with his radicalism, inspired the press to nickname him "the Red Menace." So what was he waiting for? What big or little R revolution could happen for him now? And what was *she* waiting for? For him to come alive again, to free them both? Was this the one thing she couldn't do for them? But didn't she understand this to be the one thing he no longer was capable of doing?

He paced back to the kitchen and poured another glass of cola. The Baked Dish fragrantly announced its readiness from the oven. Once, she used to call and say she'd be late, but that too had disappeared somewhere along the way.

Deforestation. Erosion. Desertification. The fight over the blue enamel paint-can cover. The fight over being overdrawn at the bank. The fight over forgetting to turn off the electric blanket. The fights over her chronic headaches, his chronic insomnia. The stalemates about love-making; poignant, ritual reachings out to each other, blunders, withdrawals, silences. Conversation strip-mined down to exchanges of function, concern, news. So much for defiance. The petty battles, sulks, grievances, and reconciliations they endured were identical with those of other married couples, including those of the same age, class, even gender. How commonplace. How humiliating.

Worse: they had been adopted, in the habit of America, as a New Commodity. The revolutionary whose khaki fatigues become chic, the ascetic flocked to by religious pilgrims, the vindicated explorer now safely bemedaled. With their own collaboration, they had become fashionable—an "egalitarian couple." Private misery packaged under brand names. And a market for the product.

Until finally they were exhausted by swimming against a tide that swept them into its current. Until finally no new escalation of the "level of struggle" could breath life into what had become the candy bride and groom on the wedding cake.

Stuck with what we now represent, he thought: the New Improved Jumbo-Size Couple. The latest trend, the "in" thing, from the folks who brought you—

He heard the downstairs street door open and close. Julian. Julian was home.

He moved quickly, as if he were afraid—which was absurd—to the oven, grabbed the potholders, and lifted the Baked Dish to the top of the stove. From where he stood he could see straight through to the loft door, watching it as her footsteps rose on the stairs.

He grinned as she entered. She dropped her suitcase.

"Hi! You timed it just right, even if the plane was late. Supper's ready. Or did you eat on the flight?"

She came over to him. They embraced gingerly.

"Eat on the plane? Are you kidding? The glamor of travel: Toy airline food on toy trays eaten with toy utensils. An endless stream of Sleeptite Motels. Sometimes a treat—organically grown beansprouts for the dinner in my honor at the Women's Center."

She peeked into the pot.

Only he would have noticed the fragment of hesitation before she exclaimed,

"Baked Dish! Great! I'm starved."

"I put your mail on the hall table, as usual."

"Mmm," she murmured. She was already peeling off her blazer and making for the hall table. "Thanks," she called back absent-mindedly.

He hefted the large pot and carried it to the table, returned and brought the jug wine. She came drifting back, sorting the mail as she walked.

"Anything interesting?" he asked.

"World-shaking. Bills. Feminist periodicals. A request for a fellowship recommendation from a woman I've never heard of. 'The Mel Chester Show' wants me again, this time to debate Hugh Hefner about pornography. They can forget it. Two petitions asking for signature, donation, support. More bills—"

"Well, leave the rest for now. Food's ready."

"—An announcement of my forthcoming appearance at a benefit for the Women's Electoral League—which I have an awful feeling I forgot to write in my datebook—and a résumé assuming I've got a job opening for the secretary I sure could use but have never had. And bills. And a rejection of the two new poems, from *Poetry America:* 'Well-crafted but too polemical.' "

"It looked like there was a royalty check . . . ?"

She sat down at the table, still scanning her papers.

"Yeah. I was saving the best for last. It's about enough to cover a quarter of the telephone bill. The vast sum of $71.38. I'm underwhelmed with gratitude. So much for writers who get rich off political movements. I better call Herb Becker at *Trends* tomorrow and tell him I'll do that five-hundred-word potboiler on women in the armed forces after all."

She rose abruptly, just as he was about to swallow his first forkful of noodles.

"Sorry. Be right back. Forgot to wash up. You go ahead, don't let it get cold," called backward as she disappeared toward the bathroom.

Laurence put down his fork and stared at the pile of mail on the table between them. She hadn't mentioned the arrival of the monthly bank statement on their joint account, though he could see she'd already opened it, too. In fact, three canceled checks lay on the floor where they'd dropped in her swirl of movement from the table. He bent and retrieved them. Damn. All three from him to O'Neil's liquor store. But she knows I often just cash checks there, he thought. Still, he placed them at the bottom of the pile of canceled checks and carefully moved the whole stack of mail to the sideboard.

Julian returned and sat down again. As she unfolded her napkin, he saw her glance flit over the table, taking in the flowers and candles.

"Oh, nice, Larry."

But he also registered—from a momentary lingering of her eyes on the glasses and silverware—that there were waterspots on the glasses and he'd put the forks on the wrong side again. Fuck it, he told himself, that's the way we did it in my part of Colorado. To hell with it. This reception, even if imperfect, is one your feminist sisters all over the country would gladly give their Valium prescriptions to come home to. But he only said,

"So what happened this time?"

"Nothing much. Sort of wall-to-wall trauma day before yesterday, before I went to the airport. I was going to stop off at the hospital and see her"—"Her" needed no further identification to either of them—"before taking off for California, remember?"

"Oh yeah. So how was it?"

"A living nightmare. I swear, Larry, the L-Dopa might reduce the tremors, but the side effects, Christ! They're monstrous. None of the doctors' explanations prepare you for it. The bouts of blindness come and go without warning. She still trembles, and her hands are beginning to stiffen and turn in at the wrists. But worst of all are the hallucinations. The paranoia. God knows she's conducted her life wretchedly, at least by my standards, but nobody should have to suffer like this. Day before yesterday—well, I was with her only an hour, because the doctor wanted to have a conference with me and then I had to rush to catch the plane. At first she didn't have a clue who I was. Then she recognized me, and I thought we were having what could almost be called a conversation for a few minutes— nothing earth-shaking, you understand, just the weather and how was she feeling and that I wouldn't be by for two days because I had to go on a trip—and at some point I realized she thought she was talking to Aunt Yetta. So I gently tried to tell her I was me, Julian, her daughter, not Aunt Yetta. Then she all of a sudden remembered that both Yetta and Essie were dead and burst into tears about how she was all alone in the world. Then she picked up the flowers I'd brought and threw them at me. In my face."

"She thought you'd look great with a flower behind your ear or what?" He helped them both to second heapings of Baked Dish although there still was some on her plate. He refilled his wineglass. Hers was untouched.

"Hardly. Behind the ear is where the adorable pink hairbow was always supposed to go."

"I hope you threw them right back at her."

"Larry, be serious. It was terrible. And then, and then—" A look of surprise washed all color from her face. She put down her fork.

"Jule? You all right?"

She breathed in deeply. It seemed to pass.

"Yes. Thanks. Just felt—peculiar."

"The Baked Dish isn't *that* bad, certainly?"

She smiled weakly. "No, silly ass, of course not. It isn't the food at all."

"Well, something made you turn a fetching shade of chartreuse there for a minute."

She pushed her plate away. "No. Really. I'm okay. Think I'll wait a bit before finishing dinner, though, if it's all the same to you."

"Oh. Yeah. Sure. Want anything? Glass of water?"

"No, thanks." She glanced at him and their eyes caught. Impossible to tell whether her look of apprehension mirrored his, or the reverse.

"Now I ask you"—she brightened into her comic tone— "what other man would have the perverse bravado to cover up his disappointment about the reception to his *cooking?* Oh, Lare. You *are* a dear person."

So some little bubble of deformed love must have mutated inside her and floated up to her mouth. Affection and pity. Thank you, ma'am. His jaw tightened.

"*No,* oh, Larry, I didn't mean it like it sounded. 'A dear person'—like some sort of charming acquaintance. Jesus but we can be supersensitive with each other lately."

"Yeah, well, 'lately' has stretched quite a while—"

"No, no. Look, all I meant. There was— She did something else that really was hideous. It's just that . . . I'd sort of put it out of my mind, didn't want to think about it. Anyway, there was plenty else that happened. A hair-raising scene with the doctor, who wanted to know—"

"But what about Hope? What did that bitch do to you now, Julian?"

"Don't call her that! She's a helpless, ghastly old woman all twisted with her disease and her unlived life, Laurence! For god's sake can't you see it doesn't help when you try to play the heroic prince?"

"Pardon *me.* For being interested in what Hope Travis-ty laid on her hapless daughter this time. Demanded money, perhaps, when she's got it all already, thanks to your child labor? Berated you about your commie husband with working-class dirt still under his fingernails? Or just managed to ignore —for the thousandth time—the fact that you're a writer, a grown woman, a political leader, my wife?"

She put her hands over her ears and screamed at him, "Stop it! Have some mercy, Larry! *Stop* it!"

Once she'd so loved his defense of her against Hope, his intransigence. The first time he ever hung up the phone on her mother—grabbing the receiver out of Julian's hand where she sat crying at the venom pouring through it in Hope's voice—

she had thrown herself into his arms with sheer gratitude and admiration. Julian had never hung up on Hope in her life; it was *her* tactic for ending an argument, one Julian neither wished to nor was able to imitate. But he, having survived the first twenty years of his life in family basic training, used to violent voices and well-aimed fists, was not intimidated. Wasn't it for this that Julian had fled to him in the first place? Why then did the same tone of protecting her now seem merely gratuitous, devoid of human compassion?

"Is it my craziness, that you seem to be getting off on Hope's downfall? Or is it just that I sometimes feel like the grass being trampled when the elephants fight?" she murmured, as if in answer to his unasked questions. They sat in a silence broken only by the clink of his fork against the pottery plate, his chewing. He refilled his glass again. Then he said formally,

"So what did the doctor want."

She bit her lip.

"He wanted to discuss 'extreme measures.' He says her heart is strong as a horse, but you never know with a Parkinson's patient, it could go at any moment. On the other hand, she could continue like this for years. In fact, they'll be releasing her again on Monday. Anyway, for the record, he wanted to know did I want respirators, oxygen tents, all that stuff, in case there should ever be an emergency." It came out flatly, like a journalist reporting on an overheard conversation in a hospital corridor.

"And what'd you tell him."

There was another pause.

"I told him no extreme measures. Let what happens, happen."

"That's decent. She'll die with dignity, thanks to you. She never lived with it."

Julian ignored his judgment.

"I must have pronounced my decision so quickly—I've thought about it for months now—that Dr. Bernstein looked at me funny." She let out a cynical laugh. "Then he said, 'You know, Ms. Travis'—he's very proud of being *au courant*, always uses 'Ms.'—'you know, Ms. Travis, the law itself says we have to take *some* measures. If your mother starts eating less, we'll have to go to intravenous. The law reads that to do otherwise would be to starve her to death.' As if, by implication, I was suggesting they do that. As if I was some kind of murderer.''

"Well, not notorious for their empathy, doctors," Laurence said carefully, as he cleared away the plates and went into the kitchen. Julian trailed after him, bringing the glasses and the wine.

"Yes, well . . . it was most unpleasant, to say the least."

"And then what?" He began washing the dishes.

"What do you mean? Here, let me wash those. You cooked."

"No, I'll do them. I mean *then* what? What was the next yard laid down in the wall-to-wall trauma?"

"Oh, sort of a blur, I guess. I rushed to the airport, almost missed the plane. Worked on my notes for the speech during the flight. Did some mail. Then there they were, waiting to meet me in San Francisco. Really good women, though."

"Yeah? So then?" His voice was raised above the running water.

"Well, so then. The usual. Motel, shower, change. The dinner—with faculty women this time, all of them struggling to keep some shred of women's studies alive despite the cutbacks. Then the speech—on battery, this one—and then the reception afterward and then the motel again and then up at six for a breakfast meeting with the women artists' group, then the midmorning guest workshop on poetry, the rush to the airport again—and here I am." She wound up lamely, standing in the kitchen with empty hands.

"Just garden-variety trauma, you mean."

"Yeah," she smiled, "garden variety. God, I'm tired, though. What happened with you while I was gone?" She yawned.

He dried his hands and strode back purposefully to wipe down the table.

"Me? Oh, nothing."

"Well, something must have happened."

"There were lots of calls for you. I put the messages on your desk. Oh, except the last one. It's by the livingroom phone. Tim Monahan wants you to—"

"I don't care about Tim Monahan." Her hands hung helplessly at her sides. "Laurence," she pleaded, "what did you do, think, feel? *Talk* to me."

He rinsed out the sponge and dried his hands again.

"Want to go out on the roof for a while? There's not many warm evenings left."

"Sure, Larry. I'd like that."

The hell you would, he thought. What you'd like is a bath and the wipeout of sleep. But you feel obligated to "communicate." So all right we'll "communicate." Julian's agenda: finish speech, autograph books, catch plane, arrive home, read mail, do telephoning, sign statements, make deadlines. Agonize over mother. Change the world. And at the very bottom of the list—usually bumped to the next day's list because of space limitations—Have Meaningful Communication With Laurence. So why do I give it to her, he wondered. Because I'm an addict, that's why. Because I'm as hooked on believing our marriage can still be transformed as Julian is on believing the world can still be transformed. Because I keep hoping maybe we can have just one conversation and keep Her out of it since we'd actually be hearing each other for a change.

The roof was quiet in the evening cool; even the traffic sounds seemed far away. How proud they both had been of having "made the tar bloom"—the pots, basins, window boxes, the hanging plants, the cherry tomatoes and lettuces, all the herbs—dill, parsley, marjoram, thyme, mint, rosemary, chives —and the ivy and the impatiens and his own beloved little avocado tree nurtured from a pit.

"All this has to come in soon," he said wistfully. "Strike the set, as you'd say."

They unrolled two tatami mats and sat down.

"I know. It's always a shame to see it go when September comes." She was the one waiting now, a signal of restraining her own leadership, of denying it.

Finally, he spoke. He could hardly hear his own voice.

"Me? What did I do, think, feel?" He laughed softly. "I should thank you for remembering to ask, Jule. Last on the list of ever growing priorities: your writing and the movement and your being the burdened breadwinner and now Hope again and doctors."

There was no reply to this. There never had been.

"Me?" he went on. "Well, let's see. I clipped an article from the *Times*. Thought maybe it'd be useful for the chapter you're working on in the new book—some new study of long-term effects on rape victims. I wrote a nasty letter to the head of the station about his refusal to let me turn over the program to women for a month next March, in honor of International Women's Day. I got an even nastier letter back from him. I got groceries. I got the stuff at the cleaners. I got depressed. I got drunk. I think I got a cold."

She plucked a dead leaf from the furled morning glory nearest her.

"Aw, Lare, something'll happen. At least it's not as if you don't have a platform for your political ideas—"

"Platform? Christ, Jule, a dip-shit one-hour weekly radio show on the local public radio station—at one a.m., yet. That's a platform? So I get to ramble on about what I see happening to this country. For a few minutes here and there. Between playing jazz records like a goddamned disc jockey. All for the munificent sum of seventy-five bucks per show. A platform. Jesus."

"You have a big following, listeners who—"

"—are insomniacs or like jazz. You should see the mail *I* get, down at the station. Though there's precious little of it. Mostly they want me to play more records and shut up about politics. Especially shut up about feminism and how men have to change blah blah blah."

"It's not your fault, dammit, that you're one of the few—maybe the only—man alive with such dedication to the women's movement. And that you risk talking about that. It's not your fault that this society is filled with sexist shitheads."

"You get published by those sexist shitheads, I notice. And invited to lecture at their colleges. And sought out for guest shots on their talk shows. And *their* talk shows reach millions of people—so *you* reach millions of people."

"Larry, I—"

"And I'm glad. You know that, Jule. Truly glad. I'm proud of you. It's just that . . ." He trailed off.

"It's just this bloody moment in bloody history, that's what. It's backlash. It's that something crawled out from under a rock and has been crouched in the White House for almost a year calling itself Reagan. It's that the only reason they publish me or invite me to talk is because women want to read and hear a woman speak on women's lives. Women *don't* want—understandably—to hear any more men on that particular subject. Unfortunately, men don't want to hear about the subject at all, especially not from a turncoat male. It makes me want to throw up."

He found himself appreciating her anger as a convincing performance.

"Funny thing, Jule," he said slowly, "at certain levels it doesn't really bother me. Sometimes I think that's 'cause I just shut it out—the bothering, I mean. But mostly I think it's because *I* know who I am, what I have to say, what impact I could make. If only they'd let me have some forum from which to make it. I'm not just another Abbie Hoffman or Jerry Rubin. Or even Tom Hayden."

"At least Tom hooked *him*self up with an actress wife who's successful enough to *buy* him a political forum. Poor Larry, you got a dud from Central Casting." Her joke went sour and she tried to rectify it. "You'll be remembered long after those Sixties Samurais—"

"I'd rather not be remembered admiringly as a footnote to history. I'd rather not wait for my posthumous vogue."

"Long before that, darling. Genius, like murder, will out. Oh, Larry, Larry, what *are* we going to do about us," she tried to laugh. "For me you'll always be as you were the first moment I saw you, at that godforsaken party given by Kent whatshisname—"

"—Campbell—"

"—Campbell, that's it. The one with the small publishing house who got so broke he was even thinking of publishing widdle pink me in a vanity edition Hope would have paid for— to my embarrassment. But he did do one good thing in his life: introduce us." She began to build her reminiscence. "How else would your universe and mine have crossed? Me, fidgeting with insecurity among real radicals, intellectuals, poets—those dirty old *and* dirty young men who kept sidling up to me drooling things like 'My dear, you needn't *write* poems; you *are* a poem.' And then—you. I'll never forget it so long as I live. Them in dowdy suits and atrocity ties, and you in khakhis and a plain white T-shirt, your body slender as a Greek ephebe, leaning against the old upright piano with your pipe in one hand and a drink in the other, talking revolution." He couldn't stop her, and he knew she couldn't stop herself. In the absence of a present, she was trying to seduce him toward the future via the past. "The sight of you standing there: cobalt-blue eyes, just the right kind of Leslie Howard lock of red hair falling over your forehead. The way you peered at me through narrowed eyes and swirls of pipe smoke when we were introduced."

" 'Laurence Millman, the Red Menace,' no doubt."

"No doubt. Well, what undereducated hardworking adolescent-of-the-world who was secretly devouring Rosa Luxemburg wouldn't have gone all weak at the kneesies? I remember you had just come from a year in Alabama, working in one of the earliest voter-registration drives. Way before they became chic for Northern white liberals. You talked about it. How the adrenaline was continually in your bloodstream and metallic in your mouth at every telephone ring, every knock on the door. The—what did you call it? 'The commonplace daily shapes of hatred.' To me, you were everything brilliant and brave. All that stuff could certainly turn a girl's head, you know."

"Certainly hadn't turned many girls' heads before," he smiled, admiring the effectiveness of her entertainment despite himself.

"Well, it gave me a permanent crick in the neck. Though god knows what you saw in *me*, through all that pinkiness." She was fishing.

"Oh, I saw under that. Pain behind the eyes. A lot of energy. A shocking brain that knew more than you thought you knew and said more than you thought you dared. You weren't just some upper-class princess. You kept . . . surprising yourself. And me. It was fun to watch. I dunno, that air of . . . possibility. A kind of I-can-do-it-whatever-it-is stubbornness. It fascinated me. And then you hit me like a ton of bricks—"

"With my lust for revolution," she whispered lasciviously.

"Yeah, that's right," he chuckled, "with your lust for revolution. I'd never met anybody who wanted to save the world so much, except me. Certainly I never met such an unlikely candidate as you. I guess the temptation to play Svengali was overpowering."

This time they both laughed. She leaned one elbow onto his tatami mat.

"I sure was ready and eager to play Trilby."

But the present did exist. And the future? He stared at the silhouette of the avocado tree.

"So who'd have thought we'd wind up playing—what did

that one leftist rag of a paper call us?—'the Ball-less Wonder and the Castrating Bitch.' "

"Oh Larry, don't think about that now. Forget them. What in hell does anybody know about anybody else, much less about any marriage? All the fine-tuned pain inflicted and exchanged in any intimate relationship—"

"You know what they'll say, don't you? If we ever do break up, I mean. They'll say—"

"I know. I can list the cliché diagnoses. Who cares—"

"It Was Competition Over Their Careers."

"Bullshit. They should know how hard you've fought for my work, how hard I've fought for yours. They should—"

"Also: That's What Travis Gets for Having Married a Person with Oh Horrors a Penis. That would be from your movement separatist groupies, of course."

"Larry, cut it out. That's not fair—"

"And we can always count on the good old patriarchy itself: That's What Befalls a Liberated Couple When He Does the Dishes and She's Out 'In The World.' "

"Why are we listing these idiocies?" she persisted. "You and I both know they'll use any rift between us to bolster all the sexist, ageist, classist, *ism*-ist, bigotries they can muster. Gnatbrains. Since when has that stopped us?"

It was too dark for her to see his reaction. But he did answer, the rewarding content of his words belied by the tone of defeat in his voice.

"Helluva good reason to stay together, huh? I mean, not to give 'em the chance?"

"Sure beats explaining things."

They sat in silence, watching a few stars trying to glimmer against the streetlit sky. Then she tried again, in a different key.

"Larry? I just want you to know . . . you're *not* last on some mythical priority list. It's just . . . Oh, I don't know. There's always so much to get *done*. And when I do ask, you sometimes act like it's an insult. As if I were probing for you to name the latest Millman Failures or something. You should know by now I don't ever even *think* of it that way."

He groped in the night and found her hand.

"I know, Jule. See, but . . . the thing is, you *are* the one

with the exciting news. Late-night meetings, urgent telephoning, trips, the thrill of political—"

"Sometimes it just feels like melodrama, Lare. You know
that. Sometimes I think it's all serial explosions triggered by a
long fuse set ages ago by *her.*"

"Yeah, but . . . I mean, it was different when we could
work together. Like in the anti-war movement. We were so
exhilarated together, even scared shitless as we were all the
time. Friends going to prison—I mean for longer than our
piddly civil-disobedience jailings—or going underground or
into exile to escape the Vietnam draft. But we had our own
private . . . *solidarity,* just the two of us. You and me together. Getting teargassed, beat up, busted, recorded in FBI
files, the works. And right through it we seemed to just—*love*
each other so goddammed much. Was that only because we
assumed we'd die any minute from some crazy shooting us
during a demo?"

"Of *course* not. But you were the one who taught me that
history moves, new contradictions surface, organizing isn't one
long glamorous siege of the Winter Palace—"

"Shit, I know those days are over. I know women had to get
their own movement together. I know the Left, Old *and* New,
fell apart in this country mostly because of the way it treated
women. I know it *deserved* to fail apart. I *know* all that. I *left*
the Left, because of *that.* Hell, I gave up a lot to— What I'm
trying to say is there's no way for me to follow you where you
are now, more than I'm already trying to. I can't even call
myself a feminist man because that would be a rip-off, co-
opting one of the few things women *name* them*selves.* I can
just . . . play a supportive role from the sidelines. Any other
involvement is instantly suspect as 'taking over.' "

"Because for a man it usually is, Larry," she said as gently as
she could.

"I know *that,* too. But you—you've still *got* it, you've got it
with other women. The shared anger, the actions, the in-jokes,
the . . . shorthand code. A feeling of being effective, of having a *community.* I hardly even have any friends anymore."

A short sigh of impatience escaped her.

"Larry, that's ridiculous. Just last week Ruby and Len—"

"Look. You know as well as I do that all the interesting
people these days are women. And they're *your* friends first,

natch, and my friends only because I'm the appendage. And the couples—yuck. I'm so tired of comparing 'struggle struggle toil and trouble' stories as social conversation I could die. But the men who *don't* live with women—or, correction, with feminist women—they're the Job's counselors I despise most of all. 'Give it to 'er, Lare! Show her you're a man. Put her in her place. All this feminist crap is divisive of Serious Politics.' I need advice like this? So. No friends. Any that might once have been mine have deserted the sinking feminist prince." He was embarrassed by the way facts kept sounding like self-pity.

"Well then, let's find us some new—"

"Jule. That's not the point. All I'm trying to get at is that your life is the one with the energy, at least the visible kind. Maybe if I were a writer or an artist . . . but I'm not. You've got that going for you, too. Your life is more interesting to both of us, I'm afraid—even to me. For one thing, it seems our survival—our literal financial survival—depends on it. For another, I *am* proud of you, and I really do believe in this politics, you know. I always wanted to be on the cutting edge. I just never thought I'd be there living vicariously, like—" He stopped himself at the border of the unspeakable.

"Like a stage mother, you mean," she said, bitterness leaking into her voice. "So I've turned you into a stage mother?"

"Well, you say you dream often enough that I turn into her."

"*You* once said that if you *were* turning into her it was perhaps a generous sacrifice to save me from knowing how much I was turning into her myself."

"Well, it doesn't matter, anyway, now, does it." It wasn't a question. "You must be exhausted, Jule-ums," he finished off, too lightly. "Tomorrow I'll start 'striking' the roof, I guess. Before the first frost. Or what New York calls a frost. Nothing like what I remember from the Colorado mountain autumns—*that* was a *frost.*"

For a moment, he glimpsed himself again—a lonely boy, an almost suicidally sensitive young man escaping the winters when he had huddled in bed with a flashlight, devouring books in secret so his father wouldn't blow up over the light bill. A strange longing lay in him for that old captivity, now recalled as a time of freedom. The rough beauty of the Rockies, pewter streams that ribboned through stands of pine and spruce a denser green than anywhere in the world. His connection with and love of the land, a connection Julian had never known, always envied.

"Yes, I guess we should go in . . . Larry?"

"Yeah?"

"We'll make it yet. Neither of us gives up easily. If we had, we wouldn't have got this far. We're survivors."

Optimism ticked on in her like a timing device wired to dynamite. He rose abruptly and began to roll up his tatami mat.

"Actually, I loathe that phrase," he muttered.

"What? What did I say?"

"I mean 'survivors.' You hear it bandied about everywhere these days. By triple divorcés. By sell-outs. Born-again-Christian Watergate politicians. People who don't give a shit about asking 'survival at what price?' There are some things one maybe shouldn't survive. I mean, unless one doesn't give a damn whose skin it comes out of."

"All right, all right. I didn't mean it like that, and you know it." She was calculating whether one more try was worth it, and he almost wished she'd give up and grant them both release. But the reflexes already had her tap-dancing before she reached a conscious decision. "What I did mean was, well, everybody's unhappy in one way or another. Whoever said relationships weren't the hardest work around? At least we're not the kind who just settle for . . . torpor. At least we're trying for something not yet invented."

"You were the one who taught me the danger of 'post-revolutionary thinking in a pre-revolutionary context.' "

She got to her feet and began rolling up her mat, too.

"Well, what the hell. Why not? The old evolutionary leap. Or a pretense of it. Pretending a virtue we don't have, like Polonius counseled. Maybe in time the virtue will become real."

"Polonius, my dear wife, was a platitude-ridden deadly bore. Shakespeare intended him that way."

"I *know*, but—"

"*I* know *you* know. Ad infinitum." They stood facing one another in vain, mutually eclipsed. "Oh, Jule. I guess we go on because neither of us can conceive how not to. Maybe that's cowardice. Maybe it's an act of existential courage. Who the hell knows. Like that line in your poem. What was it? Oh yeah.

'The pretense of pretending we needn't pretend is pretension.' Damned good line."

"Thanks," she mumbled, so low he couldn't tell whether in anger or hopelessness.

"You must be beat," he said expectantly.

"Yeah, I am," she sighed. "What's more, I have to go into Athena tomorrow, to pick up a manuscript job."

"Editing or copy-editing?"

"I don't even know yet. But Charlotte wanted me to come get it on Tuesday, and I told her it would have to hold till I came back from California, that I'd just have to make up the time and work on it over the weekend to meet their deadline."

"Can't you pass this one up? I mean with the money coming from the lecture date—"

"Larry. We're about three thousand dollars in debt again. I can't afford to pass anything up. And at least the books I get to work on from Athena Ltd. are remotely feminist. They don't make me feel as if I have a blue pencil lodged in my throat from trying to swallow some sentence about how 'he swept her romantically into his crushing embrace and felt her heart heave at him through her ripped bodice.' "

They wound their way through the familiar rooms, shutting off lights as they went, darkness gathering its fullness behind them.

"Aren't you going to have your ritual soak?"

"I'd fall asleep in the tub and drown," she called back over her shoulder. "My legendary energy. They raved about it when I was two feet high, reviewers admire it in my writing, lecture audiences now get infected with it the way they used to when I spoke lines other people had written for me. Fie on thee, I say to my fabulous energy."

"Oh, it's still there, Jule. It must suffer a sea-change when you come home, though. Or get left on the doorstep."

She undressed and quickly slid a nightgown over her head—before he might think about making love, Laurence suspected. How many millions of such symbolic acts passed as code between married people, he wondered. But loneliness or fear—or was it defiance?—drove him to deliberately ignore the code. He moved closer to her in their bed, seeking her under the blanket, the nightgown, sensing her body stiffen involuntarily at his touch. Then he felt her soundless sigh—as if something in her mind had shifted, tired of resisting, and was reconciling itself: why not? for the comfort of comforting him, at least; for the comfort of not having rejected him; for the comfort— whisper of the heart's innermost devil, though whether in her heart or his own he could not tell—the comfort of having paid one out, and being owed a night undisturbed in return.

And while he labored lovingly above her body, and while her body gave back perfectly the requisite motions in response —feeling nothing, concentrating on the effectiveness of the performance?—he tried to not think what happens to two people who still love one another but whose passion has become joyless. O murmur of the devil in the heart: Was it possible now to recall when it was *not* joyless? Had it *ever* been there?

Then, sudden and sharp as a blade, memory twisted in his ribs. The two of them, each brimming with their individual revelations, walking across the Brooklyn Bridge—what would somehow always be to him *their* bridge. Not all the violin strings in corny Hollywood movie scores could have cheapened us then, he thought, seeing once more the wind stream wild through her hair, hearing the river roar below. *The way we held one another. The glance she gave me then, before we kissed and after.* It *had* been there once. *Never disown it, Julian,* he prayed silently to her; *never forget or denounce it, Laurence,* he prayed to himself; *never let the years or the failures of nerve revise it conveniently away. If the tragedy is that by our very devotion we somehow diminished one another, why is that merely reactionary or neurotic, reducible to another brand name? Why can't that be like grace, laying waste to a profligate life in order to sanctify it?*

He reached for her and clung hard. "Oh, Jule," she heard him cry. But she mistook his sobs, and picking up her cue from that, quickened her own breathing. She vaguely understood that though he was now reconciled to not knowing what her body intended or pretended in their acts of love, he was grateful for the gesture, and he let it drive him into the doomed solipsism of his own coming, as if that were an act affirming hers affirming his, passing one another in the night again.

Afterward, lying in the dark, Julian spoke.

"It was that she lunged at me. Incredibly frail she is now. You've seen her, Larry. But something drove her up. Some

. . . hatred of me, something absolutely primeval and malignant gave her strength. She sprang from that hospital bed—I couldn't believe my eyes, I was too paralyzed to budge—and it sounded as if she was babbling in Italian. 'Avanti . . .' Impossible, she doesn't know a word of Italian. It must have been something else, but you couldn't understand her anyway, because the words were so slurred. But Larry, she flew at me—and she was massive with rage. A giant. All five feet of her somehow towering over me. Not since the night she threw the brass clock at me have I been physically afraid of her. She was totally mad. And *strong.* She went for my eyes, my throat. I kept putting my hands up in front of my face and I heard myself screaming 'Momma, Momma, why are you doing this? It's *me,* Momma. It's Julian!' It took three nurses—one of them a man—to pull her off me. God, Larry, they put her in *restraints.* Before my eyes. And me crying and begging them not to, and her shouting 'I know it's you! D'y' hear me, Julian? It's you who've done this to me! I never want to see you again as long as I live! Nurse!' she yelled, 'keep her away from me, keep that demon away from me!' She *said* that." Julian was trembling with the horror of telling it. Laurence waited. "Larry, Larry, I didn't say anything to set her off, honest. And I *know* about the medication making her paranoid and all that. But still . . . Christ, she must actually hate me for it to come out under the medication so intensely. What have I done to make her hate me like that? What have I *done?* I wanted my own life, you, us. Something real. But something must *be* real, and despicable, in her—and in me—for her to hate me like that."

Laurence Millman knew when to be silent. For this too Julian had once loved him, even though his silences were now often turned against her. But this silence, punctuated only by the tightening of his grasp on her body, was turned outward against the world, against Hope, against everything that was battering fangs and claws at their walls and windows. She murmured as she began to fall asleep on his shoulder,

"She tried to sink her teeth into my cheek, but my arm went up, and she bit into my watch instead. Broke the crystal. Bit so hard she broke the crystal. Why, Larry, why . . ."

Julian slept on undisturbed when, a few hours later, Laurence woke drenched with sweat, crept softly out of bed, threw on a robe, and made his way back out onto the roof garden alone. The stars were clearer now. He could wait out the dawn in this safe place. There was no need to wake her. There was no need to tell her that now even her dreams were invading his, hardly a space left in which to breathe, hardly a self left with which to breathe.

There was no need to tell her how vivid it had been: him crying over and over, "Jule, Jule, if only they hadn't separated us like this!" Then he'd looked down at himself and seen that he was restrained in a straitjacket just as she was, each of them with their arms forcibly embracing only their own bodies. But suddenly he broke free of his restraints and was able to fling his arms wide. He grinned and began to dance toward her. "Fuck 'em all, that's what I say, Julian. You're still mine and I love you. Hell, I *raised* you, no wonder you turned out okay! My own baby revolutionary I'm so proud of. Come to me, Julian." But she stared at him, stricken, then wheeled and ran desperately through what became a long hospital corridor. He pursued her, his cries echoing her footsteps, "Hey, Julian, wait up! Don't be scared. It's *me*, Jule. You know who I am." A frantic creature, limbs pinioned, she fled him down the corridor, doors on each side slamming in her face as she tried to dodge into them, one after another, until at last the space widened between her body and his, until he saw her now distant figure hesitate for a second before the polished steel Exit door at the corridor's end. She spun around, her arms still bound, her face a mask of flesh stretched tight by fear, saw him coming closer, then wheeled again and flung her whole weight against the door. It gave, swung open, and slammed shut again after swallowing up her shape. But still Laurence ran after her, breath coming so short it seemed his lungs would burst with longing, pulse racing in exertion and panic at losing her. He reached the door. It was locked. "Julian!" he called through it. "Julian! Come out! Don't be afraid! It's just me, can't you see it's just me?"

Silence answered him. He beat helpless fists against the door. "Julian," he sobbed, sagging against the polished steel, "I can't live without you. I don't know how to anymore. Come back to me, to the way we used to be." From the corner of his eye he glimpsed his reflection in the shining metal. "Julian," he whispered, turning slowly to look at himself, one hand coming up in confusion to touch the softening jawline, to brush back the forehead curls in wonder. "Julian," he whispered again, "come back. Please? Come back to the one who loves you best."

By that time, of course, he understood why she had fled him. By that time, it was too late. Seeing his reflection full-face, he knew. The last of the hoped-for and struggled-for transformations had been abandoned, and all the while this one had been growing to completion. Unexpected, irreversible, now it too was a perfected work. By that time, he learned from the locked door's gleaming surface, he was Her.

CHAPTER THREE
Winter, 1959–1960

This time I'll try to get it past the censor.

I doubt that Hope will ever look in the back of my history notebook. She's not very interested in my schoolwork, except in the A grades, of course. She thinks history is especially boring.

This could be a journal, the kind real writers keep. Training for observing, writing dialogue, practice of the craft, all that stuff. If she ever discovers it, I might as well step in front of an onrushing camera and end it all, there would be such hell to pay. But would I love it if these pages could be private, all my own.

Maybe then I could find out what it is I feel—if I feel anything real at all. I'm obsessed with that, with *ever* doing *anything* so completely that I can escape myself observing myself doing it—and observing others observing how I do it. I go into churches lately. Catholic churches, Protestant, synagogues if they're open, even last week a Greek Orthodox church. It's a space to myself. I even pray. But it's as if I'm that poor bastard Claudius just not getting through. Except I'm worse: I keep on hoping Hamlet *is* spying on me from behind the arras or wherever. I can't concentrate. Partly that's because I don't believe in all that mumbo-jumbo. I remember thinking there was no god when I was quite little. There were only constellations and planets, the ocean and things growing up right out of the ground—and all that was pretty miraculous in itself. This was back when I was young, about six, when I wrote that spooky little jingle before my birthday: "Some like it hot, some like it cold. I'm afraid of seven years old."

At any rate, if I didn't "believe" back then, I certainly don't now, at the ripe old has-been kid-star age of just-last-week-turned seventeen. *God,* if I can only *live* long enough to get out of the *teens!* At least I'm not Sweet Sixteen anymore, and if there *were* a god that would be something to thank him for. Now I can be Sardonic Seventeen all I want—in these pages, anyway.

But what I was starting to write about was why I can't concentrate on praying. I'd like to because I think if you can somehow go through the motions convincingly enough, long enough, then the real thing—faith or whatever—will come. I think that's the concept they call "earned grace." (For an atheist, even I find my preoccupation with reading around in comparative religions and theology pretty suspicious.) But my atheism sure does get in the way of my faith. Still, the main reason I can't concentrate on praying is even worse, the same problem that's haunted me since I can remember: what I can't *help* but concentrate on is Portrait of Young Girl Piously Kneeling. It's as if anything that *would* be the real me is transparent, one of those clear plastic pages you write on but when you pull it up from the treated slate beneath, the words vanish. An unpainted canvas, a rolled-up scrim, a blank movie screen. As if, were I to pass in front of a mirror, like some lovely doomed vampire I would show myself no reflection.

No soul, they once thought that meant.

I need somebody to want me to be something before I can become it. But then I *can* become it—and believe it. And once *I* believe it, it becomes real for anyone seeing me, and *then* I *really* believe it. So I'd need God to *want* me to believe in God before I could believe. But I guess I'd have to believe in God in the first place in order to get a hold of the script or hear the Director. Maybe I *don't* have a soul, after all.

Even now, watching myself watching myself writing, it's as if, should I turn my attention away from that watching for one second, I'd cease to exist, go up *puff* in a spiral of smoke. I wonder sometimes if I'm a nut. Once I asked Hope if I could see a therapist, but sure enough if it involves insight she won't hear of it. The only use she has for psychiatry is that I should date Jack Erdman, because although he's still only in his residency he *is* a doctor and *will* be a (rich) headshrinker. Ugh. I've given up trying to talk with her about my own maybe craziness. Her basic reply is, "Oh honey, all the world's a stage, what's the fuss about?"

The irony is she's right. Right again, maddeningly. The Wise One, the Queen Mother. I know that in one way or another everybody's always acting: not only actors but politicians and businessmen. Theatrical agents, those nausea-provoking people with their putrid Dahlings and Deahests. And spies, secret agents, double agents. And the priests and soldiers in their different costumes, like Virginia Woolf says. But they all seem able to do it at *will*. It doesn't run away with them like it does with me. Noticing the noticing the noticing, like facing mirrors reflecting each other's reflection into infinity, until I'd do anything to stop the wheels within wheels in my brain. Yesterday, I told her again I want to get out of the business. Big Fight number seven thousand six hundred and forty-three.

What she doesn't know is that I've decided I want to be a real writer.

I did try to tell her that, too, more than once. But whenever I say I want to write, she says, "Write what?" Which makes no sense and isn't the point and I can't answer. What do I say? "Anything. Everything. I don't know."? That won't get you very far with *her*.

Certainly she knows I've scribbled stories and poems since I learned to hold a pencil, but she merely takes that as another sign of The Baby's multi-talented little sickening self. Like her arranging for one of the poems I wrote when I was ten to be sealed in a time capsule along with city documents and newspapers during the Yonkers Centennial Festivities. Cutesy gumdrop poem plus a publicity shot of The Baby. To be opened a hundred years in the future. *Mortifying*. I don't want to be remembered like that. *I* intend something quite different. I've decided. As usual, I watched myself making the decision. So I even have a witness.

I think maybe the way to get out of feeling as if you're living a story all the time (though that *is* better than living a story someone else has written *for* you) but the way to escape from living even your own story would be to deliberately create other stories. If I have to go through my life like some doomed soulless creature, then I can be constructive about it at least, by learning to make it up "for real."

I've had some moments of satisfaction doing that in the business itself (damned few, thank-you-Hope). Those were when I could play a meaty part, something that demanded dramatic skill. But most parts for children aren't like that, because no adult thinks about kids as human beings with as many tragic emotions as big people. Most kids' parts are "sweet," or "cute." You also spend a *disgusting* amount of time doing personal appearances and publicity puke. Which takes *no* skill except smiling and curtsying and autographing till your hand cramps. Or getting pinched on the cheek till you're sure you'll get cheek cancer. Or having your one comfortable pair of barrettes auctioned right off your head during some TV telethon for underprivileged children. It's a rare treat to play a nice psychotic kid, or do a scene where you get to have hysterics. *Then* I felt as if I actually deserved some of the applause. It was for a moment an answer to the question I'd whisper to myself at age twelve in front of the mirror: Why are you *doing* this?

Well, you do it partly out of pride. Pride in doing the best you can, no matter how sugary the part is and no matter what anybody thinks. Also, and in complete contradiction (can such a contradiction actually exist? I wish I still had Barbara to talk philosophy with!) you also do it *because* you care what they think. A lot. They (seem to) love you for it. I guess I realized pretty early that what they loved about it was that you were fulfilling their own expectations of surprise. You were a magical toy, a wind-up doll. I used to wonder why, after I'd learned some revolting recitation for an audition (I think the "quality of mercy" speech of Portia, and Shaw's St. Joan bleating about the little lambs in the green grass will stick in my memory until I die); after I'd learned the lines to recite, I'd wonder what was the point in reciting aloud to people what they already knew in advance I was going to say? Yes, of *course* I knew what was being tested was the "delivery." But on a kid's level of logic it seemed senseless.

You also do it because you don't know what else to do. All you're sure of is that you're something other than you are. (I always think I'm really someplace else.) I can play older or younger than my age, and on radio I can pinch my voice up to sound like a breathy kindergarten kid, or wrinkle it down—I mean not in treble but in years—to sound like an eighty-year-old woman. So you're sure you can be everything, but you feel you can't be *one single thing thoroughly.*

I know, for instance, that everybody—including this atrocious new tutor—thinks my writing is proof that I'm "a dilettante." I shouldn't care what in hell they, and especially Hope, think(s). I care so much it hurts. I don't *want* to want to be what others want me to be! Is acting an addiction? Eventually terminal? I don't want to leave the business just to play-act living on a bigger set—my life.

Some days I feel full of hate—which is a feeling, in turn, that I hate. I am *worn out* with all this *feeling*.

A few nights ago I dreamt I had absolute power, like an empress or a goddess. I had them all lined up—the agents and personal managers, the old "Family" company, every tutor except Barbara, the photographers and cameramen, the wardrobe fitters sticking you with pins, the school kids who loathed my guts and tripped me and gave me Indian burns and were afraid of me and liked each *other,* all the old piano and singing and tap and ballet and swimming and accents coaches, the evil producers and the snappish directors—and there, at the very end of the line, standing apart by herself, Hope. They were all taller than me, as if I were still a child. But small as I was in the dream, I went down that line carrying an armful of sharp stakes. I drove a stake deep into each of their hearts, and as I did it I curtsyed and smiled "Thank you very much." But when I came to her, she was crying. Then I saw why. She already was riddled with stakes, a pincushion, a Saint Sebastian. There wasn't one inch of room for me to hurt her more. So I gave up and tried to embrace her instead. But as I pressed myself against her, my embrace drove the stakes deeper into her— and she and I both screamed at the same time. I woke up with my heart pounding.

I have to stop now. I just heard her come back from lunch with the broker.

I had a HUGE fight with her yesterday. About Erdman. He wants to take me for a drive on Sunday in his sports car and I don't want to go. I have to admit that he's handsome and much older than me (seven years). That's exciting when you come down to it. And he *is* already a doctor and he's done his internship and just started his residency in psychiatry. He flatters me about how "exquisite" I am but since I don't *feel* exquisite I think he's a liar. The truth is that any excuse to go out, even on a daytime "date," is like heaven to me. But the last time I had lunch with him I decided I never wanted to see him again. It went like this:

Him: So . . . hmmm . . . (he already acts like a psychiatrist) . . . you think you want to give up acting.

Me: I *know* I want to give it up.

Him: Hmmmm . . . What do you have in mind to do with yourself, then, Julian? You're a talented girl, you know.

Me: (Silently: Vomit vomit.) (Out loud:) I want to do something else.

Him: Have you thought about . . . hmmm . . . getting married?

Me: Yes, I have. I don't want to get married for a long time yet.

Him: Hmmm . . . then you must have some other plans in mind.

Me: Yes. (Silently: And I don't intend to tell *you.)*

Him: Hmmmm . . . Am I to take that mysterious answer the way I think you *really* mean it?

Me: How do you think I really mean it?

Him: I think you *don't* have any special plans for yourself, except to get away from your mother—

Me: That's not true. (Silently: You betcha.)

Him: —and I think you're scared of men and that's why you're scared of me—

Me: I'm certainly *not* scared of you, Jack. (Silently: Vomit vomit.)

Him: —and you're covering up that insecurity by saying you have all these mysterious alternate plans, when what you really want is to be married and have kids of your own. (Then he flashed me a smileful of teeth.)

Me: Then I'll tell you how wrong you are. I *do* have plans for myself. I want to be a writer.

Him: A writer . . . hmmmm . . . well, that's okay. (Another blinding toothy smile.) I can live with that. Every young wife should have a hobby. Some women do ceramics.

Honest to god, that was the conversation. So yesterday I informed her that I never wanted to see her revolting disgusting doctor-candidate for me again.

That conversation went like *this:*

Her: You're crazy.

Me: So? Then let me see a real psychiatrist of my own, Momma, not a slimy boyfriend type.

Her: He went to Harvard Medical School. His father is a doctor. He's going to be a rich man. He'll never get called out in the middle of the night on an emergency like physical doctors.

Me: He has shifty eyes. He can go to hell. And do ceramics there.

Her: Watch your mouth. You don't have to marry him tomorrow. Or ever. You could just cultivate him a little. It wouldn't kill you.

Me: Why should I cultivate him? He's not a garden.

Her: Don't get smart with me, Julian. Even the biggest stars don't always work steady. You're in an age transition. An actress could use a financial cushion like a rich doctor.

Me: Momma, you contradict yourself all the time! I'm not going to *be* an actress, I've *told* you that. Besides, according to you, there's enough money from what I've already earned so that I don't have to work a day more in my life.

Her: That's beside the point. Then what *are* you going to do with your life? The only thing you know how to do is act. You already have a career, a reputation.

Me: I didn't choose them.

Her: What does that matter? You would have chosen the same thing if you'd been old enough to and had any sense. The point is the career exists now. You can't just give it up. What are you giving it up *for?*

Me: I'm only seventeen, Momma. I'm still thinking.

Her: So while you're thinking it'll kill you to be nice to Jack Erdman?

And round and round and round again. Complete with yelling and crying and her "nerves." Until I finally hit on my exit line: "Momma, he keeps putting his hands all over me."

The truth is he never does, though his smug toothy leer always makes me want to run home and take a shower. But telling the truth doesn't pay around here. Whereas the line worked with her. Instant. Perfect. Right on cue.

The end of Jack Erdman, may he rest in peace in some future wife's ceramic urn.

Hope better never find this journal.

P.S.: Maybe someday I'll write plays.

I want to truly write about her. Starting now, with this entry and with Haydn's "Messiah" on the phonograph. She's gone out for dinner with that ghastly textile manufacturer. I wish to god she'd marry him. If she were concerned with somebody else it might take some of the pressure off me.

Truth is: I hate Hope more than anyone in the world.

Truth also is: I love Hope more than anyone in the world.

To her it's so simple. She's given me her entire life, she expects only love in return. Who could be so warped as to deny her that?

She *is* blameless. She did what she thought was best for me. That's also a truth. *A* truth. A truth caught in the subway rush-hour of truths.

Am *I* blameless, then? A child has to grow up, after all, and she's always said I could be or do anything I wanted. But if I'm blameless as well as her, why won't *she* acknowledge *that*, the way I've done in so many fights with her—saying how I *don't* blame her, how I love her, but that I can't *breathe* anymore, I don't know who I am, it's time for me to lead my own life. I'm seventeen years old, for Christ's sake. (It looks weird to swear on the page.) I'm a grown woman. Certainly *she* reminds *me* of that often enough, when she feels I've been irresponsible about something *she* wants me to do.

Another truth is: if she won't acknowledge my blamelessness (and acknowledge that I grant *her* blamelessness), then I myself won't ever really believe it, deep down. What's *wrong* with me? So then, at this point in the wheels-within-wheels brain routine, I start to feel guilty.

Because yet another mashed-up truth is: she made me.

Frau Frankenstein and her Creature.

If I like what I am (and sometimes I almost do), then how can I blame her? If I *don't* like what I am (which is almost all the time), then am I not liking me precisely in order to blame her?

She's always been a fighter, and she made me one. She

herself gave me the equipment (which I was never supposed to use, I guess, against *her*).

She's given me everything. I can't even sort out what's my own. For instance, this feeling of always wearing a mask, or layers of them in lightning-quick changes. It stirs through me so frequently, like a ladle being circled listlessly through left-over stew by an arthritic hand. (I wonder if that's good writing. No, Julian, get back to just putting it down, don't get trapped into watching the writing again . . .)

This feeling that everything's fake can be a *good* thing—in Buddhism and Hinduism, anyway. Maya, illusion; Nirvana, nothingness. Well, knowing about Maya and Nirvana comes from Barbara—but *feeling* them comes from Hope's influence, though she wouldn't understand it and would insist that I didn't feel it. But it does come from her.

Whatever confidence I have is rooted in her belief in me. And it can't endure against the opposition of the one who made it, either. I better not forget Hope is the double-message master. Like preaching material things don't count so I shouldn't have harped on having a room of my own, but meanwhile being obsessed about money herself—her stocks and bonds and Dow Jones averages. Or like the menstruation-and-sex conversation years ago, a real beauty. All that stuff about how menstruating was natural and clean and nothing shameful, how sex at the right time and with the right boy was not scary and was just grand—and me coming away feeling sort of repulsed and thinking it must be *me* because she said all the right things. And finally figuring out that she'd said them in a tone of voice just above a whisper. Double-message Momma.

She always seems to radiate unbounded confidence in her own opinions, even if they're superstitions or lies. She radiates confidence in my opinions, too—but in the *abstract*. When I express a *specific* opinion, and god forbid especially if it might diverge from hers, she withdraws her approval lightning-fast. (Of course she denies this.)

It's as if Hope has no notion whatsoever of her power over me. She can whine and she can thunder. She can crack me like an eggshell so that I splatter out in pity for her. Yet I'm terrified of her. Why can't I be selective, pick some part of her to affirm but reject the rest?

Well, this kind of writing must be real because it's making

me sick to my stomach. And my gastrointestinal system has to be authentic, even if not much else about me is. I'll stop this journal entry now. But I won't give up.

I'm going to write my way through Hope. Maybe somewhere I'll find Julian.

I just looked back at the last entry and realized that Hope's "nerves" and fainting fits and nausea is one way she controls me. So maybe it's a sign of health that I'm daring to get nauseated on my own?

Just another tactic that would come from her, and so probably be useless against her.

Everything is useless against her. I don't know who I'll be when she dies.

But more than any of my feelings *about* her, I feel *her*, somehow. I used to watch how she tried to avoid the role of stage mother. It broke my heart with pity for her. But I hated her for it, too, because it meant that in public, with Them around, she never pushed me forward, never contradicted a director, never praised me. In private, ho ho another story. *There* waited the expectations, the criticisms, the "stand a fraction upstage but if you're caught don't say I told you to do it because they'll bar me from the set." *I feel all of her, all the time.*

I'm too central in her life. And she's a giantess in mine. By the time I'm forty, of course, she won't be. But by then I'll be too ancient to do the things it's worth being free of her in order to do.

I know writing all this must be a cliché—the thing I *dread.* Though Barbara used to say a writer has to dare write his way through *miles* of clichés even for years maybe before he gets down to the creative original. With Barbara gone, it's harder to think of myself as a someday writer. As for that crap about Hope being worried Barbara didn't challenge me enough: Hope was *jealous* of Barbara. Barbara knew it and so did I.

She was like the teacher right out of "The Corn Is Green." Severe, challenging, but also mild. She even smelled good, and that fabulous grainy-gravel low voice—I used to sit fascinated while she talked about writers and language and human rights and politics and religion and anything. She never treated me like a freak adolescent performer dabbling in intellectual pursuits. She asked, she listened, she *heard*.

That first session after Hope hired her as my tutor, Barbara looked at me across the coffeetable in the livingroom (she'd asked whether we should work in my room, and raised her eyebrows ever so slightly when told I hadn't a room of my own). She leaned toward me and suggested we use the first session to get to know each other. Then she asked me who I was. And right away I knew she didn't mean my name, rank, and Employed Minor registration number. I thought I'd die.

I remember I said I was a labyrinth, a maze. (I wanted to show off how much I'd read in mythology. I was only fourteen, after all.) I said the labyrinth had a starting place and a center, but between these two was an enigma. I told her I wanted to be a writer. I'd never said that aloud before, and I was stunned to hear my own mouth put it right out there. Then I started to talk about myself as an actress—but she went directly back to the writer part.

"What kind of writer?" she asked.

I thought I'd die again. Or that I had and was now in paradise. We were off from there. It poured out of me like a flood. That I wanted to make people laugh and cry and think and change, have an effect the way I'd sometimes had as an actress, but with my *own* words and thoughts this time.

Barbara is one of those people who can sum up all your inarticulate gurglings in a few magical words and you know you've been understood.

"So," she smiled at me. "You want to be of use."

"Even worse," I heard myself say. "I want to change the world. I know that sounds hopelessly fourteen."

"Or hope*fully* a sign of positive evolutionary mutancy," she shot back. "I believe it, Julian."

And she wasn't smiling when she said *that*. She believed it. She *knew* it. She *respected* it.

So what's the use of wasting notebook pages on Barbara now? Hope managed to find reasons to dismiss her—for having committed the sin of trying to save my life. It always comes back to Hope's power over me.

Like cutting me off from Barbara, because I loved the *me* I was when I was with Barbara, and I loved Barbara. Like keeping distant any friends I might have—on the rare occasions someone near my own age has wanted to be friends with a person like me. Like managing to throw up a Dead End sign about Bramwell. For fear of *what?* That two teenage prodigies (except he was one and I'm really not) would fall in frenzied mouth-frothing love with each other and screw night and day and get me pregnant? When he has to sit at that piano of his and practice a minimum six hours a day in between *his* tutor and homework and concert tours and things that make him as disgusted with his life as I am with mine?

She encouraged it at first, like she always does. The night we met, both of us headliners at a benefit for the New York City Youth Scholarship Fund, it was Hope who invited Bramwell and his mother over for coffee and snacks afterward. When they left, she and I giggled together about how cute he was. When he came to lunch the following Saturday, I had planned to cook something but she took us both out to the Japanese restaurant around the corner. She got tickets for her and me for his next concert at Carnegie Recital Hall. She told my press agent about it and there was an "item" in Leonard Lyons' column about the two "youthful talents" being seen around town together—which made me want to shrivel up with embarrassment. But she let us be friends.

It was only when he and I started to *be* friends that she changed. Whenever I saw him, she'd ask me, sort of "girlfriend to girlfriend," how it was going, what had we done, what had we talked about. But I didn't *want* to tell her every detail. Some of the things we discussed were private. I suppose that was the kiss of death. She started sniping about him: he was too full of himself, his career wasn't going right, why didn't he take me to an opening night on Broadway where we'd be seen and it would help both our careers. She and I started to fight about it. Then he called and told me that she'd called his mother and told *her* she thought it was best "if the kids gave each other a rest because they're both so young and shouldn't monopolize each other's time." His mother was angry about that but what could she do, so *she* told *him,* and what could *he* do? There was nothing at all I could do.

I really loved Bram. Sure, probably I was in love with him, too. At least I think. It's very hard being a teenager, because you think and feel everything strongly and at the same time everyone is telling you that you only *believe* you're in love, you only *think* you're depressed, you only *imagine* you're confused. (To me in particular this feels like Charles Boyer secretly turning the gas lights up and down in order to drive Ingrid Bergman daffy.) Also, you would give anything in your adolescent life *not* to be a sophomoric "teenager." Which in fact you are. Dis*gust*ing state. So the more you try not to be all those things the more you feel yourself being and doing them. Arrrggghhhhh!!

I'd give anything to be able to peel me off myself. Then I get frightened that this is the kind of thing people who commit suicide say. But I want to *live*, not die. It's almost a surprise that I look forward to the rest of my life.

This time I want to pick up on what I was writing about Bram. Because he really *was* wonderful and gorgeous and I've never dared say or write that to anyone—definitely not him, certainly not Hope.

I'll try to describe him. That's good practice for being a writer. He had (well, he still has, I suppose, even though she managed to put him into the past tense as far as it concerned me) he *has* dark blondish hair, the color of old brass, and it curls a little at the base of his neck. He has brown eyes, but not like mine; his are glinted with amber flecks and they just take your breath away when he looks (looked) at you. He's got this divine chin. And when he sits down at a piano and rips off a Bach prelude or lets loose with a Chopin ballade, you might as well swoon. The thing is, he was only a year older than me (still is, dumbbell), but even at seventeen he had, not just sophistication, but *maturity*. He'd been concertizing since age five, playing classical music. Not a grinning, shuffling kid who sweethearted her way through one vomitously darling part after another, who got nonalcoholic drinks at fancy restaurants in New York named after her the way restaurants served "Shirley Temple cocktails" in Hollywood. Bram at least had been *himself*—even if he was put on display. But he wasn't pleased with himself, either. Because all *he* wanted to do was compose, not perform. He wrote wonderful music, too. He worried that it was "derivative," the way I hate the idea that I have to trudge through miles of clichés to reach what Barbara called "one's own unique voice" on the page. But to me, his music sounded the way I want my words to sound, lyrical and power-ful and inevitable and surprising all at the same time.

I wish I *had* slept with Bram. (Hope better NEVER find this notebook!) Frankly, I'm so tired of being a virgin I could screech it from a broadcasting transmitter. And it would've been just lovely if Bram and I had been the first ones for each other. I just bet he was a virgin, too, though of course we never talked about that. But we talked about almost everything else. Music and composers and books and how it felt to get a stand-ing ovation and how putrid most tutors are and how it must feel to go to a regular highschool and what hell it is to go on tour once you get over the excitement, and how you have no friends your own age. And about the mixed-up love and fear and hatred you feel for your parents, though in my case it was parent singular.*

Most of all Bram understood how it feels to be a child playing at being a child. How they expect that indignity of you as well, and how scared you are they'll reject you if you're not convinc-ing.

It's the reason I intend never to have a child. I think it's vicious to grasp someone's life and mould it to your own liking.

But I will marry.

She could never get a man to stay with her. *I* will, by god.

She could never imagine herself *not* being a mother (so she says). I can't imagine myself *being* one.

Take that, beloved enemy my mother. We're utterly differ-ent, you and I. Exact opposites.

* I didn't tell even Bram the most sacred secret of all, what I've put together piece by piece for years now, about in my case parents plural. I wonder if I dare trust that to this journal. Better think about that first, Julian.

All day today I've been wondering how I can be so *petty* in my feelings toward Hope. Sometimes I almost take a perverse pleasure in her obstructing me, as if that gave me more ammu-nition for eventual vengeance, as if I were storing it up to explode in one blast strong enough to fling me free of her. Eventually she'll die and I'll be left alive, the stronger even if only by default.

My god, what a terrible thing to think, and to write down, about your own mother! I *must* be sick.

Re-reading what I wrote yesterday makes me realize all over again how creepy it is that I came out of her body. I don't feel as if I'm in my *own,* but I *know* I was in *hers.* I wash me, dress me, feed me. I urinate and defecate. But where I really *live* is inside my head. I've never once cared beans for sports or athletic stuff, I guess. I do masturbate. The psychology books seem divided on whether that's good or not. Anyway, that's one thing I *do* do down in my body. Of course, never having had a damned room of my own, even here in the long-promised holy land of a Sutton Place apartment, I learned long ago how to masturbate real fast, in the bathroom. I must be the fastest hand in the East. Door locked, sink water running, zip bang whoosh three minutes flat. Then flush as if you'd used the toilet, and emerge (not even breathing heavily) before she can ask why the door is locked or say what are you doing in there that's taking so long don't you know reading on the toilet will give you piles.

Somehow it's all connected to the way I feel about my body. It's short, short-waisted, too. Small-boned, but tending toward the plump. Like hers. Yet without her good features—even teeth, pale skin, large eyes.

I make me sick. Breasts too big (and have been since I was fourteen; they had to use binders to flatten them for certain roles so I could look younger). Nose too large. Eyes too small. Hair thin and given to stringiness, though I did win the Battle of the Blonde and got her to let me return to my own color— which is, I have to confess, a revolting mousey brown. Ick. But I'm stuck with the principle of the thing. My face is still baby-fat round. *Yuchk.* Barbara said all teenage women (she actually said *women*) felt this way about their bodies—too tall or short or fat or thin—and that I was quite different from Hope and should have compassion on myself and give myself time.

Well, Barbara's gone and Hope's still here.

And face it, Julian. Even if it *was* with money you earned, Hope *paid* Barbara to be your tutor and your friend, as Hope so delicately reminded you. When the payment stopped, the visits stopped. That day I ran into Barbara by chance in the public library I was afraid I might start crying. But I used to be able to tell her things I'd never uttered aloud to anybody, so this time, too, I came right out and *said* it:

"Why didn't you ever call or write or anything, Barbara? It's been six months almost."

For the first time ever, she didn't look me right in the eye. She fiddled with her pinky ring. Then she did look me in the eye.

"Julian. I respect you. I loved . . . teaching you, working with you. You're a remarkable young person."

It was so good to hear. I had to clench my jaw to stop the lump in my throat.

"Couldn't we still— I don't mean you should tutor me or anything, certainly not for free. But just . . . I thought we were friends."

"It's not for me to come between you and your mother. She loves you and wants only what she believes is best for you."

"You mean if you and I went on being friends, it might get me into hot water with Hope? I wouldn't care, Barbara. Honest. I'm already in hot water with her most of the time. And I really miss—"

"I mean that if you and I were to be friends it would get *me* into hot water, as you put it, with your mother. I can't afford that. I'm sorry."

"You mean she would try one of those ominous threats of hers? Like saying you should lose your tutoring license because you didn't challenge me enough or some baloney like that? She would never really—"

"I mean she could . . . Yes, something like that."

I felt panicky. I just couldn't let her disappear from my life again. I started babbling.

"Barbara, look, I could explain to her," I said. "Maybe if she *understood* what talking with you means to me, that I *miss* it so. There's nobody . . . I mean, literature and art and politics and . . . even the music you introduced me to. I mean, *Bach.* I've been trying to write sonnets, Barbara. Petrarchan and Shakespearean both. I've been sending them out to the little poetry magazines. I've been reading Karen Horney's psychological books, like you suggested. I joined the NAACP and I went to a memorial rally for Hiroshima last August. I'm trying to get out of acting altogether. I—Barbara, I—"

"Julian. Oh Julian," was all she said.

Then I got embarrassed, like some nagging kid. So we just

stood there and didn't say anything. Then she cleared her throat and looked at me again.

"There are some things I can't . . . I think that your mother misunderstood the way I worked with you as your tutor. I think anything you would say to her to explain differently might only confirm her misunderstanding. And I'm afraid that her misunderstanding is profound."

"But *I* understand. I'm a separate *person* from her. Maybe we wouldn't even have to tell her? *I* understand—"

"Not everything," she cut in, with that little half-smile of hers she used to wear when asking me things like "So you feel Sophocles telegraphs his endings in advance?"

"Well, of course not *every—*"

"There are some things you don't understand that I can't teach you. For my own reasons. Not even because of Hope."

I certainly didn't understand. I still don't. But that day I just stood there feeling like I'd been left behind without even a map to help me catch up. All I could manage to say was,

"I guess that's that. I hope you enjoy working with your other students, Barbara. I envy them. I loathe the tutor I have now. You wouldn't *believe* how *revolting* he—"

"I have to go, Julian, I'm late. Forgive me."

"Sure, sure. I have to go, too. Well . . ."

"I'm glad we ran into each other. I think about you often."

"Oh well, don't bother. I know how busy you are and . . . I am, too. Actually, my new tutor keeps me hopping with assignments, so I'm really very stimulated. I'm just fine." I knew she could see right through me but I couldn't help myself.

We said goodbye and started walking in different directions. Then I heard my name and I turned around.

"Julian," she called, "send me a signed copy of your first published book someday? I'll buy all the rest of them, one by one as they come out, myself."

Then she waved and walked away.

So that was it. And I still don't understand. But I have to *face* it. It's been over a year now, with no word. In Hope's lovingly brutal phrase: "She dropped you, dear."

Well, Barbara left me something, anyway. I can retreat into my brain—away from Hope and Hope's body, my life and my body, this showy apartment and the embroidery of lies we live with here. If I had a room of my own! (Virginia, how right you were.) Then I think how Jane Austen wrote at the kitchen table while running her father's parsonage, so that's no excuse. Hope, naturally, always points out to me (and everyone else) how well off I am. I suppose I am. People are starving. But my being well off isn't of any use to *me*, so what's the good of it?

I get these depressed fits of laziness where I don't want to do a thing around the apartment, especially since it's *her* home, not mine. Then there are my weird surges of housework flurry, when I feel I can't *bear* the disorder anymore or her indifference to it. So I attack the kitchen. It drives me crazy how she never washes a pot or pan properly. What's she got against kitchen utensils, anyway? She's a lousy cook (her lamb chops always are so well done they bounce on your plate when you try to cut them, and her vegetables are so overcooked that whether they start out red, yellow, or green, they end up a uniform gray). Consequently, I'm a pretty good cook. On the other hand, she's very skillful with a needle (oh the ghosts of those organdies!), so I *refuse* to learn to sew.

Sometimes I make a foray on what I've named The Ironing Closet. The Ironing Closet is an otherwise ordinary closet into which Hope stuffs the clean laundry she insists one of us do at the building's free laundromat machines in the basement. It's so like her—to spend tons of money on this apartment but not give me a room of my own (and what about a room of *her* own?); to scrimp by not sending stuff to a laundry but then leave it indefinitely, clean but scrunched up, in that closet. So when you open the door, blouses, towels, underwear, lacy placemats, all come fluttering down on your head. She hates ironing but doesn't like me to do it. Maybe she thinks I'll burn something, like my precious commodity self. Yet she procrastinates doing it, so there always are washed but totally unwearable clothes piling up until there's a fight and she sighs like a martyr and does the ironing.

I am such a *petty* person!

Today I had to miss the class on Provençal poetry I've been attending (non-matriculating of course) at Columbia. Why? Because there was no other time in the world except those three hours for us to tape this *cankerous, suppurative* "public service" commercial for U.S. Savings Bonds. (I've been using the thesaurus, like Barbara said, and it really does expand your adjectives). Anyway, the Ideal American Girl, now Ideal American Teenager (doesn't smoke, doesn't drink, doesn't date, doesn't swear, doesn't EVER revolt, doesn't LIVE) had to tell the television audience how super-dooper it was to invest in Eisenhower-Nixon America. (I hope that Kennedy guy *does* get nominated and even elected, never mind if he is Catholic. I only wish I could vote.) Before Barbara, I used to detest doing this sort of patriotism thing just because it felt goody-goody. Then she introduced politics into my life. So now I know about the difference between socialism and communism, about how the Korean War was complicated, about South Africa. (And my own mother *believed* all that *crap* that McCarthy did a service to the country!) So now I know. Thanks a *lot*, Barbara. Now I have *more* reasons for wanting to gag when I have to go through one of these wholesome Ideal American Girl things. Like being Queen of the Boy Scouts' Ball—which is supposed to make up for my not being allowed to see Bramwell?

I don't see any way out of this except by waiting, getting older. Meanwhile, I do it: "I hope *other* young people will *realize*, as *I* do, the *vital* importance of building our country's *future* along with our *individual* futures vomit vomit."

Between the intention and the gesture falls the shadow, to misquote T. S. Eliot. (Thank you, Barbara.) I think the child actor is conscious of that T. S. Eliot gap all the time. It makes you think the whole world is a two-dimensional painted set.

Barbara used to do her Socrates act with me and ask, "Then what is real?" She'd be right. The family? Hope and I are a "family"—the widow and her half-orphan. A college degree? Which I'll probably never get because Hope won't let me go away to school and because having been tutored now for so many years since I was twelve I'm terribly uneven—graduate level in literature and philosophy and the like, but still probably hovering around grade 6 in science: there's just so many lab experiments you can do in a kitchen, particularly one with crusted pots and pans. Yet I've met college graduates who are honestly not very bright. So is their degree "real"?

Is *age* real? Not only can I act older or younger, I can *feel* older or younger, depending on the situation. Is race real? Apostate Jews that we are, is it hypocritical that Hope plans a *seder* every Pesach (lassit*ud*inous annual event attended by her broker, my agent, one or two of her "girlfriends," and helpless me)? For that matter, are Jews a religion or a race or what? For that matter, am I a Jew? Or a girl? Or a woman? Or seventeen? Or an actress? Or a writer? Or a daughter like Goneril or one like Cordelia? Or stark raving mad?

This is ridiculous. I ought to put down some of the good moments. Like yesterday, when I learned that years before I was born, she had loved a poem of William Blake's I had just discovered in *Songs of Innocence.* Who would have thought it of her? The tender moments, the way her smile can make me feel. Her sudden shocking rare miraculous *comprehension!*

She always manages to send me white lilacs on my birthday, and they're sure not in season in October. But she knows I love them, and I guess she orders them way in advance; I bet they're flown in from somewhere at an exorbitant price. The way she'll buy me a book she knows I want, but be uninterested in my telling her about it after I've read it. Still, she'll buy it for me—as a surprise, an un-birthday, or a gift for one of the billions of holidays she celebrates: Chinese New Year, Ramadan, Easter and Pesach and Succoth, *and* all the secular ones, July Fourth, Columbus Day, Thanksgiving, the works. Right around this time of year, with Christmas and Hannukah overlapping, plus New Year's, it drives me especially nuts, but I have to admit that in her frenzy to assimilate, she certainly is ecumenical.

She can be so beautiful. When I was little, I used to long for her—which was silly since we were together all the time. If I couldn't fall asleep I'd ask for her chenille bathrobe to cuddle with. Not one of my zillions of stuffed animals or the dolls—her bathrobe. Because it smelled like her: a mix of her skin and Joy perfume and sweat and warmth and sandalwood soap and something musky like cinnamon or vanilla (which I must have imagined because she never cooked with either one of them).

Oh *damn.* Why does running away from her tyranny also mean running away from her love?

So, Julian, that breathtaking comprehension you rapturized about last week, where was it this afternoon? Or does she dangle it like bait so you'll be reeled in right after you snap it up? The cruel thing is that the tenderness can so suddenly be yanked back. Then the whole world dwindles gray and literally "hope-less."

But then I think: if it can be so suddenly withdrawn, was it real in the first place?

The way she "manages." Manipulates. Flirts. The vulgarity of her at times, when she cracks chicken bones with her teeth in a public restaurant, when she screams at my agent, her mouth distorted with rage (and his secretary watching as if my mother were an asylum escapee). The safety pin that holds her bra together. Her exaggerations. Not enough that she tells me I've already earned two million bucks and her investments are so good I'll never have to work for a living. No, she has to claim to other people that I was the most highly paid child in the world. Our family doctor can't just be "good," he has to be "the finest anywhere, Arab sheiks come all the way to New York to be treated by him." Whether any of that garbage is true or not, she has to go around all the time *saying* it. I could die from embarrassment. Some of it *is* an outright lie. My big-deal evening dress, which was made by her crony the dressmaker-girlfriend at cost, became "a Balenciaga." After bloodying the battlefield to get her to permit me to attend even a few classes uptown, I hear her boasting that Julian is "going to Columbia graduate school already, and Phi Beta Kappa." When I'm still a *total* ignoramus who can't stop mixing up Manet with Monet. And the *crudeness* of her. The way she's so bossy with waiters and cab drivers, but such a toady to people she thinks can "do us good." The way her eyes go tiny and sharp, like a ferret's, watching me. The way she changes the rules. All the time.

"You'll go on to even better things, Julian, baby," she says. *How,* I'd like to know? When every move of independence is perceived as ingratitude? I *know* it can't have been easy for her. She's had to be both parents in one, she claims. But why should that necessarily make for these arbitrary shifts, like some schizophrenic deity?

My choices are:

#1) refuse to learn her manipulative tactics;

#2) imitate them as realistically as I, the trained mimic, can.

Problem with #1: then with what tools *do* I function??

Problem with #2: oh god, how horrible.

Could I ever invent my *own* tools? What*ever* I invent she takes over. It becomes another "talent." She never destroys outright. She does worse. She cheapens—and then leaves you with it.

Once, I told her that someday I'd love to have a garden. I like to grow things. I'm not half bad at it: the potted plants thrive with my help. The next thing I knew, there were these little toy-type ladyish tools—a five-inch spade and hoe and rake. But guess what naturally no garden. No window box even. (Not even a room of your own yet, so why worry about a garden?)

When I really began loving my music, back around when I was eleven, and practicing piano for my own pleasure (this was even *before* Bram) I found myself entered in yet another piano competition. So after I dutifully won, I stopped playing. The only way out.

When my French improved with Barbara (because she put me onto Camus and Gide and Baudelaire—little did you know the stuff your daughter was getting her hands on, Momma), Hope trivialized it by insisting that I order in French at chic restaurants.

When I made the *fatal* mistake of confiding that I was trying to write poetry and wanted to join a poetry workshop I heard about at Columbia, next thing I knew she'd found this *snail* of a man, Kent Campbell, and they were plotting to bring out a first book of little-heavens-look-how-she's-grown-into-a-*poet*-for-goodness-sake Julian Travis. I'm still fighting on that front. The battle this afternoon was whether we had to go, "for the good of my writing career" *(what* writing career??) to some soirée this *slug* Campbell is giving in two weeks.

"*Think,* darling, of the artists and writers you'll meet there! A whole new universe!" she says.

I could *die.* I want to regurgitate all the precious-wecious poemlets I ever penned. Now I'm supposed to smile and tap-dance my way through a whole new universe?

Oh Momma, can't you ever let anything just *be?* Can't you leave anything untouched by your white be-ringed claws? Can't you let me love some things, love *you* for that matter, without butting in?

If she were to read this.

She would be so hurt it would kill her. She would never speak to me again. She'd throw me out. She would cry until her eyes swelled, and then, still weeping but cold as the Arctic, she'd turn on me and say, "You are a petty, vile, inhuman, unfair, uncompassionate, spoiled brat. You've accepted everything and preened yourself and had the world's adoration while I lived all these years in your shadow. You haven't the faintest idea how to love. You've *played into* every bit of what you claim to detest—and profited by it, and what's more you've enjoyed it. You're just like your father. And for this I've given you my entire existence—which you've destroyed."

And she'd be right about that, too.

I've had a poem accepted for publication.

I can't believe it. It's like a voice from god saying YOU CAN BE A WRITER.

It's a small poetry magazine in Arizona, called *Cactus Wren*. They sent me a check for five dollars and a note saying they'd be interested in seeing more of my work. They didn't accept it because they knew who I was. I'm sure of that because they addressed the envelope and the note to *Mr.* Julian Travis. They didn't know and didn't care that I'd been a star. They think I'm a poet.

It's the sonnet called "Demeter and Persephone." I know it's probably not that good, but *it's been accepted for publication.*

I can't believe it.

This is February 15, 1960.

This is the best day of my life (so far).

I can't avoid it any longer. I'm going to write it down. I've got to tell it *some*where or explode. Even though neither of us have spoken about it since that nightmarish time when I was thirteen. She acts as if it never happened. But it haunts me. Maybe if I write about it here—though if she knew she'd see that as yet another betrayal—maybe I'll get free of it.

I can't even remember how it started. Freud would probably say I've blocked that. I know I'd already been accumulating clues here and there, and a previous visit of Aunt Yetta's had yielded up some juicy ones to an expert eavesdropper like me. (Train an actress, Hope, and you *get* an actress. I can walk in my sox across a parquet floor to eavesdrop without one creak of the floorboards. I can detect the difference between the shifting of her weight in a kitchen chair and the other kind of shifting, prior to rising, so as to scurry soundlessly back to bed with no discovery.)

But this time I almost forgot my technique with the shock of overhearing, through their mix of English and Yiddish, that they were using the present tense. When the rising weightshift creaked from the chair, I barely made it back to the bedroom in time. My heart was banging so loud I was afraid it would heave through my "sleeping" body when she peeked in at the door.

How many days after that did it take me to build up the courage, to wait for the perfect moment? A couple of months, I think. But eventually I must have felt the time was right. Idiot.

It was during one of those mirage oases of her "comprehension"—the ones that turn out to be quicksand. We were lying in our twin beds, in the dark, having the close conversation we seldom have—the kind that goes rancid in my memory when I hear her tell a reporter "We're real girlfriends who can tell each other *any*thing with *total* honesty and how proud I am of Julian's independence." But the opening was there, the mood was right. Ripeness is *supposed* to be all.

So I maneuvered it around to get her discussing the time before I was born, her own girlhood and adolescence and the war—all of which I'd heard before anyway. But sometimes a new nugget would drop. You never knew. Then, very softly, I asked,

"Momma? Tell me more about him."

"Him?" she said into the room between us.

"My father."

"I've told you already, Julian. You know what a brilliant man he was, what a fine doctor. The languages he spoke, how well-educated he was. We loved each other so much. We could have been so happy. It was tragic when the war killed him."

"The war killed him, Momma?"

"But you *know* that, honey. All that intelligence, that compassion, cut off in the prime. I thought I'd die of grief. I would have, too, if it hadn't been for you. There was a baby to think about. It kept me going. And I've never been sorry, either."

I could hear her voice smile through that last sentence.

I remember calculatingly putting into my own voice all the tenderness it could communicate, with every vocal skill I'd acquired in my thirteen years, whispering oh so gently,

"Momma? . . . Momma, he's alive, isn't he? He's still alive."

There was such a silence in the room that for a second it felt as if I were there alone.

"Momma? It's all *right*, Momma. I love *you*, Momma. Nothing can ever change that. But, Momma? Momma, I *know* he's alive?"

The bedtable light switched on. The room sprang into vision and her face, turned toward me, seemed to fill all of it.

"Spy," she hissed. "Traitor. Who told you? How did you find out? Who in hell do you think you are that you can—"

"Momma, Momma, dearest little Momma—" even now I can recall my panic as I ran from my bed and tried to get into hers, under the covers, the way I used to fall asleep when I was little.

She wouldn't let me in. She was sitting up in bed staring at me as if I wasn't me but some intruder, burglar, murderer. I burst into tears and tried to sit on the edge of her bed, but she stuck out a foot and kicked at me. So I stood there in my pajamas, crying.

"Momma, honest, it's *okay* Momma! I still love you more than anything or anyone! I always will, Momma, always! I just want to *know*, Momma, don't you see? Please—"

"What do you want to know," she asked, but it came out as a statement. Her tone was flat, like someone who'd been waiting years for this moment, like this had been a threatened but until now delayed sentence of death.

"Anything, Momma, everything. Whatever you want to tell me. *Please*. Please?"

"Anything. Everything," she repeated dully. "Whatever I want to tell you." Then she looked at me, sharp and deep. I could hardly breathe with fear, hope, excitement.

"Then I *will* tell you, Julian. Sit down."

So I sat on the foot of her bed. I waited. I didn't dare hurry her.

"Everything you already know is true. What I never told you . . . well, I always intended to, when you were older, better equipped to handle it. You're a highstrung child, you know, oversensitive, fragile. That goes with your talent, but still, I worry . . . What I would have told you when you were older —if you hadn't turned spy on your own mother"—the hiss in her voice rose again, then receded as if reined in by an act of will—"is that he . . . changed. I'll never know why. Maybe he wasn't ready for the responsibility of being a father after what he'd been through. He'd escaped from the Nazis, lost every single human being he'd ever loved. That must have been it. I think so. Yes. Because, Julian—since you want the truth—he deserted his wife and child. He abandoned us."

"He . . . abandoned us?"

"Totally. He disappeared. At first I tried to have him traced. I thought something had happened to him, an accident or something. But then as time went by, I realized how cold he'd grown while I was pregnant with you, how remote. Finally I got a letter from him—no return address—somewhere in Connecticut, saying it was finished. Over. And I knew how absolutely futile it would be to try and find a man who had managed to cover his tracks all across Europe—false papers, false names—with the whole Gestapo on his trail. This man knew how to hide."

"Was he— Is he— Couldn't you look up David Travis, Momma? Couldn't you just look up his name?"

"His name?" she laughed strangely. "His name was Traumstein, David Traumstein."

"Not David Travis? But Momma—"

"Why should my child and me bear the name of the sonofabitch who abandoned us? I had to recover. I had to survive. So I did. I got a divorce on the grounds of abandonment. Then I went to court and had your name and mine changed. Legally. To Travis."

"But—who's Travis then?"

"*Nobody's* Travis, you fool," she snapped, "*we* are. You and me. I made it up. I liked it. I came across the name somewhere in a magazine and I liked it. So I took it. It's a good name. What's wrong with it?" she glared at me.

"Nothing, Momma. It's a beautiful name. I like it a lot. It's just—strange that—"

"There's nothing strange about it. People change their names all the time. Just like I'd already changed my maiden name. It's normal. What do you know about life, about anything, Julian?"

"I don't. I don't, Momma. I know I don't. But all I mean is, it's . . . peculiar. Not being my real name."

"The hell it isn't!" she shouted at me. "It's legal, it's real, it's mine, it's yours. The whole goddamned country knows you by that name. That name is famous because of you and me. What could be more real? Are you crazy?"

I remember thinking: back off, don't aggravate her further, get more facts if you can.

"Momma?" I reached out and touched her hand. She pulled it away.

"Momma?" again, "And he never . . . I mean, in thirteen years he's never once—"

"Never." The word hit like a fist in my face. "And don't start to get romantic fantasies in your overheated brain, Baby, about finding him, either. Get the message? *Never.* He didn't want you. He still doesn't."

"But, how do we know that for *sure?* I mean—"

"Do you hear him pounding down the door out there to get in to see his cherished daughter?"

"No, Momma."

"He didn't want you. *I* wanted you."

"Yes, Momma."

"*I* bore you, raised you, sacrificed for you, loved you. He didn't give a damn for his precious daughter. He only wanted a son."

"He did? Did he say that?"

"He didn't have to say it. Maybe he did say it, I can't remember. It doesn't matter, I knew it. Your father, Julian, is a Prussian ice-man, arrogant and fancy, the kind from a long 'line'— and wanting to extend it. A son he would have stayed with his wife for. A son."

I just sat there, crying. She looked at me and seemed to relent.

"Baby. *I* wanted a *daughter.* What would I do with a son? Look, it's no use thinking about it. Put it out of your mind. It's always been just us against the world, you and me, remember? Back in the old Yonkers apartment, when we'd go window shopping and plan our future and bake cookies together and laugh? It used to be enough. It still is. We've got each other. That's all we've ever really had. But we're special, you and me."

She reached out her hand for mine now. I took it gratefully.

"Julian? Baby? You're thirteen now. You're a big girl with a wonderful career and life ahead of her. There's no stopping us. What's the point of mooning after some scum who never wanted you? Even if you could find him—and you can't and he's moved on by now and he might be dead for all I know—believe me, Julian, he wouldn't see you. He'd throw you out on the street. I won't have you hurt like that. I love you. I love you more than anything in the world."

I looked up at her and when I saw that she was crying too, it burst inside me and I hurled myself into her arms. This time she took me under the covers, inside next to her, where it was warm and safe.

I must have cried and cried. I remember her crying, too, and her hand stroking my hair and the softness of her breasts under her nightgown, the cloth all wet with my tears, and her murmuring,

"Some kind of inhuman monster, the war must have made of him. That he could be so loving. Marry me. Father you. Then vanish. Goodbye, farewell, *auf weidersehn,* that's it. Some kind of *creature . . ."*

The last thing I remember, before we must have cried ourselves to sleep in each other's arms, was my whispering, trying to comfort her in turn,

"Like Zeus in the myths. Huh Momma? He appeared as a swan or a rain of gold coins or a bull, and then—"

And her crying, saying softly,

"Yes, my baby. Like Zeus in the myths. Just like that. Just like in the myths."

After that night we never spoke of it again.

But it didn't leave me. The knowledge that he might be out there somewhere has been with me every minute since.

At first, I was just so grateful to her—for having wanted me, kept me—and for telling me the truth.

Then the anger started, snake in the garden. Why had she lied to me all those years? Why did she imply I was "fragile" and unstable? Why had she been so *mean* when it turned out that I knew? Then the guilt started. *Hello,* guilt. Because she *was* the one who had raised me. Then the feeling, growing like a tumor, that I owed her so much I could never get away from her. And through it all still loving her. For having survived. For having loved *me.*

So here I am, age seventeen, locked in battle with her all this time later. Still obsessed.

With the phantom of him, the reality of her, the unreality of me.

I feel only one authentic thing. Writing the secret down has proven it. *I'm going to be a writer.* Some kind of weight got removed from me just by putting it on paper. Catharsis and all that—which Barbara warned you had to be careful about. Catharsis isn't enough. You have to transform it to make it art.

But then, I'm young. As Barbara said, "Have a little compassion on yourself." I'll try, Barbara, wherever you are. I'll try, Father, wherever you are.

I'll try, Julian, wherever you are.

Oh dear god I don't believe in, please never let her look through this history notebook.

Oh my beloved mother, we *will* lose each other, you and I, just-us-against-the-world—and against each other. I lose you every time I find you. And I'll go on losing you, over and over.

Because your fierce will is mine, too, little Momma. Given into my hands by you yourself.

And I just might write more of it down.

And I just might lose Julian. And find me.

CHAPTER FOUR

Spring, 1982

Athena, Ltd., was a wonderful place to visit, but Julian had never wanted to live there. Athena was a successful feminist publishing house—a contradiction in terms unless one scrutinized the terms.

"Successful" in this case meant the firm had pioneered its way into existence to begin with and managed to stay there for nine years, sometimes teetering on the rim of bankruptcy but continuing to acquire, print, and distribute books by and about women. "Feminist," of course, had as many definitions as there were women to define them. Feminism could mean saving the world or your own soul, or both. Athena, Ltd., was less ambitious in its definition. Its founders—a group of five intrepid women weary of laboring for years in publishing industry vineyards—had conceived the idea of a house they would control, one which would publish books on every aspect of the women's movement and of women's lives, for a general, even mass, audience. They would name it after Athena, the goddess of wisdom, and because adding "Incorporated" sounded capitalistic and patriarchal, they opted for the more elegant British term "Limited."

Unfortunately or fortunately, words have a mystical power of their own, bearing within themselves like a coded RNA the capacity for reproduction, duplication, evolution—and mutancy. Or, as philosophers have guessed and poets muttered for centuries, be careful what you say: it might mean something. None of the five founders had given much thought to Athena's mythic origins: that she was the sole goddess not born of woman but sprung from the brain of Zeus—that thunderbolt-heaving, arch-capitalistic arch-patriarch. Or that Athena, tipping the scales with her decision that Orestes go unpunished after matricide, did so because she deliberately sided with the boys. Nor had they dwelt overlong on the ironic capacities inherent in the word "limited." They had no time for semantic luxuries. They worked hard. They meant well. They wanted power.

Now, almost a decade after its founding, Athena's growth showed features both of its zeusean ancestry and its limitations. Julian had related to Athena with a supportiveness that increased its vigilance in direct proportion to her growing dependence on them for work. She had seen the list expand steadily from five books the first year to ten each season. Athena now produced its own paperbacks as well as hardcovers. It had won a few prizes. Some of its authors had been translated into foreign editions. It had begun spin-off lines—in anti-sexist children's books, in health; finally, to Julian's alarm, in fashion and cookbooks. It still published some works by and about a wider constituency: older women, radical women, lesbian women, black and Hispanic, Asian-American and Native Indian women. But these had begun, around the fifth year, to be "now and thens" produced from a peevish threefold sense of principle, unavoidability, and keeping at bay the relentless criticism the women's movement reserves for its own.

Athena managed commercially on three authors. One was Elsa Levin, a humorist who wrote not-quite best-sellers with such titles as *How to Bore Your Rapist Off You* and *The Housewives' Survival Manual*. The second was Oleander Ongatari, who had been born and raised in Westport, Connecticut, and educated at Vassar, but who had learned the hard way—after unsuccessfully peddling a novel based on the life of Anna Magdalena Bach—to adopt an African name and turban before publishing her subsequent smash short-story collection: *Up Side Yo' Haid and Down in Mah Heart What's a Woman to Do Wid a Baaad Man*. The third was Fiona Trax, who wrote erotic science-fiction novels in which women in a futurist society had so much power they could afford to wear miniskirts made of silver lamé and walk around with no tops (they all had perfect, sprightly breasts) and no man dared take it wrong. Athena had recently celebrated a new triumph. They had acquired Maxine Duncan Brewer, who had never published more than one book at each of her previous six publishers, and who had left behind her a trail of broken contracts with haggard editors now prone to alcoholic nervous breakdowns, yet who sold extraordinarily well: *You Can Make It to the Top, Sister!, How to Play and Win by Men's Rules,* and *Supergal, Go for It!* had been her greatest successes.

Nonetheless, Athena still existed precariously, squeaking by in chronic debt and gamely enduring ridicule from both big corporate publishers and more-radical-than-thou feminist collectives which produced three mimeographed chapbooks of Heavy Theory a year. Its founders sometimes wondered why they had abandoned what in retrospect seemed like secure careers for the tightrope on which they now swayed. Periodically, the Athenas envied their imitators and the luxuries afforded them by geographical placement or single-issue orientation: Virago in England, Frauenoffensive in West Germany—these could afford to publish more serious works of fiction and even of feminist philosophy, because their audiences had not suffered American educations and still read for enlightenment as well as pleasure. Back home, such women's movement publishers as the Feminist Press generally restricted themselves to reprinting classic works by foremothers in the suffrage movement or publishing texts for women's studies. At other times, however, the Athenians would congratulate themselves on their Golden Mean, that they were not singularly academic, neither too radical nor sold out, that they were, in fact, performing a vital service to "feminist men and women."

Aware of Athena's behind-the-scenes difficulties, Julian sympathized with their predicament, but still found herself at loggerheads with some of their politics. Every time she went to the cheerful chaos of their offices, she felt guilty about her ambivalence and ambivalent about her guilt. She had worked there regularly as an in-house editor for a year, during one period when Larry and she were particularly desperate for the bail-out only a steady job could provide, without the occupational anxieties of free-lancing. But working in a hierarchy of women who had public nonhierarchical principles produced anxieties all its own for her. On the other hand, free-lancing for Athena could be a pleasure.

No glass-and-chrome sweep of offices in Publishers' Row, not for Athena. First, it would be a bad image. Second, movement purists might picket it. Third, Athena couldn't afford it anyway. So the company was ensconced in Manhattan's jewelry district, a brazen contradiction to its surroundings, where Hassidic men clogged the streets, wearing long black coats and black hats from which their sidecurls dangled like exotic earrings, carrying bulging black briefcases with double locks, never smiling, arguing animatedly with one another in Yiddish, German, Polish, Russian, and English about the quality, weight, and cut of diamonds, the price of gold, the latest robbery of Isaac Yeshudel's ultra-secure safe. Rising in the elevator of Athena's building was a lesson in the humility of encountering other human beings' passionate engagements with issues crucial in their lives and utterly irrelevant in one's own:

"So, Moishe. Whaddya think of the blues?"

"Ach. The rough Johannesburg sends us. Moses could strike with his rod and even he couldn't get more than a carat a cut."

"Three times as much. I pay for platinum *three times* more pennyweight than gold. So you look on the world market? On the world market it costs the same identical. Three times more for me only? What is? I'm a leper?"

"Lissen. I remember when you got factory men who were *workers.* Ya know how I mean? Craftsmen. Geniuses. Dedicated. They loved their work, they didn't care about salaries. Now you have? Spics. Not even Spanish from Spain. *Schwarzes,* darkies. And Germans. Nazis I got working for me. Whaddya wonder? It's a surprise workmanship's down? All they care from is money."

Sometimes, if Julian entered a crowded elevator and was seen to press the button for the fifteenth floor, silence would descend on the passengers as they ascended. Or a man would scowl, with a mournful shake of his earcurls,

"Building changing. Going down in quality. Those people on fifteen don't know from women. Men in pants with discontent they are, not women."

This would be followed by a low chorus of assent in what

Julian took to be a Yiddish version of 'God preserve us from such Jezebels.' None of the riders looked at one another, but all studied the fake wood-paneled elevator doors before them with the intensity of insurgents awaiting the opening of the Jericho gates. When the doors released Julian onto the fifteenth floor, it felt like coming home. Good old Athena, she thought, relief being like respect relative. "Those people" on fifteen had managed to upset their neighbors on other floors by daring to chat with other firms' secretaries on occasion, and had given some free copies of books to a few mildly interested women. For this, a formal complaint had been registered with the building owners that Athena was infiltrating floor by floor and organizing workers to rise up against their employers in a Masada-like besiegement. Good old Athena, Julian thought, everything in context.

She passed through the reception area with a wave; Manuela was at the switchboard and knew her. The clamor unique to Athena in the publishing world greeted Julian as she moved through the corridors toward the editorial section. She passed the front office of Georgina Fraser, Georgi for short, a founder and the editor in chief of Athena. Through her open door Julian could see a characteristic Athena encounter taking place. Jeremy, the three-year-old son of the art director, had wheeled himself into Georgi's office on the resident battered plastic tricycle as he made his rounds.

"Whachya doin'?" he demanded.

Georgi had stopped in the middle of dialing, phone receiver in hand, ever-present cheroot still clenched between her teeth, stack of papers sliding off her lap where she sat at her book-piled coffeetable, comfortably ignoring the desk behind her.

"I'm working, Jer. How are you today?"

"Why?"

"Why am I working?"

"Yeah. Why?"

" 'Cause I have to. 'Cause I like it, too."

"Why?"

"I have to 'cause this stuff has to be done today. But I like to because, well, this is the way I have fun."

"Why?"

"Because it is. We make good books here."

"Why?"

"Because we want to. Because people like our books. You've seen our books, Jeremy. Remember, the big picture book about the princess who fought the dragons?"

"Why?"

"Because she had to rescue the prince, remember? Your mother herself drew the pictures for that one."

"Why?"

Georgi glanced up and saw Julian in the doorway. She smiled with relief. Not only was this neither a stockholder nor a Hassid, this was a grownup.

"Hi, Georgi. Just on my way in to Charlotte to deliver a manuscript. Couldn't resist listening in on your Grand Inquisitor scene, though. Impressive. Now I know where you get the patience to deal with distributors."

"You discovered my secret. I practice on Jeremy." Spoiled by the momentary adult exchange, she turned back to the small cyclist. "Okay, Zen master, time to scram. Go visit Bess. You know she always has lollypops." His curiosity instantly surfeited at the mention of lollypops, Jeremy spun around and pedaled furiously toward the door. Julian got out of his way just in time, barely avoiding the ignominy of being run over by a plastic tricycle.

"Check with your mother first! About the lollypop!" Georgi yelled after him before resuming her dialing. Julian called goodbye to her and followed the small cyclist down the hall. Past the foreign and serial rights departments, their walls bedecked with feminist posters in German, Spanish, French, Italian. Past the art department, where the wall taste ran more to Judy Chicago. Past publicity and promotion, with huge blow-ups of Jane Fonda, Vanessa Redgrave, Lily Tomlin. Past sales and marketing, where there were carpets on the floor and where charts and calenders replaced politics on the walls (stockholders visited here). Into editorial, and its cacophony of women's voices. Here, the posters cubicle after cubicle proclaimed individuality within the parameters of solidarity: Billie Jean King and Althea Gibson vied for prominence in the health and fitness editor's cubicle; Tina Turner, Beverly Sills, and Cicely Tyson exulted above the desk of Leonora, the arts and entertainment editor; Gloria Steinem shared a wall with Bella Abzug and Angela Davis in the nest of Laura, the politi-

cal editor; Bess, the juvenile editor, had a corkboard glittering
with a button collection that proclaimed Mothers Are People
Too, Children's Rights, Boys Can Cry, Girls Are Strong, and
Free Abortion On Demand (here was the expectable lollypop
connection).

The partitions were as articulate in their varied messages as
Chinese wall posters. They certainly defied any viewer to cling
to a belief that Athena, Ltd.—or the women's movement—was
monolithic, dull, lacking in a sense of the absurd, or finished. It
was perilous to get too interested in the walls, however, because not to watch one's step meant tripping over a large
stuffed tiger or a roller skate, bumping into a Pisan tower of
transfile boxes labeled *Take to Storage Please Soon!* It could also
mean bashing into and being scalded by one of the many
coffee/tea/instant soup and other noshes islands throughout
the corridors, where electric pots bubbled as continuously as
crumbs accumulated. Julian stopped for a moment to disen-
gage a discarded lollypop remnant stuck to the sole of her shoe,
and was greeted with hello's and waves from women looking
up from telephone conversations and women hunched over
the new word processors, determined not to let tech anxiety
get the better of them.

No question, this was a "humanized workplace." Its victory
was that despite the cynical smiles in Publishers' Row interior-
designer offices, Athena met its deadlines, mollified its stockholders, pacified its authors, and got books out. Julian's Athena
ambivalence lurched toward the warmth-admiration end of
the spectrum. Feeling shamefaced at her own capacity for
judgmentalism, she finally made it through to Charlotte
Kirsch's office.

As a co-founder and director of the press, Charlotte had an
actual office, not a cubicle. Yet unlike the suites of her peers in
other publishing houses, her sole window looked out onto a
brick wall, the worn carpet retained sheddings from her two
small defiantly unclipped apricot poodles who now lay sleeping nose to nose in the middle of it, there were no flashy
buttons on her one-line telephone, and a portable radio on her
desk tinkled a harpsichordist playing a selection from "The
Well-Tempered Clavier." Charlotte's walls sported a touch-
ingly eclectic mix: a poster of Virginia Woolf, five of the latest
Athena book jackets, a petition (suggestively tacked near the

door) for saving the whales, the production schedule for this season's list, a graph of sales broken down by region, a painting she had done of her husband Zachary, a cluster of three-by-five cards with sayings she liked scrawled on them (by Alice Walker, Teilhard de Chardin, Mae West), various framed scrolls and plaques (Athena's awards), and a hand-lettered sign reading *Do Not Panic DoNotPanic* DONOTPANIC.

She too was on the phone. Charlotte sometimes complained that in a few years she would be forced to have an operation surgically amputating the phone receiver from her ear. But she looked up, saw Julian on her threshold (those few women at Athena whose offices were in possession of doors kept them open as an egalitarian statement), and beckoned her inside. Charlotte's voice to her caller was vibrating somewhere between a patronizing patience-it's-Jeremy tone and thinly disguised rage. It soon became obvious she was speaking with Maxine Duncan Brewer. Julian sank into a corner of the faded corduroy-covered sofa and waited.

She was genuinely fond of Charlotte, who understood when Julian had to turn down a job because of lecture or writing commitments, yet gave her first call on free-lance work because she knew Julian needed the money. Besides, Charlotte loved music and animals; how could you not like her? She and Julian were about the same age, and she too was married, for just under twelve years—with all the bonding such similarity could inspire between two women.

At the beginning, their colleague relationship had fed their growing friendship, not threatened it. However, as Athena suffered its sea-changes over the years, their business communications became cautious, then formal, then strained, and their private confidences showed signs of spillover pollution. Perspectives of survival figured into it—Athena's survival in the marketplace with as much honor intact as possible, and Julian's survival in the context of Athena, on the same terms. Meanwhile, both women mourned the loss of spontaneity between them as friends, but each suspected the other of mourning the loss less. Julian presumed Charlotte understood that however her loyalty to Athena wobbled in private, in public it was solid. But Charlotte, who rose to public attacks with the glee of a seasoned veteran, absorbed Julian's private criticisms as if they were personal accusations. Each became increasingly defensive in her conviction that the other must think her a hypocrite.

Now Julian, wearing a faint smile meant to communicate supportiveness, sat on Charlotte's office sofa and watched her boss send voicetone and facial expression off in two separate directions. Charlotte was nervously twisting the single braid in which she wore her pale blond hair. Strands began coming loose, like fine wisps of temper. She pushed her bangs to one side and began massaging her forehead.

"I know, Maxine. Yes, I— I *know,* dear. But you must understand that we lack the resources for first-class air tickets on the entire book tour, we . . . I know, dear. Of *course* you deserve— If we could, I assure you that we— But that won't do any good, dear. Maxine, really, it . . . Maxine. *Maxine,* I've already spoken with Pam Bently in Publicity and Promo, and I *know* the problem, it's . . ." Charlotte rolled her eyes at Julian, put one hand over the mouthpiece, and growled, "This woman is worse than *Friedan.*"

Julian picked up a copy of *Ms.* Magazine from the floor, where it had been either dropped by mistake or flung by intention. There was a paper clip on one particular page and when she saw it was a review of an Athena book she realized it had been flung. The reviewer was not only questioning the book but wondering in print whether the author—and in fact Athena—any longer had the right to the description "feminist."

Charlotte slammed down the phone after one last "Bye-bye, darling" delivered through clenched teeth. She saw Julian scanning the review, and made a gesture as if tearing out her hair.

"It's been that kind of day *all* day, Julian. As you may have guessed, that was Supergal herself on the phone, aiming for yet another Temperamental Diva Asshole Prize in publishing. And who in hell," pointing accusingly at the magazine in Julian's hands, "do they think *they* are? *Sisters?*"

"Well," Julian began, "it's hard for me to say, Charlotte." Just as Julian never considered that Charlotte might lose sleep worrying about an erosion of Athena's integrity, so Charlotte had no notion of Julian's distaste at her own behavior in having swiftly learned the revised script: what was still permissible to say and what was now to remain unspoken. "I happen to be underfond of both this reviewer and the author she's review-ing. Not as people, but in terms of their politics. *And* their writing."

"That's not the point. The point is that one feminist institu-tion should goddam well have the decency to support another. What are they, suffering from acute terminal purity?"

"Hardly. They're just trying to survive in the so-called main-stream while swimming against the current *and* treading wa-ter. Like Athena. And *they've* got the financial shoals of adver-tisers to navigate."

"May they shoot the rapids," Charlotte sputtered.

"Oh come on. Besides, they have a right to *their* integrity, too. You don't think that just because they're a feminist institu-tion they should fling orchids at every book appearing under a feminist label? How does that develop a healthy criticism?"

"No, not at *every* book." She snickered. "Only *ours.* Nor do I think we should confuse healthy criticism with a hatchet job. As for their financial shoals, I'll match our odious stockholders against their obnoxious advertisers any day."

Julian cleared her throat.

"Well, I brought back the finished Preston manuscript. All of my queries are flagged, as usual." She fished the manuscript from her book-bag, walked over, and wedged it onto the crammed desk.

"Fine. That was record time, Julian. Thanks." Charlotte rif-fled the pages and, seeing relatively few flags on the margins, seemed to relax. "I'm sorry, I didn't mean to be unfair. Un*sis-terly,* O heinous crime. Some of my best friends work at *Ms.* No, seriously. I know they're up against much the same thing we are. Everything from right-wing groups wanting to ban our books, to tons of unsolicited manuscripts from otherwise per-fectly sane women suddenly seized with the inspiration to 'write,' to what are probably the most perfidiously difficult group of authors *and* readers in the literate world."

"My my, Charlotte, we *are* tetchy today."

"I'm just fed up with the double standard that seems re-served especially for us. I mean, other houses—and all right, maybe other magazines, too—get off easy. All they have to do is be minimally interesting to a general readership and show a little profit to their investors. Piece of cake. But we're sup-posed to be wunderkinds financially; let *us* show a drop in sales figures and the New York *Times* announces that women's businesses are in trouble, that women can't cut the mustard in the corporate world, and that this means the women's movement is now yet again dead. On the other hand, we're supposed to be some sort of movement press—whatever that means. What it means in *fact* is that whatever we publish—*or* reject—provokes sackloads of protest mail from one disgruntled group of activists or another. They'd never think of doing this to Random House, you know, or Macmillan, or any of the big boys. Where, I'd like to know, is there such a thing as support? Remember 'support'?"

Julian felt a squirm of suspicion that this tirade was indirectly aimed at her, then immediately felt paranoid for having entertained the suspicion.

"Nobody promised that the patriarchy would be unmade in a day, Charlotte. You folks wanted to be a bridge between the politics and the popularization of them. Admirable, but a bridge gets walked over. That's its function, you know. What's more, some politics—maybe the best kind—usually aren't 'popularizable,' at least not until they've been around awhile: 'What? Universal suffrage? *Insane* notion!' You know as well as I do that a progressive idea takes time to filter through a culture—"

"We don't *have* time. We have *stock*holders."

"Yes. So you try to filter faster. Sometimes," Julian blurted out, "that amounts to distorting, blanding out. Maxine Duncan Brewer."

"Oh dear. Yet another lecture on our corruption. I notice we're not good enough to publish Julian Travis? She might stoop to *edit* for Athena, but she *publishes* with distinguished old Hamilton Press."

For a moment, a question poised in the silence between them: how long would it be until Charlotte would yearn for the day, painful though it might seem when it arrived, when Julian would decline the jobs Charlotte dangled—or how long would it be until Julian would wish, however regretfully, that Charlotte wouldn't offer anymore? Then both women backed away from the confrontation, each still clinging to her side of a bargain they believed to be mature and constructive, one in which skills and fees were exchanged for the sake of a differently interpreted greater good.

"Athena doesn't print poetry, Charlotte," Julian demurred, "and Hamilton does. You know my motto: Love me, love my poems; if you want my prose, you've got to take on the other along with it." She threw in a submission gesture. "I'll never be properly 'commercial,' anyway."

Charlotte sighed and rearranged the pencils in her pottery mug.

"Well, maybe I'm just in a foul mood." This time it was she who changed the subject. "So what did you think of the Preston?"

"It's—I—liked it. I mean, well, that sort of single-girl-swinger-stuff isn't usually my— but it's got a bright, sassy type of writing which I suppose . . . It's really a treat," she finished lamely. Untenable to comment that there were so few flags because she'd given up on the manuscript in despair. Then, shifting into what she hoped wouldn't appear as too drastic a non sequitur, "Of course, I still haven't got over my fan-like reaction to the last book I did for you. The Graham biography of Katherine Mansfield? Damn, but that was good. Feminist but not jargonistic. Well researched. Doesn't ignore the New Zealand years in favor of the English ones. Well written. Long overdue. It was a pleasure to copy-edit."

Charlotte beamed. As if on cue, one of the poodles woke, wagged over to Julian, and licked her shoe.

"Oh that's music to my ears. Particularly from you, Julian. Your less than subtle hoity-toity literary judgments give me indigestion sometimes."

Nettled, Julian offered a smile in response. Charlotte smiled back. For the sake of the bargain, Charlotte would swallow her humiliation at what she assumed to be Julian's contempt. For the sake of the bargain, Julian would swallow *hers* at feeling grateful for Charlotte's forbearance and patronage. They might differ on whether the contempt or the gratitude was voluntary as well as deserved, but they shared a confusion over whether the attendant humiliation was as deserved as it was voluntary. Charlotte thrust out her chin in an unconscious gesture of pride.

"You know that the Graham was rejected by twelve houses before it came to us? Leonora fought hard for us to take it on. Books like that revive my faith in what we're doing here. Of course it'll bomb commercially."

"Wait a minute, Charlotte. Not necessarily. Why?"

"A literary biography? Of a woman? And a foreigner? In the Reign of Reagan? Are you kidding?"

"But *why?*" Julian sounded to herself like Jeremy.

"Because, that's why. We'll lose money on it. But that's all right once in a while. The sales of Maxine Duncan Brewer allow us to publish people like Joy Graham." She had regained her dignity and her good humor returned with it. "How about lunch? Have you got time? Athena will treat."

Julian thought longingly of her plans for revising the new sonnet sequence that afternoon; it was to have been a self-reward for having endured copy-editing the Preston. She knew that a make-nice lunch would be helpful, though not necessary, to guarantee further work. Lies and pretense. You *are* a hypocrite, Baby, she thought. A confused hypocrite, too, because she missed their old camaraderie. She missed Charlotte.

"Well, okay. Yes. I'd enjoy that, in fact."

"Great!" Charlotte exclaimed. Then, a touch embarrassed at the pleasure in her voice, she added, "Just let me make out a payment slip to you for the Preston so I can drop it off at the business office on our way out. Then you might actually have a check by the end of the month, or at least before you're eligible for a senior citizens' bus pass."

"Oh. Thanks. Yes, sure," Julian tossed back casually, sitting down on the sofa again to wait while Charlotte typed up the form. They exchanged a quick glance, unanticipated, unsettling. A fidelity resonated between them, potent as nostalgia, a cranky recognition that they were still on the same side—though neither could have said with confidence of what—stuck with each other like family members who congregate only at births and funerals, who snarl over Grandma's silver teapot being left to this cousin instead of that one, but who are there (grudgingly) when they are (grudgingly) needed. Athena was, for Julian, like the proverb about home: the place where, when you had to go there, they had to take you in. If the banner of this particular sisterhood was somewhat frayed, Julian reflected, still it fluttered in the storm, brave and bonny.

Over vegetarian won-ton soup in the kosher Chinese restaurant, Charlotte sighed,

"Sorry about the place. As you know, this neighborhood isn't the greatest for choices in cuisine. There's the dairy restaurant, the kosher takeout hot-dog stand, the kosher pizza shop, the deli—where the food's fabulous, actually, but you emerge deaf from the noise—and dear old Mamaleh Yin Chow's."

"It's fine, Charlotte," Julian laughed. "So long as we stick to beef or chicken. The ersatz shrimp does me in. The first time I came here, I ordered Mu Shu Pork without thinking. The waiter almost expired with horror on the spot."

"I yearn for the day when Athena changes neighborhoods. I *abhor* our building. Always have and always will."

"Spoken like a good apostate New York Jew." She toasted Charlotte with a glass of tea.

"You got it. Listen, if I'd stayed on as an editor at Knopf we'd be lunching at the Four Seasons." Charlotte rummaged in her purse, came up with a bottle of extra-strength aspirin, popped two into her mouth, and downed a swig of her tea.

"You look tired, Charlotte. And it's only Monday. Couldn't you and Zach get to the country house for the weekend?"

"That, my dear, was the problem. We *did* get to the country house for the weekend. With neither of his Ivy League brats glowering at the evil stepmother. Just the two of us."

"Oh. I see. Was this a shouting-match one or an intensive let's-struggle-this-through one or a deadly silences one where communication runs the gamut from 'Have you seen the newspaper?' to 'I'm going for a walk'?"

"This was *all* of the above. This was a peach. This started with my apparently pernicious question as to why, after seven years of our having the country house, Zach still has to ask me where the plastic garbage bags are kept, when they have been in the same cupboard under the same sink for all seven years. It escalated rapidly to his unsolicited on-the-spot analysis of why I am such a hostile and neurotic person. What *is* the matter with these people?"

"You mean psychiatrists?" Julian suppressed a laugh about the long-lost Jack Erdman of her youth.

"I mean men. I know shrinks are particularly risky to be married to, but I mean the generic category itself. Don't forget I was married before, to a humble engineer. But he too alas was a man. Maybe they're really another species? A different life form, possibly? Not necessarily an intelligent one?"

"Aha. Yea, verily. This, I have frequently mused to myself, is a distinct possibility. In fact, had you asked me yesterday, I would unhesitatingly have replied in the affirmative."

"Oh. You and Larry had a fun weekend, too."

"Smashing. And I do mean smashing. He got smashed. Also some dinnerware. Revolutionary vanguardists can, when it comes down to it, find a common brotherhood with engineers and psychiatrists."

"On what grounds? Their penises?"

They both burst out laughing, and a second wave of cackles hit them when a passing waiter shot Charlotte an indignant glance at her overheard question, as he shuffled by bearing a tray of vegetarian spare ribs.

"I mean it, Julian," she went on, lowering her voice with a giggle, "and they seem to have another thing in common. They're all Jekyll-and-Hydes, have you noticed? It's like . . . well, the reason I fell in love with Zach was *because,* in a way, he *was* a shrink. Certainly Ted—he was the engineer, you never knew him, lucky you—Ted responded to any discussion about thoughts or feelings, any attempt to talk about what might be lying underneath one's actions, with a glaze of sphinx-like disinterest. Zach was willing, even eager to discuss all that. I thought, 'Here is a man who is willing to probe, who wants to know the inner me, who's not afraid of emotion.' So the flip side of the coin is that if I happen to put on a red scarf in the morning I get asked, 'Feeling confrontative today, are you?' "

Julian rose to their old atmosphere of conspiracy.

"One of the reasons I married Larry was the *intensity* he gave off. Gentle *and* intense, I thought, wow. So gentle can flip over to passive and intense can display itself in shattered dishes."

"Uh, Julian, you think maybe Larry should see somebody? I mean a shrink? Throwing things . . . well, that's sort of on another level . . ."

"Oh no, *no.* This weekend was an exception. And don't be silly. Larry would never raise a finger against me, if that's what you're thinking. Besides, he thinks all shrinks are brainwashing agents of the System. Anyway, you are suggesting maybe our eminently sane friend Zachary perhaps?"

"God no. But don't you get frightened—"

"Not really. I mean, this is *Larry* we're talking about. No, it's the yo-yo effect that gets me. You're never quite sure who'll be there in the morning—or night, for that matter."

"You mean: Dr. Jekyll or—"

"—Mr. Hyde, exactly. Oh, Charlotte, you *are* a relief. I mean, you under*stand*. The trouble with bitching about one's husband to a woman friend who isn't married—or who hasn't been married long *enough*—is that you get a blank look or else you feel creepy and disloyal or else she says something insightfully idiotic like 'So why don't you leave him?' "

"Oh, do I know!" Charlotte, too, settled into the excitement of airing emotions stamped Classified. "See, you want the understanding and the sympathy. But you also want to know that the friend you're bitching *to* knows you *love* him. I can't *stand* the oversimplifications of the movement anymore. They drive me bananas!"

Julian toyed with her chopsticks.

"Well, I know you love Zach. And I know I love Larry. It's just that it gets so . . . exhausting. If only this thing we call 'consciousness' didn't expose every level, from housework to jobs to sex to—"

"—to everything, let's face it. Maybe men are hopeless. At least at this point in history. At least to live with. Maybe the separatists are right. Maybe we should all become lesbians. Or just use men and discard them, like Kleenex, the way some men use women."

"Well, I can show you scars from years of Q-and-A after lectures, when some of my lesbian sisters made me feel like a walking oxymoron: the married feminist. I'd hate to admit they were right. I'd hate to give up. Anyway, I seem to be hopelessly heterosexual. Or hopelessly . . . Larryosexual. See, it isn't 'men' I want, it's *Larry*. He was the first person I went to bed with, you know. When I was all of, oh, nineteen. It's been Larry all along. For keeps."

Charlotte looked up, her mouth full, shocked.

"You don't mean to tell me he's the only man you've ever screwed!"

"No," Julian shifted uncomfortably in her seat, "there *was* one bona fide affair."

"Does he know?"

"Larry? Oh, of course."

"How'd he take it? When was this? Did I know you then?

Who was the guy?" The new respect in Charlotte's voice made Julian even more uneasy, but was seductive enough to compensate for the prying.

"About two years ago. Yes, we knew each other then. My month at that artists' colony, remember? A painter. Tall, dark, handsome, good in bed—that is, I *think* so, out of my hilariously vast non-experience—and staggeringly dumb. Every time he opened his mouth, he confirmed that what I was feeling was plain lust, that I was in no danger of love."

"But it— Was it—"

"It was *quite* pleasurable. Lots of getting carried away, so long as we didn't try to talk about anything challenging—like art, politics, humanity, the weather, or that the world was round. His paintings were masterpieces of boredom: splashy blobs of gray hurled against white. 'Me Tarzan, you canvas' seemed his way of relating to his work."

"Oh, who cares about his work. What was—"

"Yes. It *was* delicious in bed. Breath knocked out of my lungs and all that. Maybe because it *wasn't* complicated by loving? Because he was my first, in fact my only, 'affair'—with all the abandon that implies? Because it wasn't weighted by years of marriage? Or because it felt so . . . adult? I dunno."

"You overanalyze everything, Julian. What happened?"

"What do you think happened? He went on to his next art-colony affair and I went home to Larry."

"And he found out?"

"No. I told him."

"Omigod. You and your truth tyranny. You *told* him?"

"Yeah. The premise of the marriage has always been honesty. Oh damn—" Julian grabbed her napkin and began mopping up tea from the glass she had overfilled. "I mean, I knew Larry sometimes had lovers. Nothing serious. More in the early days when he still used to go on organizing trips, to movement conferences, stuff like that. As we both got more serious about feminism, I think that sort of thing dwindled for him, and then stopped. I don't mean I ever demanded that it stop, nothing like that. We always tried to live our life together on some free level of . . . I don't mean 'open marriage' or swinging, either. It's hard to explain," she wound up awkwardly, wishing she'd stuck to trashing Maxine Duncan Brewer, whatever different dangers that entailed.

"So Larry understood, then."

Charlotte seemed to know precisely which buttons to push.

"No, my friend, Larry did not understand. That was the stunner."

"The rules changed when you entered the game."

"Well . . . more complicated than that. I think it was one more thing he felt he'd 'given up'—for me, for feminism—only to see me get it. He said he could have understood and wouldn't have minded if it had been a woman, but another man—"

Charlotte would have none of it. Julian could see from her expression that she was about to solve a conundrum with a stereotype.

"Julian. I have to tell you that I don't think it was any of this political purity or complexity stuff, the two of you as a 1980's version of Emma Goldman and Alexander Berkman."

"Well of course when you put it that way it sounds ridicu—"

"I have to tell you, sweetie-pie, that it was a husband's freakout that his wifie made it with somebody else, when straying was supposed to be reserved for *him*. A number one cliché double standard."

"Charlotte, *I* have to tell *you* that's bullshit. Larry *believes* in feminism; he's had to sacrifice too much for him not to. I can't think of any other man who—"

"Spare me. I'm sure he believes and I know he's paid his dues. But resenting you for that is just another facet of the same double standard. You say you didn't ask monogamy of him. So who raised it then, my dear Emma? Who asked him to give up his extra-marital goodies? And then impose his new-found chastity on you?"

"Nobody asked. *He* decided to—"

"There. I rest my case. Oh no I don't," she pursued, "because you're only assuming, you don't even know for sure. He may *still* wander now and then, but when *you* do—wham!"

Julian was tempted to ask whether Charlotte really was talking about Laurence or Zach, but she restrained herself.

"I *do* know, Charlotte. I'd feel it. Larry's been voluntarily monogamous for years now."

"So? Should we send him a hero-worker medal? You were faithful for years, too, just a little out of synch. He strayed early, you strayed late. Do the rules have to follow *his* behavior, *his* timing? Besides, how can we be sure it *was* voluntary on his part? He kind of paled from public view, remember. Less travel, fewer chances, *and* more women out there who thanks to his wife were feminist and therefore less vulnerable to the Red Menace. Maybe he just got turned down more. Maybe his charisma pheremones dried up. Maybe he entered middle-aged male menopause and got less interested in women. Hell, maybe he's gay."

"*Charlotte!* Now you're talking *heterosexist* bullshit!"

"And stop laying the 'ists' and 'isms' on me. You once told me you were as surprised as I was when Larry turned househusband with such alacrity. Maybe he's a closet case who always wanted to wimp around keeping house and being supported. And that's *not* meant as anti-gay. Some of the closest—"

"—friends you have are gay, I bet. I can't *believe* you just said that."

"Well, it happens to be true, even if it's now become an off-limits sentence. Anyway, whatever the reason, Larry felt threatened when you struck out on your own. *Threatened,* sweetie."

Julian closed her eyes for a moment to gather strength for what had to be a convincing rebuttal, especially since all of Charlotte's theories had a disturbing ring of familiarity, having been whispered by voices in her own brain.

"What you don't seem to understand, Charlotte, is that the affair was a symptom, not the problem, for god's sake. Oh I know everything overlaps, but the affair was two years ago; last weekend's fight wasn't about any of that. It's . . . it's a grief, a fatigue, a kind of obstinate despair-in-loving I think Larry and I share with most other women and men who love each other at this insane moment in history when men and women speak different languages. Christ, if anything, his having the courage to 'wimp about,' as you put it, has helped keep the marriage *together* rather than hastening its demise. I mean, at least Larry had the guts to opt out of the John Wayne image *before* the he-man became unfashionable. The truth is I wouldn't have stayed with any man *other* than Laurence Millman all these years. And I sure as hell never plan to live with another man, if this marriage goes on the rocks. I've been married over half my life. The idea of starting from scratch is . . . beyond masochism."

"There I know what you mean. The barbarous ritual of 'dating' I endured between the end of marriage number one and Zach: incredible. I got so fed up with all that getting-to-know-you crap with each new guy—my likes and dislikes, his likes and dislikes—it got so I felt like sending a cassette of myself instead, with a form-letter: If the background, preferences, insights, and general tone of this tape appeals to you, mister, send me a cassette in return. If that appeals to *me,* then perhaps we can take things from there. Who had the time for this bizarre rite?"

"But you *wanted* to be married again, so you did it. I *don't* want to be married again, ever. With Larry at least I feel I've had the best that men have to offer in this century, somebody gentle and principled, brilliant, intense and . . . and, well, rebellious against all sorts of odds. Somebody with the guts for that matter to have wanted to be—and stay—married to *me.* Quite a challenge, that: from fugitive child-star right on up through shrill women's libber. Oh no, it's Larry or no man for me."

"You might surprise yourself, Julian. What else does that leave? Celibacy? Women? Poodles?"

"Oh, sex isn't important. To hell with sex." Julian tried to shift the subject. "Think they have lichee nuts here?"

"Well, women certainly don't attract *me.* Sexually, I mean. There'd be too much sacrificed by feeling erotic about women. That wonderful friendship you can have with women—like we're talking now—that confidence and understanding about love-hate toward men—all that gets lost when the tension of sex rears its head. I feel it whenever I'm around lesbian women."

"Oh Charlotte, really." Julian began to fidget for fortune-cookie time. "You *can*not generalize so deplorably: a househusband must be a closet gay man; lesbian women come on like Casanova. Christ, it depends on the individual, haven't you learned that yet? We're talking 101 here."

"That's movement rhetoric again. Don't you ever get off the podium? Frankly, I like the 'otherness' of men. Women are too . . . too familiar. Going to bed with a woman would be like masturbating with a mirror. Like incest. Like . . . loving yourself."

"I wish you could *hear* yourself. If you've seen one woman

you've seen them all? Women are too familiar to feel erotic about but lesbians are too different to be friends with? Are we going crazy here? Look. Years ago I was in a consciousness-raising group—my very first group—with a woman named Iliana de Costa. She defined herself as a lesbian woman, but she also had had a number of affairs with men, in three cases longish relationships. She's an art photographer. An Argentinian exile, radical, lively, smart. Speaks five languages fluently. She's one of the most intelligent, warmest women I've ever known. I could name at least three other examples right off the top of my head—Laura Wilton, who does your political books, for one—but Iliana happens to come to mind because she just surfaced again in New York after five years in Europe. When we had lunch it was as if we picked up where we'd left off. Exactly the kind of close, immediate comprehension you mentioned. There's never been any sexual pressure from her whatsoever. She's a *friend*—like only women can be."

"All right *all right,* I hope all the speeches are over."

"I didn't mean to make a speech. But stereotypes make my teeth grind by reflex. For a minute there, you were one step away from saying all gay men are weak and effeminate and all lesbian women are macho."

"Oh no. On the contrary. I think *all men* are weak and *all women* are strong. The opposite of what both sides give off." Charlotte, chastened by Julian's vehemence or bored by her polemics, relaxed into the banquette as the waiter cleared away the remains of her kosher chicken with broccoli.

"There we are in total agreement." Both knew it was wiser to stick to criticizing men than arguing about women. "I know exactly what you mean. The movement has denounced the he-man image because that's so obvious, but it's time we got down to examining what lies *under* that image—and not just pitying it. I mean, looking at the dependency *men* have on *women,* not the other way around. I see it in Larry, the chronic weakness you're talking about. I'm no moron. But I've also seen it in gay men, old men, young men, reactionaries and revolutionaries, black and white. Always—whether we dare show it or not—the women are stronger. The terms must have got bifurcated: men think strong means tough, so they act like lethal klutzes. But most women affirm their strength through beast-of-burden endurance, as if it's got separated from assertiveness. What a mess."

"Well, that brings us full circle, doesn't it? Maybe neither men *nor* women are intelligent life forms," Charlotte groaned, pouring more tea into the glasses.

The two women sat in silence.

"So did you and Zach patch it up?" Julian lit a cigarette.

"Not really. You've got to stop smoking. But it usually gets better during the week. I have the office and he has his nicely successful practice with plenty of loony patients; they must make even me look good. And dealing with women as I do all the time, in the evenings even *he* looks good. However. Of late the happy little weekends when we're alone with no distractions have been nightmares."

Julian snorted. "Familiar. At least during the week there's work, colleagues, friends—"

"—reality-checks. People who think you're a decent human being, not some neurotic inept. Not for me lately the Thank God It's Friday sentiment."

"Charlotte! How about you and I form a Thank God It's Monday Club? You know, women who can't wait to get back to their jobs and away from their cosy husbands and homes after the weekend."

"Love it! TGIM! *Think* of it. Women will *flock* to join. Our membership will run into the millions within weeks. Except of course for the odious few, like Angela Stanley-Marks, my nemesis, who—"

"Wait, I missed a beat. Who's she?"

Charlotte gave a vicious crack to her fortune cookie and beamed a Pollyanna smile.

"Angie is our new editor. You haven't met her yet. She does health, fitness, nutrition, all that hearty stuff. *Angie,*" her tone growing more sarcastic, "is a tall, willowy WASP who is somehow always tanned, who tosses her mane of russet curls about and *reeks* with good health. *Angie* has a *perfect* marriage to a *perfect* anti-sexist tennis-pro husband who even changed his name so they could be perfect hyphenates together." Charlotte saw Julian catch and return her own wicked smile. "*Angie* 'shares' tips for perfection with the likes of me. They consist of 'Only fifteen minutes a day' of back-brushing your hair, flossing your teeth, certain exercises, gargles, creams, meditation—like that. Add up all her fifteen minuteses and you'd have a thirty-hour day in which there'd be no time to run Athena. But *Angie*"—Julian began to giggle helplessly as Charlotte wound toward an inspired climax—"is straight out of Brewer's *Supergal.* She and her hyphenate husband and their four perfect children eat only proper things and go every weekend to perform perfect jock seizures in which they flail their sixteen collective *perfect* limbs in *perfect* unison. *Angie* probably conditions her pubic hair. *Angie* is perfectly *maddening.*" Charlotte dumped a seditious amount of white sugar into her tea.

"Maybe life will be kind and spare me meeting her. I never work on your sports books anyway."

"You could if you wanted to."

"No, thank you. I'm the sedentary type who thinks a football is something you hit a home run with, remember? I may be the only forty-year-old woman you will ever meet in this culture who doesn't know how to ride a bicycle."

"Well, that's because of your kooky childhood, Julian. Otherwise, you survived it fairly sane."

"Yeah . . . and a lot of that, like it or not, is due to Larry. All the other kid actors I knew wound up addicts of one sort or another, or on their fifth marriage, or in the funny farm, or having attempted suicide. Nothing so dramatic for me. I wanted art. And revolution. I got Larry and the women's movement. Pretty good."

"Julian, my dear. That you survived your childhood is due not to Larry but to your plucky self. I remember when I first met you. I thought, 'Yoicks! That's ex-little Julian Travis, whom I used to watch every week as I was growing up.' You were my idol. I wanted to *be* you. So I was positive you must have become some kind of twitching flake as an adult, I mean having all that adulation as a kid."

Julian obligingly began to twitch.

"No, but that's the point," Charlotte laughed, "you were . . . normal. Well, a little 'intellekshul' and snobbish about books and politics, maybe. But a human being. With a sense of humor, yet."

"Thanks, Charlotte. The older I get, the more I value a sense of irony and a sense of humor. Maybe they're two sides of the same coin. I swear I don't know how people without a sense of humor survive. I mean, what do they *do?*"

"They turn into Larry or Zach."

They both burst out laughing again. Charlotte wiped her eyes and read out her fortune in a sonorous voice.

" 'To respect the mother is to enter the heavens.' Zack's kids should've got this. What a crock of shit."

"You think that's the Chinese influence or the Orthodox Jewish?"

"Jewish first part, but 'the heavens' plural is decidedly Chinese."

"Well, mine is more mundane, but just as preachy: 'Talent is not Wisdom.' As if I needed to be told."

"Whatever happened to the good old days when fortune cookies prophesied things like fame, wealth, and a gorgeous stranger?" Charlotte made a face and then signaled for the check. "How *is* your mother these days, speaking of entering the heavens—or shouldn't I ask?"

"No, it's okay, you can ask. I can't answer, that's all. I haven't seen her in, oh, almost eight months now. Last September. She still won't see me, ever since she flew at me the last time she was in the hospital. Slams down the phone on me, had the locks to her apartment changed. At first I kept track of her indirectly via her broker, her doctor, and two women—old friends of hers from way back. But then about three months ago she apparently stopped speaking to them, too. And changed doctors and brokerage houses. So my observation routes have dried up. I still call about twice a week, thinking it might change, but no. The minute I say hello, bang down goes the telephone. At first it drove me up the wall with worry, but then at least I learned from Mrs. Dudinsky—she's the woman who used to come in to bring groceries and make an attempt to stir the dustballs around—that even though she was fired, too, Hope has hired a part-time companion. Somebody Mrs. Dudinsky just happened to know, from the same agency. It seems this woman comes in less often than Mrs. D. used to— only about three times a week—but gets on all right with Hope. So at least I know somebody's looking in on her."

"Christ, you go sort of gray when you talk about it."

Julian shrugged as they gathered up their things.

"What can I do, Charlotte? She won't let me in—not in any way. I don't know if it's the medication that's made her so damned paranoid or if it's just exacerbated all her old feelings of betrayal from when I first left the business, then left her, then married Larry. I don't even know for sure that she's *taking* the medication . . . All I do know is, once in a while, I'm able to get through a day without obsessing about her. And then, too," Julian added drily, "life is so charitable. It gives you respite from one wretchedness groove by scratching your brain over onto another with screechy regularity. Of late, the marriage misery has taken precedence, I confess." Julian started to rise from the table, but Charlotte stopped her, laying a hand on her sleeve.

"Not been the best of years, has it, Jule?" she asked quietly.

"No, not the best. I tell myself, you just put one foot in front of the other and keep on. But sometimes it gets . . . just very . . . tiring."

"Have you tried writing about it? Hope, I mean."

"I can't see any way to do it, Charlotte. I've tried. Thanks for being an intrepid editor at heart, though."

"A little nudge never hurt now and then. I'd be willing to look at whatever you'd like, at any stage, if it would help. Maybe it would be just the thing to get it—"

"—out of my system? Thanks, but this isn't 'flu, it's more like malaria. Recurrent bouts, lifelong. I've tried to exorcise it—in poems, nonfiction 'political analyses,' short stories. Besides, 'catharsis' in art is deadly. Forget it." She rose again, and this time Charlotte followed her, still trying, as they made their way out of the restaurant.

"What about a play?"

"A *play?* Are you nuts, Charlotte? Has Zach finally driven you round the bend?"

"No, I'm serious. Maybe that way—"

"I can see it now: 'Enter the Mother, the Daughter/Wife, the Husband—from stage left, stage right, and upstage center, respectively. Each is armed with lethal weapons. They proceed to massacre one another. No dialogue except screams and groans. It's a pantomime. Curtain.' Short play, Charlotte. Very avant-garde. Just the thing to make me the rage on the so-far-off-Broadway circuit I'll be the toast of Peoria."

"Well, not a theater play, then. What about a television script? I mean, the medium you know best, the one that's probably in your blood? Just using that *form* as a way to—"

"Oh, even better! '*Will* Laurence and Julian find their way to happiness? *Will* Hope answer her daughter's phone calls? Tune in tomorrow and find out!' Maybe I can sell the idea to Paola Luchino as a soap opera—but set in the Riviera for lush visuals." They emerged into the street. "Look, love, thanks anyway, I'm afraid it's not even worth a try. Oh," she changed the subject, "it's starting to drizzle. *Just* for *us*. Because you and I came outside, Charlotte. Targets. Make no mistake." They embraced. Some atavistic training rose in Julian. Always leave 'em laughing—and wanting more.

"Oh Charlotte," she brightened, pulling back from what felt to her like pity, "so you won't think my life is too much Perils of Pauline, I have two new feminist jokes for you. Picked them up last month after a speech in D.C."

"D.C.? They can't be very funny, then."

"No, really. Nice nasty man-hating jokes."

"What are you waiting for? Tell!"

"All right: What is 250,000 men at the bottom of the ocean?"

"Uh . . . I give up, what?"

"Not enough."

Charlotte smiled. "And the other one?"

"How many men does it take to tile a bathroom floor?"

"Um . . . none, unless they're paid more than any woman?"

"No. Only two—if you slice them *very* thin."

"A little hostile, aren't they, these jokes?"

Bombed, Julian thought. On her way back toward the office, Charlotte was already donning her Athena sensibility.

"Oh, I don't know. Even if they are hostile, don't we deserve some recompense for all these centuries of farmer's daughter and mother-in-law and dumb-blonde jokes men tell?"

"Well. Anyway, Julian, I hope it gets better for you. And for Larry, too. And with your mother and everything. It was good to see you."

The best move now would be as graceful an exit as could be managed.

"Thanks for everything, Charlotte. It was good to see you, too. And I hope we won't have to stay in the TGIM club for too long. Give my regards to Zach—if you're still speaking to him, that is."

"I will. And mine to Larry."

It was like the married women's reassurance ritual: All Will Be Well. Commiseration Now Closed. Business as Usual.

"And thanks for lunch, too."

"Quite welcome," Charlotte called, starting off in the opposite direction. "Take care, now!"

Julian watched her disappear, swallowed up among the black-coated men swarming the streets. Then she turned toward the bus stop to go home.

It seemed to her these days that every motion required an act of will. From the big ones: keeping her forced exile from Hope in perspective, holding on to the love for Larry, trying to find a moment of time for writing anything of her own in between political articles, traveling, speeches, free-lance editing. To the tiny ones: remember to confirm air ticket for Wisconsin next week. Missed the bank today, go first thing in the morning and deposit the new royalty check and ask for immediate credit no delay please. We're almost out of toilet paper. Call Mrs. D. in case she has any update passed on from Hope's companion. Soon as check has cleared go with Larry to buy him two new pairs of slacks. We need milk. Check-in calls to Scribner's and Knopf, any new free-lance stuff available? Fix alarm clock or buy cheap new one. Remind Larry he needs a haircut. When at bank get quarters for laundromat. Soon as check has cleared—remember to nag that college in Oregon where *is* check?—pay urgent gas and electric bill. Remember to draft press statement for Welfare Women's Coalition press conference and get it to Renée Fitzpatrick before Wednesday. Take boots to shoemaker for resoling . . . She thought of the famous tombstone epigraph of a witty suicide: *All this endless buttoning and unbuttoning.* She didn't want to go home. But where else was there to go?

She zipped up her windbreaker and hunched under a building overhang nearest the bus stop. An April downpour had begun in earnest, rapid needles of rain seeming to perforate the asphalt as if it were a black satin pincushion.

Sometimes the will cracked, but before it could break outright, exhaustion rushed in. She could summon the energy or, if necessary, project a façade of serenity when around other people. But not with Larry. And not when alone with herself. Fatigue at the bone, at the brain, in the pores. Fatigue beyond depression, and certainly beyond the anger depression was said to conceal. Truth tyranny! Lying about finding that odious Preston manuscript tolerable. Opportunist. Manipulator. Put one foot. To what bloody goddamned purpose? Then the other foot. For the approval of Hope? (That's my baby trooper!") For the approval of Larry? ("I'll say this for you, Jule, you've got staying power.") For the approval of the movement? ("You give me courage" . . . "How can you be married and call yourself a feminist" . . . "I know this is crazy, but weren't you the little girl who" . . .) For the approval of herself? An approval from which she lived in eternal exile?

A bus loomed along the rainslick avenue. Julian boarded with the other waiting would-be passengers, becoming entangled in the aisle with a Puerto Rican woman attempting to juggle two large shopping bags and two small children who whined continuously in Spanish at their mother. Mothers and children and exiles, Julian thought, and you carp that *you* have it bad, you self-indulgent turd? Think about Iliana, for that matter. Christ, she's been an actual exile for most of her life. Try that one on, Julian. A rebel against *her* mother, too, against her entire family—refused to marry, rejected the Church, defied the sexual codes by daring to sleep with anybody she chose, man or woman. Defied the social codes by becoming an art photographer when that was unheard of—in Argentina, yet. Defied a totalitarian political system, first by her incendiary photographs, then by her open anti-government activism, finally by going into exile. At age nineteen, for god's sake, Julian. When you were all atwitter with the major cosmic crisis of trying to "find yourself." Then roamed the world: New York, Paris, Madrid, then back to New York, the early CR group— then Europe again. And always the necklaces of cameras, always adorned by the precious lenses through which she saw the world in her unique way, always registering that, capturing it on prints that now hung framed along the best gallery exhibition walls. Inventing and reinventing the world through her own eyes. By sheer will. And you talk about will, Julian? Gameplayer. Better self-disgust than self-pity.

Very well, she confessed to herself, so it is a game, this trying to get through each day. A gambit. A technique not only to survive but to teach oneself some meaning in this otherwise distasteful process called daily life. You learned all over again to improvise, the skill an actor needed as much as—no, more than—the ability to memorize.

The Game was like a dare. Seeing how long you could let the exhaustion prey on you, how remote you could let the will become before catching it again, pulling it thread by thread like a spider would out of some place in you that you still trusted could secrete it.

She dismounted the bus at her stop and started the two-block walk to the loft. The rain had stopped. Maybe Larry would feel like talking? Maybe she could secrete from herself the will to talk, too. Maybe there was hope beyond Hope. Because if the Game was still a shake of the adolescent fist, Prometheus against the gods, it had also become Job refusing to curse God and die. The Game was more than to suffer and survive. The Game was also to find or forge some moment of beauty, of grace, at least once a day. Say "Thank you" to the harassed bus driver and he might light up with a smile of surprise. Praise something. The shape of a rainwashed nectarine in a street fruit-stand, its self-contained sunburst colors. The way an ailanthus tree flourished up through a subway grate. A moment of laughter with Charlotte, however much the two women misunderstood that they understood one another. The brief freshness of city streets after a thunderstorm. Praise *some*thing. Vignettes of a York Mystery Play inserted into this Samuel Beckett life.

If the Game succeeded there would be a small flare inside, a kindling of energy at having affirmed some particle of existence.

She let herself in at the street door.

If the Game failed there would be a hollow sensation: of hypocrisy, of Norman Vincent Peale positive thinking, of competing for some Plucky Wench of the Week award. If the Game failed it would feel as if the attempt to affirm had in itself been stagey—so that the bus driver would approve, so that Charlotte would approve, so that whoever Julian Travis was, *she* would approve. Circular thinking, the way the damned would brood in hell. If the Game failed, it was just another scam, the legacy, the only heirloom Hope bequeathed. If the Game failed, you had to wipe it out of your mind and start all over again. Put your right foot . . .

Julian passed the hall mirror and stopped to look. There she was. Can I love her, even *like* her? Some days she looked younger than forty, because of the cursedly round face that had been so adorable for the first ten years of her life. Today she looked older than her age. Olive skin drained ashen by the fluorescent hall light. Short straight mud-colored hair. The mouth fleshy, too sensual for what it had never dared. The eyes dark and large—like Hers. The one good feature, like Hers. She tested a smile at Julian from the mirror.

"Who are you, Julian?" she murmured to the glass. "Is it as bad as all that, that Hope didn't just rob you of yourself but you never even got a chance to create a 'who' in the first place?"

The eyes in the mirror started to fill. Julian always can cry on cue, she thought scornfully.

"I'll tell you who you are, Jule. *Julie. Baby,*" she muttered. "You're a fake. 'Write it as a TV script,' Charlotte says. Little does she know you, *Julie.* You're a self-pitying bitch, a failure and a phony and a fool. You wouldn't know reality unless you'd *learned* it in a script. You have nothing, *nothing* in the whole vast universe to do with me here inside myself, do you hear me? I hate your phony faking guts, Julian Travis, your lovey-dovey affirmations, lies, martyrdoms, goody-goody bids for ego worship. I hate your garish face over my immaculate skull. You don't even exist. *God.* You're all I have, I've got to live with you until we both die, and you don't even exist."

She turned her back on the mirror.

"And if you don't exist," she whispered into the dim hall, *"then who in hell am I?"*

She had an answer the instant she walked into the loft. A piece of paper tacked up on the cork bulletin board accosted her with ragged block-printed capital letters:

DEAR POWER-BROKER,
I CAN'T STAND WHAT YOUR LIFE IS DOING TO OUR
LIVES. I'M BEGINNING TO HATE YOU
FOR WHAT YOU'VE DONE TO
WHAT IS (LAUGHINGLY CALLED) MY LIFE.
I'LL BE OUT ALL NIGHT IF NECESSARY DOING
WHAT I DON'T EVEN ENJOY DOING ANYMORE
THANKS TO AMERICA'S TAP-DANCING
REVOLUTIONARY DARLING. PLEASE GO TO HELL BEFORE
I GET HOME. URGENT URGENT URGENT THIS HURTS.

ALL POWER TO THE WOMEN!
   YOUR LOVING HOUSEWIFE FORMERLY
   THE RED MENACE NOW THE GRAY MOUSE,
   LAURENCE (TRAVIS)

CHAPTER FIVE
Autumn, 1961

This was really happening: she was on her way to meet him.

Five years it had taken. Five years of sleuthing, patching the evidence together from all those eavesdropped-on conversations between Hope and Yetta or Essie, library trips on literary excuses in order to research her way through the telephone books of every major and many smaller cities in Connecticut. Five years of imagining what it would be like. What *he* would be like. Five years of fantasies. The fantasy in which he refused to acknowledge her, in which she was denied outright, annihilated on the spot. The fantasy in which he physically threw her out the door. The fantasy in which he burst into tears and flung his arms wide, unabashedly sobbing, "My daughter, my daughter. I always knew you'd find me someday." Five years of lying in bed at night imagining how he would look; what she might recognize in his features of her own face; what his voice, his accent, would sound like.

A curtain had been dropped on the subject since Julian was thirteen, since the confrontation that had broken open the lie that David was dead. Hope's version had simply picked itself up that night and ambled sideways, settling down again not far from where it had been: so he was alive, what of it. He had deserted them. Why be curious about a so-called father who had never taken one particle of interest in his own child—

especially when such curiosity wounded the other parent whose entire existence had been given over to that child? But the obsession wasn't so easily exorcised. Julian knew that Hope neither understood nor would grant one millimeter of sympathy to the obsession: it was done, over with, finished; there was nothing to learn from or about David Traumstein; he *was*, in effect, a dead man. And so should he be to Julian. Hadn't eighteen years of his silence made that clear?

The obsession went into hiding. Julian's imagination took inventory of all the ways he might have tried to contact his daughter, but been impeded by Hope. Had she destroyed letters? Deflected phone calls? Julian knew that nothing was beyond Hope when fighting for what she thought was her survival and her daughter's love. So the powerful mystique of him endured and ripened, nurtured in secret by Julian's care. Sitting stiffly in the window seat of this dingy bus en route to the university town of Storrs, she began for the thousandth time to number the minimal facts she had about him, telling the beads of memory through this last novena.

He was a doctor, a pediatrician. Born in Vienna, of a "good" family, upper-middle-class, well educated. About ten years older than Hope. A linguist: spoke German, English, French; supposedly had excellent Greek and Latin. Had read the classics in the original, for pleasure; particularly relished Greek drama. Knew and loved music—but Hope would go into no details there. Was brilliant, handsome, arrogant; could be cold, cruel, emotionally aloof unto "sadism" (Hope's word). Indeed, Hope's virtuosity for exaggeration had to be weighed against every detail, at every re-listing. To drop one's guard about that for even a second was to be assaulted by such doubt and fear as to the possibility of actually connecting with him that Julian would again give up the whole idea. This had already happened three times, this reconciling herself to eternal ignorance on the subject, even after she had finally learned where he was—the city, the address, the telephone number. That moment, sitting in the wooden library chair with the phone book for Storrs in front of her: how the room froze, how still everything became when the name leapt at her, in the same fine print as those above and below it but with the impact of emblazoned letters flaming ten feet high—DAVID TRAUM-STEIN, M.D.

In the little games she played with herself, this had been the next to last trip to the library phone books she was going to permit. It was ludicrous, futile, thinking someone might still be where he was eighteen years earlier—if he had been there to begin with at all. Like an alcoholic trying to clamber on the wagon, Julian now had a history of refusing to permit herself further self-indulgence. She first stopped searching for him after confiding the matter to her journal. But when Hope began showing an interest in her writing, Julian had shredded and flushed the journal pages. There was no evidence. Safety. There also was no exorcism of *him* remaining—on the page. So long as he had been confined there, Julian had earned a relative peace of mind. Now he was loose again, and the library trips started. Then, with only one more self-permitted trip to go, it was suddenly too late. She'd found the name. Now none of them could escape from any of them anymore.

It was hot in the bus and the window was stuck. She felt her palms begin to sweat and stripped off her gloves, remembering how her hands had shaken the day she'd made the first call, in a British accent—pretending to be a researcher doing follow-up on Jewish war refugees—to confirm that this was indeed the same Dr. Traumstein who had emigrated from Austria in 1941. The very thought of that phone call, just before her eighteenth birthday, still could make her hands tremble now, a whole year later. How in hell can I carry off a face-to-face meeting, she worried, nervously smoothing out the cotton fingers of the gloves.

The wife had answered. Julian hadn't known that at the time; possibly the nurse-receptionist, she'd thought. But those well-contrived questions of the follow-up researcher from the mythical American-European Jewry League had amazingly enough elicited a fair amount of information—certainly sufficient to brood over for another year—until the next call, this last call, the fatal one, to make the appointment toward which the bus steadily sped her.

"To whom am I speaking, please?" the British researcher's voice had inquired.

"This is Mrs. Traumstein, the Doctor's wife. I also work in his medical practice, his office."

"I see. And may I ask how long you and the doctor have been married?"

"Since 1941."

"1941?" Impossible.

"Yes."

"I see. Any children, might I ask?"

There was a pause so slight it might have been imagined by the British researcher.

"One child."

Acknowledged. Acknowledged, after all. And how did the current Mrs. Traumstein cope with that for so many years?

"And may I have your maiden name, please?"

"I was born Weisstern, Minna Weisstern."

The accent, though faint, was there.

"Born in Vienna, as well?"

"Yes. The Doctor and I were childhood friends."

"And you emigrated in—?"

"In 1941, the same year we were married."

Each answer blasted open further underground deposits of questions. But these were questions no American-European Jewry League volunteer could get away with asking. Besides, although she retained her cool British tone of inquiry, Julian had to get off the telephone quickly now, because more than the hand holding the receiver had begun to tremble.

Who would have thought it might be so easy? Just say thank you for your cooperation and hang up the phone. Then sift for months, solipsistically, through the new information—which didn't jell with information she had already lived with for years.

So he had remarried. Yet he still acknowledged the child of the first marriage. Then why had he never—or had he?—tried to be a presence in that child's life? Furthermore, the second wife, Minna, clearly knew about the child. Or did she think the child was dead? And how could they have been married a year before the child was born? Why hadn't the League volunteer pressed for a bit more information about the child? Minna's respect for authority seemed so entrenched that she might have gone on answering whatever questions were put to her.

At times, Julian's brain reeled down side paths that led to dead ends, swamps, precipice edges. What if Hope were not her biological mother? Nonsense: the genes showed themselves physically. What if David were a bigamist? What if Hope had told him the child had died, just as she had told the child that he was dead? A rat in a laboratory maze, Julian's mind traced and retraced every path, no matter how irrational. Always the end returned her to the starting place.

The riddle goaded her on, depleted her, drove her to desperate invocations of peace. Put it out of your mind, she'd chant to herself. Forget it. So she'd landed a job, freed herself of her virginity with Laurence, found an apartment, moved. Surely sufficient rites of passage? Forget the other. What will matter in your life is what you make of your life, not your ancestors, ethnicities, superstitious genetic influences. You can be anything you want to be. Then she would remember who had taught her that. And she would enter the labyrinth again, the chthonic place of mystery, terror, longing, nausea—the only place she now felt truly at home.

Julian glanced at her watch. The delicate gold face—Hope's gift for her eighteenth birthday—announced they were only twenty minutes away from Storrs. This was happening. She was approaching the core of the labyrinth.

She brushed a piece of lint from the jade-green wool suit in which she had carefully costumed herself, and readjusted the collar of the white blouse. Stocking seams straight, she could feel them. Black high-heel pumps, new, still unscuffed, still uncomfortable. Beige gloves in lap, matching beige purse. The well-dressed young woman, self-contained, prepared for anything.

She had lied to Hope, of course; the genes showed themselves more than physically. She had told her mother not to phone as usual at the literary agency or at the Yorkville apartment because she was taking the day off to spend it with Laurence, knowing that Hope—still enranged about their affair—would never phone at his loft. She had lied to her boss, claiming that a family illness necessitated her absence. She had lied to the wife-receptionist in order to make the appointment. Although, she told herself, *that* had been more of a hint than a total falsehood. But its being a hint depended on how valid Hope's stories about him had been. Lies teetering on a foundation of truth? Or the reverse? At this moment, everyone concerned had been lied to, everyone concerned thought Julian was elsewhere than where she was. At this moment, only Julian Travis, riding in a bus somewhere in Connecticut, knew who she was going to meet.

Think tactically, she had directed herself. Plan it; stage, light, costume it; it's the only way you can get through it. He was a classics scholar, Hope had said, and he loved Greek drama in particular. He'd refuse to see you, Hope had said, he wants no part of you how stupid can you be can't you figure that out after all this time. Calculate. How can you make an appointment, be assured you get to see him? Certainly *not* warn him it will be Surprise Daddy. Hope just might have been telling the truth. But can you surprise him totally? The man was a concentration-camp victim, an escapee, a refugee. How merciless can you get? What if he has an on-the-spot heart attack from your little surprise? What if you murder your own father out of curiosity? Plan it. Stage it. *Do what you know how to do.*

Give him at least a hint, a half-lie but a clue—the way you have lived with hints and clues all your life. Something with wit. If he's as smart as you think he is, as educated as you've been told he is, as obsessed with his child as you've dreamt he is —then he'll figure it out. He'll know and be prepared for the young woman who walks through his office door in time for her 2 P.M. appointment on October first, 1961.

So she had made the second call. And again got Minna. This time Julian wore a French accent—but a light one, to confuse things safely. She wished to make an appointment to discuss her child's health problem even before bringing the child in for an examination. Why? Well, the child was, uh, fragile. She had not expected to be asked who referred her to Dr. Traumstein. It threw her. But the years of training, rehearsals, live television performances when if something went wrong you improvised, carried her through.

She tossed out a made-up name: an old friend who lived in Connecticut had praised Dr. Traumstein highly. Since she herself had only recently moved to New York from California and had no pediatrician of her own, why no it wasn't too far to travel an hour or so to find a really good doctor.

But, ventured Minna, the name of the referrer was unfamiliar, not one of the Doctor's patients.

"Ah, yes, but of course. My friend has recently remarried and I never *can* remember his name. I always knew her by her widowed name. Doubtless she is registered with your office by her new husband's name, you see."

Minna saw. Minna, faithful to her role as a walk-on character unwittingly furthering the plot, helpfully made the appointment. In the name of Atreus. First name or initial, please?

"E."

If he knew his classics, then.

If he remembered.

If the House of Atreus put him on alert.

If the name "E. Atreus" snapped into place unerringly as the final missing piece of the puzzle; if the magic words opened a door to a path that curved inevitably around the last turn of the labyrinth he too might have been treading for almost two decades; if Sophocles and Euripides were still read by him for pleasure; if he were brilliant or merely cared, if he were vigilant or even wary, if, *if.* Then he would not be surprised. Then he would be well warned that no one in the world but his daughter would be appearing in time to keep the appointment of Elektra Atreus.

And if not? If he were stupid or unsubtle, uneducated or forgetful, complacent, dense? If he hadn't ever cared at all?

In that case—some Sophoclean chorus intoned softly inside Julian's proscenium brain, an ancient menace of revenge hissing through its sibilant innocence—*in that case, let him be surprised.*

She was suddenly sleepy. Absurd to be sleepy now, when they were entering the outskirts of this quiet New England town—neat lawns, tidy white houses, windowbox nasturtiums, trees already flaring gold and crimson with autumn. It was as if the years of lying awake were only now taking their toll. Years rebuilding his face from one faded photograph, decoding, tracking him down—his daughter the post-war Gestapo. Years of Elektra living under Clytemnestra's ruthlessly loving hand, hunching at the palace gate on guard for the encounter that would set in motion a final avenging of her father's honor, the meeting that would at last tell her who she was. Suspense shriveled to boredom, curiosity to indifference, as those years drained out of her mind. All she wanted was to pass the stop, let it slide past the window; to stay on the bus so its motion could rock her to insensibility. Stay on the bus and never go back, not to him, not to her, not to any of them. Stay on the bus and get off someplace else. Become someone else.

"This isn't me," Julian whispered to the gold watch-face, "I

didn't write this. I don't want to live this. It's all the fault of the
script."

But the bus stopped. She rose, tottering slightly on the new
heels, and straightened her spine as if she were about to make
an entrance.

And so you are, she added silently. You will get down this
aisle—*there*—and off this bus—*there*. Now you will look around
for a taxi. *There's one*, that's it. Now you will give the address.
There.

This was happening. She was on her way to meet him.

The taxi reached its destination with alarming speed. Two
blocks to the right, a turn, three blocks to the left, compacted
labyrinth, and the houses became larger, more imposing, the
front lawns more lush, the azalea bushes luxuriant even in
autumn. There was no mistaking *the* house. She sensed it
ahead just as the taxi began slowing down. The corner house.
There, in polished brass swinging from two posts on the lawn,
his shingle. The Doctor's House.

Not the gates of Mycenae, but formidable all the same. The
Doctor's House differentiated itself from the uniform white of
neighboring homes on the block. This one was painted a soft
gray; the sun-porch around the back half visible from the side,
glass-enclosed for year-round use. A back-lit stained-glass
panel—imported, from the looks of its quality, possibly an antique—had been mounted in the front door: opalescent water-
lilies undulating against a milky green background. The block,
the neighborhood, the town itself might be "suburb," but the
Doctor's House proclaimed itself "Old World Europe."

Julian tried to ingest and process the moment as she paid the
cab driver. Twitches of emotion—excitement, fear, urgency—
were now so continual in their shifts that she could barely
separate them one from another as they jerked through her
puppet self. But there was no time to wait them out. She didn't
dare linger too long on the sidewalk. It wouldn't do to appear
suspicious until the moment itself. The twitches danced their
puppet up the front walk. She was still fearful of telegraphing
herself, that her identity would be discovered before she got to
him—that the audience would then be snatched away, the
visitor rejected before she reached the inner chamber of the
throne room.

The doorbell of this home-office didn't buzz like most American doorbells; it chimed deeply, echoing from somewhere inside the bowels of the house. A respectable wait. No answer. Julian pressed the bell again, watching her gloved hand begin to tremor slightly. Control yourself, she thought. What is this— stage-fright, like a baby? Had she—or Minna—got the date wrong, or the time? Had all those damned fake accents confused the facts of when and how? Had David read the Atreus clue *too* clearly, and summarily cleared out rather than face his Elektra? Was he even now hiding inside the house, refusing to grant her admittance?

The door swung open. A plump, dark-haired woman in her early fifties stood there, offering a tentative smile.

"Yes?"

"I have an appointment with Dr. Traumstein?" The statement came out as an appeal. Correct the tone. Needs more authority. And don't forget the French flavor.

"Ah. You are Mrs. Ahtrayoos?"

"Miss Atreus, yes." *Stupid*, Julian. You're a *Mrs.*, you're the mother of a child, he's a pediatrician, remember? And why repronounce the name more accurately? Maybe nobody got the clue just because of Minna's mispronunciation. Because this, definitely, was Minna. The "other woman." The woman who'd displaced Hope. The stepmother, wickedness and all. No mistaking the voice, or, for that matter, the type.

David Traumstein was in one thing, then, consistent. He had a weakness for a particular type—the Doctor's Woman. Short, *zaftig*, with dark hair and large eyes. Minna and Hope could have been sisters, Julian thought. But she couldn't avoid noticing the milder quality of this woman, an almost deliberately projected pliancy, perhaps required to conceal the strength of the woman who had won. That vibrant, often offensive, sometimes electrifying energy Hope radiated was lacking here. Where Hope would confront and defy, Minna would appease and manipulate. Where Hope would manipulate, Minna would concede. And where Hope would (hard to imagine) concede— which would be done with privately articulated vows of vengeance—Minna would surrender tractably. This was a more unsavory, because more genteel, version of Julian's mother. Even the physical features, Julian thought with some satisfaction, were coarser: the eyes not so lustrous, the hair not so fine. The skin was ruddy, unlike Hope's cream alabaster flesh. The voice was a shade too high-pitched, too cheerful in its hausfrau poise. Julian, following the jelloid hip-motion of Minna down the Persian-carpeted dark foyer, felt startled to discover in herself such unforeseen loyalty to Hope. Nonetheless, she couldn't help thinking that David Traumstein had settled for a Roman copy of the Greek original.

Minna ushered her into the waiting room. It was Modern American Doctor, an abrupt departure from what little she had been permitted to glimpse of the rest of the house. This room might have been moved intact to any twenty-storey "professional building" of doctors and dentists: pastel yellow walls, the wifenursereceptionist's desk toward which Minna homed like a self-satisfied pigeon, a tweed-cloth-covered sofa on which sat a tired-looking woman not much older than Julian, with a toddler asleep on her lap. The requisite coffeetable displayed copies of *Time, Newsweek, Ladies' Home Journal, McCall's*. These were joined by a stack of pamphlets: "How to Raise a Healthy Child," "What Every Mother Should Know" (in a pink cover), and "Fathers Can Help, Too" (in a blue one). A vase of silk flowers stood on Minna's gray metal desk, where that pudgy dovelet now sat, proffering a clipboard and pencil at Julian with her ladylike menial air.

"You will please to fill out the information form, Mrs., uh—"

"Yes. Thank you."

Julian swallowed a tiny bubble of panic when she glanced at the form. Mother's name. Father's name. Date of birth. Hers? Or her imaginary child's? Medical history. But the Greek chorus remained steadfast inside her head, swaying slightly in rhythm to their chant. *It's a standard form. Make up any answers you like. He'll have his answers soon enough. They don't matter. What matters is how close you are now, all but inside the door, that door, there, which must lead to his office. You're inside the gates, now get inside that door.* She scribbled her answers rapidly and handed the board back. Minna disappeared with a courtier-like scuttle through the door to the inner sanctum.

Julian sat down on the sofa, smiled nervously at the young mother, and looked at the sleeping child.

"Not seriously sick, I hope?"

"No, I don't think so. I sure hope not," the woman sighed. "I don't have an appointment, I'm just waiting for an opening. I

sure hope not," she repeated. "I've got a newborn at home—
my mom's with him now—and he's had colic. I dunno how I
can handle two sick kids at once."

Julian nodded, trying to act sympathetic but feeling a
twinge of guilt that she was not about to offer her own appointment time so that this woman and child could go first. As it was,
every second of waiting for Minna to emerge seemed intermi-
nable.

"I think it's just a cold," the woman rambled on, reassuring
herself, "but she has a low fever, so Dr. Traumstein thought I
better bring her in, to be on the safe side. What with a new
baby in the house and all, you know."

Julian nodded again. Then it came out before she could
censor herself.

"What's he like? Dr. Traumstein?"

"You never met him? You never been here before? Funny,
you look familiar."

"Uh, no. A friend recommended him. I, uh, wanted to meet
and talk with him before I brought my child in."

"You got only one?"

"Yes. Yes, only one."

"Lucky. But you should have another. They say an only child
is lonely. And spoiled. Best thing is to have 'em close together.
Then they can play with each other, you know? Kids are such a
joy," she yawned.

"I'm sure you're right," Julian said, glancing toward the door
to the inner office. "What *is* he like?"

"Dr. Traumstein? Oh, he's real good with kids. My sister has
two of her own, one's in his teens now. She's been bringing 'em
both here for years. Kids seem to trust him. He always gives
'em candy after a shot, tells 'em little jokes. Real good with—"

The door opened and Minna emerged. Julian stood up.

"He will see you soon, Miss Iytreeoos. The Doctor."

Minna pronounced his title with such reverence one could
hear the undertones: Herr Doktor. Poor Minna, Julian wondered, had she once, like her predecessor Hope, dreamt of a
different life? Had the handsome young doctor swept her off
her feet, too, promising romance and a vicarious career as the
soulmate of an altruistic physician and chatelaine of his manor
—only to wind her up here, in however fancy a house on a
suburban American street, doubling as his receptionist? Surely

this demure creature had never envisioned herself a second wife, co-conspirator with her husband for years about the Gothic-novel secret of a skeleton-child rattling in the closet of his past.

But Minna seemed the essence of *Gemütlichkeit*, puttering contentedly away at her metal desk among his papers, bills, appointment books. Julian tried to picture them in bed together, her father and this placid woman, an exercise in imagination complicated by her ignorance of his appearance. It was not possible to conceive of anybody making love to Minna without sinking into her ductility like a dazed child into a featherbed. Hope—whom Julian had never seen in an erotic situation with anyone beyond the flirtations conducted with brokers, agents, and headwaiters—Hope was as clearly, and with as little evidence, capable of passion. Grand passion, probably, Julian supposed; ever-hyperbolic Hope.

"Please to be patient," Minna simpered.

Be patient. Almost there. Get inside the door. With an effort, Julian slowed down her pacing.

Minna pantomimed formally toward the couch—she tended to make gestures out of a Schnitzler play—but Julian declined and continued to stroll around the room. The windows looked out onto carefully barbered lawn. The pictures on the walls were stock prints of landscapes; mediocre, not worth a second glance. Only one, on the wall beside his private office door, showed authenticity. It was a deep-framed engraving printed with sepia ink, a nineteenth-century view of a river valley, the water flowing between two gently sloping cliff walls, the ruins of a castle high on a distant rock overhang. "Dürnstein an der Donau," read the legend at the bottom. The Danube valley. That had been part of home for him.

The intercom on Minna's desk made a burping sound—like a cyanide pellet dropped into acid under the seat of a condemned prisoner, Julian thought, shocked by her own mental association. Then Minna was already hanging up the phone and rising, again smiling that ingratiating *mou* of sycophancy.

He knows. He read the form and found the answers peculiar and suddenly put it together with E. Atreus and he knows and she's about to politely throw me out. Oh dear god, what if he knows? And what if he doesn't?

"The Doctor will see you now," bowing her head toward Julian.

She opened the door beside the Dürnstein print and took a step backward. Julian walked through and heard Minna muffle the door shut behind her.

This office was only slightly smaller than the reception room, but just as impersonal. This desk, however, was not metal, but burnished mahogany, facing into the room in front of glass double doors that looked out—as he now did, his back toward her—over what appeared to be a modest flower and vegetable garden. Another door led to what must be the examining room. The details around her would blur forever in Julian's remembrance, except for three specific imprints: the dapper-suited back of the man of medium height who stood behind the desk, and the two large silver-framed photographs that sat on a side table. One was obviously the young Minna, that obedient smile well in place decades ago. The other was an instantly recognizable baby photograph of Julian herself.

She stood just a step inside the closed door, waiting. Everything seemed to have stopped: time itself, her own heart. He turned, his gaze fixed on the clipboard in his hand, and glanced up at her. What she saw, more than registering any of his features, was a man's face suddenly paling to chalk before her eyes.

"Hello, David. I'm Julian. Your daughter."

His eyes jerked involuntarily down to the clipboard, then up again to her, then down again, then up. So he had not deciphered the clues. She could hear his mind skidding, braking, careening in the silence of the room.

He regained control, and looked at her evenly. By the time he spoke, the voice was already contained, almost suave.

"I know."

"Oh? May I ask how? You seemed surprised."

"You look— very like your mother did when we—when I knew her."

So that, too, had worked. Set the stage, design the makeup, let no detail escape you. She was wearing her hair as Hope had worn hers in old pictures—parted in the middle, with the sides loosely brushed back, shoulder length—even though she herself usually wore it knotted in a bun, to look and feel older than eighteen. So it had worked.

He came toward her. Each gesture now was weighted with years of fantasy scenarios, and as the movement rose and entered reality so rose the possibilities. In that instant, as it hovered, his motive hung in a balance equal with exquisite likelihood. Then, as it chose one action only, the other possibilities fell away for all time, as the striking of a first chord ends all music.

He did not embrace her. Instead, he continued past her, opened his office door, put out his head, and curtly told Minna that he wished not to be disturbed. Then he shut and locked the door. So died forever part of the hoping, while part of the panic was resurrected in its place, wildly, irrationally. They were locked in together. What did that mean? Why had he done that?

He retreated to the safety behind his desk.

"You will please to sit down?" He all but clicked his heels. The Viennese accent was pronounced, unmistakable, as if intentionally retained.

Julian moved to the seat in front of his desk and sat down.

She saw before her a man in his late fifties or early sixties, well preserved and well dressed—spotless white shirt, a discreetly expensive tie, cufflinks. The silver hair was worn in a fashionable haircut, but slightly longer than common, more in the European style. The features of his face offered her nothing of herself.

The eyes were dark gray, the complexion a smooth-shaven olive. The high forehead rose from a long straight delicately flared nose. There was a slackening line around the jaw, from age, which didn't belie the full, sensuous mouth or the thrust of a square chin below it. Hope was right, there was a real dimple in the chin. And when he had been younger, and blond, and the face and body lines sharp and lean, Julian could see that he must have been handsome.

"Well," he said, leaning back in his chair, now in possession of himself, "I can say I *am* a bit surprised."

"I . . . wasn't sure you'd know who I was."

"I knew who you were the moment I saw you. You really do look very much as she did."

"Any other features you recognize?"

"I see nothing of myself, if that is what you mean."

"Well, the genes must be there. I wasn't born by immaculate

conception." She'd meant to sound witty, but the words came out edged with sarcasm. Bad beginning. She flinched. His eyes narrowed, the physician making a diagnosis.

"Please, why have you come? What do you want?"

So this was to hate him, then.

That the same man who had against all explanation kept her baby picture on his desk for almost nineteen years could, on finally meeting her, think of nothing to ask but "What do you want?"

"I want nothing of you. As to why I'm here, I should think that was obvious."

"Perhaps. But frankly, I do not know."

"For all of my life I've wanted to meet my father. Is that so very strange?"

He shrugged elegantly. "A great many people have never met their parents. It doesn't seem such an uncommon thing."

"It's uncommon enough to have become something of an obsession in my case."

"That's unfortunate. I understand that girls often are melodramatic . . . ah, intense, perhaps. But surely the world does not revolve around anything so trivial as—"

"Forgive me. But you can't possibly realize my position. It isn't a trivial concern to me." Perhaps if she shifted from the emotional realm, demonstrated the intellectual . . . "Look. If I had been a son in search of my father, I would have been re-enacting a major archetype. Oedipus. Theseus. Christ. Does my being a daughter in search of the same thing make it a trivial quest?"

He shrugged again. "And so you want . . . ?"

"Only to have met you, seen you face to face, talked a while with you. Heard your side of the story."

"My side?" he smiled. "There is, I am afraid, very little story."

"Nevertheless, I would like, more than you can imagine, to hear it from your lips. And that's *all* I want." She added, trying for a note which would betray neither humiliation nor bitterness, "I haven't come to blackmail you, you know. Or to harm you or your new wife in any way."

"My new wife? You mean Minna? What is so new about Minna?"

"Well, I mean . . . your second wife."

He swiveled slightly in his chair.

"I see," was all he responded. Then he leaned forward and began playing with the silver letter-opener on his desk.

"And may I ask," he murmured in a lower tone, "why the elaborate pretense? This strange false name in which you made the appointment? And why after so long, suddenly? Is your mother no longer alive?"

Something was going wrong. It was she who should be asking the questions, not he. But the impetus of interrogation already lay firmly in his grasp, and so eager was she to show herself to him—to have him understand the burden of ignorance she had borne for years, to have him comprehend the frail indomitable stubbornness of her pursuit—that she knew she would reply to any question he put her. *And,* chanted the chorus, *it must mean he too is curious. He cares. He cares. He always cared.* Some vestige of pride helped her to ask, with her most disarming smile,

"You mean the false name I gave means nothing to you?"

He studied the clipboard.

"No. I am afraid not. And please to not play games with me."

Another chord, the death of more music. So this is what it was to fear him. She struggled back to her own ragged courage.

"It's not a game, and I'm not playing. My mother is still alive. She doesn't know I'm here. I gave a false name because, quite honestly, I had no idea whether you would receive me as myself or refuse to let me come. I traveled a long way to this meeting, and not only in mileage. I didn't intend to be turned away. But I gave that particular pseudonym as a possible clue to you. Please understand that I have been told very little about you. But I *was* told that you were once apparently fond of classic Greek drama. Aeschylus. Sophocles. Euripides."

"That was many years ago. I fail to see—"

"Miss Atreus. From the House of Atreus. That house had only one daughter with the initial 'E.' Her name was Elektra. In case, as it seems, you have forgotten."

He looked mildly amused.

"And I was supposed to decipher this as some sort of clue? How very ornate, my dear."

Her tragedy, interpreted by him as farce. So this is what it was to recognize each other.

"Perhaps not ornate to someone who remembered his Mycenaean history," she ventured, as politely and insultingly as he had. *You are his daughter,* the chorus murmured, *you can hold your own with him.*

"Perhaps not. But a great deal of modern history has intervened and—preoccupied me somewhat." He forced a short laugh.

So this is what it was to feel a lifetime of defenses shatter in tenderness. *This is your father, Julian, and he only has escaped alone to tell thee.*

"I—I would like to ask *you* a few questions . . . You don't have to answer anything if you don't want to, of course," she added hastily.

"I may not know the answers, and I have no idea—or perhaps I do—what you've been told, but . . ."

Like an ancient biblical blessing: the permission. Of all the firmament of questions, where would she begin?

"Why did you never . . . Did you ever try to see me?"

"I saw you once. You were an infant, a few days old only."

"That was all?"

"It was . . . unpleasant."

"Seeing me?"

"The circumstances. Your mother, her sisters . . ."

"And you never tried to see me after that one time."

"No."

"How could you—I mean, did you never want—"

"It was not that possible—or that necessary—to follow up. Those women—your mother and her sisters—made it difficult. Distasteful. They were, I regret to say, quite . . . vicious at times. And—"

"Vulgar."

He raised his eyebrows.

"Yes."

How would it ever be possible for her to discern in her memory of that gaze the shadow of approval cast by his surprise? Or ever to differentiate what she saw from what her desire cast, a shadow itself, over his face? And if it were, ever could be, approval, at what cost? That she deny the flesh which had cared for her sufficiently to live the lie that permitted the living? Somewhere in all this famishment for acceptance, she had to find an appetite—that much if no more—for honor.

"How did you imagine they'd regard you? As a prince with *droit de seigneur?* I realize, of course," she threw in casually, speaking of her life in the third person and the passive construction, "that the child was unwanted. But you were the doctor, after all. You were the one who might have thought about a contraceptive."

"I had other things to think about. Food. Shelter. Survival. And survival as much as possible on my terms. Or what the world had left to me of my terms."

"It . . . could appear to some as a convenient excuse."

He shrugged. "You are your mother's daughter."

One honor gained, another lost. Pain rusted through her as if a scalpel carelessly left in the intestines from some long-ago operation had suddenly been twisted.

"I am also your daughter."

An indifferent smile. "On one meeting?"

"No. Not on one meeting. Merely on fact. Or do you deny it?"

"I don't deny it, my dear. But I think it has little relevance to either of our lives."

There was no key and no way to batter against a door sealed with such Old World politesse. Julian sensed treacherous tears rising. She forced them down. *That he will not have. He will not see you cry. Never.* But the voice that asked the next question embarrassed her by its thin, childish quality.

"Did you—ever love her? At all?"

"What a traditional question for a modern young woman." Was he trying to tease her, his way of being kind? "But I fear I must tell you: the answer is no."

"Never? Even—"

"Even when you were conceived? No. Oh, yes"—that smile —"you are shocked that I knew what you were really asking? You forget, you see, I am a pediatrician—which means I know women. I know their sentimentality about conception. Nature herself is not sentimental about it, you know."

"She loved you. You knew that."

"I knew that, yes. And certainly I was—fond of her. Your mother was an attractive woman. And she was good to me, I will say that. But she was totally unrealistic in terms of what she expected from me. A possessive woman, Hope. She wanted my whole life, my soul."

"She wanted you to love her, perhaps. That might be a simpler reason for what later became her possessiveness." How odd to defend the rights of one's enemy, as if to keep the adversary worthy of what had been one's own best, in a lifelong contest of wills. "She shared her life with you. Was it so bizarre for her to want you to share the building of your new life with her? It wasn't as if you already had an established way of existence. You'd lost your entire family, you'd crawled through the nightmare of the camps, you were a fugitive from the hell that Europe had become—"

He shifted abruptly in his chair. The posture stiffened, as if an old fencing master had entered the room.

"My dear young woman. I cannot tolerate all these maudlin assumptions. I am not responsible for what you have been misinformed about my life. But since you ask, I tell you a few hard truths for a change. I was never in a concentration camp. Nor were any of my family. I already was a full surgery and medical graduate, about to commence my practice in Vienna. My father had died five years earlier, peacefully, in bed. My mother wished to emigrate to Israel, and my sister accompanied her. But it was felt that there were more career opportunities for me in the United States, and so it was arranged, with considerable bribery and through friends with influence, that I be put on the priority list of emigrés with the Jewish refugee committees, although the company I had to keep in that category was often . . . unpalatable."

"You never escaped from a camp?"

"It would have been difficult for me to 'escape,' as you put it, since I was never in a camp to begin with. As for escaping from concentration camps—that was hardly a common occurrence, my dear girl."

"She said—she said you'd crawled through the sewers of Europe to survive, that was her phrase. She believed that. She's always believed that was the reason for . . . that explained your . . . callousness. My god, lies upon lies, endlessly. You lied to Hope."

Again the aristocratic shrug. "*I* did not tell her those things. She had her own preconceived notions. She assumed many things. I simply refrained from telling her otherwise. It seemed kinder. And she was, for a crucial period of time, my lifeline."

"My god," Julian murmured again. "It's stunning. You really

are an incredibly cruel man. You 'simply refrained from telling her otherwise.' My god."

"And why should I have told her otherwise?" His voice never rose, but the accent became more clipped. "Your mother believed what she wanted to believe, what they all wanted to believe. She believed it even before she met me; it was like one of your pre-cut mass-produced American coats that she slipped over my shoulders when I walked off the ship that January. She never bothered to ask whether I liked it or not—but my clothes had always been custom-tailored, you see. All the American Jews pitied us. And some of us were indeed pitiable. But *every* one of us *needed* that pity. To survive, begin new lives. Many, even most, who came here were not only pitiable, they were contemptible—less than human. Long before the Nazis, they had been like this. The stock your mother comes from: peasants, *shtetl* dwellers, peddlers, ghetto inhabitants. Little or no education. Little or no culture."

"My mother's father was a rabbi. He—"

"You asked. So then be answered. To American Jews, already in their cushioned nests, all European Jews who were war victims were the same—even worse—than their own immigrant ancestors had been before coming to the so-called New World. We were all of course scrawny, hungry, filthy, desperate, groveling, half-crushed insects. Objects which were pitiable—and a little disgusting. It let them feel how far they themselves had come from being what we still were. The Infanta and her dwarf—for contrast. Ghetto mentalities, Yiddish-speakers, whiners, *mussulmen*—the skeletoid walking dead of the camps—that's what we all were supposed to be. The world's most reliable victims: the first and last resort for persecution. Greasy, itinerant, superstitious. Am I to help it if your mother projected *her* family background onto *mine?*"

"Her family—"

"And tell her otherwise?" he snorted. "The background differences, yes. They were evident, anyway. Also, I could not always stop myself from speaking aloud the . . . enormity of my loss. Not people, not family, no. But an entire way of life. You could never understand that. A rhythm, a pace, of generations. Certain rituals—the opening night of the Philharmonic, the sound one's footsteps made on the marble of the Kunsthistorische, summers in Bad Ischl, winters on ski holidays in the

Austrian Alps, the spring excursion into Grinzing to sample the new wines . . . the young Schwartzkopf in concert the first time she dared attempt 'Im Abendrot' . . . the Ringstrasse, the Stadtpark . . . these things mean nothing to you. To us they *were* our life, leisurely, graceful, a commonplace beauty that gave form to the seasons. My great-grandfather was a surgeon-captain in the Austrian army—and he was not the first nor the last Jew to hold such a rank. My family was *Austrian,* you understand? Even more than that—*Viennese.* All of us— architects, surgeons, solicitors, professors. And the women— accomplished, elegant, able to draw nicely, to play at least one instrument, to dance charmingly, to preside over a well-kept home . . . These things I could not stop myself from saying aloud to Hope, as if I were mourning Kaddish like a devout simpering synagogue fanatic—which no one in my family ever was."

Julian stared at him. He rendered her a brief laugh, at ease in his bitterness.

"What little I did tell your mother only made me more pitiable in her American Jewish eyes. Lo how the mighty have fallen. I could hear it in her voice, suffused with a love only the powerful can afford. But destroy *all* of her pre-cut illusions? If she had known that I never, how you said it, crawled through the sewers of Europe, never was in or heroically escaped from a camp, would I then have been a sufficient victim? I think not, my dear. And there was something more. I had my pride. Which no one—not the peasant Jews of Europe, not Hitler's lack of discrimination, not your mother—could take from me. With that pride I survived. Not a crude pride of endurance, like the Orthodox peasant scurrying around beneath Cossack hooves. A pride of blood, a long line—"

"So you not only didn't love her. You loathed her."

"Oh, really. Such youthful excesses of language, such psychologizing. I was fond of her. Grateful, even. I could perhaps have remained a friendly acquaintance, except that—"

"A friendly acquaintance with your deserted ex-wife, the mother of your child? A *friendly acquaintance*—"

He rose to his feet, and for one terrifying second she thought he would order her from the room. But he turned, paced around his desk chair, and stared out the window. When he spun again to face her, she was confused by his expression—

what seemed a clumsy encounter between compassion and his features.

"Julian," he began softly, "you came here seeking some revelation, some happy ending to all your girlish fantasies. When you have lived longer, you may understand that there are no happy endings. But there are revelations. Some of them by their nature preclude the happy ending."

She folded the gloves in her lap and forced her hands to lie perfectly still.

"I do understand," she said evenly. "I'm not afraid."

"That is good. It is best to not be afraid of the facts. So then. I will take you at your word that you wish to know what there is to know."

He returned to his chair and sat down. She waited. All the years of waiting densified into this moment.

"So then," he repeated. "Your mother is not my ex-wife. Minna is not my new wife. Minna is my only wife. Your mother and I were never married."

Certain statements fall, through stratospheres of shock, with the gravity of the inevitable, as if always intuited, merely delayed en route to their eventual doom of confirmation.

"Minna and I have known one another since we were children in Vienna. Our families were old friends. We grew up together. We knew someday we would be married. We were already betrothed when the war came. She went to England, I came here. As soon as I could, I sent for her to join me."

"Did Hope know this?"

"No. That was not possible to tell her. You see, at first it seemed not necessary. Then, later, after I came to understand that she had been making all these plans in her mind—well, I still needed her. Then she claimed she was pregnant. So it became unavoidable not to tell her. She was of course upset. Her family was . . . hysterical. That I should marry her."

"And you? You weren't 'upset'? You felt no pity for her?"

"My dear child. We came from two different universes. We really had nothing in common. She wanted what little I still possessed: the education, the culture—and also the suffering. It would never have worked. I suggested she find an abortion, but she would not hear of it. It was her own decision. She had miscalculated, that someone whose world had been destroyed by the coarsest of people for the coarsest of reasons and through the coarsest of means, could still feel—pity."

"So you just—abandoned her."

"That is harsh. I suggested she not have the child. When she refused, what else could I do? At her request—her pleading—I did see the child. I know she thought I would be so moved by this monumental event that I would be overcome with love for both her and her offspring and—well, the happy ending. It was, instead, an unpleasant occasion, as I have said."

"And that was it? You never tried to connect with the child again?"

"It was too strained, too difficult. I had my own life to think about, to begin again from fresh. There was no way I could keep track of—"

"Actually, David, I would have been a hard child to lose track of. You can't possibly be unaware that at a certain point I was the most famous small person in this country?"

"I heard something about that. But I rarely watch the television, you see. And after all, it was none of my business. Even Hope, by that time, would not have welcomed my interest. The name had been changed—even from her own maiden name—since you had never borne my name. And, again, you see, I had my pride—"

"Yes. Your pride." Stung, she began to speak rapidly. "I'm beginning to understand. Tell me, don't your bastards carry the same bloodcells, the same genes of such pride?"

Had his expression not been so controlled, she might almost have imagined that he winced.

"I really can't say, my dear. One doesn't—"

"Follow them up. So how would you know, indeed. Or is it that you follow up the sons but not the daughters? Surely not those from peasant stock."

"Ach, my dear Julian," he laughed, "so you are the young radical, too. A television star, and also a revolutionary. How very American. Like President Kennedy. But perhaps that is more excusable in someone like you, only twenty years old. I too was once going to change the world. I almost became a communist, you know? It was the chic thing for Vienna intellectuals between the wars. Such fervor! Such self-righteous anger!" He chuckled, inviting her in as an accomplice in his bonhomie.

"But once in this country, you settled into the comfortable life of the bourgeoisie. You got over all that youthful idealism, I gather?" She heard her own sharp parry with the question, but her interior self was alive to something else he had said, something that had not even been aimed at her but which had penetrated fatally and was coursing through her veins, an embolism in the blood.

"Once in this country, I determined to survive and build a life here. I knew that even after the war would be over, Vienna —my Vienna, as I and my family had experienced it—would never be the same. I've been back to visit, naturally, many times since. But to be 'repatriated' and 'recompensed' like the merchant class, that was not for me. And today, well, there is a McDonald's hamburger-stand not far from the Belvedere Gardens. Not for me. No, I determined to survive *here*. More than survive—to prevail. That is why I changed my field from surgery to pediatrics. Caring for young life in this world . . . it seemed . . . positive. When I came to this country, you see, I learned that my medical education—the finest, in the world's most honored medical city—was not good enough for raw young America, so self-confident of its own destiny. It would have taken more years of being dependent on and possessed by your mother, to take the required additional courses and board examinations for surgery, my old specialty, than for pediatrics."

"And the latter was also easier, perhaps?"

"Easier? Oh my dear child—"

"Please don't call me that." The embolism still groping through the veins, approaching the brain. What was it he'd said, *what?*

"My apologies. It is a manner of speech. But 'easy'? Do you know, can you imagine, what it is to try and cure a child scientifically, despite the ignorances and superstitions of its mother? Her possessiveness, her lack of judgment? Her excessive alarm over minor illness and her self-deluding home remedies for major diseases? They *resist* you, these mothers. They ask for your help and claim to obey your advice—but they fight you as if to the death. It doesn't matter what age the child is, the mother—"

There it was.

"You said . . . something. A moment ago. You said something about my being a young woman twenty years old. You must have lost track of that, too, David. I'll be twenty *next* year. I'm just about to turn nineteen, a week from today."

She couldn't tell whether the astonishment in his expression was from her having dared to interrupt the direction of his thought, or whether it was the content of what she'd said. Then his eyes narrowed again and he leaned forward across the desk.

"No. You are about to turn twenty a week from today."

This was a direct engagement, a face-to-face duel, one she must win. For her mother's sake? For the few things she, Julian, had believed solid among so many shifting unrealities? Or was it one she hoped to lose—for the savage, awesome freedom it implied?

"I was born on October 7, 1942. This is 1961. I'm about to be nineteen."

"You were born on October 7, 1941. You are about to be twenty years old, Julian."

They stared at each other. Then he rose, strode to a filing cabinet across the room, took out a set of keys on a silver pocket keychain. He selected one and unlocked a file drawer. It took him only a moment's search to find the paper. Julian watched him, mesmerized.

"This is your birth certificate. Perhaps you have never seen it."

She started to speak, then stopped herself. How suddenly irrelevant to explain to him that there *was* no certificate, that there had been a fire in the city registry and all the records had been lost, that it had been necessary for Hope to swear a deposition to a judge years ago so that a new certificate could be issued. She stopped herself—one last helpless gesture of protection for the young mother whose despair, she now realized, must have been all-encompassing.

But there it was, in her hand. The real one, the original one, the one with the seal. Julian, female, born to Hope Baker, née Hokhmah Broitbaum; father unknown, October 7, 1941.

"It's . . . a strange feeling. To suddenly lose a year of my life."

"Your mother lied to you? You thought—?"

"No . . . No. She's . . . never lied to me. She—I think we both knew that it was helpful in my career. To, well, shave off a year. But as time went on I must have . . . lost track myself."

Not enough to have had your own radio program at age five; more precocious at age four. A whole year that you lived somewhere, somehow, doing what, utterly lost, vanished forever. To cover the shame of a woman who did the only thing she could do—pretend. Pretend the real into being, by pure will. And he speaks of pride. *Nothing* about you is real, Julian. You are a figment of the imagination of Hope Travis. You are a hallucination, an invention, a *golem.*

"Would you like to have this?" he asked gently.

"I—yes, I would."

"Keep it, then. I have no use for it. I do not know why I saved it all these years."

He began to straighten out small items on his desk. It was time to exit before the room spun completely out of control.

"Well. Thank you, David. For seeing me and telling me what you've told me. And, for this," gesturing with the paper. "I— wish you well."

"Thank you," he replied formally, "And—may I ask—what you intend . . ."

"I will never bother you again. I agree with you. Our . . . relationship seems irrelevant." She lifted her chin and smiled, both prides—her mother's and her father's—alive in that smile, but recognized by neither, nor by their daughter. "And I don't intend to tell Hope of this meeting. Not for a while, at least. It would only—distress her. So. Then. I'll be going." She rose to her feet, her eyes sweeping the room to record it a last time. "Oh, there is one thing more."

"Yes?" he asked, and with a final burst of longing in some vessel of the heart she thought she heard an eagerness in his question.

"David. Why does the man who only saw his child once and never 'followed up' still keep, ninet— twenty years later, her baby photograph framed in silver by his desk?"

If it could have been said—*I exist, look at me, tell me, let me know, speak it once and for all O my father, let free whatever shred of love for me you might have hidden all these many years*—if it could have been spoken, that which resonated in her question, poised waiting in her eyes, spined her whole body upright as she stood by the door of his office while her nerves hummed like tuning forks for his answer, *if.* If it was ever to be learned, let it be learned now.

He looked at the picture. When he turned again to her, his expression was tinged with what once might have been grief, and something else she could not perceive: the addictive self-contempt known only to a survivor.

"That photograph is not of you. It is of my son. He is three years younger than you. I am sorry, Julian."

"Thank you, David. For— Goodbye."

You smile, she directed herself. You exit with dignity. You thank Minna in passing, you do not break your stride, get out of this corridor now and this stained-glass door and to the street and walk in the general direction of the bus depot somehow you do it a bastard a year lost wiped clean out of your past a brother one child she'd said on the phone how could you have thought wishful hearing 1941 half-crushed insect a year the son he always wanted she was right she lied he never loved her never wanted you he lied she never wanted you a son she did want you she lied you were wrong wrong always wrong. The only real choice in your life is a choice between mendacities.

But by the time the bus deposited her back in New York, she had remembered that there was one human being on the planet in whom she could confide these bleeding new truths. One person who would hear her, understand, still be able to see something real, something Julian, in her. One person so scarred from his own bleak and violent family love that he would care. One person who knew that if you could turn it into something of use, into art, into politics—yes David damn you naïvely save the whole vile hateful lying ravaged bloodsick world with it—then you could do more than just survive it, callous and brutalized. Then you could understand it, forgive it perhaps. And not repeat it.

She ran to the first phone booth she saw after disembarking the bus, and dialed. Please god let him be in, please god.

The familiar voice answered.

"Laurence? Oh thank god you're there."

"Oh, hi, Julian. You okay?"

"Laurence. I—I need to talk to you. And Laurence, can we take that walk across Brooklyn Bridge you always said we might someday? I've still never been."

"Uh, yeah, sure, Julian. Wait a minute, you mean right *now?* Aren't you at work? Oh, I couldn't poss—"

"Right now, yes, right now if that's humanly possible. Please.

There's stuff I've—I've got to tell somebody. Meet me in fifteen minutes at the Manhattan side of the bridge? Please?"

And he said he would. And he wasn't lying.

He did.

CHAPTER SIX

Autumn, 1982

Emerging from her darkroom, Iliana de Costa blinked at the afternoon light slanting through her windows. Large, she supposed, bemused at the notion that windows of such size could be clucked over reverently in Manhattan, while they'd be considered average to small in Venice. There, her flat had cost one-quarter of the rent this one did, and had been almost three times the size. There, the incomparable light had lavished itself through floor-to-ceiling French doors that opened onto her terrace-balconies on the Riva degli Schiavoni overlooking the laguna. There . . . But what was the use of comparing? Venice was past. Like the Paris years. Like those in Barcelona, in Rome, and the abominable month in London, which she disliked almost as much as New York.

Yet here she was again, back in New York: this massive impersonal city where the light's repertoire was usually limited to charcoal through slate, the textures on which it fell flattened to steel, concrete, granite. What New Yorkers called "the" park, she thought, would not be "central" but one of several in almost any major city in the world, nor did she find this lack ameliorated by the scrawny trees pathetically lining some (only the more affluent, she noticed) blocks. This time, however, Manhattan seemed more tolerable than it had in that first devastating encounter with the city almost thirty years earlier, when she had arrived from Buenos Aires with the equivalent of twenty-five U.S. dollars in her pocket and not a soul to contact. The cherished Hasselblad had to be pawned after three days. Later, when she returned to retrieve it with her first week's salary from the factory job, the pawnbroker refused to honor her ticket. No use shouting at him in clear English; to him a Spanish accent meant a Puerto Rican and a drug addict. Nor would she assert that she was neither, feeling that would constitute a betrayal of the thirty-nine Puerto Rican women with whom she had shared that first week of hell, all of them hunched over sewing machines in one drafty room.

This time she had returned to New York in what they said was triumph. The reviews of her one-woman show at the Focus Gallery were uniform in their praise. Her work sold well. This time, all the cameras and lenses remained with her; no pawnbrokers need apply. This time, she could afford a high-ceilinged sunny flat in Greenwich Village, assemble her prized record collection from storage in three different cities around the world, purchase a fine set of components, and hear music again. This time, she was back as Iliana de Costa, and nobody dared ask why.

Nobody but Julian, of course—who had leaned across the table at their first lunch after her return last spring, inquiring earnestly just that: why had she returned, hating the city as she did? The answer had been easy enough, Iliana remembered, plumping down now onto her cocoa velvet couch, the still curling prints of her darkroom session in her lap for sorting: the Focus show, naturally. And then again, how weary she was of Venice.

Weary of Venice! Where every object extolled the light, which in turn wooed everything it caressed! But where the light never lingered its glance on Julian Travis. That, to be sure, she had *not* said to Julian. And never would say.

"Never." Iliana commanded aloud, an order to her solitary self.

But Julian lay now in her lap, new photographs, the first contact sheets from the session for the jacket picture of Julian's next book. Roll upon roll—she, who never descended anymore to "portrait photography," who had volunteered this, as a friend. And a flesh-and-blood Julian would be walking through the door in fifteen minutes.

Iliana cast a practiced eye around the room, then screwed her mouth up in a pout of distaste. Too little a space, too bland an architecture. Here, what had been the artlessly graceful dishevelment of her Venetian rooms became mere clutter. The Murano blown-glass vase on her coffeetable loomed too large for its setting and sparkled dully as if sulking at the quality of light it was given to reflect. Books, recordings, and tapes spilled over from their shelves onto every tabletop, onto some of the bentwood chairs, onto the floor itself. She could never find anything in this ridiculous flat about which everyone oohed and aahed. No space in the bedroom for a proper dressing table; her colognes and lotions had to balance, living dangerously, in the bathroom medicine cabinet or on the back of the toilet commode. No room in either of the postage-stamp-size closets for her Cerutti suits to hang without creasing, for the silk shirts to emerge without their sleeves fixed in freakish gestures—refugees from the work of a Diane Arbus, perhaps, not from a de Costa.

She sighed and poured herself a glass of sherry. The one worthwhile taste England had taught her—and *that*, she smiled, originated in Spain. Hot-dogs and pizza and garlic bagels learned from New York. Schnitzel and *Café mit Schlag* from Vienna. Fresh-baked baguettes and *café* with a *grande crème*, from Paris. Sensual pleasures. But no flavor like the *asado* from home.

Home. What an insipid notion, she reminded herself. If a revolution occurred tomorrow, she still couldn't return to Argentina. Even were there to be an end to the shifting military coups and corruption, *her* revolution would still be a long way off. As a woman, a Latin woman, a Latin woman artist.

She picked up the magni-viewer and began squinting at the contact sheets. Yes. And yes. There. Oh yes. She had caught it again and again, the quality Julian always tried to project but no one except she, Iliana, had managed to see, much less catch. Here it was, captured, an ultimate possession in black-and-white, forever. Smiling, serious, brooding-author-fit-for-book-jacket-shot, impish, sullen, enticing—*there:* laughing so hard as to be almost unrecognizable, smile unplanned, hair tousled to a loveliness no comb could elicit, throat arched back and free. Possessed. Iliana savored the memory of that session: of taking Julian as she wished, telling her what to wear, how to sit—then surprising her *between* poses, from every angle, the challenge of mating unhinted passion with technique to focus on this particular subject! It had electrified the result, as Iliana guessed it might. *This* perspective of that belovèd face was now forever Iliana de Costa's.

She sat back and sipped her sherry. It would be interesting, now, to see which of the shots Julian would gravitate to, as opposed to which she might ultimately pick for the bookjacket, which involved other considerations. But there would be a message in which print would shock its subject, rivet her, make her uneasy—deliciously so. Most interesting.

All the Julians, she concluded with satisfaction, were on these sheets, stripped bare by the perception of her lens, as if the subject of that lens herself, luminously naked, lay open, laughing, ready for love, on the bed in the small room beyond. At least all of the *so-far* Julians. The one she had first met almost ten years ago during her second New York sojourn—the period volcanic with Seventies politics and personal epiphanies—the Julian she had encountered in that early CR group, where the North American women were irritatingly astonished at how "feminist" a Latina could be. Patronizing *gringas,* she scowled. But there had been Julian. Who was not in the least surprised, who loved the writings of Sor Juana de la Cruz, whose eyes widened with recognition when Iliana mentioned that back home she had studied—the only woman student ever—under Enrico Martínez.

"The 'Latin Stieglitz'!" Julian had exclaimed. Then quickly added, blushing, "Oh, I'm sorry, Iliana. I didn't mean to define him in such ethnocentric terms." Amazing, for a Nordeamericana. Then, later, there had been all the other Julians.

Images poised one by one before Iliana's memory vivid as the contact sheets in her lap. She shut her eyes, the better to see them. She and Julian, the compulsive ones left at 3 A.M. after the rest of the group had begged off—husbands, kids, a hard day tomorrow—left alone to finish mimeographing leaflets for the next night's demonstration. The two of them giggling uncontrollably in karate class, to the frowns of their feminist classmates and the fury of the Sensai. The two of them, sharing literary and artistic bonds beyond what either shared politically with the rest of the group. The two of them, sometimes just walking around the Lower East Side—Iliana furtively snapping her camera at certain street faces, objects in the gutter, doorways of boarded-up tenement buildings; Julian learning to see with Iliana's eyes; Iliana refining her English by getting Julian to talk about poetry. The two of us, she remembered, comprehending each other across chasms of culture and language—finding in that an exhilarating victory, a promise for humanity. She opened her eyes and peered again at the spectrum of expressions in her photographs. The pity of it. Hidden somewhere behind those smiles there was a secret smile waiting all this time to fling itself across the face with an abandon no motive but desire could provoke.

But never. Never said and never would be said. Even though Iliana had more than once felt invitation was being given, clues dropped. Deciphering those clues, imagining a hidden reciprocity of obsession, could lead to lunacy, she had warned herself, and as her private passion for Julian grew, she resolved that the only way to banish the unilateral love but preserve the bilateral friendship was to go abroad again.

Not back to Latin America. She would return to Europe. It might heal her, as it had the first time. In Europe she had learned to see through an Old World sight, tearless with watching generations of revolutionaries, lovers, tyrannical idealists and their victims alike pass beneath windows leaded like half-lidded eyes—a gaze of jaded sanity, despair suspended daily more through acts of wit than will, a diffident altruism leavened by personal responsibility for one's own existence.

To this day she could remember the disappointment moaned by their group. Just *now,* to leave the States? When the movement was taking *off,* when press coverage of feminist issues had become *serious,* when Hispanic-American women were "getting involved" . . . Even more could she remember how forlorn Julian had been. But all Julian had said, wistfully, was,

"It will be hard for me, losing you. We'll miss you."

There it was again, the double-entendre code. "Hard for *me,"* but *"We'll* miss you." Was that the editorial "we," the speaking-on-behalf-of-the-group "we," the royal "we," or some hint about all the Julians in tandem? It was the confirmation Iliana dreaded: she must get away from Julian in order to get over Julian in order to love Julian safely.

So there had been Venice. *"Pas mal, pas mal de tout,"* Iliana murmured. Venice was decidedly a consolation for almost any loss. Her reputation had grown, and her financial means, and her capacity to enjoy herself. Venice had taught her that art was the only lasting revolutionary gesture, and that whatever helped her accomplish her art, made life more comfortable or more interesting, was not a luxury but a necessity.

Oh, if the old CR group could see her now! Sold-out hussy, they would grumble, running dog of a capitalist-imperialist swine! Well, who cared; most of them by now were probably back in bland suburbia, the remainder still clutching bleached denim "workers' " shirts to their downwardly mobile selves. Let any of *them* manage to smuggle film out of Argentina under the eyes of the notorious torture police. Let *them* work in a sweatshop without the benefit of a union, live through a bone-chilling New York February with no winter boots. Let *them* scar their vision with one-tenth of what hers had seen and recorded. Then let them discover Venice: sensual delight, and the personal "self-indulgence" which was only a fraction of what she might now avail herself if she chose. Because it was true that she still was more at home in her coveralls, pockets bagging with lenses and light meters, than in designer clothes.

There was only one problem in Venice. Even there she saw Julians: street-urchin small girls, militant feminists, intense women poets. Negatives. The original developed print remained in a far country but haunted her, the ghost of an exposure improperly set. There were the letters, too. Julian-on-the-page unconsciously knew how to give Iliana hope that the never-yet-manifest smile might one day dance, Salomé in a luxuriant *éclat*, across the real Julian face.

There had been distractions, to be sure. Work, laughter, diversions. Lovers. Two years with Beth, the Canadian expatriate who tutored English for a living, whose accent and political radicalism made her a temporarily satisfying Julian-surrogate. Then the aimless year: long sidewalk-café conversations with Giorgio about the futility of love. Her agent and confidant, he was the one person with whom she ever discussed Julian. Then the last two years, with Christina, a Latin and an exile like herself, but from Brazil—and as different from Julian as a glossy finish from a matte. That affair had expired finally when there were no more tempestuous fights to be stormed through. Iliana had tried the imitation and the contrast; both had their compensations, neither quenched the thirst. Venice began to feel played out, a stopover. It was Julian who had now become "home."

But Iliana waited. Everything she knew and was helped her wait: the exile's patience, the artist's discipline, the apostate Catholic's fatalism, the pride of the pampas *caballero*. She had waited without hope.

Until Julian's letters confided difficulties with Laurence, then mentioned him less and less. Until the loss of Giorgio, months of visiting the hospital as he wasted away, an early casualty of what they now called AIDS. When he died, carrying with him Iliana's secret, she found herself for the first time in years thinking about a return to New York. Then it came— the coup for which Giorgio had worked so hard but never lived to see:

"A one-woman show at the finest photography gallery in Manhattan," she muttered aloud through clenched teeth.

The justification.

The doorbell shrilled, announcing Julian. Iliana started with excitement—like an absurd schoolgirl, she thought. She forced herself to move calmly, sliding out from under the contact prints and carefully placing her sherry glass in its crystal coaster on the coffeetable. She could feel herself rapidly trying on a wardrobe of different smiles, despite the ripple of rage this realization sent through her. She glanced in the hall mirror, to see who Julian would see. Then she went to the door.

This would be the woman she had wanted more than she thought such wanting possible. For eight years. This would be the woman she loved now as tenderly as she might once have loved Enrico Martínez's aborted child. This would be her old comrade and friend. This would be Julian.

"*Querida!*" she cried gaily as she swung open the door and enveloped Julian in a hug, feeling the upper half of Julian's torso respond with warmth. The physical message of terror from a heterosexual woman to a lesbian friend: a peculiar spastic bend at the waist, a posture in the shape of a number 7, the lower torso kept arched away at a safe distance. She released Julian and stepped back, holding her at arms' length to have a look at her. "But you're fatigued!" she proclaimed immediately. "Come, right away, take off your things. Put down all the cases, little shopping-bag lady. Is it cold out? What would be good? Coffee? Tea? A drink? Have you eaten?"

The worn face smiled at her.

"Actually, I'd love a drink. No, wait a minute, better not. I have to finish an article tonight, no matter how long it takes. Better make that coffee, okay? Sorry I'm late—"

"Not okay. A *little* drink, just a mild one. Then coffee. And you eat something."

"Honest, not hungry."

"Ta ta ta." Iliana enunciated her nonsense words of dismissal with firmness. "I know what I say. A glass of burgundy gets the blood flowing. I promise that you will write your 'whatever' better, even if you have to stay up all night to do it, you workaholic."

"All right, I surrender, I give up," Julian grinned. She loves being gently bullied, Iliana thought, loves being taken care of. *Mi preciosa.*

"Oh!" Julian cried, spying the contact sheets on the sofa. "Is that *them?* I can't wait!"

"Oh no you do not, Juliana my friend," she yelled, rushing to sweep the sheets up onto her corner desk. "You just wait. Sit down on the couch and relax. I bring you a glass of friendly St. Emilion. You clear your fevering brain of whatever has made you tired, so you approach de Costa pictures with the clear mind and eye."

"Dear *dear.* I did *not* mean to offend the great de Costa," Julian answered, but the mischievous note in her voice already showed signs of recovery from exhaustion. "I'll be good and wait. But I'm *dying* to see them, you wretch!"

"Soon, soon. Patience is good for the soul," Iliana called from the kitchen. Swiftly she assembled a tray: the wine, a stem balloon glass, an oven-warmed baguette, a slice of truffled pâté, a crystal bowl of cornichons. She didn't like Julian's brittle-boned look. It brought back her own days in Paris, when to eke out a meagre survival as a model, she had sucked in her cheeks affecting high-fashion gaunt, all the while living on bread and coffee. "Sustenance first, comprehension after," she announced, bearing the tray into the livingroom.

"But I told you, I'm not hung— Oooo it looks delicious," Julian admitted, throwing Iliana the look of a child caught denying it wants to steal from the cookie jar.

"So, hunger artist, you can perhaps stoop to nibble something?"

Julian produced an exaggerated sigh. "For you, my dearest friend, only for your sake, shall I force myself to taste, chew, and even yea swallow, a morsel of this lowly fare." Then, changing voices to that of a gangster, "Outta my way, lady, unless you wanna get run over in my lunge toward that pâté."

Iliana's laughter rang out like a bell at matins. Every time she estimated what Julian needed and discovered herself accurate (despite any of the stated or unstated demurrals) was another sign, a nuanced promise that the Salomé smile was slowly, tantalizingly, dancing its way up to the surface of that face. She watched with satisfaction while the food was attacked. But between bites, Julian accused,

"You're not eating. I notice you're not having any wine, either. You don't practice what you preach."

"I *always* practice what I preach. That's how I learn what is good to preach and what is disastrous. But I've been drinking sherry. To mix sherry with burgundy is an insult to the sensibility, a confusion to the palate, and an invitation for revenge from the stomach. Although I might have a—'nish'?"

"Nosh," Julian laughed.

"Nish, nosh, of the pâté. *And* I make us some coffee. Since you insist on chasing this inoffensive St. Emilion with a blast of caffeine, what can I do?" She got up and went to the kitchen, pausing on her way to put a record on the turntable.

How could you convince someone like Julian of the necessity to feed one's own hungers as well as those of the world? She measured fresh beans into the coffeegrinder and flicked it on. Its roar drowned out the music from the other room, and the fragrance of coffee, as always, brought a pang of sense-memory from home. Denial, that's what it was, self-denial. A censorship of personal hunger—and not only for food—as pernicious as any government censorship. She filled the pot with water. Denial of hunger, of thirst. But when you tried to tell them, what happened? When you forced them to look at the faces of starvation in La Villa Miseria, Buenos Aires' worst slum, what happened? They suppressed your photographs, they censored you, they drove you away. She lit a flame under the coffeepot. How do you convince them that all the hungers are connected? How do you convince them so they don't drive you away?

She returned to the livingroom.

"Excellent," she nodded, glancing at Julian. "You must have been famished without knowing it, *pobrecita*. You are far too thin these days."

"Don't be silly. You know what they say: you can't be too thin or too rich. Well, I'm certainly safe from being rich. But it's the first time in my life I'm thin from not dieting." Julian mumbled out of a full mouth. " 'Course, it's a cloud-covered silver lining, that. The Grief Diet. I mean, I'm so damned busy or anxious or depressed or nauseated these days I don't have time to eat, much less appetite. But it's not intentional. If I croak from stress at least I'll be a glamorous corpse."

"You are too young to be planning your corpse-hood, my dear. Yoy, yoy, yoy," Iliana shook her head, "the incorrigible actress is among us. Listen to me. I mean it. You are getting bony."

"What? You want me to be the little roly-poly I was years ago in our group? Fat *and* miserable you want me to be, is that it? Some buddy *you* are."

"All you North Americans are obsessed with weight. Anorexia must be a national disease here." Iliana popped a cornichon into her mouth. "Food is a great sensual pleasure— not for gluttony, for discriminating delight. So, I might add, is flesh. And you need not have worried, *chica*, about a diet. You have a Flemish body, from the Dutch masters. A Flemish body and a Renaissance mind."

"And Walt Disney reactions: Gee. Golly. Gosh. Are you supportive! You sure learned your CR-group lessons well. Do you ever know how to make a girl feel better! And what," Julian shifted, "is that gorgeous music?"

"A new record from Composers' Forum I just bought today." Iliana noticed the resistance, the change of subject, and turned back toward the kitchen. "A woman composer with an unpronounceable name," she called back over her shoulder. "Just want to check the coffee. But it's marvelous, no? So eclectic. She uses everything—instruments, synthesizer, voice . . ."

She came out of the kitchen, carrying a second tray with two cups and a steaming pot of coffee.

"Anyway, I *do* know what I say," she persisted, edging the tray beside the first on the shrinking coffeetable surface. "Take it from one who has a Renoir body and a Quixotic mind— which is not a bad combination either, I might add. You should make yourself eat a little more, drink a glass of wine, enjoy some of the comforts life has to offer."

"So offer me one," Julian demanded. Then quickly specified, *"Now* can I see the contacts?"

The invitation. Then the caveat. Iliana smiled and proffered a damask napkin. "Now," she said, bringing over the sheets from her desk and placing them gently, like a gift of myrrh, in Julian's outstretched hands, *"now,* yes, you may have the reward."

Julian looked up at her.

"Iliana. I—I want you to know . . . I want you to understand that *I* understand what a great personal favor this is. I know that you never do this sort of photography anymore. I want you to know that I'm just—very grateful."

Iliana brushed the thanks aside with an indifferent wave of her hand which betrayed none of that hand's yearning to stroke the wisps of hair beckoning from Julian's forehead. She contented herself instead with a shrug, and settled down beside her friend, handing Julian the magni-viewer and saying casually,

"I wouldn't have volunteered the session if I had not wanted to do it. It gave me pleasure. So do the results. I hope they please you, too."

To watch the profile of that face, the neck like a lily stem bearing its small graceful head, light brown fronds of hair— that strange hair which in certain light, like this November dusk, was hazed through with a greengold gleaming . . . *mi corazón, mi sueño.* Little martyr, innocent of pleasures foregone as yet untasted, little ondine of the seagreen hair. What a luxury, this, to watch freely with justification expressions play across that face as it bent to perceive *her* perceiving of it, a wordlessly provocative communication. Julian began to smile. Then she laughed, then became grave, then smiled again. She glanced up at Iliana, her eyebrows raised in respect, then looked down again, drawn back to this irresistibly alluring cast of all the Julians as perceived by all the Ilianas. She began to murmur how fine they were, how remarkable, how extraordinary, how hard it would be to choose one for the jacket. Then she stopped her chatter and peered more keenly through the viewer, her body language changing, her surprise palpable. It was precisely the sequence Iliana had anticipated. There, yes, she saw it. She saw what Iliana had seen. Undeniable now. The photograph worth not only a thousand words but the one which cannot lie.

"My god," Julian murmured, "I've never seen this face before. I— I don't know this woman. It's—it's like a double. Can this— Is this really me? I mean, I know it's me, of course, but . . ." She looked up in awe. "I've seen literally thousands of pictures of me, 'Yana. From gurgling age two straight up through simpering sixteen, from young married matron to police mug-shot, feminist militant to studious poet. But I've never seen this woman. She's . . . she's beautiful," Julian's whisper was barely audible, "She's . . . she looks so *happy.*"

Break, my heart, not to touch her, enfold her utterly at this proximity, Iliana thought. She is seeing herself, penetrating herself with the eye of someone who has loved her for so long, in such silence. This may be the one offering she ever will accept from you, oh break my heart, break with this joy and this torture.

Julian's eyes were moist when she looked up again. "Thank you," she said quietly, "oh, thank you. I— it'll take me a bit of living with them to choose one for the jacket. What's here is, well, quite a lot to digest all at once. Oh, but thank you," she whispered again, "I'm . . . so surprised at what you saw."

"I've seen that for some time, my dear," Iliana answered lightly, "and also known that you had never seen it. That was one reason why I wanted to shoot the session. Perhaps I shall always see in you what you have not yet perceived in yourself. Perhaps the eye of de Costa, or just the eye of your . . . old friend and sister 'Yana, yes?"

"Yes," Julian nodded, her gaze returning magnetized to the images of a joyous, voluptuous woman who wore her own features but expressed no emotion she could recall feeling. "Yes," she repeated, "perhaps all of the above."

"Today, for example, I see sorrow shadowing the eyes, a hunger that cannot be pacified with fresh bread, no? A hunger for serenity. Do you want," Iliana probed, "to talk about it? Or better at this stage to not?"

She poured two cups of coffee and handed one to Julian. This simple kindness seemed to unhinge its recipient, who put down the cup and burst into tears. Iliana fetched a box of tissues, placed it on the table, and sat down again on the sofa, restricting herself to putting an arm around Julian's shoulders.

"What, *mi niña?* What is the worst of it? Is it Laurence?"

"Larry?" came the muffled reply. "Oh hell, poor Larry, what an unholy mess *that* is. We were going to change the world. We can't even free each other from our own ghosts. Intellectual and political equals, the new revolutionary woman and man. Don't make me laugh. At this point, he'd probably regard a gesture of love from me as pity and I'd probably construe one from him as need. Oh Christ, what I've done to poor Larry!"

"Julian. Forgive me, but I say this from the heart. And remember I have always liked Laurence immensely. From the first, he reminded me of my brother, the one who was 'disappeared.' "

"I know," Julian interrupted, stalling whatever Iliana's forthcoming insight might be. "He used to say you were the only one of the CR group with whom it was possible to have a civilized conversation. I remember," she sniffled, blowing her nose into another offered tissue, "the night I finally gave up and stomped off to bed while you and Larry sat up for hours dissecting Latin American politics." Julian hiccupped. "I was so glad, too. That he had a peer to talk with. That you respected him and—*understood* why I was married to such a person.— Especially since . . . Oh hell, 'Yana, you know the trouncing some lesbian feminists have given me for being a corrupt married woman."

"I know. You have been praised and you have been slandered. With me I would like for you to just be yourself. So that is why I tell you—reminding you that I have always liked Larry —that you have things sometimes out of perspective, and it does no good to either one of you. Remember that I too have loved certain men, so it is hardly for me to judge you. All this sophomoric Anglo-Saxon either/or bird-holing about sex—so tedious! Such a failure of imagination!" She paused. How to say this? How to say that homelessness was preferable to a denial of hunger, that freedom was no abstract concept but a sequence of exactitudes which included loving yourself—and whomever else you chose to love, when and where you chose

—without guilt? How to avoid old misunderstandings and new exilings for insisting that a woman's intellect, aesthetics, and sexuality were inextricable—a traditional enough idea, Iliana thought wryly, where a man was concerned? How to say this to Julian, of all people? As a friend. Carefully. Lightly. She adopted a conspiratorial tone. "You know, sometimes I think a secret heresy: that heterosexuality is a sign of youth, of altruism. A rite of passage. Every woman should indulge in it for a time—before she is ready to mature into the complexity of loving a woman." Carefully. As a friend. "But be that as it may —and Santa María strike me dead if *that* should become a political 'correct line'!—I must tell you that you are too hard on yourself. You defend Laurence, always Laurence. One must approach a subject from different angles. It takes two to destroy a relationship, you know."

Julian wiped her eyes. "Yes, but to paraphrase Solon or some other Greek, 'To a really good woman everything is her own fault.' Who said that? Socrates? Larry would know . . ."

"Whoever it was said 'man,' not 'woman'—and that *is* different, since most men do *not* assume responsibility and most women do. Beware Greeks bearing axioms, my dear."

Julian chuckled. A sign of life again. *I am good for her,* Iliana realized, a pod of sweetness bursting inside her with the discovery: thank you God for letting it be that I am good for her.

"What I try to say is," she continued, "that you have been defending him for years—way back in the group, remember? At first it was how wonderful and easy the egalitarian marriage was—"

"Oh but I—"

"No, let me finish. What an exception he was. Even when you finally spoke some of your other feelings, still you accused yourself, insisted *you* must be failing in some way. It was classic."

"But also true. He never meant—"

"Juliana. You forget that you and I were among the so-called pioneers of this thing called consciousness-raising? Don't pull this, what you call, bullshit, on Iliana. Listen, my friend, sometimes you are so into martyrdom I think you must have been secretly baptized Roman Catholic!"

This time they both laughed, but Iliana raised her hand to forestall another interruption.

"When you wrote me in Venice about your affair with the beautiful dummy—forgive me, I mean no disrespect to your art colony boy. But my dear, *really*. Well, I was amused—and glad—that you had at last exploded in some healthy human lust, little workaholic. But I admit I was also astonished that you wrote Laurence received the news so badly. No, wait, first I was astonished that you had to go and babble all to him. Again, my dear, really. All this whoring after honesty. Sometimes I want to scream, 'Hypocrisy, where are you? Come back, kind, sympathetic Hypocrisy, all is forgiven!' I might add that Europeans and Latins know how to do this sort of thing more gracefully. Still, you told him. That was shock to me enough. Then, the shock was compounded by his reaction. *Tiens!* I had believed this was the modern-day Bloomsbury couple! How can the standards be so different for *her?* Is then my old bohemian radical friend Laurence just as sauce-for-the-duck-but-not-for-the-hen, or whatever the saying is, as the average macho Argentinian male? *Holá!*"

Julian's shoulders tightened, and when she raised her head this time her eyes flashed with defensiveness. "You can't just simplify it to men, dammit, 'Yana. In certain ways of course you can. But don't let's pretend between you and me that women are paragons. We both know that relationships between women can involve the same agonies—possessiveness, jealousy, power imbalance—the same old what my dear departed Aunt Essie would have called 'dreck.' "

"Since when have women ever hurt you as much as men have?" Iliana countered, pouring out another round of by now tepid coffee and not noticing the temperature of the pot, preoccupied by the heat generated between herself and her companion.

"Women have hurt me more, in some ways. Because I'm no longer vulnerable to men. Except to Larry. But I don't think of him, somehow, as a man."

"That," Iliana snorted, "might be the problem. But perhaps you are just suffering from feminist burn-up?"

"Burn-out," Julian corrected listlessly. "Oh, you don't know, Iliana. That . . . *trust* from the early days, it's . . . I don't know where it went. Forced into externals; necessary ones, maybe. Into marching, I guess, and lobbying. Legislating. Building battery and rape shelters, fundraising, godknowswhatall. But at what cost. It's rare these days that I can talk to a woman the way you and I talk. With no . . . hidden agendas. I miss that. Terribly."

"The way you and I talked was always rare, I thought," Iliana submitted, stirring her cold black coffee with a gratuitous spoon.

"Sorry. You're right. But you know what I mean. *Women.*" Julian spat out the word as if it were a clot lodged in her lungs.

So it wasn't about Larry after all. Not the worst of it. It was older, more noxious than that.

"There are as many subtle tortures as there are torturers and victims," Iliana hazarded. "Tell me, if you can. If you wish to," she added softly.

"I'll tell you," Julian said in a rush, turning full face to her friend, "It's the hypocrisy everywhere. Go away hypocrisy all is *not* forgiven. Like at Athena. Their hypocrisy in how they survive, in why and what they publish. And mine, by god, in why and how I relate to them, and collaborate and reinforce and justify that. It's my own hypocrisy about—and *to*—Larry. It's my hypocrisy in knowing that you're attracted to me and have been for years—and my taking refuge in thinking that for me to name that would be megalomania. But *not* to name it is to play the cliché heterosexual woman who invites yet eludes the issue in counterfeit innocence. Hidden agendas. Damn right. It's my dying mother's hypocrisy—for years and years now—lying about my birth, my name, my age, her age, her illness, our 'fortune.' Which I at least thought would safely keep her in creature comfort until she died, never mind whether any was left over or not. So then, through my channels of spying on her since she won't see me, I learned two little stunners of fact: first, she has to go into a nursing home. The woman who looks in on her says she's worsening rapidly and that the doctor insists she have continual supervision. Second, I learned today—after two weeks of phone calls and meetings with her brokers and attorneys about which I won't bore you—that there is barely a penny left of my childhood earnings, which were according to her in the millions. Though if Hope stumbled and fell flat over a truth she wouldn't recognize it; for all I know I earned fifty cents total. Which has gone over the years into bad investments, apparently. The upshot— if you want hypocrisy—is that Julian, this loving wife who has destroyed her hubby, is now about to become the filial daughter who must sell her mother's apartment right out from under that lady, to pay for a nursing home and the medical bills. What's more, Regan-Goneril here must first *find* a suitable nursing home by touring one of the grimmest circuits of all: every old women's home in this city. Because I *won't* put her someplace where I can't visit her every day. If—" here the rage gave way and the voice broke into shards of pain "—*if* she'll see me, that is. *If* she'll recognize me. *If* I can find a place that's decent, humane . . ."

The sobs broke out again, but this time Iliana gathered Julian full into her arms, rocking her against her breast as she might have rocked a child. Be still, my heart, she thought, leave be for now the middle part of what your Juliana said aloud—that she knew, that she has known for a long time, that she loves her Iliana anyway. Be still, be still. Something stronger, more lustrous than desire, was kindling in that heart —a love she had whole lives and continents ago given up feeling, something chaste as her iconic childhood angels, something that glowed annunciation at her now through soot-streaked windows, a nimbus of *caritas* enveloping their *pietà*, suffusing her, widening her soul. Juliana.

"Hush," she crooned, *"carissima,* hush. Leave be. Leave everything be. We deal with one crisis at a time, yes? Nothing more need be said. For now, we focus on the mama, no? And if you let me, you do not go alone into those hell-holes. Iliana comes with you, stiffens the spine, makes you eat a little something, maybe even makes you laugh for a moment. And we find for the mama a good place, where she will be comfortable, where you will be at peace to have her. Together we go through what you've told me is her koo-koo flat and dispose of things and clean it up and put it for sale on the market, and that will pay nicely for as long as she needs the home. You'll see. All that is necessary is not to take oneself too tragically. I know what I say."

Julian blew her nose but didn't move from the comforting embrace. Her voice, spent, almost sleepy, floated up to Iliana from that ample bosom.

"God, you're good, 'Yana. How'd you get to be so goddamned wise? That's what I want to know. You're only six years older than me. It's mortifying."

Iliana's laughter bubbled out, a spring of contentment fountaining in her throat. "I did want always to be wise. I hardly think I have attained my goal. But sometimes I think I show a *bit* of promise, I do confess it. You do, too. Your sense of humor serves you well."

"But you . . . *clarify* things. You sort out the crazy from the sane, the real from the false. There's something so . . . *solid* about you."

Iliana gave Julian a playful shove away from her breast and thrust another tissue at her. "Santa Lucia! Don't start that 'what is real' whimpering again, *chica*. You go loco on the subject." She studied Julian for a moment. "I want to show you something." She went to the littered desk and shuffled through manila envelopes and cardboard binders. "Ah. Here it is, yes. Now look," she commanded, returning to the sofa and thrusting a photograph at Julian. "What is that?"

Julian saw a play of light dappling a progression of fine and then coarse-grained textures in a windblown pattern, an undulance of motion and shading. "It's ravishing, Iliana. It's, well I can't be sure, but I think it's a branch of a tree, isn't it? Is this from your Black Forest series?"

Iliana let out a small hoot of triumph. "Ha! So, Ms. What-Is-Real! *That* is a microphotograph of a human hair, my dear. And this?"

"An incredible fast-speed shot of a whirlpool," Julian guessed, her eyes beginning to sparkle with the game.

"Wrong again, you blind poet. It's a close-up of the gnarl, the —what is it called?—the *whorl*, in a cypress tree. And this?"

"Three strikes and I'll be out. Ummm, that must be a shot of the desert. A dune at sunset? Wow, is it breathtaking!"

"Breathtaking yes, desert no. It happens to be the line of a hipbone, nude female in dawn light."

"Ta ta ta," Julian retorted, raising her eyebrows roguishly. "Well who would have thought it."

"Certainly not you," Iliana parried with equal rascality. But the promise shuttered open again in her that Julian could tease this way. Gently, carefully, my heart. "You see," she went on in a restrained voice, "dear fool, 'real' is relative. All a matter of perspective, speed and exposure, proportion, shadow. Most of all, of light."

"In a photograph, perhaps. Life's not a photograph."

"To hell it's not. Even the sainted Marx said it was a moving picture, if not a still one. Look, my darling dense Julian. When I left Argentina, I did so by disguise. I think I never told you this. It's quite hilarious: I left as a nun, a virginal novice. The good sisters—the original ones, before the feminist 'sisters'—helped smuggle me out. Under those venerable robes were negatives and cameras and whatever else was really 'me.' It was most revealing, this concealment. Suddenly I was treated not as a woman, and not as a man either, but as a safe sexual cipher. I have gone to convent schools—and I assure you that nuns are not sexual ciphers," she injected with a twinkle. "But a totalitarian country had as unyielding a perception of religious fanaticism as of political fanaticism. I should have expected that. Don't forget, I grew up with both the myth and the reality of Eva Perón. I was seventeen when she died. And she was neither the demon nor the angel she has been depicted as being. She gained divorce rights for women—and the vote. Even if it *was* always as appendage to Juan. She also did collaborate in his fascism. She affected us all, deeply, with her peculiar magic. Evita, my dear"—she chucked Julian under the chin—"was an unregenerate actress who turned political."

"Thanks a lot," Julian moaned.

"Ah, listen, gloomy one. Sometimes a disguise is the emergence of a new skin, as an old one is being cast off. To change, to grow, that can feel 'unreal' because it's unfamiliar, don't you *see?* Dear idiot," she sighed impatiently, "there's a Malraux line I once memorized, from *La Condition Humaine*. In English it would be something like: 'A costume is . . . sufficient to permit one escape from oneself, sufficient to find an entirely different life in the perception of others.' You say you know of my attraction to you, and we will perhaps speak of that another time—no, not now." She raised her voice against Julian's reply. "*No*. Believe me. But my point is that I didn't see you on the television when you were a baby star or whatever; I hadn't even read your books when I first met you in our old group. I had no preconceived notions of Julian Travis. It was *you* I saw. You I still see," gesturing toward the contact sheets, "and you I will always see, no matter how you try to hide from me. It's no special virtue on my part; perhaps it will be my doom, who knows? I can't help it."

"I wish I could—"

"*I* wish you could love Julian as I love Julian. That simple. I'm only afraid that, *not* loving her as you do, you nurse a secret contempt for anyone who does. I should not like to be the target of that contempt."

Julian stared at her.

"So that is why I tell you it would be a mercy to everyone all round, I think, if Julian were to love Julian just a little, not with her ego but with her heart; a mercy to her poor mother, to Larry, to me. But most of all to Julian. This 'self-lessness' is an evil word, if you think about it. Ayee, *mi amor,*" Iliana urged, "don't you see! After Eva Perón there was Isabel Perón trying to become Evita! We *all* invent ourselves, every minute of every day! That's all there is!"

The room was blue now with dusk. Iliana heaved herself up from her place beside her stunned visitor and snapped on a lamp.

"So," she cleared her throat. "A little wine, food, coffee. A little visual art. Some basic consciousness-raising. And a Latin sermon. Are we feeling better?"

"Much better, thank you, 'Yana." But Julian still stared, unmoving, at the space Iliana had vacated beside her.

"Then I think it's time you better go and plunge into the whatever article—in which, no doubt, you will tell other women what they should do to love and liberate themselves."

Julian looked up at her sharply, then one corner of her mouth twisted into a grin. "Yeah. Charlotte Kirsch—she's a friend, works at Athena—told me once that I ought to drop my preachiness and instead write out all this chronic crisis as a TV play. That was almost a year ago; by now it would be a miserere miniseries." She rose and stretched. "But you're right. The article awaits. Come back, Hypocrisy, all is forgiven!"

Slender fragile strength in that body. Subtle, resilient strength in that mind. Flemish body and Renaissance mind, my own private primavera, pure and impure, *mi mujer* whom I love enough to refuse myself to, you whose proximity intoxicates unknowingly, intentionally. Careless seductive cat who mourns yourself as declawed when your talons sank themselves long ago into my vitals. My Juliana.

They walked to the door and Julian shrugged into her coat.

"Holá! I forgot. I have a present for you. Hold there for one minute." Iliana returned with a bottle of cologne and tucked it into Julian's satchel. "It's Amazone. You always comment that you like it when I wear it. So this time when I got myself some, I got some for you."

"Oh 'Yana—"

"Ta ta ta. It gives me pleasure. And maybe it will remind you that even if life isn't, how do you call it, a bowl of rosebuds, still, a pleasing fragrance now and then, a mellow wine, a little laughter . . ."

Julian turned in a blur of hall light and flung her arms around Iliana, the whole body this time, no part held back in fear.

"Dearest friend, I love you and respect you and am more grateful to you than I know words for. I've never in my life been so . . . taken *care* of. All your generosities—the photographs, the thoughtful little gifts, the offer to help with Hope. Even just listening to me, letting there be one place where I can pour *all* of it out. The wisdom you give me. *And* the pâté, too." Iliana could feel Julian's breath warm with laughter against her ear. Then Julian drew back and peered at her.

"De Costa," she said, "you know how to love. You're a cornucopia, spilling energy. Thank God for you in my life, de Costa."

Hail, heartbloom, full of grace, tower of ivory mystical rose, be still, be still. She took Julian's hands in hers and said simply, "It matters. And it's possible."

One look. Then Julian whirled and was gone.

Iliana stood gazing out into the apartment corridor, past the doors to the other flats, and heard Julian's footsteps pad down the carpeted brownstone stairs. She shut her own door and leaned against it, feeling her heart pound through her body—throat, wrists, genitals, knees. Then she went to the bookshelf, sought and found what she wanted, and carried *The Revelations of Divine Love* by Juliana of Norwich over to the lamp. The book opened naturally to the heavily underlined passage she so loved: "I saw no difference between God and our substance, but saw it as if it were all God . . . virtues come into our soul at the time it is knitted to our body. In this knitting we are made sensual . . . Thus I understand that God is in our sensuality, and shall never move away from it . . . We cannot be entirely holy until we know our own soul—and that will be when our sensuality . . . has been brought up into the substance."

Yes, she decided, moving to the window and watching the

figure diminish in the fading evening light, bent into the wind, that is my belovèd. It mattered not to her, the real story of Julian's name which she had been told years ago, even before genderless names became fashionable in the women's movement: how Hope had expected a son and chosen the name for its assimilative elegance, and because of the Huxleys, whom Hope had read in her brief sojourn at university. How the mother had kept the name for the son born a daughter, as if to feminize it would signify defeat. None of that heritage mattered to Iliana. This heavily marked passage of devotions, she believed, was the true heritage of Juliana, the name that chimed with her own, and one that she, Iliana, had been sent to reveal—the annunciatory angel.

Julian's figure had become barely more than a speck in the Goya-blue street, then it turned a corner and disappeared. But if, with that vanishing, the last of the light seemed to drain from the sky, Iliana could now believe in the return of dawn. Even in such a city—the renewal of radiance.

"Mi Juliana," she prayed aloud to the descending darkness, and pressed the book close to her breast, where that head had lain, in a momentary peace.

CHAPTER SEVEN
Winter, 1982–1983

"Family"

A Television Drama

Time: A winter evening   Place: A Chelsea loft in New York City

Cast

Julian Travis	Elizabeth Clement
Laurence Millman . . .	Lansing Harris
The Mother	Hokhmah Broitbaum
The Child	Julie Traumstein

Assorted Extras and Library-Morgue Film-clips

(Fade in on close-shot of woman's hand pressing a doorbell, then pick up sound of a buzz-back. Widen out to medium-shot of Julian, carrying suitcase, letting herself in on the buzz-back and starting to mount a flight of loft stairs. Cut to: Laurence, at upstairs loft door, looking down anxiously. Pick up perspective from behind him, angle over his shoulder, as Julian enters the loft, moves past him without embrace, then drops her suitcase. Widen to two-shot:)

Laurence:

What happened? Why'd you ring instead of using your key?

Julian:

I seem to have lost my key. Maybe it just slid to the bottom of my bag, but I couldn't stand on the street all night trying to feel for it in the dark.

(Rapid flash-cut to close-shot of a wedding
ring, then flash-cut to The Mother yelling
"Use your key!" Cut back to two-shot of
Laurence and Julian:)

Laurence:

Oh. You're real late.

Julian:

I know. Sorry, Lare. The plane circled for half an hour—

Laurence:

You hungry? I got take-out Chinese, but I don't think there's much left.

(Pan Julian as she moves toward sofa, then
seems to change her mind and sits in
overstuffed chair, lowering herself heavily:)

Julian:

No. Thanks. Just want to sit and never move again. A coma would be nice. Fed intravenously, other people responsible for my vital signs and bodily functions. Deliberate consciousness-lowering.

(Widen angle to show Laurence come over,
hesitate, then sit on sofa opposite her.
Medium two-shot:)

Laurence:

I know what you mean. *(A pause.)* Mail's on your desk.

Julian:

Can't cope with it right now.

Laurence:

The, uh, phone calls . . . well, I've been ignoring the phone for about three or four days. On Monday the utility company called—some Mr. Fiorno or something. Says we're a month overdue, if the bill isn't paid in five days they'll cut us off. Told

him you were away and I, uh . . . I said I was just staying here.
Said I'd give you the message. Then I decided to hell with the
phone and didn't answer it anymore. Nobody ever calls for me,
anyway.

Julian:

(Eyes closed, wearily:) Okay. Okay.

Laurence:

(They sit in silence for a long pause.) So. How'd it go.

Julian:

Usual. I arrived to find Middle Cal State had titled my speech
"Gender Roles: Progress in the 1980's and Beyond." They
knew I was going to cover rape, battery, child molestation,
poverty, the works. Plus do international issues like genital
mutilation, suffrage, dowry murder, and and and. Gender
Roles my ass. What a euphemism. Revolution has become a
dirty word all over again.

(Cut to Laurence:)

Laurence:

Yeah. But the audience liked it, huh? I mean—

(Cut to Julian:)

Julian:

Oh sure. There's always that moment of connection, like an
electric charge. But these days you get the feeling you're a
radical fix that'll wear off soon after you leave town. *(She sighs.)*
And there was the other moment, good ol' reliable. Just as I
was finishing the talk, a young woman leapt to her feet—
unfaded blue jeans, newly hacked-off hair, combat boots still
shiny from the army-navy store, uniform complete—and heck-
led, "How can you call yourself a feminist and still be married?" Little did she know how major a part she plays in keeping this marriage defensively intact merely by virtue of her
opposition.

(Cut to Laurence, close-up:)

Laurence:

Thanks. That's a helluva thing to just walk in and lay on me.

(Cut to Julian, close-up:)

Julian:

(Wearily, as if by rote:) Sorry sorry sorry. Didn't mean it that
way. Just meant it's such special purgatorial fun—being virtu-

ally the sole publicly known married radical feminist "spokesperson."

> (Wide-angle shot, while Laurence rises
> abruptly, goes to cupboard and pours himself
> a shot of brandy. Cut to close-up of Julian
> watching him. Her face changes to guilt with
> a fleeting shade of panic:)

Larry, all I meant was— Oh shit, you *know* what I mean.

> (Cut back to two-shot, as he wheels on her,
> angry:)

> Laurence:

You think it's paradise being my half of some model feminist marriage? I just wanted us to be *us,* not worshipped or attacked or made goddam responsible for anybody else's life. So here we have me—remember *me?*—who thought feminism "made sense." Shared housework, shared politics, save the world, all that crap. But who began to realize, somewhere back in the Pleistocene Age of our coupledom, that all the changes I've gone through would never be sufficient. The affirmative-action *feminist* double standard—which in less civilized days used to be known as revenge.

> (Cut to two-shot:)

> Julian:

What's the *matter* with you? Why are you dumping this on me when I'm barely through the door?

> Laurence:

(A beat, then:) I got fired from the station.

> Julian:

Oh my god. Oh Larry—

> Laurence:

Mr. Shit-for-Brains, our program director, decided I should be the vanguard of the cut-backs. Just like that. Nothing political about his motivation, of course.

> Julian:

They can't do this to you. We'll fight it. I'll call him first thing in the morning—

> Laurence:

I don't want you coming to my rescue. I don't want your tactical advice, either. It works fine for you but when I adopt it it turns rancid. Like the time you advised me not to take on being co-director of the Mobilization Against Poverty campaign because a woman should get the job and because the other director was Winston Peterson and *he's* a notorious *sexist.* Not only would that have given me back a national forum, but it was a year-long project—with a salary, I might add. Then you managed to lower yourself to speak at the same rally with old Win—because "it was important that a feminist presence be there."

Julian:

That's not quite how it— Larry, be fair.

Laurence:

Why? You wring your hands over my predicament and tell me how "Life is unfair." You confuse life with yourself, Julian. The two are not necessarily equivalent.

(He drains his glass. Cut to Julian, biting her
lip. Then, in a controlled voice:)

Julian:

Larry? Don't let's do this to each other. I'm beat, and I know you must be flattened by this double-cross at the station. It's rotten. Maybe we can both think more clearly tomorrow. I know there must be *some* way to fight it. If you don't want me involved, okay, fine. But—well, one way or another . . . something'll come up, you'll find something else, or—

(Cut to two-shot, as Laurence leans forward
from the sofa:)

Laurence:

Oh for crying out loud, Jule! Cut the crap! Little Ms. Supportive! Go write out more checks to the women's movement. Leave me in peace. Go sit for another session with Iliana, so she can drool over the object of her lust. Another book, another jacket photo, another admirer to feed your omnivorous ego.

(Cut to tight-shot of Julian's hands gripping
the arms of her chair. Quick cut to Laurence
in close-up, wincing at what he's just said.
Quick cut to Julian, her jaw tightening:)

Julian:

Watch it, Larry. I'm so tired I might say what *I* feel for once. Don't take out your wretchedness on me. *Or* on the one friend I can trust.

(Cut to Laurence, seeing it's too late to take it
back, unable to stop now:)

Laurence:

Wow, I'm pleased to know that twenty-one years together
don't earn us a friendship we can trust, whereas the properly
credentialed Third World dyke can waft in out of nowhere and
become the one friend you can trust. Sorry about the boring
decades of commitment, ma'am. I guess I haven't washed
enough dishes, given back to you enough flattering images of
the great Julian Travis to qualify.

(Quick cut to Julian:)

Julian:

God *damn* you, Larry! Iliana's not your rival, *you* are! I'm still
so gripped by the person you *were* and could *still* be that I can't
confront the you that *non*-exists *now!* I'm so bloody tired of
bottling up my rage I could burst! The fact that I'm so *little*
potentially lesbian has helped me stay with you in spite of
enormous pressure from within *and* from without. And you
know it!

(Widen to long two-shot, to emphasize the
space between them and their smallness in
the loft livingroom. Julian buries her face in
her hands, but the voice that comes out of
her leaks rage:)

Iliana *loves* me—and she knows how to *show* it. She's never
approached me sexually, though Christ knows what that's cost
her. The so-called flattering images she gives back to me happen to be of a me I've never *seen* before—

(Cut to Laurence, his rage open now, meeting
hers:)

Laurence:

—not dreary and drained by *me,* I suppose. No, for me you save
the tight-lipped long-suffering saint face, the silent accusation.
Never once in over twenty years celebration never . . .

(Bring down his voice level to barely audible
except for the refrain of "never," and fade up
superimposed over his furious face montage
clips in fast-paced sequence:)

You never trusted me. Never loved me. Never let your tight puritan self go with me. You always held back. There are places in me you've never touched, never dared reach for. Never never never . . .

> (Montage: Julian and Laurence flat on their backs in bulky coats, lying on snowy ground, waving their arms and laughing wildly. Dissolve to: Laurence and Julian, hammers in their hands, flailing at tearing down a wall in the loft, giggling at one another through clouds of plaster dust coating their hair. Begin rapid montage: Julian tearing herself out of a helmeted cop's clutches and racing toward Laurence, who is being nightsticked by another cop; Julian running offstage from a lecture into Laurence's arms where he waits in the wings to welcome her with a hug; waist-shot of young Julian sitting cross-legged on the loft floor, looking up at Laurence with adoration; Laurence and Julian striding down the street, arms around each other, singing at the top of their voices; Julian at stove, stirring, as Laurence comes from behind and embraces her; Julian naked in bed, her arms lifted, reaching up. Dissolve montage down and bring up Laurence's close-up face and voice:)

Never a moment of joy never a simple giving of the self never a trust! *That* you save for others! That was never on the Larry Agenda, never.

> (Cut to close-up of Julian, dry-eyed with equal fury:)

Julian:

Sorry I was such a failure as Mrs. Red Menace, not providing you with rose-covered wife, child, home. Poor little boy, terrified of his daddy, lonely for his momma, out to change the world *not* to save humanity but because he was scared shitless of functioning minimally in it as an adult.

> (Medium two-shot:)

Laurence:

(His face contorting deliberately:) Gribbitz.

Julian:

What did you say?

Laurence:

Gribbitz. Gribbitz grunt oink gribbitz.

Julian:

Are you insane or what? What are you *say*ing!

Laurence:

Croak. Gribbitz. It's no good talking to America's Darling; she's deaf to anything but praise—except when she's doing self-lacerating self-criticism in order to co-opt anybody else from it. So I won't talk. The Feminist Prince is dead. Long live the Frog. Gribbitz.

> (Julian rises. Dolly back to show her starting
> toward her suitcase.)

Julian:

I won't descend to this. I'm going to bed. Maybe tomorrow we can talk in real lang—

> (Laurence follows her, shouting:)

Laurence:

Gribbitz! Croak! Gribbitz!

> (Julian spins to face him. Fast up superimpose
> shot of The Mother's face, screaming with
> anger, then Julian in close-up, her features
> following the same lines:)

Julian:

You wanna croak instead of talking, then *I'll* talk, by god. Except it's hard to know where to start, considering all the items I've shredded in the Unspeakable Bin for years—

> (Cut to close-up of Laurence:)

Laurence:

—and saved like stored-up ammunition for just such a moment! The little martyr shows her hand? The victim picks up the electrodes she's actually wielded all along?

> (Cut to: rapid montage of students rioting in
> the street, throwing Molotov cocktails; The
> Mother's face; a Chinese mother binding the

feet of a weeping child; The Mother's face; a *chador*-garbed figure spreading the legs of a girlchild and bending over her with a razor to clitoridectomize her; The Mother's face. Bring up close-up of Julian, spitting venom now:)

Julian:

It's time. *Time*, Laurence. Time you grew up and became an adult. Time you hung up your clothes. Time you hung up your clothes. Time you answered your mail. Time you earned a living, yeah. Time you remembered to do a laundry yourself without it getting so bad I have to remind you we don't have any clean clothes left. Time you came out of catatonia and made some contacts which could actually godforbid I know the thought alarms you come through with some actions, projects, better jobs for a change. Time you learned how to wash a glass *clean*, not just as a reward for nagging old me. Time you stopped leaving dirty sox and shoes and underpants strewn through rooms that I happen to share—which do *not* contain piles of *my* clothes all over the place—

(Cut to two-shot:)

Laurence:

This whole *loft* used to be mine! First we had to tear *down* walls to accommodate the great Travis. Then the terms changed and we had to *build* 'em so *you* could have a study. Now we have The Julian Sector. The Laurence Sector.

Julian:

(Undeterred from her assault:) Time you learned that the dropping and breaking and losing of tools and cups and gloves isn't a cute trait but shows stupidity and contempt for other people's consideration, comfort, even basic rights. It's time you *noticed*, after twenty years, where the wooden spoons go in the kitchen, and where the knives go. If you don't like their placement, *say* so and *change* it. But the truth is that all along the Feminist Prince has been too froggishly busy proclaiming allegiance to the abstract politics to give a shit for such "petty" details!

(Top-shot down from catwalk, showing each of them isolated in a pin-shot of intense light,

the room around them now in darkness. They
face each other as adversaries.)

Laurence:

You're a loveless robot. You're a leech. Christ, you've stolen my
soul! What'd you do, fold it and put it away in a drawer 'cause I
left it lying around somewhere?

Julian:

For that matter, it's time you goddamned learned how to take
decent criticism—and I *mean* decent. I'm sick of your emotional blackmail in claiming that any criticism of you at all
undermines your frail self-confidence at this point in your frail
life! Which has been for *years*. It's time you actually put
records back in their jackets. Every time I want to play some
music, I find records—some of which I had before I knew the
eternally promising young Lenin, Laurence Millman, and others of which I went to delighted lengths to acquire for you—
left in heaps, scratched beyond use, or stacked on the floor with
cat-hair crudded over them. Because you apparently believe
in vacuuming only on the equinoxes and solstices. This isn't
fragility. It's *plain male bullshit and laziness*. It's *time* you put
the toilet seat down, don't you think? *Time* you changed the
bed linen *on your own*, without its being a major production or
waiting until the bed is ready to get up and walk or *out*waiting
my waiting to see if you'll notice until I give up and finally do it
myself. Petty, *petty* complaints. Just like "The Politics of
Housework" noticed so long ago in some damned feminist
anthology or other. Just like you yourself proclaimed on the
radio in order to receive the curtsyed praise of feminists,
grandstanding for the sake of appearances!

(They circle each other, combatants. Cut to
long-shot of them pooled in reddening light:)

Laurence:

Appearances! Look, *look* world! *(He spreads open his arms in
appeal to invisible witnesses:)* Look who's talking about appearances! This is *real life*, Julian! It's scummy and unromantic!
It's filled with shit and piss and cum! It ain't pretty! And Julian
Travis is *not* the star of it all, with everybody else relegated to
playing Rosencrantz or Guildenstern or Hope in her various

ugly faces or the phantom daddy David! People live and work and get depressed and try again and fail and have kids—

> (Quick flash-shot of The Child, about age
> three, running laughing through a park; cut
> to close-up of Laurence:)

—and love and suffer and die! You go through life like some infant yowling for its mommy's arms,

> (Quick shot close-up of The Mother's face,
> smiling, suffused with love; cut back to
> Laurence:)

some infant lying in its crib while the muscles in its face try on expressions it doesn't even know how to feel yet. I've *watched* babies, I know! *(Laurence begins to cry.)* I'll never have one of my own, I know that. I know I'll never be a father. But I watch 'em—in the street, in carriages and strollers, in the supermarket carts—other people's kids, other people's lives, other people's . . . *(He breaks down and sobs.)*

> (Dolly in to loose two-shot of them standing,
> his head hanging like a beaten dog's. She too
> cries, soundlessly. Slowly, as if heavy weights
> were attached to each wrist, she raises her
> arms toward him. As she touches him, he
> changes, lifts his head, and snarls at her:)

And I don't want your pity-garbage, either. Why are you *doing* this to me? You wouldn't *be* who you are if it wasn't for *me!*

> (Flash-shot of The Mother's face, shouting,
> crying; quick cut to Julian in close-up, her
> expression hardening. She yanks back her
> hands as if singed.)

Julian:

Why am I doing this? The question I've asked myself for the last ten years of our exercise called a marriage. For love? Larry, you wear down my love day after week after month with your sulks and your fourteen-hour depressive sleeps. For sex? Don't make me laugh, I might get truly hysterical!

> (As she continues the following J'accuse, her
> voice level drops to almost inaudible, with
> only the emphasized words coming through
> clear; her image fades in slow dissolve as we

get another rapid montage: a younger
Laurence in tight close-up, smoking a pipe
and talking; Laurence in blue jeans and
T-shirt dancing with a broom; Laurence
chairing a meeting, looking at Julian suddenly
and grinning; Laurence shouting into a
bullhorn, finishing to rally-cheers, turning to
Julian with a roguish wink.)

Does it never occur to you that whenever you express interest
in what I'm doing, it's in the power and public aspect of what I
do for our survival? You love what you attack me for: *appearances.* The same tacky kid doing her tap-dance Portia routine
to support another version of the same loving *family* which in
turn will claim it has Given Its All to Make Her What She Is
Today. That's not *me.* I have my own business being alive on
this planet and in this skin and in this brain—and it's *not* to
provide *you* with a lifelong fellowship-grant and confidence-
boosting. *Never, never, never* consideration from *you,* never
any courtesy, any kindness.

(Montage continues: Laurence giving Julian a
back-rub while she sits at her typewriter;
Laurence hauling shopping bags of groceries;
Laurence presenting a bunch of flowers from
behind his back with a flourish; Laurence
grabbing the telephone receiver out of
Julian's hand as she sits weeping, and hanging
up with a bang; Laurence interposing his
body between Julian and three white men
menacing her in a civil-rights march:)

Never never any communication or intimacy anymore

(Montage: Laurence and Julian in a rapid-fire
series of two-shots at different ages over the
years—hunched together over an open book,
necking on the floor before a Franklin-stove
fire, walking together down the street—
always animatedly talking, talking, talking.)

God! The *waste,* the living death of this situation! I'm so tired of
being the decider, the doer, the energy source, the strong one!

(Quick flash to The Mother's face, and bring
up fragments of her words: "He's a weakling!

They all are! You could be anything you
want!")

I could be anything I want! I don't have to choose this death-in-
life that began with you!

> (Rapid cut to Laurence, stunned, his face
> turning almost unrecognizable with hurt and
> hate:)

Laurence:

Began with *me!* You began it! I was a full and happy human
being before you!

> (Quick flash-shot to Laurence in bed, angrily
> turning away from Joyce, who stands crying,
> her outstretched hands open in a plea.)

I began it? *You* began it!

> (Tight combination shot, first of Laurence
> over Julian's shoulder, then of Julian over
> Laurence's shoulder:)

Julian:

You began it!

> (Rapid montage: street riots in Northern
> Ireland; Arabs lining up at West Bank
> checkpoint for strip search; missiles rising in
> silos. Both their voices at the same instant,
> crying out in voice-over:)

Laurence voice-over:

Jule!

Julian voice-over:

Larry!

> (Quick dissolve to loose two-shot again, wide-
> angle of them still circled by darkness. The
> light cools from red to blue-violet. Julian and
> Laurence freeze. Superimpose over their
> figures, in slow-motion, lyrical, soft-focus: a
> younger Laurence and Julian walking over
> the Brooklyn Bridge and following the action
> described in the ensuing voice-overs:)

Laurence voice-over:

We finally walked over it, the great keening Brooklyn, the span of passage. She phoned me in her despair and shock, the child of her trying to balance gamely on Hope's quicksand of lies. And I went with her—

Julian voice-over:

—hand in hand under the Gothic arches through the hum of energy along steel ropes expertly stretched to carry whatever weight necessary without breaking—

Laurence voice-over:

—that was the day after, I remember. After the night I'd seen Joyce again, for the first time in three years, and knew I still wanted her. Told her I'd finally even marry her now. But it was too late. She told me it was over. For all time. And I went into hell and finally fell asleep after dawn—

Julian voice-over:

There was one human being on the planet who could understand, still be able to see something real about me. One person who knew that if you could turn it into art, turn it into politics, save the whole vile hateful lying brutal bloodsick world with it, then you could forgive it, not repeat it—

Laurence voice-over:

—but how could she have known? Feral child, driven by her own loss: "I need to talk to you," she said, "Can we—

Julian voice-over:

—walk across the Brooklyn Bridge like you always said we might someday? I've still never been."

Laurence voice-over:

Tidal wave, ship's prow bearing down on me while I was drowning, no way to resist her.

Julian voice-over:

"Meet me in fifteen minutes on the Manhattan side? *Please?*"

Laurence voice-over:

And to my own astonishment, I did. Heaved myself up from my bed of mourning and I did. Whatever words poured out of her that day, I hardly heard. I was too busy seeing her: ship's figurehead into the wind, hair rushing backward like plumes from the warrior-queen helmet of her skull. The wise child who knew enough to want something different from what she'd been trained to want. The virgin who'd trusted me and already given herself into my hands. The friend who loved me. Seeing her as if we'd just met. The raw possibility of her, vibrating—

Julian voice-over:

We swayed toward each other, so slowly. And the Bridge swayed in the wind. And the gulls wheeled bloodwinged in the twilight, and the towers of the city loomed toward us in envy. Everything—bridge arches wings waves current concrete granite translucent grains of air everything yearned toward us at that moment, toward who we were and who we might become—

Laurence voice-over:

—where we stood, eye to glistening eye, mouth against mouth, body to body shaking with the wind and the force of that touch. And I said

Laurence:

Julian—

Laurence voice-over:

"Julian," I said. "Julian," shouting above the wind and the shrieking of the gulls, "Julian," I yelled in recognition in full joy and never abandoned not by anyone all grief evermore struck from me by the dazzle of her face, "Julian," I said, "Will you marry me?" And—

Julian:

Yes—

Laurence voice-over:

—she said. "Yes," she sang back through wind and river-rush. "Yes."

(Fade out superimpose of Bridge scene. Hard focus back on the two of them in the livingroom. The blue light fades and the light around them begins to come up. The features of the room return. Both are utterly spent, arms hanging at their sides, shoulders sagging, expressions drained. They turn from each other and stumble back to their original seats on chair and sofa. Pan back with them, then

dolly in and up to a high-shot to emphasize
the fragmentation. A long pause. Then:)

Laurence:

(In a low voice, no energy:) I don't care. You decide. Do whatever you want to do. Live your life any way you want.

Julian:

(Also with no energy:) You think I'll ever escape your judgment if I leave? Then this passive-aggressive torment will turn
into how I took the best years of your life and threw you out to
starve.

(Cut to tight-shot of Laurence's face with his
voice-over saying in his mind: *"She'll never
leave. Practice losing her. You'll have to drive
her away."* Cut to Julian, medium-shot, as she
sits with her hands limp in her lap:)

Julian:

I'm no kid anymore. I can't keep up the fight.

(Quick flash to The Child, age nine, in a
street brawl, falling down in the gutter but
still fighting from a prone position. Cut back
to Julian:)

So where does that leave us? This cowardly clinging together
on the wedding cake? Larry, if you won't try to change us
together *with* me, then I *will* do whatever I have to to change
us by myself.

(Cut to Laurence from over Julian's shoulder,
her perspective, as he rises wearily and goes
to the cupboard for another drink.)

Laurence:

Big surprise. 'S what I already said. You decide. You always do.

(Camera stays with him, but we see in the
foreground Julian's hand reaching out in a
desperate gesture toward him:)

Julian:

I haven't been fair tonight. I haven't talked about "not as-
signing blame" or about "our pattern." I haven't apologized
for all the ways *I've* been wrong, cruel, responsible for this
mess-up. But Christ, you yourself used to tell me I had an

"overly developed capacity for self-contempt." I want to *be, do, live,* something else now. I want more time to myself—not just stolen minutes in a taxi or plane or motel. I want some *fun,* some sweetness in my life. I've only ever wanted that with *you.* But if I can't have it with you, I want it *some*where, somehow.

> (Laurence turns, stands with glass in his hand.
> Dolly in to close-up of him. A grief-stricken
> smile haunts his face.)

Laurence:

Where does it go to when it goes? Those tender magnificent mescaline trips you and I used to take back in the Sixties. I remember one early trip when we lay in bed while dawn came through the loft windows in flakes of light. There was a full-blown rose, creamy white, in a glass on the orange-crate bedtable. We looked into it and then at each other. I saw both the rose and you overlapping on my retina, your petaled face unfolding before my eyes, your cells bleeding out love for me. We turned into everything we wanted to be for each other. A young Viking warrior queen. An ancient Zen master. An old peasant couple serenely working their fields. Then you were suddenly Joan of Arc and I was just as suddenly your best girlfriend—someone you called Bunker—and we were female and male all mixed and twining . . .

Julian:

(Very quietly:) I want . . . some graciousness, some affirmation, in my life. I can hardly breathe without them any longer, Lare.

> (Pan Laurence back as he sinks on the sofa
> with glass in one hand and bottle in the
> other.)

Laurence:

I can't either, Jule. I can't breathe at *all* anymore. You eat up the air, there's none left for me. *(A pause.)* I honest-to-god don't know what more to do. Every time I've met your New Woman demands—to be more sensitive, divest myself of power, be more supportive—I can almost feel your contempt coming at me for having met them. So now you see this blob, this passive, dependent hiccup of a human being for whom you feel loyalty, pity, affection, responsibility—but no attraction, no respect. I don't know what more I can *become*. Dead? Do I have to die?

> (Cut to Julian, shot from over Laurence's
> shoulder, his perspective:)

Julian:

(An attempt at a lighter note which goes awry:) Your preoccupation with death has always been the kind of luxurious self-indulgence available to someone who intends others to do his living for him, darling. *(Then, in a more earnest tone:)* I never wanted your guilt *or* your passivity, Larry. I only want you to take responsibility for your own life, not—

> (Dolly in slow arc going full circle, from
> behind his shoulder to frontal two-shot, to
> him from her perspective, through rear two-
> shot against wild fourth wall, back to original
> camera position, during the following
> exchange:)

Laurence:

—I'm beginning to understand, with a dull, rising nausea, that this is not going to change. I begin to understand how much you hate me.

Julian:

I *don't* hate—

Laurence:

Yeah. Hate me. I begin to realize that I can't even recognize the depth of my hatred for *you*. And how dangerous that is for us both.

Julian:

Larry. *I'm* not the enemy. For god's sake, I'm on *your side.* How can I make you realize that?

> (Quick flash-shot to a small black girl running
> away; back to two-shot as camera continues
> circling them:)

I've stood by you and stood by you. I've always believed that if there was a genius in this house, it was *you*.

> (Quick flash-shots in rapid montage: smiling
> Eva Braun, smiling Evita Perón, smiling
> Coretta Scott King, smiling Zelda Fitzgerald,

smiling Nancy Reagan, smiling Frida Kahlo,
smiling Isabel Allende, into still photo of
smiling Clara Wieck Schumann. Rapid
dissolve back to two-shot as camera continues
to circle Laurence and Julian:)

You know how desperate your career-situation makes me, how
I've tried— but those are boring old stories. *I* begin to realize
that if I'm destroyed it doesn't save you. I admit I've thought
that at times. Like that whole year when I just . . . stopped
writing anything, for fear it might find an audience. Why do
my only choices seem guilt or anger?

(Quick flash to The Mother's face, nodding
approvingly, then cut back to scene:)

Look at me, I'm not even crying. That scares me. Though
you've made such fun over the years of my faucet-ready eyes—
not imagining, I guess, how ominous the absence of those tears
would be. I'm so afraid . . .

(By now camera should have completed its
full circuit; pull back to full-length two-shot of
them sitting in front of dying embers in
Franklin stove.)

Laurence:

Getting cold.

Julian:

Yeah.

(Wordlessly, each of them reaches out a hand
to the other, but they are too far apart, and
neither seems able to move. Zoom in close on
the hands straining to touch and the space
between; flash-cut to a low-shot of the
younger Laurence and Julian, same distance
apart, high on the Brooklyn Bridge, as they
begin to lean toward one another; dissolve
back to the hands reaching.)

Laurence:

(*Softly:*) Oh dear god, the pity of it. Poor child. Poor, lost child
that never even got a chance to be born.

(Cut to Julian, her face in shock as she thinks
Laurence is referring to her secret abortion

and years of deception about being unable to
bear a child. Stay with her in tight close-up
through next speech:)

Julian:

So you knew, after all. So that's why . . . Laurence. I can
never tell you how sorry I am—for you—about my abortion.
But I had to terminate that pregnancy. I couldn't face it. I
couldn't stall your obsession to be a father anymore. I took the
cowardly and manipulative way out. The secret abortion. And
then, for years, the pill. In secret. Yes, I lied.

(Flash to The Mother's face, in pain; cut back
to Julian:)

Like Hope lied to me. Like David lied to her. Like you lied
about your affairs outside the marriage. Like both you and I lie
to the world—telling the truth but not the whole truth. I lied.
Part of me always wanted you to catch me in it. But once it got
started, the lie had a life of its own, and I . . . I'm sorry. I
just— never could be a mother, that's all. I'd have been an
awful one, I've always known that. It's not for me.

(Flash to The Child on a huge parade float,
smiling, waving, curtsying. Cut to Laurence,
his face full of horror, each word wrenching
itself loose:)

Laurence:

I—didn't—even—mean—that. I meant *you*. The child that
never got born in Julian Travis. Now you tell me . . . you tell
me that all this time . . . Julian! *I believed you!*

(Cut to Julian, realizing her blunder in telling
him the truth, now terrified; cut back to
Laurence, his eyes wide with fear of what is
rising in him:)

You bitch. *(He gets to his feet unsteadily; the brandy has taken
its toll.)*

(Voice-over in his mind: *"Gotta drive her
away, gotta drive her away."*)

You living toxic mortal wound!

(Cut to wide-angle shot of room as she rises.
He totters for a moment, then rushes out. We
hear him charging up the stairs to the upper

loft floor, the sound of objects falling and
breaking, his footsteps stomping. Julian stands
where he left her, paralyzed. She stares at the
ceiling, following the direction of the noises.
Silence, then another crash. We hear
Laurence's footsteps dash down the stairs in
the outer hall, hesitate for a second at the
door to this floor, then rush on down. The
street door slams. Camera stays on wide-angle
of Julian alone in livingroom as she slowly
begins to move through it, talking out loud to
herself:)

Julian:

If I'm wrong, I'm insane. If I'm right, it's even worse. I *have* to
learn where he leaves off and I begin. I have to learn.

(She opens the hall door and mounts the stairs
to the upper loft floor; low-shot watches her
ascend; upper-floor camera picks her up from
high angle as she rises, then follows her
through door and onto the upper floor,
moving behind her back, focused over her
shoulder, so that the lens sees what she is
seeing at the same moment. She enters her
study. Her desk chair has been overturned, a
potted cactus plant swept off her desk surface
and spilled onto the carpet. The shade of her
desk lamp is swinging wildly, alternately
casting enough light and shadow over her
desk for her to see a piece of paper lying on
it, pencilled in block letters. She draws
nearer. Camera angles over her shoulder to
read what she is reading:)

I LOATHE YOU FOR WHAT YOU'VE
DONE TO MY LIFE, YOU VAMPIRE.
MURDERING BASTARD. FUCK YOU.

(Julian touches the lampshade to stop it from
swinging. Dolly back as she rights the chair,
starts to gather up the soil and plant back
into its pot, stops. She rises from squatting by

the plant and moves again, like a sleepwalker, toward another door:)

Julian:

(Out loud, to herself:) Careful. It isn't the first of those notes. You've read them before. He doesn't mean it. Tomorrow he'll cry and you'll cry and the two of you will have a real talk. Breathe. Idiotic to shake like this, Julian. You're not physically afraid of Larry, you know he wouldn't hurt a fly. *(Internal voice-over in her mind:) You are not a fly. You're a fake and a phony and a coward. You're a bastard. You're a fool and a hypocrite, a murderous martyr. (Out loud:)* Calm. If he gets crazy you must act all the more sane. Focus on details and reality. Function. Burn the note in the Franklin. *(Internal voice-over:) No. Leave it there, don't touch its poison. Maybe he'll think you didn't see it, that you're unscathed by the madness churning through the house. (Out loud:)* Move out of this space. Breathe.

(Pan with her as she opens the other door and enters his study. It is in an even more severe state of breakage than hers. Broken glass lies all over the floor, a standing lamp has been knocked over, the desk chair lies on its side, castor-wheels still spinning. A revolutionary poster has been ripped from the wall; we can see it is a picture of Ché Guevara, the legend reading, "At the risk of sounding ridiculous, I would say that a real revolutionary is motivated by great love." Then Julian sees the block-letter printed note propped up against his desk lamp. Zoom in on:)

KILLER. YOU'VE STOLEN OR MURDERED EVERYTHING I EVER LOVED: OUR CHILD, MY POLITICS, MY ENERGY, MY REPUTATION, MY LOVE FOR YOU. KILLER BUTCHER THIEF SADIST LIAR!

(Aloud again to herself:) Careful. Calm. Breathe. Ignore it. *(She sees cockroaches feasting on the Chinese-food carton left on his desk.)* Don't get drawn in. Don't start cleaning up. The more you clean up one thing, the more you'll notice something

else needs doing. Go into the bedroom. Lie down. Sleep. Forget.

> (Pan with her as she moves back through his
> study door into the outer corridor, then
> through another door, to their bedroom.)

Fear. God, this is real fear. Of Larry?

> (Dolly in behind her as before, to see what
> she sees: the bedsheet of the double bed is
> ripped in half from top to bottom. In the
> center, legs twisted, arms sprawled, lies a
> faded Raggedy Ann doll. Stay on doll while
> Julian says aloud:)

He found it. He took it out of tissue paper in my drawer and—

> (Her hand reaches into the camera frame to
> lift the doll. Then she and we see another
> note lying under it:)

> ALL THESE YEARS I MIGHT AS WELL
> HAVE MADE LOVE TO THIS RAG DOLL
> AS TO YOU. DESTROYER! DEFENDER
> OF OUR MARRIAGE TO THE WORLD AND
> VICIOUS LIMP RAG DOLL TO ME. YOU
> DON'T EVEN HAVE "I LOVE YOU"
> PRINTED ON YOUR HEART. DROP
> DEAD, SNOW QUEEN. FROM THE CANDY
> GROOM ON THE WEDDING CAKE, THE
> NEVER-A-FATHER FOOL.

> (She drops the doll onto the bed. Pull back to
> show her full-length, standing by the side of
> the bed. Julian voice-over in her mind:)

Get out of the bedroom. Deal with it later, change the linen, put the doll away, be grateful he didn't rip her apart. (Out loud:) He wouldn't do that, there's not a violent bone in Larry's body. Breathe. Think. Get out of the bedroom.

> (She walks slowly, an automaton, back into
> the corridor and toward her own study door.
> Long-shot follows her figure. A sudden
> telephone ring shatters the stillness, and we
> see her start, shudder, then run toward her
> study.)

See. There. It's him already. Maybe already sorry. Maybe on the way home. We can talk, make a fresh pot of coffee— *(Julian voice-over:) This is Larry good god (Out loud:)* This isn't some brute batterer psychotic alcoholic this is *Larry. (She stands by her desk for a second, then picks up the phone.)* Hello? Hello?

(Tight head-shot of Julian; we can hear the filtered voice coming over the receiver.)

Man's Voice:

Miss Travis? Is this Miss Julian Travis?

Julian:

(Holding her hand over the receiver, whispering to herself in a rapid prayer:) Dear God, let it not be the police about Larry. And let it not be that maniac breather who wants to throw acid on the women's libber's face. Most of all let it not be something bad about Larry please God.

Man's Voice:

Hello? Hello? Miss Travis?

Julian:

(Uncovering the receiver and speaking into it:) Y-yes. Who's speaking, please?

Voice:

It's Dr. Grimes, Miss Travis, your mother's doctor. I'm relieved to finally reach you. I've been trying to locate you for two days. Nobody's been home, and I had no other number—

Julian:

(Her face showing momentary relief, then new anxiety:) Oh. Oh, I'm sorry. The—the phone's apparently been out of order. And I was out of town. Is she— Nothing's happened, has it?

Voice:

I'm afraid something has, Miss Travis. Not critical, but serious. And it makes the matter we discussed a week or so ago—a nursing facility—urgent. She's been brought to the hospital again, day before yesterday.

Julian:

Is it—is she—how—

Voice:

Forgive me, but I haven't inquired of you . . . I take it you are, ah, estranged from your mother, Miss Travis?

Julian:

Yes, Dr. Grimes. You could say that. I think I told you that for some time now, she's refused to see her friends, her former doctor, her former housekeeper. What I didn't tell you is that she's also refused to see me, for over a year. Whether it's the L-Dopa hallucinations or not, she apparently felt we were all in a conspiracy against her.

Voice:

I see. I have to tell you that this is not uncommon in some of these cases. Sometimes I wonder which is worse, the disease or the medication. But surely if she had been on a regularly monitored dosage—

Julian:

Dr. Grimes, I've been through this now with four different doctors over the years. That was always the trouble, you see. She wouldn't go for regular monitoring. It was a source of friction with all her previous physicians. But can *you* tell *me*—

Voice:

Who was the most recent—

Julian:

(Her eyes shut, as if by rote:) Dr. Jacob Bernstein at Manhattan General. I can give you his number if you—

Voice:

No, no, that's quite all right, I can get it. I've been trying to learn who he was from Mrs. Travis, but she wouldn't . . . uh, your mother is a difficult patient, Miss Travis.

> (Julian's mouth twists into a rueful smile. Pan
> back to show her free hand nervously tidying
> her desk from Laurence's rampage.)

Julian:

I understand that, Dr. Grimes. Now please *tell* me . . . what, I mean how did she come to be back in the hospital?

Voice:

She fell, I'm afraid. At this stage a Parkinson patient really should be accompanied at all times. But as you know, she insisted she could manage by herself with someone looking in only every few days.

268 DRY YOUR SMILE

Julian:

Yes, yes, I know. But what—

Voice:

It seems that five days ago, not long after her cleaning woman had left, your mother stumbled to the bathroom and fell. She broke her hip. By the way, how old is your mother, Miss Travis?

Julian:

(Her hand twists and untwists the phone cord unconsciously:) I'm sorry, Dr. Grimes, I have no idea. I imagine she must be in her mid-sixties. I wish I could be more precise. But she came of an immigrant family, and the records in those days . . .

Voice:

That's all right. It would be helpful, but it isn't that important. Actually, I'd estimate her to be more in her early seventies.

(Dolly back and pan down to show Julian
stoop and begin with her free hand to gather
up the spilled plant-pot soil, absent-mindedly
trying to stuff it and the broken plant back
into the pot as she listens:)

Julian:

Please go on. Then what? It took you *five* days to find me?

Voice:

(After a pause:) Two days to find *you*. Three days to find *her*. She'd cut herself off from everyone so effectively that not even a neighbor wondered at anything peculiar. It seems her cleaning lady had a personal family tragedy of her own—her brother died suddenly—and when she couldn't make it to your mother's but got no answer on the phone she started calling you. But your phone, as I mentioned . . .

(Julian has frozen in her squatting position,
her hand still full of earth)

. . . It seems your mother lay on the bathroom floor, unconscious for a while, and then began to crawl toward the phone.

(Julian slowly slides forward onto her knees.)

Miss Travis? Are you there?

Julian:

(With effort:) Yes. Yes, I'm here. Please go on.

Voice:

Obviously it was extremely difficult for her. And with the hip fracture, quite painful. She's dehydrated, and her EKG shows that she might have suffered another slight stroke in the process. Oh, I meant to ask you: I do detect signs of an earlier minor stroke episode, don't I?

Julian:

(Barely able to manage the word:) Yes.

Voice:

She must have passed in and out of consciousness a number of times. But she continued to inch toward the phone. Finally, three days later, the cleaning lady—Mrs. Washington—reached me. We gained entrance via the building superintendent and brought your mother in right away.

Julian:

(Trying to rise, not managing it:) I'll be right there, Dr. Grimes.

Voice:

Oh, Miss Travis. I think you should know one more thing.

Julian:

(Sharp, brittle:) What?

Voice:

Well . . . your mother doesn't want to see you. She is probably not capable, of course. But then I'm not an attorney. I think you should know that when I told her we had to ring you, her reaction was, uh, extremely negative. But you *are* the sole living relative, aren't you?

Julian:

(Bitterly:) Depending on how you define living or relative, Dr. Grimes, yes.

Voice:

I don't understand—

Julian:

I'm sorry. Never mind. Yes, I am her sole living relative. And I'm grateful to you for persisting in trying to reach me. I'll come right away, whether she wants to see me or not.

Voice:

Good girl. *(Julian's mouth tightens involuntarily.)* We also need to discuss some procedural matters about her care, the future, the various—

Julian:

Yes, various costs. I understand, Dr. Grimes. I'll be there as fast as I can. Thank you.

> (We hear his end of the line click off. Julian
> remains on her knees, clutching the receiver
> as if some last message might be forthcoming.
> Then she reaches up to the desk and hangs
> up the phone. Dolly in to tight close-up of
> her face, as her voice-over takes us into her
> mind:)

Julian voice-over:

Three days. And three nights. The light coming and going across the strands of the filthy Bokhara. How close your face would be to the carpet, Hope, your view of the room the same as that of the roaches who amble over the floor. The light coming slow and then fading slow and heaving your bulk through another sear of pain to inch another space closer. And the phone never ringing, the doorbell never ringing, the key never heard in the changed lock I would have used oh yes if it had fit. Who did you think of, Momma? Me? Mrs. Washington? Mrs. Dudinsky? David? That it maybe was finally really happening, and you alone, crawling across a dirty floor, crying out in your barely intelligible speech for help?

> (Julian bends to all fours, putting her face
> deliberately close to the soil-strewn carpet, to
> try to see what Hope saw. Dolly back to take
> in the setting, the floor around her. Cut to
> what she sees, a close-up of the nap of carpet.
> Cut back to Julian, on all fours, crouching;
> move in again to tight face close-up with
> Julian voice-over:)

More than seventy hours, with the light coming and going slow through the blinds. Had the television been on for company? Did it play out its entire repertoire of soaps and game shows and cop shows and family sitcoms and news and late shows until the national anthem and the sound of static? For the darkest hours of night, static? Until the light started to leak in and the anthem broke into the channel signal again? Or was it silent except for a traffic horn, a siren? Were you trying maybe to call *me*, Momma? Or even just get an operator? And the pain shuddering out from your splintered hip-bone through your whole body? Or did the stroke wipe everything clean from the brain, like that magic slate I had as a kid? Did you think of nothing except maybe "phone" and "help"? *Three nights and three days. (Julian opens her mouth to scream, but no sound comes.)*

Hope voice-over:

I never want to see you again, Julian. You did this to me.

Laurence voice-over:

You rotten bitch, you ruined my life.

Julian voice-over:

There must be some kind of atheist's god all my own, to help get me through this. There must be some place not brimming with horror. Joy exists somewhere, people have written about it. Or did they make it up? Does everyone? Seventy hours. You've got to do something. You've got to be calm and get down to the hospital and first change the linen no leave him a note careful most of all don't curse the universe and die you've got to be strong you can do it pull out the will who in hell do you think you are bitch bastard destroyer killer.

Julian:

What is it I do wrong?

Julian voice-over:

Never mind for now. *Think.* Get up and start moving. One foot, then the other. Women are the strong ones seventy hours *she crawled* to the phone. That's your heritage.

Julian:

I can't. I can't be strong anymore. All the will, it's drained out like pus from a lanced boil, leaving a welt of shrunken skin. *(Louder, almost a shout:)* I want someone else to be strong. I want to lean on someone else for a change! *(She looks down and notices that one hand is still clutching the spilled plant soil. She opens her fingers and watches it sift through them.*

Then, laboriously, like an old woman, she starts getting to her feet.)

> (Widen frame to take in Julian standing,
> leaning for support against her desk.
> Suddenly she raises her head like an animal
> caught in a trap, and howls:)

Laaarry!

> (The wail echoes through the empty loft.
> Faintly, from the street outside, sounds drift
> up of a quarrel between a prostitute and a
> pimp. Julian stares at her own hands with
> curiosity. Then she watches as one of them
> reaches out and lifts the telephone receiver.
> All her actions are done very slowly, as if
> underwater:)

Julian voice-over:

I'm not here. Not really. I'm a stranger, a detached observer self at the scene of the accident wondering which of all these feelings playing through me is my own. What's the motivation? Will this be a cry for help—from a woman who *could* make it to the phone? Is it a gesture toward freedom? A self-conscious heightening of the melodrama? an admission of defeat? another doomed inevitable scene to be played out? What kind of mad creature would so inflate an ordinary call into a fateful act? *What are you really feeling,* Julian? *Can* you feel? *Who are you?*

> (We move into a tight close-up again, and
> hear through the receiver a ring on the other
> end of the line. After only that first ring, the
> filtered voice of a woman answers:)

Woman's Voice:

Hello?

Julian:

Iliana?

Voice:

(Instantly:) Julian.

Julian:

Yes.

Julian voice-over *(rapidly:)*

Quickly. Quickly, now, before the tears rising in the throat break through—

Julian:

Yes. It's me.

(Fade-out. Bring up crawl of credits, black and white. No music. Dissolve to black.)

CHAPTER EIGHT

Spring, 1983

March 15, 1983, 8 A.M.: Day One.

The morning of the Ides of March. What an ominous date to begin keeping a journal again.

Awake early, at Ginny's, in her bedroom. She insisted on sleeping on the couch, generously giving me the privacy of a closed door.

I'm still numb. Haven't eaten since day before yesterday. Went off tranquilizers three days ago, but took two last night, to sleep. Dropped off like a stone at 3 A.M. Now I'm irritated to find myself awake so early, unable to go back to sleep. What a disappointment. I had hoped, given the exhaustion, that I'd sleep much longer, all day perhaps. What I wouldn't give to sleep for days, weeks, to escape feeling anything!

I feel bitter, injured, self-pitying, self-righteous. Scared. A little excited, too. Curious as to how Laurence is taking it.

Strange, but I'm not lonely yet. Although last night, after having left the loft, I felt horribly alone and cold. The long, aimless bus rides were like trips through hell, a surly Charon for a driver, my few companion-passengers the tired night-shift workers of the city—watchmen and guards, telephone operators, nurses, hospital aides. The late-night drunks and shopping-bag ladies who huddle for temporary warmth into the fluorescence of a bus, not caring where it takes them. The laborers of darkness. The homeless.

Me too. I had nowhere to go. Too many friends who would have received me with unabashed glee—what Larry has rightly termed "Job's counselors"—who would underestimate what he and I mean, together or separately. To their hospitality I could not sink. To Hope's empty apartment, for which I now have a key again—out of the question, even with her still in the hospital. That would be trying to escape from one panel of a Bosch painting and finding you've taken refuge in another. I must admit that I considered it. Amazing how swiftly the niceties of emotional anguish get put into perspective by the basics: little cash in wallet, late at night, no place to stay.

But I decided against it. So I rode the buses of New York for hours, finally winding up at Times Square, where the movies run all night. Except that most are porno and sado-masochistic flicks, with audiences of middle-aged men hunched over the secret in their laps, jerking off under folded raincoats. Then there are the young men, gay hustlers taking a break from their rounds on the cold streets, and of course more drunks, snoring off their stupor. Astounding, too, how the basics lower one's judgmentalism and spontaneously heighten one's capacity for compassion: I have a newfound sympathy for drunks—I, who enjoy only a rare Bloody Mary or glass of wine with dinner, but who have never particularly understood the much-vaunted fun aspect of it all. Poor drunks. Maybe they're just trying to sleep off life. I can relate to that.

But I knew that the Apollo theater on Forty-second Street was the one all-night so-called art movie house in the city. Sure enough, they were showing a re-run of *The Great White Hope* —the tragic love affair between two people who tried to transcend being "Other" (in their case, a white woman and a black man), who were nevertheless destroyed by their times and themselves. The film still moves me deeply, even knowing as I do that many such real-life couples were drawn together during the Sixties and Seventies not always for such idealistic reasons. I'll never forget Leonora telling me how, in her experience as a black heterosexual feminist, it was always the black woman who got screwed. Or, rather, didn't. Because her black brother was after having what the white woman "represented" (class, power, success) and her white sister was after what the black man "represented" (sexuality, rage, assuagement of white guilt). But neither can I ignore how the lovers in this particular film really do try to scale the cliffs of those stereotypes to attain some visionary summit. Before they push each off, that is. Intense identification with Laurence and me.

What a detour. This must be what tranquilizers do for you. Relax your brain so much it toddles off in any direction toward which you give it the slightest nudge. Thank god this is a private journal. At last, to begin keeping a journal with the certainty no one will look into it unless at my specific request! This in itself is a great leap forward. Why did it have to wait until I'd left Larry?

Left Larry—how odd that sounds. Unreal. (What else is new?) I sat in that damned movie theater, watching another damned pair of damned failing lovers, and crying like Niobe. I also kept getting up and phoning Ginny every fifteen minutes or so until she returned home. The ideal host, Ginny, for someone like me: literary agent, friend, someone who would sympathize but not moralize, leap to no major conclusions, neither pry nor psychologize, be discreet, leave me alone, and let me spend the night. At last she answered the phone. I had found a refuge.

Now, this morning: resentful, worried, yet strangely relieved. I can't believe the separation is other than a trial one, can't believe that Larry and I won't still "come through." My face is bloated from crying. My body aches. I feel like I used to after big fights with Hope—needing to sleep, to heal, for days afterward.

I have actually left Laurence.

I can't help being stunned that things have gone this far— for *us*, who were going to be different.

But I have hope.

Why *do* I have hope? (And definitely with a *lower-case* "h.")

Because there's nothing else for me to have.

March 27, 1983. At Charlotte's.

Well, the keeping of a daily journal seems one resolution already gone down the tube, along with my home of almost twenty-two years and the idea of a rapid reconciliation. So much for what I think was secretly in the back of my mind when I wrote the first entry in this blank book: Julian's one night of running away from home.

I stayed at Ginny's for four days, but couldn't impose myself any longer, not that she made me feel as if I were an imposition. But with only one bedroom and her insistence on sleeping on the couch, it was absurd. So I returned to the loft, ostensibly to pick up some clothes. I had been living in the same jeans, shirt, sweater, and boots during the interim—a condition which brooks no excuses for not washing one's underwear and sox *every single* night. Actually I returned to the loft hoping that L. and I might exchange one look and fall into each other's arms, music up, slow fade-out. This did not happen. I was met by his physical absence but his psychic presence, in the form of one of those chilling notes laid on top of a pile of my mail, reading: "Please attend to rent payment which was due on 15th unless you wish me thrown out into the gutter along with your books and manuscripts which I'm sure mean more to you than I do."

So much for imminent reconciliation. Picked up mail and a few changes of clothes; made some calls giving Ginny's phone as the one for leaving messages in case of free-lance work. Hung around getting tearful over the cats. Started to water the plants, but he'd done that. Secretly hoped he'd walk in and we'd take one look, fall into each other's etc. Gazed longingly at my study, desk, typewriter. Gathered up a few file folders and the draft of the current chapter in the middle of which I supposedly am. Felt silly and dazed. Left again.

But one of the calls I made was to Athena, and when I said to leave messages with Ginny, may the angels forever bless her soul Charlotte instantly put one and one together and did not come up with two. She came up with one separated from one. She casually asked—making no production of it—whether by chance I could use a place to stay for a while "to get some work done in quiet." Why good heavens yes however did you guess my dear, said I. She then said that she and Zach were going away for two weeks (she on vacation now that the spring list is out of the nest and to accompany him to a shrinks' convention in Europe, and then a holiday) and it would be a terrific favor to *her* if I'd apartment-sit and poodle-sit. Charlotte, thought I, never mind your publishing all the Maxine Duncan Brewers in the world: you got class, kid.

So here I am at Charlotte and Zach's. Which is eerie, considering how often I've been here as a dinner guest; rather like getting to go backstage and see the workings of a particular production you've viewed many times from out front. But it's lovely having a large, comfortable apartment all to myself, even unto two dogs who try but fail to play cat-surrogate for the much-missed-by-me loft cats.

I had one out-of-town-overnight, a speaking date in Chicago, but came back here and have almost another whole week to go. After that, I'm not sure. Some stubborn part of me trusts that by then L. and I will have worked it out—whatever that means. Some vigilant part of me worries that we *will*, but only by patching a Band-Aid over a festering wound. Other parts of me are engaged in excitement at the prospect of being truly on my own, in (premature?) mourning for our marriage, in rage (against him, me, us, history, and patriarchy), and in (very large part of me occupied with this one:) panic.

Iliana has been an incredible friend. She immediately offered her place to me—on not one but two careful counts: she reminded me that her sofa opened up into a bed, and said we could set up a cardtable as a makeshift desk, so that the living-room could become "my space"; she *also* offered to go and stay with friends so I could have her apartment to myself in "privacy." Stunningly generous. But I told her I wouldn't think of evicting her from her own hard-won turf, that I was set for the moment at least. Everything is up in the air. It's dizzying to realize that I have no idea where I'll be a week from now.

No savings account, of course. Nor can I suddenly cease paying the loft bills; it is, after all, my home. Besides, Laurence has no income right now, how would he survive? Furthermore, I may be back there in some resolved manner by next week. This time everything is unreal for real.

I've seen Iliana every day, except when I was out of town. She's loaned me cash, made me eat, even made me forget all this misery for a moment or two and laugh at the madness of it. She's never bad-mouthed Laurence, yet she's managed to be a remarkably strengthening presence. Never a reference to any sexual matter between us; in fact, a flat refusal to discuss the subject when I've tried to raise or clarify it. I have a dread of seeming to "lead her on" but she keeps waving all such discussions aside with one of her wise crone "I know what I say" dismissals.

This evening, at dinner, we arranged to go together tomorrow and attempt the first siege on Hope's apartment. It can't be put off any longer. In fact, somewhere in the midst of my own vagrancy, I've got to make the time and find the stamina to face disposition of that co-op, as well as proceed with the nursing-home odyssey.

Good god. Doctors, lawyers, Laurence, bills, no roost of my own, more speaking dates coming up but little money now and it's always a four-to-six-week lag between the date and the college actually sending the check. My papers and files for the current book sitting in my study at the loft. Hope in the hospital, staring straight ahead of her whenever I go to visit, which has been every day except for when I was in Chicago. Not knowing whether she's deliberately un-seeing me or if that's part of her condition; suspecting the former.

I sit at the side of her hospital bed and study her. All that power, that archetypal numinousity—now so enfeebled. Lavender veins prominent in her chalky, flaccid skin; the bones of her skeleton already beginning to flirt through her surfaces— in the grimace of teeth, the claw of a hand. Her skull hints its contours more boldly through the lifeless strands of graywhite hair. Sometimes she sneaks a glance at me, but mostly she won't even look in my direction.

I still fear her. *Damn.* This moronic *fear* in me—of what? She's far too weak to hurt me physically. She's even incontinent. Parkinson's, strokes, the cast on her hip, dehydration, the ever-present danger of pneumonia in a patient so bedridden— what more do I want? She's powerless. How can she possibly hurt me now?

She does have power. She has the power to not love me.

Is that where it all begins? The power to withhold love, the primal cause of all violence? She never did actually withhold it (I *think*). But she must have used the threat of doing that in a manner so subtle and effective as to have created in me this gaggingly desperate approval-search, this supposed devotion to "selflessness" that literally, as Iliana points out, means a lack of self. Making waves everywhere but in my own private life. "Supporting" as the only way I know how to express love. Even turning at-first independent people like Laurence into dependent ones, so I can play the indispensable martyr-mother. Not for nothing was my nickname for her "Little Momma" when I was only four years old.

So now what? I guess just go on. Here we go again, but more so: one step at a time, put your little foot . . . I keep bursting into tears at the oddest times—in the shower, on the bus, in the plane's lavatory, standing at a curb. Waiting for the light to change. And always in bed at night, crying as I try to fall asleep.

Then there's a blissful split-second in the morning, on awakening, when I haven't yet remembered what's happened, where I am and where I'm not, what I must face in general and on that particular day. Then the wake-up tears start.

Still. I'm fortunate, I tell myself, given the circumstances. Thank the universe for Ginny, for Charlotte, for the women who want me to come and lecture at their schools. Thank the universe for Iliana de Costa.

March 28, 1983

I've been to Hope's apartment. I literally don't know what I would have done had Iliana not been with me. No words for it.

Flimsy approximations: squalor, chaos, filth, jetsam of a life, madness. The condition it was in when I was last permitted inside has worsened to a state I couldn't have imagined. If I were ever to put such a scene into a story, I'd have to reduce it, bring the details down into some border-reality, or everyone would think I had a wildly exaggerative runaway mind. She had become a total recluse. Her mail—including a few puny stock-dividend checks, millions of stockholder-meeting proxy notices, appeals for donations to various synagogues and Jewish hospitals and children's homes—is heaped in piles all over the place, unopened for months. Layers of dust blanketing everything, plaster peeling from the ceiling, windows opaque with grime. Cockroach metropolis in the slimehole of a kitchen. Green mold scumming whatever used to be food in the refrigerator; just to open the fridge door could knock you over with the stench.

She must somehow have got it together to scribble a few checks each month for Mrs. Washington to mail—the co-op maintenance, telephone and utilities, Washington herself. But Mrs. W. tells me she hasn't been paid for a month, so I sent her my own check for what was owed her; what else could I do?

It'll take weeks to sort out what's left of Hope's "financial affairs." Meanwhile, the notion of attacking that apartment, cleaning it up, and getting it on the market as fast as possible so there's money for the nursing home—it's overwhelming.

I vomited up the light lunch Iliana made me eat before going there. I stood in Hope's shit-streaked bathroom, leaning over the sink heaving and weeping—because it was there she fell, it was from there she'd started her creep toward the phone. Iliana cleared a space on the sofa with one efficient sweep of her arm, sat me down, plonked herself beside me, sighed, and announced that if Hercules could manage the Augean stables alone, then two women ought to be able to handle this together, since the jobs were about on the same level.

How can you not laugh through your tears at the preposterousness of this situation? How can you not love a friend like that?

I'm too wasted to write more now. I think I'm even beat enough to fall asleep without the usual Thinking About Everything first, which would be a blessing. Tomorrow we start the clean-up. And tomorrow I find out if I can stay at Ginny's again; she'll let me know for sure if she's decided to go to the West Coast Book Fair. And tomorrow I have to call Laurence and let him know that I need to make another loft-raid, for some work-clothes in *which* to approach Hope's Augean stables. Tomorrow and tomorrow and tomorrow . . .

April Fool's Day, 1983.

I can go to Ginny's, thank god. Excellent timing, because Charlotte and Zach return on the 4th and that's when Ginny will be taking off for California. So I'll apartment-sit and plant-sit there for five days. That takes me to the 9th. Then what?

The irony is that if I didn't have to sell Hope's co-op in such a rush, all the work to clean it up could have yielded a more permanent-temporary place to stay. Hello irony, old friend.

We certainly have started cleaning it up.

First there were the huge plastic trash bags we'd brought with us, into which we threw the contents of the fridge and the pantry cupboards, the old magazines and newspapers and circulars and junk mail, the gummy stuff in the medicine cabinet and on the bathroom shelves, and the barely touchable stinking bed linen. Then there were more huge trash bags, which we filled with old clothing of hers that she hadn't worn in years —high-heeled platform shoes, moth-eaten fur hats, holey-fingered gloves, the works—to be donated to the hospital thrift shop. *Then* there were the plastic bags for the Julian Travis Shrine in the bedroom: in went the doll collection, the 1950's Teresa Brewer–Pat Nixon-style dresses, all the wee pastel-dyed slippers—also destined for the thrift shop. Iliana refused to let me throw out the photographs or awards; she thinks I'll write about all this someday and they might be useful to jog my memory. Hilarious thought: that I could ever write about this, and that my memory—which wants nothing more now than amnesia—would need jogging. But she insisted, so those went into the "for storage" pile. (Arguing with Iliana when one is feeling strong is a job in itself; in my state, forget it.)

The rugs were picked up to be cleaned and kept by the cleaners in summer storage, an arrangement they little know could go on for many seasons. The pots, pans, and cutlery are hopelessly beyond scouring and had to be thrown out. The dishes mostly cracked, chipped, not worth saving or selling. The same with her appliances (rusted iron, battery-corroded radio; three lamps with electrical shorts, broken bases, and torn shades; a crudded and inoperative toaster, similar-state electric fry pan, and so forth). Records and books will go into storage, along with the scrapbooks—through which Iliana began to leaf during one of our container-coffee-from-the-nearby-deli breaks. I tried to stop her, but she's unstoppable. To my surprise, her eye saw things in the photographs I've never seen: a set jaw, a sidelong sullen look, expressions of rebellion in my five-year-old face, a whole body language of resistance . . . I've neither the time nor the interest at this stage to re-examine the copious images of The Ideal American Girl, but something in her perceptions of those artifacts felt cleansing. All I've seen whenever I've looked at them was an obedient, grinning little monkey. I don't think Iliana was seeing solely through eyes of love, either; when it comes to a photographic image, she's uncompromising.

After four or five hours of wading around this charnel house each day, both of us are bushed. Yet she manages to get us back, either to her apartment in the Village or to Charlotte's uptown, for showers, and then she sweeps me off to a "decent" (her word) dinner, whether I'm hungry or not.

Dinner for Iliana is a ritual of civilized behavior: a not necessarily posh restaurant but one with a leisurely atmosphere, good food and service, a bottle of wine. At first it felt like an indulgent waste of time, but it does work. I relax for a bit. It's extraordinary how she manages to create graciousness in the midst of my furor. She's like a walking incarnation of that line of Baudelaire's: *"Luxe, calme, et volupté."* What a bizarre thing to pop into my memory so long after Barbara introduced to me Baudelaire . . . Anyway, we sit there at dinner and for a moment I almost forget what a mess my life is. Of course, it's as daft as if the two of us were having a nice meditative chat in the trenches while the next day's battle rises over us with the dawn. But I do love being with her—and it's more than gratitude, which is also boundless. Yet I'm terribly afraid. I don't want to fall in love with Iliana. I don't want to fall in love with anyone. I don't want to prove Laurence right. I don't want to use her as some sort of liberating angel. Most of all, I cannot handle one more iota of stress.

Meanwhile, it's equally true that she relieves the stress. Shopping-bags full of Hope's unsorted financial papers, stock certificates, etc., get carried back to her Grove Street apartment each night—because it's the one place they can *be* until I organize them for the attorneys; they can't go to the loft and they certainly can't ricochet about with me from stayover to stayover. This weekend we'll take a break from cleaning the co-op and I'll go to her place and begin the sorting out, because at least some of the papers should be in the hands of Hope's lawyers before I have to go out of town next week on two speaking dates.

Meanwhile, too, back at the hospital, *she* just lies there. Dr. Grimes is being quite helpful. He says he'll have her condition stabilized in about three weeks, barring complications—but that if I can't find a nursing home and get the apartment sold to pay for it by that point, he can perhaps manage to stretch her stay in the hospital for another week or two beyond that. She has no place else to *go.* Neither does her daughter. The two of us, as she used to proclaim merrily, against the world.

Oh, Momma.

April 12, 1983

Now at Leonora's. I've been trying to keep the separation under wraps, but word is out at Athena. It's just as well, since I frankly need to know who's going out of town when, and for whom I can house-sit. Besides, as Iliana chortles, it's good for the soul to learn a little humility. If I ever doubted that women were the best folks around I'm certainly learning it all over again.

There it was, out of the blue, a call from Leonora saying that she would be taking her vacation to visit her family in Alabama for two weeks at Easter, and "would appreciate it" if I'd stay at her place on the Upper West Side, cat-sit, and look after *her* plants. No questions asked. The "feminist diplomacy" of women is awesome, though. When I went up to Leonora's so she could give me keys and instructions, she managed to reek sympathy for my situation with no mention of any situation over which she might be reeking it. She showed me around her apartment, briefing me on its idiosyncrasies, and *happened* to explain that such-and-such vase had been a wedding present to celebrate her first marriage, such-and-such candelabra a wedding present to celebrate her second, and such-and-such items (microwave oven, cable TV) divorce presents to herself to celebrate her liberations. "Sweetie," she tossed off in passing, "I've now been married to a white man and to a black man; one from Group A and one from Group B, Chinese-restaurant-menu style. The white one wore a gold earring, the black one wore a Brooks Brothers vest, neither one took out the garbage, and both claimed I was indispensable to their happiness. Of course," she wound up slyly, "that was peachy by me—until I saw through the satisfaction of being indispensable for irrelevancies."

That was it. Nothing more was said.

So here I am. My major problem in this apartment is that Leonora is five-foot-ten, tall enough to be a high-fashion model —"the Radcliffe Kikuyu," she calls herself—so I am forever climbing up on things to get at other things. I'm sure the cat food, for example, is placed at normal height for her to reach; to me it seems stored at attic level.

The only other problem is that Leonora's is quite a distance from Hope's apartment and from the hospital. I spend my life in buses and subways; only when approaching drop-dead state do I indulge in taxis. There's the co-op over in Sutton Place, way on the East Side in the Fifties; there's the hospital, also on the East Side, but twenty blocks north; there's the loft, on the West Side but farther south in Chelsea; there's Iliana on Grove Street, also on the West Side but way downtown in the Village. Yesterday—or was it the day before?—I seemed to circle the whole of Manhattan. That's not counting trips to the lawyers' offices (which are midtown), or to Athena (over in the West Side Forties jewelry district). It seems I go to Athena a lot these days, to deliver or pick up people's housekeys, to pick up or deliver free-lance manuscripts. Charlotte seems acutely sensitive to the money crisis: I'm still waiting for colleges to pay, I'm still carrying all the loft bills, I've had to cover some of Hope's urgent bills and make a payment on her medical costs as well—since her insurance records are in a mess and it will take time for the lawyers to straighten that out. Nor can I get a bank loan, because I'm free-lance and have no collateral. Never mind waving copies of your published books at a bank. They wouldn't give a two-dollar loan to George Eliot if she rose from the grave and needed a twentieth-century shirt on her back; if she didn't have a regular payroll salary, she could go floss her mill. Familiar problem: I remember Rick McPherson moaning about actors' being unable to get bank loans because of being employed "irregularly."

Today Laurence and I crossed paths. It was at least civil. So naturally I cried for an hour afterward, sniveling on the street and pretending I had a cinder in my eye when people gawked. Also today, Hope looked directly at me, then shut her eyes against me. I sit each day for at least an hour by that hospital bed and try to talk with her:

"Hello, Momma. It's me, Julian. I love you. How're you feeling?"

Silence.

"Spring's hinting around out there, Momma, just faintly. It's still chilly, but there's a mild touch to the air."

Silence.

"Hey, Little Momma, the doctor says you're getting better. He says your heart is strong and you're a real fighter. But you and I always knew that, huh?"

Silence.

"Would you like me to get you anything, Momma? Now that

you're off intravenous and you're rehydrated, they say you can
and should eat. 'Course, I know how vile hospital food is. But I
could bring you some soup, or custard, or ice cream? Maybe a
little chicken? You love barbecued chicken. I could smuggle
some in? . . ."

Silence.

"Sorry I wasn't here yesterday till the evening, Momma. I
came right from the airport. I had to give a speech in Kansas."

Silence.

"I got paid for it, Momma. It wasn't a benefit."

Silence.

I discard the wilted flowers I had brought a couple of days
earlier. I put fresh flowers and fresh water in the vase on her
bedtable. Silence. I kiss her hello. I kiss her goodbye. No physical response. Silence. It took me some time to get up the
courage to ask Grimes whether this was her condition or not.
The reply, as I feared, was that she *is* capable of speaking and
does so to the nurses and to him, though in slurred language
and sometimes in a "displaced, depersonalized, and disori-
ented" fashion. But apparently there are also times when she
recognizes her favorite nurses and garbles on chattily with
them. For me: silence.

The co-op dissolution moves on apace, thanks to Iliana's
help. She's a dynamo. Bossy as hell, sometimes, but then again
she's usually right. I simply do not see how any of this could
proceed without her. She claims she has the time and the will
to do it, that helping "gives her pleasure." I fail to see how
scouring that filthy apartment could give anyone pleasure, to
which she replies with the omniscient "Ta ta ta." What's more,
she can be irresistibly funny in relating details of all her phone
conversations about this: a crazy Argentinian exile keeping
track, while I'm out of town, of the status with lawyers, real-
estate agents, co-op-building board, furniture and antique ap-
praisers. I must sell whatever *is* minimally valuable—which
seems to amount to the sideboard, the Sèvres plate, a few
pieces of silver, her mink coat, and her jewelry—because she'll
lose money on the apartment sale since there's no time to hold
out for the price such a co-op normally would bring. Someone's
going to get a bargain.

In the middle of all this, here I am, turtle with her home on
her back, having schlepped my portable life—file folders and

suitcase—to Leonora's. Each friend's home yields its own phenomena. Ginny, for instance, has few records but lots of tapes, most of them of the voice: operas, lieder, English folk songs, Bach cantati. Charlotte and Zach's tastes run to symphonies (Beethoven and Brahms), Liszt, and scads of Broadway musicals. Now I've hit Leonora's—which turns out to be Mozart, Aretha, and Grace Jones. It's all very educative.

Leonora's Siamese cat, Uhura, has great dignity yet seems content to tolerate me as her bedmate and servant in the absence of her usual attendant. It's a comfort, being around a cat again, absorbing the presence of a creature so self-possessed, so seductively demanding that her own needs be met, so liquid in her satin mobility. If only it were possible to put oneself first with the same primitive innocence. *"Luxe, calme, et volupté,"* indeed. Uhura is a welcome break from Charlotte's dogs, who were, I suspect, not fond of me, probably intuiting cat-prejudice on my part. But they really were sweet, though I hadn't particularly liked poodles before. It turns out that Charlotte herself never wanted poodles: she just loves animals and would've preferred plain mutts. But Zach would have none of that—any pets *he* was going to have must be pedigreed. Charlotte's quiet revenge is to refuse to have them clipped, nail-polished, or beribboned, "like some chic ladies'-magazine editor's pretentious petsies forgodsake." The upshot is that Charlotte and Zach have two pure-bred poodles who contentedly shaggle about looking like mongrel lambs. Marriage, like politics, is the art of compromise—and of guerrilla war. Anyway, Charlotte claims the poodles are highly intelligent; this was not always evident. The female, Sido, acted most of the time as if she'd been secretly hitting the gin bottle: gazing at me with bloodshot eyes, leaping at shadows, dribbling slurpy kisses on my hand, face, ankle, whatever she could get hold of. The male, whose name is the basic Fido but spelled, according to his food bowl, "Phideaux" (which is either witty or fatuous, I can't decide), he's another matter. I'm not just being feminist about this. Walking those two dogs was a challenge in balance. Sido has a sauntering, weaving style. She ambles. She stops and stares at the sidewalk. She tries to kiss the shoes of strangers. Meanwhile, Phideaux was busy walking *me*. He liked to lunge down the street with me racing after, then to brake abruptly at an appealing hydrant and fling up his leg. Since he never slowed to give warning, I would go hurtling on past, dragging poor Sido with me, and frequently bowling over innocent passers-by in the process. Phideaux also thought it amusing to attempt rape on every female dog he encountered, and to growl fiercely at every male dog, especially those twice his size. The Killer Poodle, I named him. We had some anxious moments with Great Danes and Dobermans. I also spent quite a bit of energy on these walks affecting surprise at his behavior. "Why, *Phideaux!*" I would exclaim loudly, so that I could be sure of being heard by the owner of the female dog who was eyeing us with alarm and trying to extricate dog and self from the instantaneous leash tangle. *"Phideaux!* What a thing to *do!* That's not *like* you!" when actually Phideaux's character seems to be a cross between Don Juan and Genghis Khan.

I must be losing my mind, writing down such details. But writing, as always, is such a clarifier. Like prayer is for some people. Besides, moments alone like this, late at night, after editing a manuscript and before trying to fall asleep, with (somebody's) music on the phonograph, curled up in (somebody's) bed in (somebody's) apartment writing in this *(my!)* journal, are the only ventilation I have. Now I know why bag ladies mumble to themselves. I've talked myself out with Iliana, so that she now demands we talk about *any* other things —the news, art, books, politics, philosophy—to get my mind off obsessing about Hope-Laurence-co-op-nursing-homes-money-book-deadline nightmares. She's right. Although I haven't had a moment to read anything other than Hope's papers or manuscripts for Athena, or see a movie, or go to a museum or gallery in longer than I can remember. Politics of course goes on no matter what: went to a press conference last week in support of our protest against the drug companies that produce unsafe contraceptives, filled in on the picket line against the latest porn "snuff" film; did letters, petitions, lobbying phone calls. Every day I feel more like a juggler, trying to keep all the balls in the air.

Larry is alternately nasty as hell or coolly cordial when we speak by phone about logistical matters. He prefers to be out of the loft when I come by for mail or whatever, which is probably sensible. But not knowing what the mood is going to be when I ring up to alert him that I'm coming makes me prey to the yo-yo effect. There's a sub-level, too: when he's nasty, it hurts but feels bracing, it gets my self-righteousness up, makes me think I was right to leave and who needed that crap anyway. When he's "nice"—as in expressing sympathy about Hope, however hypocritical that might be—it tears me apart. (Come back, Hypocrisy?) Attacks of guilt, sorrow, and longing ensue. But if we attempt to talk about my coming back, the conversation soon veers off into accusation and diatribe—and he hangs up on me. Borrowing *her* technique, the one he knows always made my brain melt with frustration. Once he and I did cry together over the phone—but then, within seconds, it turned venomous again.

My eyelids are drooping, so I'll close this entry. What a cheerful journal this is! It could've been written by Typhoid Mary or Little Nell. Tomorrow should be a beauty. Now that I've winnowed down the nursing-home list the hospital social worker gave me, tomorrow is the day Iliana and I start visiting them.

This too will pass, I tell myself. When? I ask myself. *When?* And *how?*

May 1, 1983

Well, well, Happy May Day to all. Now at Georgi Fraser's apartment: career-woman-modern-Danish functional. She virtually lives at the office from early morning to late at night, keeping Athena afloat—and the apartment shows it. Diet soda, one wilted Singapore orchid, vitamins, and three containers of yogurt constitute the total refrigerator contents; diet sweetener packets, a tin of pâté de foie gras, a jar of instant coffee, and some stale Earl Grey teabags are about it for the cupboard.

But it's splendid, because she has a spare bedroom, and she isn't even in her own bedroom very often, traveling around to distributors and book fairs, wheedling manuscripts out of various authors, zipping off to Europe to buy or sell foreign rights. Even when she's here, we're mostly out of each other's way, and she actually seems to enjoy my presence when we do cross tracks over a late-night cup of coffee or snack. She accuses me of having a closet domestic personality, since I've stocked the fridge with such minimals as English muffins, butter, cheese. When I'm not having dinner with Iliana, I either skip food from lack of interest or wind up snacking while standing at the open fridge door. It's too expensive to eat out all the time, and neither can I let Iliana keep on "keeping" me like this.

It would be enough of a miracle if all she'd done was accompany me through these past days, my Virgil in the circles of the Inferno. We've been over to Brooklyn and up to the Bronx, out to Staten Island and back to West End Avenue, down to the Village and up to Yorkville, casing the "homes."

The homes. What abominations. And these are the *better* ones. Some secular, some run by Jewish organizations. We even checked out a Catholic one which was supposed to be nondenominational in practice. But the minute I saw nuns and crucifixes I knew that Hope, however out of it she is, would be sufficiently sane to think I'd walled her up in a convent. Most of the homes seem to be in one way or another religious; there's no Old Atheists' Home in New York—and if it isn't here, it isn't anywhere.

The simpering euphemisms: Senior Citizens, Golden Age Clubs, Girls' Floor and Boys' Floor (some are "coed"). A saccharine patronizing of the occupants, combined with an indifference to them as individuals. The sham busyness: "craft therapy" (baskets, painting by number, clay molding, paper cut-outs done with blunt kindergarten scissors); "social events" (the monthly "prom," the weekly movie showing). Civility as oppression. At the West Sixty-sixth Street one, the admissions supervisor recognized me and asked if I'd be willing to come and volunteer a short lecture about feminism to her "ladies." I was touched by the request, and said yes. But when I phoned the next day to check with her about a specific date, she embarrassedly informed me that her director had turned down the idea as being "too contemporary and agitative" for the patients. Tell it to the Gray Panthers.

It's mentally and emotionally bruising to tour these places. What must it be like then to *live* there? We haven't yet seen one where I'd stoop to put Hope. For one thing, despite their antiseptic atmosphere (complete with plastic flowers), they're not even very *clean*. When I saw a giant waterbeetle scurry out from under the wheel as one old woman tried to turn her wheelchair around in the "day room" I thought I'd pass out. We've now learned we must demand to inspect the kitchens, where sometimes shining cauldrons hang for display from the ceiling but muck-rimmed pots are in use on the stoves.

They're all stupendously expensive: the cheapest we've seen is $2500 a month, *not* including physician's services, prescription drugs, and any "special equipment" a patient requires. Not surprisingly, we've seen only three black faces in all the homes so far—among the patients, that is. Among the probably underpaid aides, there's a disproportionately high number of those faces.

Most of the facilities verge on the totalitarian in their rules: We don't allow private radios or TV's in the rooms because our ladies might use them to disturb others (!) or get agitated at what they hear or view (!!) and "inmates" (!!!) can go to the day-room television if they like—at certain hours. Visiting admitted only at certain hours. Telephoning in—or out—only at certain hours (most don't even permit private phones in the rooms). We allow one or two pictures on a lady's nighttable, but we really can't have them bringing in a lot of personal items; it makes for clutter. We permit only three nightgowns and one "wrapper," plus two changes of front-closing day clothes; the closets are small and we really can't have *clutter.* (It seems these days that no sooner do I arrive at one conclusion than it's immediately overturned: so much for being judgmental about the state of Hope's co-op; it was her apartment and her clutter and her *right,* dammit!)

But the worst of seeing "facilities" is seeing the women in them, both staff and patients. The worn, harassed, exasperatedly beaming faces of nurses and aides, their singsong whine as they address the patients, acidic burn-out eating through the tarnish of efficiency. Not even to blame: witnessing such daily suffering, with no prognosis of recovery except the inevitable release of death, must necessitate calluses on the soul. Because *what* they see—dear god.

The patients sit in chairs or wheelchairs or lie in bed, each utterly alone in herself. Each alone in her room, alone even in her attempt at fractured corridor conversation as she laboriously inches her wheelchair along, or shuffles by leaning on her walker with intense concentration. Step, drag foot, slide walker ahead, step, drag foot, slide walker ahead—futile reflex courage. I don't know which are more shattering—those faces blank of everything but expectation of the ultimate blankness, perpetually silenced in a waking stupor, all expression except a fleeting wince or shudder wiped from the wrinkled features, or those who still cling to a frayed connection with living, who smile crookedly back at you, try to respond to your passing greeting, attempt a gesture of communication despite the censoring nerves, muscles, bones. Some even risk fighting back.

One woman confronted an aide in the corridor, daring for a second to release herself from her walker so she could shake both trembling fists with rage, shouting, "I *want* to! I *want* to! I have some rights!" What did she "want to"? Go to the toilet by herself? Watch the "agitating" television news? Make a phone call? Visit a prisoner in another cell? Boycott the prom? Just make it down to the hall's end and back without being hovered over?

I seem to have developed a twitch in my left eyelid, which Iliana claims comes from too much seeing. Yet she herself watches everything without flinching: the patients, the "caretakers," details of filth or signs of authoritarianism that have slipped by a dazed me. She brought a camera to the first place we went, but it was confiscated at the door ("for the ladies' privacy, you understand"). She has since resorted to an ingenious little pocket Pentax, so small it fits in the palm of her hand. Whenever I see her linger by a nurses' station or a wall bulletin board, or stop and casually chat overlong with a patient, I know she's focusing by her Braille-like feel, her fingers moving on that camera hidden in her pocket, her brain estimating approximate distance, light, exposure. Then she backs away a bit, slips it out of her pocket, slides it up alongside her hip or makes a fiddling waist-level gesture with her belt, and swiftly gets her shot. The click is a soft whirr inaudible to anyone not standing right next to her. It's a marvelous act to watch. It also works. Just yesterday I saw the first prints. They're absolutely staggering.

So we go on our way, witnessing. The doors to the rooms are almost always open. As you walk along the corridors you get quick-shot glimpses into what's left of whole human lives, framed in those doorways. The woman rocking back and forth, scanning her window to the blank wall beyond. The woman who sits there crying soundlessly, clutching a picture frame to her chest. The woman who waves shakily at you and beckons you in, but when you're stopped by the aide accompanying your tour, turns her head aside in bitterness. The woman trying gallantly to rearrange a pillow behind her back without calling for help. The woman who cries out weakly, "Nurse? Please? I need a pan? I've been calling and calling . . ."

Then there was the door that rooted me to the spot until Iliana drew me away, the door that framed a vignette of death playing itself out before our eyes: three staff members in rough, rapid labor over an inert body, two of them taking turns pushing down violently on the chest, the third giving mouth-to-mouth resuscitation, a pantomime of frenzied action—until one of them suddenly stopped, listened at the heart, shook her head, and pulled the sheet up over a gape-mouth, dessicated face.

Oh Hope, where can you live where *I* can live with your being there? No home of my own to take you in—not that it would've worked back at the loft, even if I were still there. Where can you go that you won't wake into a slice of sanity and see how I betrayed you by putting you there? How can I live with your thinking that?

I can't write anymore. Too beat. Georgi just knocked at the door to the spare bedroom, back from some late-night hassle over the impending printers' strike, wanting to unwind and have a cup of tea. It's the least I can do.

There's not much, it seems, that I *can* do.

May 18, 1983

Not a moment or a jot of energy to write anything here since the above entry. Almost three weeks of blur.

The Feminist Grapevine is onto the separation. Which means that whenever I make the error of going to an unavoidable meeting, at least five women approach me and express differing concerned versions of "How *are* you?" It also means that everyone sooner or later asks the Feminist Question: "Why did *you* leave? Why are *you* homeless while *he's* comfortably ensconced back there?" So I go through the thumbnail-version explanations: how I had more options than Larry, more friends; how it's just as well, because I'm on the road so much; how it's all really temporary anyway. What I rarely say is that I've discovered first-hand certain realities our political rhetoric has so far failed to penetrate. Fight back? Throw *him* out? Stand up for *your* rights? There's more to "victimization" than that. For one thing, there's pity—the feeling that I'm "strong," he's fragile. Then there's fear—that *he's* strong and *I'm* fragile. It gets all mixed up with love and optimism and pride and memories and humiliation and disbelief. Finally, there's weariness—the yearning for peace at any price, to hell with "honor." Some women understand when I say this, some don't (as *I* haven't, for years, emitting pompous-ass answers in Q–and–A sessions). I've begun to dread being "supportively" interrogated. That's the bad news.

The good news, though, is that with only a few exceptions of snide remarks ("So *that's* where the perfect marriage wound up!") most of these women have been managing to act in a "postrevolutionary manner" even in a "prerevolutionary context."

Marie reappears from the old 1960's firehouse women's center collective: she has a Central Park West apartment now and her two kids are off to college; do I want to stay there indefinitely? Sue shoves a note into my pocket: "Anything, anytime, anywhere. Not much money and a Lower East Side fourth-floor walk-up but it's yours and I can stay with my lover as long as necessary." Clare leaves phone messages all over town, at Athena, at Ginny's, at Georgi's: "Single mother with little space and two yowling children can't offer home but would be delighted to extend dinner, solace, bitchery at men, whatever." Karen has one of her aides track me down and calls (from *Congress!*) urging me to use the New York flat which she's "only in on weekends, anyway." Betita wires from Los Angeles that she'll be on location filming for the next two months and why don't I chuck it all, fly out, and stay in peace at the Malibu house. Marta magically always has an extra ticket for a concert, Alida surfaces from the imminent deadline on her own new book to offer a small loan, Kathryn and Carol want to know if I need help with any errands—cleaners, laundromat, jobs regarding Hope, anything. Blake wangles her department chairman at Manhattan University to offer me a poetry reading for three hundred dollars. Edith places her husband (did she *ask* him??) at my disposal, together with his rental limo, when he's not on a hire-job. Lesley volunteers to visit Hope in the hospital anytime I can't make it, " 'Cause I live just a block away." Suzanne, Joanne, Pat, Glo, and Bunny invite me to join their Brooklyn living collective, no rent contribution required. Marilyn drags me off to the gift of a Shiatsu massage, where the Korean masseuse diagnoses my neck and shoulder muscles as being the Great Wall of China. Toni offers free legal advice, Fran free medical advice, Vivvie free couple-counseling if that would help Larry and me, Loretta free typing of the book manuscript if any of it is ready.

Shock. Hilarity. Miracle. I must be carrying around the most distinguished set of feminist keys any hobo activist ever possessed. I've been at five, no six, different apartments since Georgi's, from which I had to move on because her sister was coming for a visit. Iliana calls me "dear derelict" and thinks I'm crazy not to just come to her and light in one place from which I'll know I won't have to move on. But I resist that, particularly since she and I grow closer all the time and the energy between us is becoming rather charged. More than I could handle in a living situation, I think.

There are places I could stay longer than a few days or a week, of course—like the Brooklyn collective. But I don't want to be over in Brooklyn and I've never been big on collective living and this is not the time for experimentation. I also feel awkward putting too much weight on any one friend for too long.

Besides, curious as it seems, there's a grotesque freedom to all this. Some days it feels like I'm simply on a prolonged lecture/organizing trip, that home will be there, reassuringly familiar, at the end of it. I prided myself on knowing how to pack, how to travel efficiently. But now I'm learning for the first time a kind of nomadic, pared-down existence—and there's something chaste, almost purifying about it. Only those clothes you can carry with you, layering or unlayering for variety or as the season shifts. Discovering that time and energy are more important even than cash, so *take* cabs if you have to and don't feel guilty about it. Delegate tasks wherever you can, unlearn shame at depending on people if they truly offer, and don't feel guilty about that. It's a strange weightlessness that I've only ever experienced before while in jail, where you're stripped of your material possessions but realize they can never strip you of yourself. There's a discovery, an elation in that, which is difficult to explain, even to Iliana.

It's also a heady sensation to feel so amazingly, undeservedly *loved.* By women friends and by less-close women acquaintances. By all the gestures of consideration, affection, generosity. The net that I and hundreds of other women have been weaving together for decades actually is now being stretched out by their hands to support *me*.

Those are the good days, anyway. I cherish them. There is, to be sure, a flip side. Like the pure fatigue and despair when *it* hits, from the tiniest details like last month wanting my warm gloves for the sudden cold snap—except that I'd left them all the way up in Riverdale at Korynne's in a box of winter stuff she's storing for me and how in hell could I disturb her for a pair of gloves but it was cold and I hadn't the money to buy another pair and my hands couldn't just be shoved into my pockets because I'm carrying things all the time so then I decided I better just put it out of my mind and have cold hands. Or how the shoulders ache from simply *carrying* everything all the time—the clothes one is sick to death of re-wearing, the file folders (labeled General To Do, Phone Calls, Urgent Mail, Hope Medical, Hope Co-op, Hope Insurance, Hope Stock Tangle, Hope Legal, Hope Bills, Laurence Bills, Hope Nursing Homes, Hope Furnishings Sale, Outstanding J.T. Loans, Upcoming Lecture Notes, Athena Memos, Book Chapter). I have so many lists that I now have lists of lists. I cart around more books than the inventory of that tiny Yonkers library I went to as a kid. Then there's how it feels to mentally run one's fingers over the loved features of well-worn possessions in rooms where one no longer lives but where part of oneself remains alert and waiting: that particular book, right now, when I need it for a reference; that particular third dresser drawer that always stuck and squeaked in a friendly manner; the fifth cut on that particular recording; the glazed plum pottery mug that meant comfort just to hold no matter what warmth filled it. But the worst of it isn't material or physical. It's the gradually accumulating prostration of saying thank you to well-meaning friends. It's the suspicion that one might have overstayed one's limit, pushed beyond unspoken boundaries, begun to be perceived as a soap-opera character; that one has somehow "asked for this" by one's galloping neuroses, that one might begin to be viewed as A Problem.

Still, there are lessons emerging in what Charlotte has termed "all this sleeping around without sleeping around." Things you learn about others: the ways they really live their lives, the small specifics—how they arrange their homes, kitchens, books; what they're obsessively clean about and what they leave dirty, which articles they really use and which merely exhibit, how their private space differs from their public personae—tiny, touching, infinitely tender details that teach compassion about the peculiar species called human. Leonora, for instance, loves soul music but loathes soul food; she's a closet vegetarian. At Charlotte and Zach's, all *her* cosmetics and contact-lens cooker and other toiletries are crammed onto half a bathroom shelf—while *his* electric shaver occupies the other half in solitary splendor. Karen's Manhattan pied-à-terre is resplendent with petit-point cushion covers she herself has made —the way, she confesses, that she keeps herself sane much less awake while listening to her stultifying colleagues in the U.S. House of Representatives. Marie, who's a superb cook, has always longed for a garlic press and a good cleaver, but thought them self-indulgent; she jumped up and down with delight when she found I'd bought them for her. *Nobody* remembers to water their plants; consequently I'm getting a reputation for being a green-thumb genius.

But I *want* to be of use, to give back not just in gratitude but (how strange to feel this under these circumstances!) in *celebration*. Such a rare privilege of glimpsing all this intimacy can develop the eye, can teach one what one likes or abhors (and didn't even know one liked or abhorred), can sensitize the vital capacity to *notice*.

Even more crucial are the lessons I begin to see are there for learning about myself. Because in this situation, after a while, anyway, the skillful tantrums don't work, the shaking of the Promethean fist. All one's fine words about existential risk not only come home to roost but lay (rotten) eggs in one's face. Patience has to be—finally—engaged and wrestled with, and patience is not some shy Griselda sitting dumbly at her spinning wheel. Patience is Cerberus at the gates of hell, wrath held in inertia only by the force of awe, a giving when one feels one has nothing left to give, a waiting that is atomic in its motion, an active stillness. I thought I'd already learned patience. But patience, I begin to see, isn't so easily seduced. I find I keep mistaking patience for mere depression, despair, or indifference. Authentic patience, when I do glimpse it, is for me accompanied by certain characteristics—humor being the chief one.

The lesson of absurdity is central. A sense of the ludicrous, the ironic, a *positive* value in the surreal—how that dwarfs the other sense of injustice, malevolence!

I mean, it *is* side-splittingly incongruous to find yourself pulling up to the lawyers' offices in the momentary luxury of Edith's husband's chauffeur-driven free limo, from which you emerge complete with briefcase, handbag, backpack, and two paper shopping bags. Then you proceed on in to meet for an hour with two attorneys who explain that your mother is a pauper but cannot claim indigence or Medicare because she legally owns a Sutton Place co-op and besides she's in trouble with the IRS for three years of unfiled tax returns. Then they discreetly inquire why you never sued her for your childhood earnings and you remind them that the "Jackie Coogan law" came into effect in New York State fairly late and though you could have slid in under the statute of limitations it was difficult to stomach the idea of hauling your mother into court. Then you ask if you might use their phone to make a few local calls. You call Laurence, who shouts that you have vast power, influence, and support-systems, and since he has none he is the proletariat. You call Charlotte to apologize that you'll be late on tomorrow's editing delivery. You call Iliana to find out if the Oklahoma State Women's College check got forwarded *yet*. You call your bank, to say you realize you're overdrawn but there's a deposit in the mail to cover that (a lie). You call the Happy Sunset Home Admissions Office, to confirm that you'll be coming by tomorrow. Then you reassure the lawyers that they'll be paid their fee as soon as the co-op is sold, and you express repeated gratitude for their forbearance. Then you give them one of the shopping bags, containing the latest batch of Hope's gradually-being-sorted papers. Then you scrunch yourself into the subway to be lurched to Georgi's, where you are now staying again because it's the most centrally located and you have a room to yourself there, which she has by now named "The Julian Travis Memorial Den." On the subway, your brain won't stop buzzing. By this time, you are a composite of even more selves than Virginia Woolf's Orlando on her way home at the end of the book. But *you* don't *have* a home. Later, in the middle of the night, you get up to go to the bathroom but being groggily half-asleep turn right instead of left and bash your face on the wall. Georgi's bathroom is to the left; it's Charlotte's that's to the right.

If this isn't farce then I have forgotten my Marx Brothers—Harpo, Groucho, Chico, Zeppo, and Karl.

What a blessed respite humor provides! Perspective, dimension, balance, *mercy* (for one's self as well as others)! How the "If-onlys . . ." and the "I-never-should-haves . . ." melt away until they sound like distant mumblings of a megalomaniacal mind babbling to itself (like Doris Lessing's "I I I . . ." in *The Golden Notebook)*, babbling out into massively shifting patterns of some profound galactic brain which has far better things about which to think.

Best of all, the humor and patience give courage, too. Not "strength," *courage.* I'm getting awfully sick of strength. A wall can be strong; so can some hulk pumping iron, a slave, a dictator, a torturer, a rapist, a mule. Courage, on the other hand, requires intelligent *attention,* which can't coexist comfortably with depression or despair. It has more to do with humility and buoyancy.

I begin to sense that all the places my trajectory now transits are rich with wisdom, mine for the finding. It's up to me to learn how to use this creatively. I sense, too, that the anguish recedes in direct proportion to the creative use I can make of it.

May 23, 1983

Still at Georgi's. Still playing to mixed notices:

—Hospital situation remains largely the same, though she has flickers of acknowledgment for me lately. I was spooning her some ice cream today, thought she didn't want anymore, and started to take away the remains. Suddenly she drawled imperiously, "Mbaby!" and opened her mouth as a sign she wanted more. I thought my heart would burst. Dr. Grimes is holding to his promise of trying to keep her there until a nursing home manifests itself, despite her not being an emergency anymore. Then again, he says that the cough she's developed bears close watching: the old threat of pneumonia.

—Nursing-home situation still unresolved. Iliana and I have endured seeing eleven so far: hell-hole after hell-hole. Still another four to go on the "preferred list." There *must* be a tolerable one in all of New York City. What this society does to old people is unspeakable. Charlotte's droll comment that we ought to be thinking about creating an Old Feminists' Home should be taken in dead earnest.

—Co-op situation improving. The apartment is finally emptied: trashed, sold, or in storage. The floor sanders have finished, the painters started today. It's already being shown to prospective buyers, with instructions to the agent that speed, not the highest price, is the priority.

—Legal situation proceeding. *Ugly.* The lawyers have had me declared Hope's guardian and conservator. The formalities involved depositions from her doctors and a hospital visit from the court-appointed expert, these atrocities to save her from a worse one, a competency hearing. I fought the entire competency approach. It had me vomiting for two days (that was at Marie's, I think), but apparently there was no other way to formalize my authority to sell the co-op. When the court expert asked her what date it was, she stammered furiously that she wasn't crazy or a child and that they both knew damned well it was September 15, 1938. (What happened to her on that day, I wonder?)

—Money situation grave. I'm still trying to juggle her bills (for which I may or may not be able to partly reimburse myself after the co-op sale, depending on how much it brings). I'm also still supporting the loft, though that does begin to feel masochistic. I know Iliana despairs of me for this lunacy. But I really don't see what else I can do.

—Travel situation beginning to get me down. Thank god the weather's warmer, but I've still got a low-grade fever hanging on from the cold I caught in Canada. Squeezed in three more speaking dates in the past weeks. Have to accept as many as possible, and sandwich in the Athena editing on planes, in motels, in airport waitingrooms.

—No movement on the Laurence front. Sullenness alternates with tears, hints of tenderness (from both of us) with viciousness (from both of us). Mostly the cruel freeze of "civility." Stasis. Numbness.

—Timing front formidable. In the next month it all has to mesh like clockwork or the whole thing will fall apart: nursing home to be found and, since they won't hold open a vacancy for more than a week, co-op must be sold by then so as to *pay* for nursing home. Both must happen before Grimes can no longer stall discharging her from the hospital into nowhere.

Lawyers will not handle tax problem without being paid up in total for their work thus far. Co-op sale mustn't be *so* cheaply sacrificial for the sake of speed (but then again it must be); there has to be enough money for her mounting legal and medical bills as well as to keep her for as long as necessary in a home. And I've *got* to be able to reimburse myself for at least a few hundred bucks or else the June loft rent can't get paid.

Panic is rising at the back of my brain, because soon colleges close for vacation and the lecture season is over until mid-fall. I can't do the intensive free-lance work required to tide all this over during the summer while in transit, crouching in various friends' spare corners. *What will I do?*

And how in the name of anything am I supposed to be writing a *book* in the middle of this? I haven't touched the suspended chapter in months, am falling way behind in delivery schedule, and can't extract more of the advance money until I have more chapters to deliver.

Panic. So much energy needed just to stave off the panic. What in hell am I going to *do?*

May 27, 1983

Yes, there *is* a Goddess, after all—and not merely because, as Iliana claims, garlic was discovered to be good in cooking.

Dear magnificent munificent sold-out compromised Athena has offered me an in-house editing job for the summer. The salary is small, but they're hardly financially secure. Besides, it *is* a salary, and a steady one. Rescue! I start on the first of the month.

It looks like we've got a prospective buyer for the co-op. What's even better, he's a relative of somebody on the co-op building's board—which means the board probably won't take forever to clear him as a potential tenant.

Iliana and I have actually seen one tolerable nursing home, a place called Peacehaven. Right on Seventy-seventh Street, non-religious, almost humane—although by now my standards have been thoroughly humbled. But it's clean and the walls are painted bright cheerful colors. The admissions director referred to the women as "clients," and "residents," not as inmates, patients, girls, ladies, or "them." The kitchen seemed spotless. They permit TV sets, radios, and phones in the rooms (all at extra charge, of course). Visiting hours are anytime between 9 A.M. and 7 P.M. The staff didn't look too tired, cynical, or sadistic, though you never can tell. Iliana and I have learned that if you can sneak away from the tour guides, you ask the women themselves whether they "like" the place. That's a risky business, because often they burst out crying that they want to go home, or they nod in silent terror. But sometimes they whisper facts about the kind of care they receive. At Peacehaven we were free to snoop where we chose, and the women we asked chatted openly about finding the place "not bad, for these places." It's wildly expensive, naturally—$3200 a month. Breathtaking. The other catch is that there are no vacancies at present or foreseen in the immediate future. I find myself shamelessly walking around with my fingers crossed that one of the poor souls who live there will conveniently croak—but only in time for the co-op closing. I have no principles left.

Hope does have a mild case of pneumonia, but Grimes doesn't think it too alarming. They have her in an oxygen tent, though, to ease the breathing. Yesterday she smiled at me for a moment through the plastic.

Spring is in full exuberance. Iliana "abducted" me on a walk through Central Park to remind me that "magnolia exist, my dear." I've got such a lightened heart today, I can hardly believe it. When Iliana and I were having dinner in a little Italian restaurant, complete with red-checked tablecloths and drippy candle-in-old-winebottle, we toasted the Garlic Goddess and then each other. Our eyes held in a long look, before I blinked mine away. But I thought *This is possibility, this is excitement, this is pleasure!*

The next time our eyes caught, I held her gaze.

June 2, 1983

Started at Athena yesterday. A desk! A file cabinet! A phone! A typewriter! A steady salary! I reminded Iliana that the Garlic Goddess also blessed us with shallots.

I'm back at Charlotte's, since now Georgi's brother is visiting her (tight-knit siblings in that family). Charlotte and Zach always take their wedding anniversary as a vacation week to spend alone together at their country house (poor Charlotte?). I have figured out the way to deal with the poodles: separately. Walk (drag) Sido, return. Then walk (fly after) Phideaux, return. It makes for four dog-walks a day. Thank god it's summer. If it were still winter, I'd wring those dogs out over the sink.

Iliana is possibly the most *alive* human being I've ever met. Yesterday, to celebrate the Athena job, she sent a dozen exotic silvery lilies and a bottle of Moët to me—at the *office.* Quite a few eyebrows hit quite a few hairlines. I think I blushed for the first time in my whole life.

(I loved it.)

June 3, 1983

With only three more bags of Hope's papers to sort through, this evening at Iliana's I came across a black pocket-notebook filled with yellowing pages: entries about Hope's girlhood trip to Mexico. Iliana held me while I cried uncontrollably.

Then another entry, after a lot of blank pages, right at the end.

> So much to do, learn, become. Maybe it's not too late to begin singing again. If I work hard enough and I'm strong enough, I can be anything I want to be. There's talk about war but I refuse to believe it. I'm so full of hope that today I decided to call *myself* "Hope" from here on in. I'm going to create a whole new me. Today is the start of a fresh chapter in my life. It's going to be a perfectly *beautiful* life.
>
> September 15, 1938

June 4, 1983

Went to the hospital directly after work, filled with love for her. She's out of the oxygen tent. She sometimes talks to me now, though not always to *me,* it turns out, but to Yetta or Esther. I don't contradict her anymore. When she does speak to *me,* just the garbled "Julian," or even "Baby" lisping out of the side of her mouth is a triumph for both of us.

But today she was drooling a lot, and I kept blotting it away as gently as I could, each of us sending out shy smiles to the other. Then—and I meant it as a little joke, god forgive me I thought she'd chuckle with recognition about it—I wiped up another dribble and I said encouragingly, "Come on, Little Momma, dry your smile."

Horror spread over her face as though I'd struck her. She squeezed her eyes shut and wrenched her head away from me. For the next two hours I pled with her. I wept, tried to explain the joke, apologized, tried to coax her back to me, told her how much I loved her. But she sealed off completely. I couldn't get through. Then I was forced to leave because visiting hours were over.

Coming down from her floor in the elevator, I felt like a monster. I called Iliana from the lobby phone booth. It all poured out. When I was finished, Iliana said simply,

"She knows."

I didn't understand, and began to repeat that I'd humiliated Hope hideously, that I'd rubbed in the fact of her disease by way of a long-ago reference she didn't even remember. But Iliana's voice rang firm over the phone:

"Juliana. I tell you she knows. Not just the reference to your childhood saying, though she knows very well where that comes from. That's why she can't face you. *She knows what she's done to you.*"

As I walked out of the hospital, the realization of what Iliana meant hit me. Then, almost simultaneously, it dawned on me that Hope would eventually die, and I would live. I would outlive her. I was alive in the young summer evening.

It was odious because I thought I'd reached the other side of forgiveness. But this didn't feel like revenge, only exuberance. It came as a shock—which is idiotic, because most children do outlive their parents. It's not that I'd really believed I *wouldn't;* more that she and I couldn't both be genuinely *alive* at the same time. Now that she begins to fade, I begin to *be.* Is that vampirism or rebirth? There was some anger along with the euphoria, but it tasted clean. Not a ready-to-dance-on-her-grave anger, because it contained no celebration of her dying. It felt instead like a ritual festival, the breaking of an old spell. It's hard to put my finger on it. I was appalled at the intensity of my elation. But strangest of all, I felt no guilt.

I think I don't want to return to Larry.

I think I want to get my own apartment.

I think I'm falling in love with Iliana de Costa.

June 9, 1983

Miracles fluttering down all over the place, like magnolia

blossoms from the trees in the park. The co-op's been sold. A vacancy opened up at Peacehaven. Hope's recovered from the pneumonia, though she still won't look at me or talk to me. Charlotte says I can have the Athena job for as long as I want it. I'm back at Georgi's in the J.T. Memorial Den and Georgi's going to Europe on the fifteenth for an entire month so I can have the apartment all to myself. That means I can begin to write again. I can pay Hope's bills and she can be moved into Peacehaven day after tomorrow. I've been trying to prepare her for that, to explain she won't be going back to the co-op and why. But she won't respond in any way, not since the "dry your smile" day, not even with fury.

Last night, after Iliana and I had a celebratory dinner with champagne (every fragment of good news is an excuse for her to declare another celebration), we walked arm-in-arm through the Village. When I left her at the street door to her apartment, I kissed her full on the lips. Then I raced off and leapt into a taxi. All the way up here to Georgi's in the cab, I trembled as if Parkinson's were a hereditary disease.

I think I definitely want my own apartment, and a more permanent separation from Larry. In fact, I think I'll have to tell him that as of July first I won't be able to shoulder the loft bills any more, because I've got to start saving for a place of my own. It's time he was nudged out of the nest, too.

It'll be hard, telling him that. He'll storm and rave about me destroying him all over again. It'll be specially painful, because in just the last three or four phone calls, he's been quite understanding. Like the original Laurence. He even came to see Hope at the hospital one evening, not that she recognized him. But then, she hasn't seen him in years. Or maybe she did recognize him but wouldn't concede that. In any event, he and I went for coffee after. There we were, Laurence and Julian, sitting in the hospital coffee-shop talking politics, deploring the latest round of Administration cutbacks in social services, trading bewilderment over Reagan's grip on the public imagination. I reminded Larry that Reagan was an actor, albeit a lousy one, and we both started laughing. I'll always love Laurence Millman. He might never believe that, but there it is. Just as Hope will never understand or believe that I'll always love her, but there *it* is.

I told all this to Iliana at dinner tonight and her reply was,

"Not surprising. Julian Travis might never understand or believe it, but perhaps you're beginning to love *her.*"

My god. I hope she's right.

June 18, 1983

Stunned, exultant confusion.

I've been to bed with Iliana.

Utterly different. Eerily *familiar.* Absolutely astounding. Totally "natural."

Explosions going off in my brain:

How startling, at my age, to encounter this whole new sexual terrain in myself—as if I'd been color-blind to certain parts of the spectrum, and now, suddenly, can see shades and vibrancies of unnameable intensity but undeniable reality. It makes me furious that I missed so much for so long, lost so much time. It makes me giddy, childishly gleeful—that this gift of savage delight came to me at all, that I escaped going to my grave in ignorance of its existence. It makes me mournful beyond outrage—that the organic *normalcy* of this state of loving, its *ease,* its (there again, I can't think of any other way to describe it:) *familiarity,* is a target for fear, hatred, bigotry.

I don't understand the force of this "epiphany," for me especially, since I've been to bed with women before, and it failed abysmally. I think back to all those years, particularly during the 1970's whirl of organizing and traveling, where I'd wind up in a sleeping bag or on a spare mattress or sofa at some women's collective after a day of meetings and demonstrations. There was inevitably at least one young woman who'd been at my elbow for hours, struggling with having contracted a severe crush but not wanting to come on as a "fan" or as what Larry used to nastily term "your lesbian groupies." I developed my own brand of feminist diplomacy to handle such situations with as much tact, evasion, and delicacy as I could muster. But after years of this, I began to feel cowardly and narrow-minded. What's more, my old approval-desire syndrome was being activated by what felt like a steady assault on me as a publicly heterosexual feminist ("How dare you call yourself . . ."). I just got tired of saying No. So there I'd be, huddled in the sleeping bag, satisfied with what I'd accomplished, but desperate for five hours of sleep before catching an early plane for the next town. Suddenly there *she'd* be: a young woman filled with longing and loneliness and a hunger for the feminist energy I guess I represented to her. She'd sit on the floor and tell her life story and we'd both begin to cry with a mutual yearning for some other way of living. I'd hold her while she cried, and then she'd ask—so vulnerably—if she could crawl in with me. Out of pity or embarrassment or tiredness (like god knows how many wives to how many husbands), I'd sometimes give in. It was easier than saying no. Though I sensed it wasn't me who was being desired, but Julian Travis. Though I felt nothing but tenderness and a sorrow for both of us as women. Though I knew I might experience a residual bitterness—at finding myself a feather in someone's cap, a notch in someone's belt. Though I knew *she* might experience a residual bitterness—that I didn't fall in love with her, that I left in the morning.

It didn't happen often. Perhaps five or six times over all those years. And sometimes we'd just sleep. But it happened enough to convince me that I must be an unregenerate heterosexual, despite what was my search maybe for it to work, and despite my fine intellectual beliefs that sexuality was a single continuum, that society was the culprit for devising categories and pigeon-holing people into either/or boxes. When I told Larry, he said he understood—though during the later fights he'd ammo it up in terms of my being incapable of saying no to anyone except him (untrue). He even wondered aloud whether it might be interesting to try for a "threesome"—him and me and another woman—a proposal which seemed sickeningly close to a harem scenario, though he floated it as an exotic experiment in "sexual revolution." I declined to organize such a meeting.

So this revelation with Iliana is all the more odd, for me. As usual, there's an irony in attendance. I've spent almost two decades fighting for the right of sexual preference as one of the central issues of women's freedom. If I've been straight-baited by some women I've also been gay-baited by right-wingers who assume all feminists are lesbian. Hello! Surprise! Here we are now, part and parcel of the group we thought we were safely crusading for as an outsider. Like the work on behalf of abortion rights—with Julian's private secret locked tight in the back of her throat during every speech. I better be careful about which oppressed group I defend. One of these days I'll wake up as a peasant in India.

Still, more than irony and amazement, there's the confusion. I find myself thinking about Larry, and a great calm undramatic bell of grief strikes and tolls through me. I think about Hope slowly beginning to die, and somewhere in my bowels something cries out *My God My God* but all regions between that cry and the surface of me feel numb, as if I've sleepwalked the past twenty-two years with Larry, sleepwalked the previous twenty with her, hearing messages of myself but from far away, underwater. I think about Iliana and I know that being drawn to her woman's body is connected with Hope and Hope's dying. Beyond that, I know only my own ignorance.

No, that's not true. I discover my own—bizarre to feel this at such a crisis-laden moment in my life—capacity for happiness. Shock upon shock. With so many details crowding my brain, my thoughts keep going back to Iliana: anticipation at seeing her, excitement at being with her, the *combination* of *intimacies*—friendship (the type one can only have with another woman, *yes* Charlotte) *simultaneous* with an erotic charge! Not having to sacrifice one for the other! So many layers of emotion oscillating at once. Even the pain, homelessness, fear, gets put to use by this new energy. I feel I'm internally hemorrhaging Life.

Is that the difference, then, from those other times, with women reaching for me like lost daughters in the night? That here *I* reach back—and find? That I'm cared for, tenderly and raucously, reminded to eat and sleep and relax, coaxed into laughter and pleasure? And how distinct the lovemaking: to be wanted for one*self* with such passion that one glimpses that self through the eye of one's lover—as desirable, sexual, actually beautiful!

Is that the difference? That with my entire life lying in ruins about me, I'm in love? I'm *in love*—with a woman?

CHAPTER NINE
Summer, 1983

"It's Independence Day," Julian said softly. "Independence Day," she repeated, her awestruck whisper echoing the first thought that had come into her consciousness on awakening. She lay still, letting the smile of that revelation play over her face. Then she turned her head to look at Iliana, asleep beside her.

My friend, she thought, easing herself up carefully on one elbow, the better to watch that sleeping face in morning light gauzed blue by the curtain. My . . . lover. The word still stammered in the brain. Yet there the lover was, her breathing calm, her hair tousled against the pillow, those beryl-gray eyes —the color of rain, Julian had declared—moving rhythmically in a secret dream visored by the lids and the lashes that curved over the cheek. Full and rich, the features of that face, even when in repose, but never more so than when animated in conversation. The cosmopolite with the naughty smile, the connoisseur of wines and cheeses, olives and Caravaggio, music, chiaroscuro. The patient watcher, who knew how to wait— and then how to woo when the time was right. How to bring Julian slowly, through these weeks of lovemaking, into responses at first passive, then awkward, then gradually sensual, open, less afraid. Oh how different, Julian grinned, how different to find a mutual desire heating in the blood, tensing the muscles, quickening the breath. Her trepidatious lovemaking to Iliana had elicited reactions so generous they seemed to Julian out of proportion to her own ineptitude. But last night, she thought, with a shameless blush this time, the very previous last night, something had broken loose in Julian, reverted to the wild, surged through her, resurrecting in her a lover whose arms, legs, torso, hands, mouth, seemed to remember a primordial cuncipotence of what and how, where and when, if, yes, now, there, yes this way, yes, yes. This time she had seen astonishment widen Iliana's eyes, felt it shiver through Iliana's flesh, heard it answered in her own body. And Iliana had opened with the abandon of an antelope to a leap of air.

Julian stretched languorously, her brain stretching, too, into twenty directions at once. How depraved it was to imagine or impose fixed roles in such a fluid situation! When the whole energy resided in this dancing balance—to take and be taken, give and receive, flicker effortlessly from one fever of surrender that lost nothing but regained one's self to another fever of passion that seized the surrender of the lover to the lover's self!

She yawned luxuriantly as a cat, congratulating herself on this dazzle of insights occurring for the first time ever in history, to her, Julian, the Chosen One. Fireworks of the intellect. Happy, oh happy Independence Day, she sang to herself.

Iliana stirred, opened her eyes, focused on Julian, and promptly announced in a sleepy voice that she was famished for breakfast but neither could she imagine ever being able to move again, considering what Julian had accomplished upon her last night.

"Then *I'll* make breakfast and we can have it in bed," Julian shouted giddily, bouncing up to a sitting position. "What have we got? What would you like? Quail eggs? Truffles under crystal?"

"Dona nobis pacem. Such energy," came the muffled reply, "We're out of everything but canned tins and condiments. I haven't had a chance to get to the market in days." Iliana emitted a human purr as she rolled onto her back. "I want . . . croissants," she blinked.

"Croissants you shall have. Fresh flakey croissants adrip with butter. Poached eggs greenly flecked with marjoram. Sizzling bacon, crisp as your laughter. Fragrant steaming espresso with a pungent curl of lem—"

"This is torture," Iliana growled. "Don't describe it. Wave the wand and make it to *happen.*"

"—thick pulpy orange juice brassy as your smile, a triple-crème cheese *wantonly* gooey as your—"

"Juliana! This is not Tom Jones in a book! This is your starving lover whom you have incapacitated and who if you do not manage to feed soon will devour whatever is near," Iliana slithered closer, smacking her lips menacingly.

Julian leapt out of bed and grabbed for her jeans, sweeping them up off the floor where they had been unceremoniously deposited the night before.

"What?" Iliana wailed. "Where are you going?"

"To the deli, silly twit. To wave the wand and make it to happen."

"Wait, I'll go with you. Don't move so *quickly,* for god's sake."

"No you won't. You'll lie there like an odalisque and I'll be back in a flash with a feast."

"But I *want* to go with—"

"Please? I'm crackling with energy. Let *me* do something for a change?"

Iliana flopped back onto her pillow. "Just as well," she groaned. "For me, I am not the same woman who went to bed last night. I will never be the same. Now I know how Atlantis felt after the tidal wave."

Julian had already strapped on her sandals. "Then just lie there and float," she called back, wriggling into her T-shirt as she stumbled toward the door. "The tidal wave is ebbing. But only for the moment."

Running down the brownstone stairs, she hummed to herself, "Independence Day, Independence Day, I'm crazy and happy, does this mean I'm gay, tra la."

Grove Street was serene as a sabbath, because of the national holiday. Only one other person was out so early, Jim Kwan, the always impeccably attired Hawaiian computer expert who lived just downstairs from Iliana. A short, rotund man in white linen shirt and shorts, he was walking his dachshund, the two of them a study in contrasting shapes. Julian called out a hello, wanting to address them as the Line and the Circle.

"Beautiful, *beautiful* amazingly *brilliant* day, don't you think?" she added, not waiting for a reply, but beaming as she swung past where the dog and his walker, pooper-scooper in hand at the ready, were stopped beside a tree. Fortunate man, she noted, the dachshund was at least a hundred and two years old and barely able to waddle; walking *him* could not be half so difficult as reconciling Sido and Phideaux in their polar temperaments and "sex role" styles.

Incredibly *reductive,* her fireworks brain flared again, to think of women playing *roles!* You didn't want an imitation man. You wanted another *woman. That* was it. Of course, the psychologists (the better ones) termed all this the "animus" or "anima," the "male in the female and vice-versa." Which not only missed the point but substituted another point entirely, still attributing action to some abstract male principle and reception to some abstract female one. Nor had the political rhetoric—lesbian, feminist, lesbian-feminist, or feminist-lesbian—really approached the implications of what such a glimpse of freedom might mean—for everyone, female and male, with a same-sex *or* opposite-sex lover. And for the *self.* Political insights at profound genius level, Julian congratulated herself.

She strode into the deli and danced through it rapidly, gathering up croissants, butter, cheese, eggs, and bacon into a small basket. Then she paused in front of the corner refrigeration bin. It was impossible to get at the orange juice. A low wall of stacked soup-can crates not yet unloaded barred her way. She looked around for the deli owner, but he was in conversation at the register with the sole other customer in the store.

"I tyell yoo dee Gaud's chonyest troot," the customer was saying emphatically. "Deece dee honely cyontree for to bee frree een hyere."

"You got it, buster. You're tellin' *me?*"

"Uh, please?" Julian called.

"Hi *knyow.* Hi cawm from Roosia honely seeks montas. Hi now trive tixi kib 'nd beink frree in Beeg Happle! Halso I vork as moofer and hahf my own wan."

"Could somebody possibly help, uh—" Julian sang out again.

The deli owner rang up the man's purchase and pushed a paper bag toward him. "Yeah, the land o' the free. You people oughtta know."

"Hi tyell you Hi *do* knyow! Commoneests hahfraid of Hamyerika, hahfraid of strunk cyontree 'nd strunk Preesiden' Rrrhaygan, ha ha." He pounded the counter happily. Julian spied the Stars and Stripes tatooed on his forearm.

"Pretty bad in Russia, huh? I mean what's it *really* like over there? Ya hear all sorts of things." The deli owner leaned across his counter in anticipation of *National Enquirer* gory details.

Julian sighed and looked longingly at the orange juice. She could just pass it up. But in the context, that seemed like a personal concession to the ultra-right wing.

"Hell, no," she muttered, setting down her basket. She heaved the soup-can cartons one by one to the side, grunting with the effort, until she could reach the juice. Only when she approached the counter did she realize her effort had interrupted the solecisms of socialist sorrow. Both men were staring at her.

The deli owner rang up her purchases in respectful silence, apparently not daring to request that she perform Amazon act number two and re-stack his cartons. But the emigré cab driver was not so restrained.

"How cyome yoo such strunk geerrl?" he asked admiringly.

"Maybe because I'm a woman," Julian snapped, counting her change. Then, suddenly remembering her one phrase of Russian, learned at the Crossroads Conference of International Women six years earlier, "Dóbro projálabat vy vismyrni feminísm," she smiled nastily at him, adding, "Welcome to international feminism," for the deli owner's benefit. She gathered up her paper bag and stalked regally to the door. Behind her, the cab driver appealed to the deli man.

"Vhat Hi deed *say?*" he cried. "Hi honely be frreendly!"

The deli man shrugged. "Forget it, buster," he grimaced. "Ya can't win. A guy can't do nuthin' right these days."

His customer nodded sagely. "Hi knyow. Vimmin is crazy hall *hover* dee vorld."

Enchanted with her riposte, Julian forgot her irritability the moment she hit the street again. She clasped her parcel as if it were her lover, and immediately re-immersed herself in her ruminations.

The *romance* of all this! This makes romance possible again! Her brain exuberated. Dear old Eleanor of Aquitaine and her daughter Marie de France . . . the concept they invented . . . it was to protect women from being abducted and raped in the Middle Ages—romance, gallantry—long lost, especially

to feminists . . . But every woman secretly *wants* romance
. . . Some acknowledge it, some deny it, most feel guilty or
childish about wanting it . . . It seems like a sign of weakness
. . . This makes it *possible* again.

She raced up the stairs, unable to tell if her heart thumped
from excitement or exertion. She could hear Iliana singing in
the shower. It's *not* weakness when it's between two women,
she reflected, unwrapping her parcels and starting breakfast in
the kitchen. In the past weeks, Iliana had sent her flowers,
toasted her with champagne, splashed her with rosewater—
and Julian had learned the freedom, found the permission, to
do the same things back. *That's* it, she concluded, that's why I
don't feel compromised or purchased. Why hasn't anyone *told*
everybody about this? She knitted her brows with concentration while setting the breakfast bedtable tray. And what do I
care, care, care, the blood sang in her veins, I'm in love and I'm
happy and it's Independence Day!

She bore the tray like an offering to the bedroom, where a
revived Iliana, re-ensconced in bed, watched with evident relish as Julian swiftly undressed again and then maneuvered
both tray and herself through the bedclothes. "We'll be Ro-
mans," Julian directed. They fell to, ravenously, stuffing their
mouths and conversing with their eyes. But Julian's mind kept
sparking with her new insights and she was impatient to share
them.

At last Iliana exclaimed a small burp of satiation and leaned
back against her pillow.

"That was delicious debauchery. An orgy for the taste buds.
Juliana," she enunciated with deliberate intensity, fixing her
eyes on her subject, "I *never* so long as I live want to *ever* again
hear you bemoan yourself as not being sensual. If you picked
up that nonsense from Laurence, then he really—"

"No! *He* didn't— Well, he did say that he had come to believe
I didn't live in what he called 'a physical world,' because I was
always in flight from physical pleasure. But it was true, 'Yana. I
mean it's not his fault. That's mostly all he ever saw or felt
coming at him from me. Denial—or at best a grudging admission. What you call the little workaholic he termed the puritan
—but they *are* related, you know. I'm not talking about the real
obsessive love I do have for my work. I'm talking about using

that as escape. I've always assumed it was part of the legacy from Hope, my particular matrilineage of flesh-loathing."

Iliana set down her coffeecup with a clunk. "If he didn't see or feel it, then he didn't elicit it. I'm sorry, but I—"

"No. He tried. He really tried. Oh, I don't know. I'll be years figuring all this out. All I'm sure of is, I've at last enrolled in Remedial Living 101."

Iliana sighed and closed her eyes. "At the rate you are proceeding, *preciosa,* you must be aiming to graduate summa cum laude within weeks."

"Ah well. Always been too goal-oriented, you know. But it *has* been said that I'm a quick study." Julian arched one eyebrow rakishly.

"What you are, my dear, is an incredibly passionate sensibility enwrapped in an exquisitely fragile body. Holá, what a combination!"

"Holá, what a compliment! Don't anybody move till I get that engraved in granite."

"No, *mi corazón.*" Iliana's smile softened. "I mean it. If only you could see what I see, love yourself even the tiniest bit the way I love you. The strength of you and the frailty. The pagan in you and the romantic."

Julian edged the tray to one side so she could wiggle closer, then slid down under the covers so her head could rest on Iliana's shoulder. She inhaled that body's warmth and nestled deeper until her temple found the cushion of a breast's amplitude.

"Iliana," she murmured, "I was just thinking about that. I'm so profoundly ignorant. It appalls me. God, how could anybody get to age forty-one and remain so stupid. Maybe I'm just the latecomer rediscovering what's already been obvious to others for a long time. But— oh, I don't know where to start. For one thing, I'm just so shocked at the *romance* of all this. You say I'm a romantic. But I thought I'd had to murder that part of myself, because it always led me to destruction, to melodrama. And it left a sour taste in the soul. Of . . . of *compromise.* This is so different."

"It's love, that's all. It matters—and it's possible."

"Larry and I also loved one another. I don't want to oversimplify *or* overcomplicate. But context really does have something to do with it." She snuggled closer, then began haltingly, "Take romance."

"With pleasure," agreed Iliana.

But Julian was undeterred. "In these past weeks, we've walked in summer rain together, played Chopin nocturnes on the tape deck, we've . . . my god, it's been one great luscious melting *swoon* of romance!"

"I should hope so," came the answer.

"But I haven't felt 'compromised.' It's felt liberating, not the way it would if a man—even Larry—sent me flowers, champagne, perfume. I'd feel . . . *bargained* for in some way, pressured. And as much as I'd love the doing, I'd become suspicious of the doer. See what I mean?"

"Is that so complicated, *chica?* Those actions have *been* used by men as 'bargainings'—the Don Juan cliché, the Casanova."

"Yes. Exactly. But my point is that I'd still *long* for them. I longed for them from Larry—the little considerations as well as the grand gestures. What I'm suspecting now is that on the occasions he *did* do them, it felt foolish, it made me nervous. So he stopped. Or else he sensed I would have put them down as nineteenth-century corny male manipulations and consequently rarely did them in the first place."

Iliana shifted position slightly. "Larry. Always Larry."

"Anyway, it all comes back to *power*. I can revel in your heady swoonful actions *because* we're both women. The power is balanced . . . But then I suppose I've wound full circle into a feminist platitude: that women and men won't be able to understand one another, much less love one another freely, until the power imbalance between them is removed. Pretty obvious. But there's more *to* it than that . . ."

"Much more. You don't have to use a diaphragm. O brilliant feminist theorist, my arm is falling asleep. Do you think I can bestir you a few centimeters?"

"I'm *sorry,*" Julian cried, rearranging herself into a cross-legged sitting position but still engrossed in her ideas. "It all has to do with sameness and difference. I think of that lovely quote of Kate's—"

"Millett?"

"Yes. On one of her posters. Something like: 'Because we're the same—different but the same—comes the danger, the perfume, risk, glory.' "

Iliana shrugged.

"All human need has its own veracity. The only thing we have in common is our difference."

"But the thing is— I'm still *'me.'* More 'me' than ever. And there's a me that's *always* been, beneath the virginal Julian or the heterosexual Julian or the, now, I guess—how funny to think of it—lesbian Julian—"

"My dear," Iliana interrupted, "forgive me, but you are so focused on these discoveries that your euphoria could be a little perilous. You do understand, I hope, that you will not necessarily be perceived as being 'more you.' I mean, if you plan to go and do one of your Tell the World honesty pronunciations."

Julian looked at her.

"You make it sound like . . . exhibitionism. A ghetto sensibility shouldn't be *fostered. 'Yana!* It's political!"

"That's what I was afraid of," Iliana muttered, heaving herself up on her pillows. "Juliana. Darling. Listen to me. Please don't go babble all this to Larry because it is 'political' and you're certain he will therefore understand—"

"But it's important that—"

"He won't understand. Believe me. He will be furious, even the great Bloomsbury-lifestyle-radical Larry. Most people will react negatively. Some of your women friends, even, will be made uneasy. A few may turn around and support Larry in this—"

"Oh Iliana, really. I haven't looked for approval to the outside world in years. If anything, I've looked too much for approval *within* the movement, large parts of which have castigated me precisely because I *wasn't* a—"

"Please. Hear me. I know all that. I don't wish to become a movement credential, for that matter, either. But it *is* the outside world I'm trying to warn you about. My love, I can't remember a time when I didn't live with the knowledge you're now discovering. I *know* that your whole life is involved with women and the movement, but that's not the same. It's not the same to wrestle with an issue like this intellectually as it is to live it. You will be astonished—and, I fear, hurt—at the way some heterosexual friends, even feminist ones, will be alienated from you."

Julian was silent. Ginny, Leonora, Georgi, Edith. Oh god.

Charlotte. She recalled with a flush of shame how she had used Iliana as an example to Charlotte during lunch, enumerating Iliana's bisexual credentials, praising Iliana precisely because she was able to "pass" so convincingly as a heterosexual friend. And were those qualities part of what made Iliana an acceptable woman to fall in love with? Oh god, Julian thought. And then would Julian herself be regarded . . .

"Or *you* will begin to alienate yourself from *their* friendship, for fear of being perceived . . . differently. Exotically. They will find that they have to explain you, and their friendship with you, to their husbands—especially since you are a heterosexual woman who will be thought to have 'switched.' You will be perceived as a threat. Like what you call a domino theory. You will be feared."

"But I'm still just *me!*" It came out like a wail. "I know all *about* the asinine bigotries: housing, jobs, child custody, the works. Iliana, I've been a women's organizer half my life!"

"And I am telling *you*, little lecturer, that the legalities are only part of it. I've rarely had to cope with that, at least not since I left Argentina. I move in the art world, among so-called bohemians and intellectuals. But as my old friend Celia says, you can't legislate consciousness."

Julian fiddled with the sash of Iliana's robe, reknotting it.

"You're talking like some kind of separatist. I never thought you, 'Yana, of all people—"

Iliana sighed and reached for her. "Julian," she said gently, "you know I'm no separatist. You know way back from the CR group that I've loved at least two men in my life. I'm just trying to protect you. You *must* develop a healthy vigilance."

Julian sidled closer, her own voice mellowing. " 'Yana darling, my greatest vigilance . . . well, I can say this to you *because* you've loved certain men . . . I confess that my—"

"You can confess in comfort," Iliana snorted, pulling Julian's head down again to its nest. "Now. Make your confession."

Julian hesitated for a moment.

"My worst terror is of tripping over some separatist 'line' that reduces the intricate nuances of our loving into a . . . a bludgeon, to batter so-called straight women. I wear too many wounds, cranial *and* aortal, from that bludgeon to ever use myself or let myself be used that way: as a guilt-provoker, a one-upper, a pseudo-feminist paragon of contempt toward *any* woman's choice in loving. I've *been* there, on that 'side.' I'm blessed—or cursed—with double vision."

"So? Don't you think *I* am? Don't you think many women who love women are, whether or not they've ever loved a man? Don't you think we all had mothers? We're *all* raised to marry. No woman is *raised* to have a woman lover, you know." Iliana's voice floated down to Julian through her own hair.

" 'S just that, oh, I dunno . . . I'm *happy,*" Julian murmured to the smooth curve of Iliana's breast, "and I'd like the whole world to celebrate it. It's not *fair.*"

Iliana smiled at the ceiling. To such a core of simplicity had all her little organizer's ramblings come. She eased herself lower in the bed and ran her hand along the fine down on Julian's back, feeling the spine tense and then arch toward her with desire. Not all the barrage of fear and hate, not all the rhetoric of equality, she thought, can define this splendor—lips brushing lips and nipples rising against nipples, muscles knitting with eagerness, gossamer words of nonsense nibbling around the ear, liquidity melting toward liquidity, lungs swelling with breath ripe for the plucking, a glad dizziness that swirled them both up into blinding darkness. *Juliana, oh Juliana.*

Later, Julian mumbled into her shoulder, "Want to tell you something."

"Tell me anything you want," Iliana whispered, "so long as it's not another political lecture, please. By the way, do you know that it's fortunate we finished the coffee, because the tray is somewhere on the floor?"

"I want to tell you," Julian persisted drowsily, "that all I meant before was . . . the erotic pull between us, it isn't . . . fragmented. I have as passionate a lust for—for the fullness of your mind and soul as I do for your body. I want to *work* with you on something that will change the world. I want to make love and have fun and cry and listen to music and share poetry aloud and learn to ski and sail and catch a damned ball and learn to ride a bicycle and a horse—*and* a camel and a burro and an elephant, if you like." Julian heaved herself up to a sitting position, her eyes now glowing. "I want to eat garlic pickles with you, and argue, and probe our mutual neuroses together—if I can *find* any of yours—and plan political agendas and go dancing and to galleries and ballets and flea markets and conferences and marches. And jail, if necessary. I want—"

"*Sí, sí, mi niña.* You just want joy. I don't like the jail part— and to a Latin the best part of skiing is the *après*. But it's *joy* you want. Oh, my *child.*"

Julian's eyes darkened. She stopped her frolicsome bounce on the bedsprings.

"Well. Enough of my blathering. Sorry. I don't usually foist philosophical conversations on people right after breakfast."

"No, no, I love it. Why— What, where are you going *now?*"

"To take a shower and get dressed. It may be the Fourth of July to my countrymen and women, darling, but I have to make a visit to Hope and then go on into the office."

Iliana sat straight up and yelped. "To the office? Today?"

"Uh huh," Julian said, gathering up the breakfast tray and its former contents from the floor. "Oh, lucky, nothing broke."

"Hope, I can understand. I'll go with you, in fact. But why go into Athena?"

"Because. Nobody else will be there. It'll be quiet. I can sit at my desk and pretend it's my own study and maybe do some writing."

"But this is a holiday in your country. You're *always* working, going, doing. Can't you take one day and just *be?*"

" 'Yana. You know me. You know my situation, what a swamp of work there is to do on every front. The notion of being able to sit uninterrupted for a few hours at a typewriter on my own real work—come on, you ought to know what that means to me."

"Well, why can't you work here?"

"Because you don't have a typewriter. Because I've now switched my copious traveling files to a home, however temporary, in one of my desk file-drawers. Because I need to riffle through some business stuff—all of which is also there now— before I can even tackle my own work."

"Then I come with you and help you." Iliana swung her legs over the side of the bed.

"No, I— I'll ring you later so we can decide about dinner, whether here or at Georgi's, okay?"

"I came with you last Saturday and Sunday to the office. The weekend before that, too. Now I get in your way or what? I disturb you or something?"

Julian's smile tightened.

"Iliana. For heaven's sake. Of course you don't disturb me. But—you have nothing to *do* there. You just sit and read and pace and get restless. The office is stuffy. It's a lovely summery day. And I get to feel . . . pressured. Guilty because I've chosen to be there."

"Then choose *not* to be there on a lovely summery day," Iliana bantered, throwing open her arms to emphasize the logic of her solution.

"But I *do* choose to be there. Look, just for a few hours, okay? I'll dash up to the nursing home and then to the office."

"Then I come with you at least to visit the mama."

"*No.* Darling, look, I'm sorry. It's no rejection of you. Really. But you've been there with me every visit this week. Momma must think she gave birth to Siamese twins. It's too much to ask of you, and I never get . . . Well, anyway, it's way uptown. Listen, I'll call you when I get into Athena, okay? Then I'll just dash off some checks and stuff, do a few minutes of writing, and—"

"You still are paying all the expenses on the loft, aren't you?"

There was a moment's silence.

"Yes. As a matter of fact, I am."

"I thought you were going to stop that as of last month. You procrastinate making him live for himself."

"I was. But now that I have this job . . . and Larry has no other means yet— Oh for god's sake, 'Yana, don't look at me as if I were a naughty child. He's a human being, you know. Besides, I think it'll resolve itself. He's seeking work again. I don't think I'll have to shoulder the bills for much longer, and—"

Iliana took the tray out of Julian's hands, then pulled her down to sit on the edge of the bed again.

"Juliana. You know I never saw myself as trying to come between you and your husband. That's why I went to Europe. But things have been breaking down between you for some time. Even when I began to think you and I might become lovers, I didn't regard that as something 'against' Larry. Things seemed over between you. But now . . . I have to tell you that the way he has behaved these past months, knowing how you are homeless and how your mother is dying, that to me is *not* the behavior of someone who loves. Yet it seems to move you closer to him—or at least it doesn't drive you away."

"That has nothing to do with it. We're talking about almost twenty-two years, a shared history."

"Let me finish, please. You say I know how to love. Yet you try to 'scape me again and again. Any time I mention the obvious answer—that you come here to live with me, or that together we find a bigger place so you can have your own study —your face grows stormy and you . . . distance yourself from me. Yet you say—and I feel it to be true—that you love being with me. I want to be with you for the rest of my life. I've told you that. So this confuses me. It . . . activates my oldest fears. More exile, more not knowing where I stand. All I can think is that you like yourself so little you have contempt for anyone who truly does love you—and who risks showing that."

Her eyes were brimming by the time she finished. Julian took her in her arms.

"Oh, Iliana. Dear love. Maybe what you say is true. About the contempt, I mean. But that's not the whole of it. I just— I don't know what will or won't happen yet with Larry. And I can't exile him, either. Or the me that's married to him. I also can't continue this nomadic existence indefinitely, I know that. I'm beginning to wear down all my friends, not to speak of being at my own wits' edge. But I can't . . . If I do definitely end things with Larry—and I admit that something in me *still* can't fully comprehend that—then I wouldn't want to live with anyone, not for quite a while at least. I've never had a space all my own, except for a few months back when I left Hope's. Even then I ricocheted into marrying Larry. I've *been* married, 'Yana. I'm too . . . flayed to plunge right in again. Besides, I'm always with people, relentlessly. I never have any solitude, any terrain to myself. Oh, can't you understand?"

"I have already become 'people'?"

"No no *no*. But Jesus, let me *breathe* a little, can't you?"

Iliana's eyes flashed with pride. "And who do you think you have learned to breathe *from*, Juliana, please to remember?"

Julian stiffened and released her, rising from the bed with a set smile on her face.

"Of course. I remember. Then . . . could you let me practice what you've taught me? On my own terms? Don't . . .

suffocate me with quite so many perfumed sprays of possession?"

"Juliana! How can you *say* that? I *love* you! I *never* pressure! I
only want—"

"In god's name don't—don't *whine* like that!" Then seeing
the insult shudder across her lover's features, she sat down and
again took Iliana in her embrace. "Dear one," she said, striving
for a warmer tone, "it's another version of our old argument
about Nin, remember? You claimed that *House of Incest* was
the precious Anaïs' best work. I agreed only to the extent of
saying it was the sole work of hers I could bear to finish without
feeling I'd been force-fed five tons of honey; that her overglut
of ambergris and molasses and peacock feathers so smothered
me I longed to walk barefoot on a rocky winter beach? It's
like—"

"I really cannot take a literary lecture on top of the political
one, Juliana. Do what you want to do. I get out of your way. You
don't want me with you," she sniffed, "then I leave you alone.
But I don't understand any of this. *I* have such a conviction
about us . . . I wish *you* shared that conviction."

"I do, oh I do. And you're not in the way. Oh, honey, this has
all happened so fast. And I . . . I just can't stand one more
pressure."

"I'm *not* pressuring you when I say plain out I love you and
want to live with you the rest of our days and die with you!"

"All right, all right. Let's talk about this later, can we? Tell
you what. I'll go up to see Hope and then I'll skip the office. Or
you can meet me up there, if you like, and we'll go to the park.
It *is* a lovely day. You're right. We can watch the fireworks
later. I suppose there's nothing at the office that won't
wait . . ."

Iliana enveloped Julian in a hug. But had she at that moment
been the keen-eyed photographer de Costa standing behind
herself, her lens might have caught an expression on the face
that appeared over her shoulder, through their embrace—and
the expression would have been a study in chiaroscuro.

Waiting at the bus stop, Julian made an effort to shift her
attention from Iliana to Hope. You have to refocus your mind
to take on each new crisis, she reminded herself, learn to take
your rests wherever you can, go numb in between, wipe out

the scene just completed, try to get fresh for the scene about to be played. But what if Iliana is right, she wondered, *do* I feel contempt for those who love me? Do I view loving me as a sign of weakness or dependency—neither of which was permitted to The Baby? Is that why I'm still playing the Earth Mother role I got cast in when I was only Earth Toddler? Weakness. Dependence. Those would have been unlovable traits. The Baby wanted not, oh not, to be unlovable.

For this, David had assimilated. Not to be seen as weak. For this, Aryan demolished Jew; Dravidians, Etruscans, Albigensians, the more peaceable tribes of West Africa—seen as weak. For this the Tibetans, the Mayans, the Iroquois and Hopi nations, the female people—*the female people*—went under. Waiting and hoping, until it was too late, to be seen as lovable for daring to be other than strong.

"And I still feel unlovable," she murmured, anticipating the visit to Peacehaven, where she would sit at her mother's bedside and feel her largesse dwindle under Hope's inability or refusal to communicate. She hailed a cab in defiance, and deposited herself in the back seat. Do this in memory of yourself, kid: a gesture of indulging Julian, beholden to no one. Sweet battered interior of a Manhattan taxi, the only true room of her own.

Compassion for the strong and contempt for the weak? For how many years had she motivated the emotion of compassion for Hope by seeing her as a larger-than-life Mother Courage character—the shrewd brutal peasant forced to survive by cunning, no matter who she used or in what manner? For how many years had she felt self-contempt for feeling that compassion—*and* for not feeling it? For how many years had she picketed the threshold of Hope's love, trying every password for admittance?

Even now. Was this new splendid celebration of her own body merely the latest gesture toward that dessicating maternal flesh, toward that same trembling woman whose hallucinations were more beset each day by paranoia? Always to be in flight toward *her?* Always this tearing and being torn, this peeling the surface away to find another layer enmasked beneath it? Always this repetition?

Torn now between Laurence and Iliana as well. Just now, when Laurence was being both spirited and gentle again, showing optimism and an understanding that could refer to years of shared verbal shorthand. *His* daring to be other than strong, what about *that?* His saying he wanted to "fight for us, for what we had been and dreamed of becoming." Just now, when Julian had broken through to some untamed creature in herself—only to find, layer on layer enmasked and tearing, that there was in Iliana, too, the exquisitely tender tyrant of loving: the possessor.

And am *I* not the ultimate possessor? she debated. Or the greedy child who never dared be greedy when I *was* a child? She fumbled for her wallet as the taxi paused at a red light one corner from the nursing home.

What in hell have you done, Julian, she reflected, complicating things to further thicken your life's plot? What *is* this? Emotional dilettantism? Cowardice? A failure of nerve? Happy Independence Day, my foot. Aren't you ashamed to be playing a middle-aged woman as if she were an ingenue? Enough navel-gazing. Pay attention. Practicalities. Taxi pulling up to Peacehaven. Conference today with Dr. Grimes. Poor Grimes, he must think the daughter is as loony as the mother; he's been given so many different telephone numbers to try in case of emergency he's now set aside a whole page of his address book for Julian Travis. Come to think of it, where are you going to *go* after July 15, when Georgi returns from Europe? The heat is on to move in with Iliana. But you'll get no writing done today. The heat is on to return to the loft, too, both emotionally and financially. Would that be the easy way out, the Hollywood ending? Or the brave one, the refusal of defeat? Going home. To a desk of one's own, a study of one's own, one phone number, cats, dishes, kitchen, plants of one's own. Laurence.

Dr. Grimes was waiting in Peacehaven's medical conference room—neat, perky, efficient. Although this was to be the standard bi-weekly conference now that Hope was stabilized, he looked grave.

"It's nothing in particular, Miss Travis. That is, well . . . we won the last round with pneumonia, though I sometimes wonder . . . they always call pneumonia the friend of the dying, the gentle end. The hip is healing satisfactorily. The bed sores —they're inevitable to some degree in a bedridden patient, no matter how often the patient is turned and shifted. Debriding them gives her discomfort, of course, but it's necessary to avoid infection and the danger of gangrene. Her mental state, well, I understand you're here every day so you know . . ."

"I know. Lately the hallucinations have been intense."

"Yes. As I've told you before, there's not much we can do about that. She's terminal-stage Parkinson's. I don't think she has more than a month or so left. But as you know, no one dies of the disease itself. The medical profession is still, as I'm sure you've noticed through these months, very ignorant."

"Your humility about that is unusual—and touching, Dr. Grimes. I know you're doing everything you can to make her comfortable. Then what is—"

"She's getting weaker all the time. Her heart is still astoundingly strong. But she's barely eating enough. Please try to convince her to eat. Otherwise . . ."

"Otherwise?"

"The IV doesn't give her sufficient nourishment. We'll have to tube-feed her through the nose."

"Oh god, Dr. Grimes, isn't there any other—"

"Yes. You're her daughter. Get her to eat."

Hope was asleep when she entered the room, the face relaxed in a momentary freedom from eye twitches and tremors. The distorted mouth was at peace, not twisted, not drooling. Julian slid into the bedside chair and watched her.

Force-feeding. Like the jailed suffragists on hunger-strike— throat torn, nasal passages scraped bloody. Her esophagus would be as wounded as her spine now was. Julian had insisted on attending a debridement, to understand what Hope was having to endure. She had seen the frayed wick of spine protruding through the waxen skin embroidered with bloated wheels of scab, each of which were regularly scraped raw to be cleansed. Hope had lain curled on her side, eyes closed, passively letting Julian grasp her talon-like hands, only whimpers escaping her side-wrenched mouth. It was Julian who had wanted to scream. Christ, that such pride, beauty, energy— however abused by others or Hope herself—should come to this!

The mother dreamed now beyond her reach, eyes rolling under translucent lids.

"I wish I could have saved you this," Julian whispered, leaning to stroke away what could not be erased even in sleep: the forehead lines that drew to a knot of tension just between the eyes.

But when Hope did wake it was in bewilderment, demanding to know if anyone had checked on the baby in the crib.

"Momma. Momma darling? There's no crib, no baby. I'm the baby, and I'm grown now, Momma. But I still love you just as much. Even more."

"No!" came the cry of anguish. "The m-baby! Go chuck on! Can't geddup m'sel'! *Please* go chuck! See Joolyan's awride!"

Layers on masks on flesh, she thought. *Do it. Feed her the lines she wants to hear, you know how, you do it with everyone, you've done it all your life. Have mercy. This once do it for real.*

So Julian rose and walked in the direction toward which Hope's head jerked in frantic pointing. She bent over the invisible baby Julian lying in an imaginary crib. She smoothed the covers. She tucked the child in.

"Yes," she smiled back at Hope. "Yes, Hope. She's all right, she's asleep and just fine."

"Ah, thas' good. Ya' shld singaher. Sha likesat. Lurrby 'n g'night. You do't."

Sing to her. "Lullaby and Goodnight," "Brahms' Lullaby," which she remembered Hope crooning someplace, backstage or off-camera, to that youngster trying to nap between scenes. Eerie to find yourself jealous of how loved you were as a baby— before you were fully you.

"Singaher? Pleasse?"

Sing to yourself, Julian. Sing to the invisible imaginary lost child trying to nap between scenes, sing.

So she sang, bending over the space in the corner. When she finished and returned to the bedside, Hope's face peered at her quizzically, almost with trust.

"Liss'n," she whispered in her slurred speech, beckoning with a jerk of one clawed hand to this stranger who had sung to her daughter, "Liss'n. Ya wanna help me? I need . . . need . . ." The dark eyes filled with tears. "Need friend. Need friend."

"Yes, oh yes. I'll help you, I'll be your friend. I'll do anything in the world to help you." Julian leaned over the bed, hovering above this other child in this other crib. "Just tell me."

Hope beckoned her nearer, and she bent deep into the odor

of fetid flesh. *From this you came. Here you were born. All acts in your life have been metaphors for this beckoning.*

"Yes," she whispered, "tell me."

The black eyes glittered, spilled over. The words were forced, timed between spasms.

"Home. Wann' go. Take me? Don' b'long here. Bad here." The whisper sibiliated into a hiss and exploded the next word like a curse. "B'othel! B'othel! Ma un modder pu' me here. C'n ya 'magine at? Ma on modder! Ina b'othel!"

Julian's brain raced frantically to translate.

"Your own mother put you where? Where did your mother put you, Hope?"

Just as desperate to be understood, the other jerked even more spastically, blistered lips forming each word with enormous effort.

"Here. Here. Bad. Go home. Wann'a. *Pleasse. Now.*"

"What is bad about this place, darling? Tell me and I'll fix it. I swear it to you. Is anybody— Has anybody been cruel or—"

"Nononono. All ver' nice*toonice* see? All day nicesweets. Bud then, then . . ."

"Then? What then? What happens, what?" *God, please, give her the language to speak to me, give me the power to hear her at last.*

"They c'm 'n . . . s'bad place. B'othel! Ma on mudder!"

"B'othel? What do you mean, oh darling, what—"

"Hoehus! Hoehus! Sha thinks Umma h-h-hore. So sha pumme here! Home? Pleassse? Now? Friend?"

"Whorehouse. Your mother— your mother thinks you're a whore. She put you here. Brothel. Dear God."

The head tried violently to nod between jerks of a neck that kept shuddering it sideways.

"Y'ss! Y'ss! Ya unndersd'nd! Y'ss!"

Somewhere in this whole vast bleak merciless universe there must be a space free of suffering, somewhere.

"Awww, h'ney. Thas' nice. Ya cry'n fa *me? Fa' me?* Aww. *Nice* frien'. Nodda hore. C'n ya he'p me?"

Feed her the lines. Collaborate. Feed her the lines as you would the soup cold now by the side of her bed, like cues for a script, feed her, nourish her. You know how to do it.

"Yes. Yes, I'll help." Julian cleared her throat and dropped her voice to the conspiratorial level of Hope's. "Well, first of all, you're not a whore. Anybody can see that, plain as day. Now. Tell you what. I have a plan."

The black eyes brightened, watching her with rapt attention.

"We'll smuggle you out, okay? But it'll have to be very well planned, you understand?"

The eyes blinked rapidly with excitement.

"The trouble is, you're weak right now, see? And we can't get you out of here if you're so weak. We've got to build up your strength first. It's very important, you understand?"

Frantic nodding.

"So I want you to let me feed you some of this soup here. Don't worry, it won't burn you. It's room temperature by now."

"Mide be p-p-poy-poy—"

"No, it's not poisoned. I'll have some first, so you'll know it's safe. See? It's all right. I swear to you."

The eyes opened wide again, trusting. A split second of almost recognition, almost mistrust. Then it passed, and Hope began, spoon after slow spoon, to swallow the soup.

Exhausted by this effort, she fell into a doze almost immediately after Julian put down the empty bowl and sat, her head drooping, her arms loose in her lap. *You must come now not just once a day but twice at least. She will eat for you, for the friend you can convince her you are. Only you can keep her alive.*

She stared at the black-and-white tiles of the nursing-home floor. No ambiguities now. No time now for anything but this. No time for the sweet wild freedoms of long-ago last night, or the would-have-been writing of this afternoon. No time for anything but Hope: her life and the losing of it, her fears and the calming of them, her soul and the reaching of it. Strip it down to this. One last try.

She rose and tiptoed toward the door, but froze at the scream that cleaved the air behind her.

"I see ya Joolyan! I see ya tryinna s-sneeek oud affer steeelin' all ma forchun! I woan leaf ya nuth'n—ya hear? I see ya!" But when she turned, Hope only glared at her for an instant, then shut her eyes like a mechanized doll and fell to sleep again.

Mrs. Costello, the day floor-nurse, approached Julian as she waited for the elevator.

"Miss Travis? May I speak to you for a moment?"

Julian gave her an automatic smile. "Certainly, Mrs. Costello."

"Did you— Have you seen the doctor today?"

"Yes. And I got her to finish the soup you'd left. I'll come both at lunchtime and after work each day now. In the mornings, too, whenever possible. To try and get her to take food from here on in."

"Oh good. Though I know it's an awful strain on you. But that wasn't what I wanted to talk to you about."

Julian straightened for whatever would be coming. She noticed the copy of an Athena book tucked under the nurse's arm.

"Your mother's been a bit of a problem lately. Oh, she can be terribly charming when she wants to be. But you know, well, she's been upsetting some of the other residents."

"How?"

"She . . . she *sings.* Quite a bit sometimes. Quite loud, too, sometimes."

Julian began to laugh.

"No, really, Miss Travis. At first we thought it was pleasant. Cheerful, you know. I mean better than having them rave or cry. But your mother never seems to know when to *stop,* she—"

Julian was laughing uncontrollably now, leaning against the wall, her knees sagging. The nurse giggled.

"I know, sometimes it gets to you. But there *is* a serious side. Truly, Miss Travis. Let's be realistic."

It sent Julian off into another gale of laughter, brought to a halt only by Mrs. Costello's voice cutting through.

"She's been exposing herself."

"What—do—you—mean." Each word came out of the laughter as if suddenly drenched with freezing rain.

"Just what I said. She exposes herself. To the nurses, the doctors, the male aides when they come to wash the floors. Even to the window-washer-man. She somehow manages to throw back or kick off the covers, lord knows how, and lies there with her private parts exposed, and even—well, she deliberately winks. Last night she shouted for about half an hour that she was 'Queen of the Whores.' Unfortunately, her speech was perfectly clear at the time. It took a while to get her settled down, I assure you."

Julian looked at the nurse. A closet feminist. Keeps herself sane by reading Athena books. A nice woman. Compassionate. Possessed of a sense of humor. Tired.

"Mrs.—Ms. Costello. I don't know what to tell you, but there's nothing I can or *would* do at this point to stop my mother from doing whatever on earth she wants. If singing loudly gives her pleasure, I suggest you all learn somehow to enjoy that with her. I can imagine the awkwardness her other actions create for you, and I'm sorry for any inconvenience. But frankly, if that's her way of affirming what's left of her body, then I applaud it. It's her body, her voice, her labia and clitoris, and if she wants to sing out any or all of them to the whole goddamned world, it's about time. She's paying a considerable rent to be here, and she has a right to her . . . eccentricities. Don't take this wrong, please, Ms. Costello. It's nothing against you. But do understand clearly that if I ever see her put in restraints for this harmless behavior—however socially unacceptable others may find it—I'll *sue* Peacehaven for one hundred thousand dollars per every pubic hair of hers that's been ruffled. I'm on *her* side, Ms. Costello. Let's never forget that."

The elevator doors opened. Julian stepped in and turned around, pressing the lobby button. As the doors began to slide shut in a narrowing frame around the stunned nurse, Julian called, "Happy Independence Day."

CHAPTER TEN

Autumn, 1983

Twice a day then, for the rest of the summer, while Manhattan turned livid with August and the streets seemed in danger of buckling from concrete-reflected heat, Julian appeared at Peacehaven. She brought flowers three times a week, marking time by the seasonal shift: as tulips had given way to lilacs, so iris ceded to freesia, roses to tiger-lilies. Chrysanthemums began to bristle in the shops, heralding autumn. Every day she brought offerings of sustenance—custard or ice cream, soft Chinese noodles, breast of chicken—whatever might tempt the interest of the old woman who was waiting for her, waiting to get strong again, waiting to go home.

Julian was waiting, too, though for what she wasn't sure. The remainder of her hours not spent at Peacehaven volleyed between Athena, house-sitting friends' apartments during their vacations, weekends at the office trying to work on her book, and time spent with Iliana—or with Laurence. Each time she saw Laurence, she came away convinced she was waiting for the breakthrough which would permit her, too, to go back home. Each time she saw Iliana, she came away suspecting she was waiting for something else, some definitive sign or act that would propel her forward. Each time she saw Hope, she came away with the unsettling belief that such a sign would come neither from the husband nor the lover, but from the mother.

By the end of August, Hope's plaintive refrain, "Home, go home," seemed the sign, though Julian chided herself for falling prey to infantile magical thinking in interpreting it as such. But being in Hope's presence had become a peculiarly safe activity. There, despite the grief and pre-death mourning that characteristically prevail at such a bedside, a restful cocoon enwrapped both mother and daughter. Some evenings Julian would simply sit watching Hope sleep, a slumber so deep she might already be exploring the outskirts of a region distant from consciousness. Some days Hope would listen, with the intense absorption of those who don't comprehend, while Julian told bedtime stories of a future, shining and peaceful, that waited as soon as Hope was strong enough to be smuggled out of the brothel.

Weeks had passed since the mother last recognized her visitor as her daughter. Julian wondered whether that was not the reason for the serenity between them; she was now "Friend," the familiar stranger who could be trusted to watch over the baby in the crib, who brought food safe to eat, who had miraculously been sent to help plan an escape. The ache of longing to be recognized as Julian, to be perceived as herself by her mother, was acute. But it was an old ache, after all, and she was becoming reconciled to the certainty that recognition would never now anoint them both with a mutual healing. Instead, the autonomy and authority this new role of Friend conferred on Julian was its own relief. Somewhere buried beneath the ache, she was as grateful to Hope for freeing her from Julian's identity as Hope was to Friend for promising freedom from the brothel. The eagle of guilt at last seemed to have lifted its wings from the two women, while they waited, suspended in time, ignorance, and merciful pretense, for the perfecting of their relative liberations.

But the eagle perched on the nursing-home portal, to hover over Julian the moment she stepped out through the door. Guilt about Laurence. Guilt now about Iliana. Guilt about myriad details which seemed daily to sift through her fingers.

She had not been able to do a penny's worth of fundraising for Jenny's state-assembly campaign. She was late on her deadline in writing the promised foreword for Sabrina's book. She had reneged on attending the press conference for the Reproductive Technology Alert Network and even forgotten to send a statement of support. She had declined countless invitations to lunch, dinner, coffee, "just talk." She did manage to get out to Staten Island to visit Anna, recovering from a hysterectomy, only to find Anna accusing her of being anti-social, withdrawn from everyone: "You've *changed*, Julian." It made her wonder whether the grapevine was onto her relationship with Iliana— "another heterosexual bites the dust"—but decided that was paranoid and attributed the accusational tone to Anna's depression. There was no way to explain her own crises without still further exposure, further provocation of advice. Besides, Julian was finally bored with talking about her own crises.

Had she changed so much? She told herself she was not being irresponsible, that there were other priorities, that she was merely trying to survive, that the sheer expenditure of energy involved in juggling emotional and physical demands depleted her. As much for practical support as for affection, she spent more time now at Iliana's, which contented her lover but increased Julian's guilt—especially whenever she saw Laurence. The Independence Day revelations already had faded dim as if they were epiphanies of a previous incarnation. She told herself that her salvation would be honesty, so she kept Iliana informed about the relaxation of tension with Laurence. But this was done at the cost of increasing tension with Iliana. There was only so much space for air in the balloon; if you compressed it in one place it bulged in another. There was neither time nor space to integrate all these rapid, drastic rites of passage. Obsessively, futilely, Julian interrogated herself. How had she got herself into this triangle? Did she secretly relish it? Was she reenacting center-stage melodrama at the cost of real people's real pain? Which brought her full circle under the beak and wings of guilt again, until she looked forward to those sheltered moments at Hope's bedside, where the priority of performing Friend convincingly was so great as to cleanse her awareness for a time of all other considerations.

"Home. Go home." Julian knew it was the cry of an old woman wanting to return to cluttered rooms that no longer existed, to walls no longer bedecked with images of The Baby but now freshly painted and hung with artifacts of new inhabitants who walked the scraped and gleaming parquet floors. Yet despite Julian's knowledge, "Home, go home," sounded like a mantra of wisdom mystically communicated from one

who stood now at the final gates of awe, one who no longer had any need to lie.

But where was home for her? Not with Iliana, at least not yet, not for a long time. Not the briefly dreamt-of apartment of her own: no money, no time to apartment-hunt, no energy or vision for the enormity of such an endeavor. Back to Laurence, then, and the loft which had been home for so long? She was afraid. Just that, afraid—of more scenes, more possession, more repetition. But Laurence had changed . . .

There would be one step, perhaps, a test of both herself and him, which might hint a prognosis about their marriage. There would be one step—simultaneously a defiance of Iliana's advice, a gesture of the sort Laurence claimed she no longer offered him, and an act of ethical integrity. There would be one step, she told herself, which might show her if only by default the direction she really wanted to follow—the way a child plays chance counting games when unable to make a decision, and discovers in the process what was desired all along. Not until the last number falls does the child realize that this choice confirms or disappoints the real wish—and if the latter, the child can always count again, until coincidence and desire cohere. She would take the step. She would tell Laurence about Iliana.

It was a Saturday afternoon, when she had come back to the loft to pick up a book from her study. Laurence was home. He asked if she wanted some coffee. So they sat in her old study, drinking coffee and chatting amiably, as if at home together again. The atmosphere was peaceful, the tone intimate. She told him.

"I assumed as much, Jule," he said hoarsely, "and if it's what you want, I'm glad for you. Honest . . . But I wish—" He looked up at her from where he'd been staring into his coffee cup. For a moment, intensity radiated from his eyes the way his lust to change the world once had. He took a deep breath. "I wish," his words spilled out, "that you'd give *us* another chance. At least as much a chance as anybody new, even if it *is* a woman. We've come so far, changed so much, together *and* apart. What a loss. That there's no Kent Campbell around to introduce us. That the person you are now and the person I am now won't even get a chance to meet."

Whether it was her own lack of marginal strength, or Hope's

chanted instruction, or what shone through his eyes in that appeal, Julian didn't know and no longer cared. A sense of inevitability, a fatalistic optimism, were at work in her. That evening, in tears, she told her lover she would be returning to her husband.

Iliana smiled and shrugged, not trying to hide her attempt to hide her pain.

"I expected this. I knew it. Well . . . you must try again if you feel you must. Whatever you suspect about me, Juliana, I do want to love you in freedom, not in captivity." Iliana permitted herself a philosophical laugh, but it emerged trailing an afterbirth of sarcasm. "How I do abhor clichés, and how I've walked right into one."

"You could never be anything but an absolute original," Julian cut in fiercely.

"Oh no, my love. A cliché as tedious as a photograph of a baby nose-to-nose with a kitten. The lesbian lover who infuses her heterosexual belovèd with energy—which then gets drained from that relationship and reinvested in the belovèd's worn out marriage." Iliana laughed again, openly bitter this time.

Julian cast an unconscious, desperate look around her, searching for a way out. "That's not what's happened—I never meant—I never promised—"

Her anguish seduced Iliana away from her own. Iliana felt the strengthening self-preoccupation of irony ebb from her like a donation of blood for transfusion. She reached for Julian, knowing herself a battlefield between warring armies of lofty and base love, but unsure which was which.

"I know, *mi sueño*, I know. You never promised. You never meant. Forget what I said. We're neither of us clichés. It's just that . . . I will worry about you. You will be careful regarding Larry?"

Fresh tears, a more urgent clinging.

"I'll be careful, yes. I love him, Iliana. But not in the old way. It will take a long time, I'm afraid, to build back my trust of him. But I've got to give it one more try, 'Yana. And I'm too tired to run anymore. I want to go home."

The silence was a din of words checked, reined, unsaid.

"You— You will call me?"

"I will call you every single day, 'Yana, if you permit it. I can't endure the thought of not seeing you, of not— May I? *May* I continue to see you during this . . . whatever, this trial period? . . . As a friend?"

"As whatever you see when you look at me, *mi amada.*"

So they had wept together in each other's arms. *Another mourning,* Julian thought, *another murder, more pain I've caused. Another stereotype enacted, another straight woman returning to her man after playing with a woman who loved her.* But there were other ghostly refrains, too. *I made you, I taught you, I showed you.* Then Julian would think of her desk, her bookshelves gleaming in the lamplight, her own doorkey. If it was all to turn out the same, then why not the familiar mode? Why fly to others that we know not of?

At first it did feel like coming home. At first she and Laurence talked—about everything: Hope and Iliana and the money burdens, the politics and pain and caring and the waste it would be if they failed one another. At first they tried making love, awkwardly, finding their way back to one another like strangers, but lacking the armor of superficiality strangers wear. At first, when she met Iliana for coffee, she had to admit that yes, they were really trying and yes, it seemed to be working. At first, when her friends at Athena congratulated her on having "worked it out," that felt good.

Never to know or comprehend why knowing and comprehension weren't enough; when or how it began to dissolve. Never to fathom how, so swiftly, toward the end of September, it already was re-enacting a quiet hell. Reopening the scabs. Debridement.

By then, when they talked, she and Laurence talked *at* each other, then in circles, then in accusation, finally in monosyllables. By then, when they walked together on the street and passed a child, their silence turned palpable, an ice-scrim between them. By then, when they tried to make love, he felt her body trying not to fight his; she felt her brain impose itself between them, shrilling through every pore for some denied limbspread freedom each part of her had tasted and could not now forget. By then, he began to take late-night solitary walks again. By then, she knew Iliana could read the desolation in her face each time they met. By then, the repeated expressions of support by Athenians for the reconciliation of her marriage began to appear excessive, vehement, homophobic.

Julian moved into her study, sleeping on a rolled-out piece of foam rubber on the floor. No time now, for a repeat flight. No will. No energy for anything but Hope, who had begun eating less again, and sleeping more. The nurses and Dr. Grimes confirmed her growing weakness. Then, on the first of October, the pace accelerated. The fall lectures began. Another chapter was due on the book. Athena's schedule intensified for the winter and spring lists. What Julian had estimated as the outer reaches of tolerable pressure expanded to a seemingly limitless terrain in which she dwelt, disbelieving in the possibility of rescue, able only to react from day to day. Iliana would just let her sit in silence when she came to visit, or sometimes Julian would fall asleep, her head in Iliana's lap, Iliana's hand lightly stroking her hair.

It was in the middle of the night when Larry knocked and then pounded at her study door, opening it before she could reply, and thrusting himself inside. He was sobbing. She raised herself up to one elbow from her pallet.

"Larry! What is it?"

"It's you. Me. Us. Jule, I can't stand it anymore. I can't stand any of it—your wheeling and dealing to try and get me jobs, the way I know you really want to be with *her* but stay with me, the way—"

"Please, Larry, have mercy on both of us. It's three in the morning. We've been over and over this."

"—I never get *heard*. Can't breathe, can't speak. No forum. Why'd you come back? Lemme *go.*"

"For crying out loud, Laurence, will you stop your self-pity for a minute? You deserve better. From yourself, from the world—"

"Lemme *go.* Stop pursuing me with this death's-head deathless love of yours. Enough of the tests. I'm a dead man, a guy who drowned one day a long time ago in a mysterious leap off Brooklyn Bridge. I'm not even identifiable now, washed up on some midnight dock. I can't— I can't—"

Julian sliced through his appeal, indifferent to whether outraged love or the nausea of repetition was forging this new adamance that made the incision.

"Go to bed, Laurence. You're drunk. I'm too empty to have another scene. I've got to get up in four hours to catch a plane."

He stared at her. "I'm in real trouble," he whispered, baffled, "I—I'm scared I'm not gonna get through this alive. I'm scared I'm—"

Julian lay back down and closed her eyes. "Laurence," she sighed, "I don't want to hear your emotional blackmail. Go away, Laurence. Go to bed."

She heard him murmur, "There's no more 'us.' It's you or me. Gotta practice losing you. Gotta." Then she heard the door close behind him.

Empty, she thought. Like the Yeats line, "Too long a sacrifice can make a stone of the heart."

There was no more respite in sleep that night. She tossed on her pallet like a dazed shipwreck adrift on a raft, visions assaulting her in punishing waves. This death's-head deathless love of yours. I can't afford this, she prayed to herself, I can't afford a nervous breakdown. If there were only a way to halt the cacophony, to stop the brain from its obsessive pattering to one blocked exit after another. Then it was morning, and the brain was commandeered to drive the body again.

When she stepped off the plane in New Mexico that afternoon, the women who met her—without knowing anything about her other than her public self—saw their guest speaker near collapse. The pre-lecture events were canceled. No book signing, no poetry reading, no guest class, no faculty dinner, no women's center reception.

But that night, she mounted the podium to speak about the institution of the family in patriarchal society. Her voice rose and fell in familiar cadences and phrases.

"The average North American homemaker works a 99.6-hour work-week with no pay and no respect; it's not even considered a job . . . One out of every four women experiences sexual abuse before she's four years old . . . 40 percent of all women killed in the United States are murdered by their spouses . . . Every eighteen seconds a woman is beaten by her husband seriously enough to require hospitalization . . . the Reagan Administration's assault on reproductive freedom . . . the infant mortality rate in Detroit now has passed that of Honduras, due to social-welfare cutbacks . . . needed re-definitions of 'family' . . . freedom of sexual choice . . . custody rights of lesbian mothers . . . children's suffrage . . . rights of the elderly . . . internationally . . . child marriage, forced marriage, polygyny . . . dowry murders . . . divorce rights . . . marital rape . . ."

The audience leapt to their feet at the end. Those who had heard Travis speak before marveled how she never seemed to get burned out, how this was the finest speech she'd ever given, positively electric, especially with those quotes that kept coming in: "The quality of mercy is not strained," and that peroration about one's right not to be shut away from the free air and the lambs in the meadows, something about rejecting perpetual imprisonment. The English majors in the audience smiled at each other in recognition of Shakespeare's Portia and Shaw's St. Joan. But all agreed that Travis's image of a woman huddled on the floor of a spare room—the woman she said all women were—was unforgettable.

Julian went directly from the airport to Peacehaven, not bothering to brace herself any longer for whatever might await her. But Hope was asleep, jaw slack, mouth open with labored breathing, the lines a tortured knot in her forehead. Her daughter sat beside her, waiting. Perhaps she would wake up and take a little food. Perhaps she would sing for Friend. Perhaps she would tell Friend that The Baby had given a good performance, like a real trooper.

But Hope slept on, and the night nurse looked in at the door to warn softly that visiting was about over. Then, as Julian began to gather up her raincoat and suitcase, Hope opened her eyes.

Brilliant and clear they were, black crystal stars in the bone-colored pottery bowl of her skull. They focused on the woman standing before her, suitcase in hand.

It was a woman in her forties, slender, looking as if she hadn't slept much lately. Light brown hair beginning to fleck silver. The eyes appeared overlarge in the drawn face. But the smile was friendly, almost familiar . . .

"Julian!" she cried. *"Julian!* 'S *you!* You came home!"

Her daughter watched through a blur of tears how the forehead knot began slowly to release its lines, a rose window radiating light, making of the entire face a sanctuary. Brilliant and clear, the dark stars glowed recognition and love. Then that whole sunken, twisted constellation of features caught and blazed recognition, the dry lips leaking spittle but cracking into a luminous smile.

"Yes, Momma. It's me. It's always been me. And it's always been you. Yes, Momma," Julian wept, dropping her suitcase and rushing to the bed to gather all that decaying matter into her arms, "Yes. Oh yes, Momma."

Hope looked up at her, the face incandescent with love.

"I missed ya so, Baby. I'm so g-glad ya finally c-came home."

"I've been here all the time, Momma. But I'm sorry it took me so long. I love you, Momma."

" 'Course you do, h'ney. Never doubted 'at. It'll all be okay. 'N I love *you*. Ya know that now, don'ya?"

Julian nodded, seeing drowsiness already reclaim Hope in its embrace. Still, she held on to the old woman, rocking her softly as she lapsed to sleep again, until the nurse came and repeated that she must leave.

It had been a moment only, yet who could measure one length of grace against two lifetimes?

She tried to tell Laurence as soon as she got home. But he turned on her, too full of his own grief to hear about anyone's even momentary cessation of theirs.

"I can't listen, Jule. Jule, I'm afraid we've lost each other. For good. I'm afraid . . ."

He stalked into his study. Fear for him rose in her beyond what she'd ever felt before. But when she tried to follow he barred the way, and spun on her with eyes now livid in hate.

"Do you know that today was October fifth, our twenty-second wedding anniversary, Julian?" he spit at her. "Do you know? Do you care?"

She spread her hands helplessly. "Larry. Honest to god, I knew last week, and then . . . it got driven out of my mind completely. I'm sorry. Things have been so heavy—"

"Oh heavy, yeah. Carrier of the world's burdens. Bringer of peace to Hope, love to Iliana, feminism to the world. But never to me, who's been broken so many times on the wheel of loving you he doesn't even know how to stand up straight anymore. Who's played your daddy. Who's played your son, the one you denied us so you could pretend you mothered *me* and wouldn't have to face dealing with a real-life child. Who's played your political tutor and housekeeper, secretary and laundress, at the cost of my own manhood. Who's even played your husband. But never been auditioned for the part he wanted most in all the world. To father our child. And to be to you the beautiful man I might have become."

"Larry, I'm going mad, please—"

But he careened past her, down the stairs and out the front door, slamming it behind him.

Julian dragged herself into her study, spread out her pallet and threw herself down on it, fully dressed. She took the phone from her desk and placed it on the floor beside her head, in case. Then she fell instantly into a dreamless sleep, her final thoughts clasping the memory that Hope had recognized Julian, and without hatred.

The phone didn't ring. But she was roused by the slam of the street door. The luminous hands of her desk clock read one o'clock. Five hours he'd been gone. She heard Laurence, cursing her with new damnations more fierce than any uttered before, and suddenly there was alive in the house a presence of danger so vivid it woke her to full alert. She heard him enter his study. She heard the familiar crash of glass, the thud of furniture falling. She heard him shouting.

"Gotta kill it, once and for all. Drive her away. *Kill* it! Wipe it out!"

Julian sprang up from her pallet and locked the door to her study. She ran to the phone.

"Bitch! Bastard! Murderess!" he breathed into her ear from the extension in his study. "Oh no. Not gonna call your precious dyke for the gallant rescue. Phone's gonna stay off the hook in my little closet here, see, and ain't nobody calling out from nowhere. Gonna wipe it all out once and for all. Drive the vampire away, stake in *your* heart jus' like you put a stake in mine years ago and called it love."

She hung up the phone. Think. *This is Larry, forgodsake, he wouldn't hurt a fly You are not a fly.*

"Once and for all, wipe it out," he was shouting. "No more candy groom, no more candy bride."

Think. You can't get out of the building. Too high to jump. No fire escape. Can't get into the hall and down the stairs without passing his study door. Can't phone. Think. He'll calm down we'll talk the door is locked don't panic think.

"Vampire! Vampire!" He was in the hall now, his voice coming toward her study door.

So this is to fear him. Snow angels hear me now. Bridge and gulls, all you candy grooms and brides trying to love from your impossible perches, oh Hope and David this is your daughter calling now in need. Be calm, don't panic, try to talk with him. Love drives out fear. No no something's changed him maybe the war yes that must be it. I wasn't wrong oh sweet snow angels all my mescaline freakouts with him foresaw this I knew I knew. Fear drives out love. Forty percent of all women killed in this country . . . Not me This can't be me This is Larry forgodsake.

He was pounding on the study door.

"Come out, Vampire! It's after midnight now, you can show your real face, your fangs, your claws, my heart's blood dripping from your greedy mouth. *Come out or I'll come in!"*

This is really happening It can't be Not us Not to me This is the man I've lived with for twenty-two . . . That's what they all say . . . This is what the battered wife feels . . . Dear snow angels Momma help . . .

Julian picked up her desk scissors, holding them open. A weapon. *Fight back, we tell them. Fight for your lives.*

But her entire body shook so hard she couldn't keep her balance. *This is how they all feel at this moment, this precise moment with the door beginning to give on its hinges Snow angels With the large stranger beating fists against wood against skull against bone Not him forgodsake Not me Not us He doesn't mean it We're different That's what they all say . . . Family tragedy in Chelsea loft last night the well-known political couple . . . No woman is raised to, you know, quite the contrary . . . Forty percent . . .*

"I've been outside this door in both your nightmares and mine for years, Vampire! *You hear me?* This time, damn your vampire soul to hell forever, I'm going to get through it!"

She felt the scissors, slippery in her sweating hand. *Fight back we tell them. No.* No, *some*where the killing must stop. *Not through my hands, not against someone I've loved No . . . That's what they all say, that's what they all think until it's too late* No! The door was splintering. One of his fists crashed through it.

No!

She threw down the scissors. She pushed herself away from leaning against the desk. *Somewhere in you there is a courage precise to this moment.* Stand up, don't lean, *stand* even if you tremble like an aspen leaf like your mother like every trembling woman in the world *stand up.* She stepped to the middle of the room and stood, arms fisted at her sides. She faced the doorway.

Now, O angels! Throw a bridge between our sufferings, let the screaming gulls and stone towers sway toward us in pity, let the current carry us, let bloodsunset wings, waves, arches, lean all their weight against this moment, Momma be with me now and in the hour of our death—

The door gave on its hinges and he burst through. Wild disheveled stranger, eyes red-rimmed with rage. Who is this man? He was shaking, too, but with fury.

They poised in the roar around them, staring into each other.

Laurence dropped his head into his hands. His words sobbed out mangled.

"Run, Jule. Get out. I'll be okay if you get out. Grab your coat and go. Please. *Hurry.* Fast. *Run, Jule, I don't wanna . . . Go.* I gotta drive you away, doncha see?" He fell to his knees, face still buried in his hands. "Oh God let her hear me! *This once, let her hear me!*"

Above every one of her nerves sirening toward him, above the din of longing to rush and fold him in her arms, Julian heard. She grabbed her coat, pushed past him through the splintered doorway, raced down the steps and out into the street.

No wallet. No change with which to make a phone call. Nothing to do this time but run until the lungs burn and the body sags against a lamppost.

"Ten dollahs, Baby? Give ya' a tenner for a quick blowjob, whaddya say?"

Then run again, run south, through the city's night chill, to the Village, to Grove Street, run and slow to a walk when you can't run anymore and then run again. Don't think. Think if you have to think only about the blood pumping from your heart, the legs moving. Slow to a walk if you have to. Then run again. Run.

While she waited for the buzz-back at the Grove Street house she glanced at the neon clock over the corner deli. Two-ten. Still, it was only a moment before the buzzer sounded.

Run. Into the hall, up the stairs. *Breathe as you climb, breathe. You're safe now. Nothing can hurt you.*

Iliana was already at the landing, waiting.

"I knew it had to be you at this hour."

"I . . . He . . . Nothing hurt . . . Had to go . . . It's over."

Iliana half-led, half-carried her into the apartment.

"Oh my love," she said, as she sat Julian down on the sofa. "You're an exile, too. But . . . welcome."

It was more than an hour later—when Julian had swallowed some brandy and was undressed and huddled in a borrowed robe and blanket, lying on the sofa, trying to tell it, trying to exorcise it—that the phone rang.

"Oh my god. It's going to be Larry."

"Then I do not answer it. It's three-thirty in the morning."

"No. We have to. It might be Dr. Grimes. We have to."

The phone insisted shrilly and the two women clung to each other against whatever message it threatened.

"When did you last see her?"

"Just this evening, yesterday I mean, last night. She was all right. She even knew me."

"Then I do not answer it."

" 'Yana! Even if it *is* Larry, I've *got* to *know!*"

So they had had no time to prepare for Julian's hearing Dr. Grimes's voice.

"Miss Trav—Julian. Thank goodness I found you. Your home phone's been giving a busy signal for over two hours. I'm sorry to tell you that we've had to rush your mother back to the hospital. This time it was her heart. You'd better get up here. She's sinking. I'm afraid this is it."

EXPRESSIONS OF LOVE
(conclusion)

PART FOUR

January, 1986

"You're still waiting for her. What will it take to make you learn?"

"I tell you I'm not waiting. I've done with that." Iliana gave an irritable squeeze to her lemon twist and dropped it into her campari and soda. "Why do you keep saying that, Celia? Would I be in Paris if I were still waiting for Julian Travis? I proceed with my own life now, for a change."

"I *keep* saying that, *vieja*, because you talk about little else but her. Here you are, back for a visit. In triumph. Rehearsing the European debut of a major composition. Lionized by all us worldly debauched emigré Nicaraguans. Yet most of what I hear from you has to do with a crazy confused *gringa* lover far off in New York. I *keep* saying that, my dear, because I have known you since we were both six years old, and I can read you very well."

Iliana shrugged. "What can I do? We were lovers for only a year and a half, and I had her actually living with me for just a little over one year. But the scar—it's deep."

"Iliana. You have been with other lovers for much longer, you—"

"Time is not the point. I've known Julian for years, before the Venice period. Since we were in that women's group. Even then, there was—an electricity between us. I set some of her poems to music, did you know that? I understand her so *deeply*, Celia. Then again, I wonder if I understand her at all . . ."

Iliana gazed absently through the café windows fogged with condensation from a January frost outside on the rue Cujas. Celia lit a Gauloise, watching how her friend's hand unconsciously tapped a syncopated rhythm on the marble-topped table.

"You know, you *want* to get on with your life, Iliana," she mused. "Part of you is conducting the new piece even when you don't know you're doing it."

Iliana gave Celia a sharp glance, then looked down at her own hand. She withdrew the hand to her lap.

"*Sí*. But even the new piece leads back to her."

"Why? Because you began it during—"

"Because it is dedicated to her mother. Her mother's name was Hope. She died—oh, two years ago last October. My god, is it that long? Twenty . . . seven months."

Celia pushed up the sleeves of her oversize sweater and leaned forward with new interest. "I didn't know that about the piece. I thought 'Réquiem para la Esperanza' meant—"

" 'Requiem for Hope' in general? I suppose you could say that, too. No more hope. For love. For politics. For going home. But it also is a requiem for a real woman. And her daughter."

"Ah," her friend exhaled, mulling this bit of fresh information. "So your Julian . . . That explains something about your Julian."

"What?" Iliana asked listlessly. "That she became a mourner?"

"Death changes people. Especially the death of a mother."

"Yes. I've thought that. Much. Strange, I even find myself imagining that the mother died in childbirth." She signaled to the waiter for another drink. "I don't mean literally, of course; I mean that when she actually did die, that's when Juliana finally was born."

"That happens to all of us, one way or another, when a parent dies, no?"

"But more so to Julian." Iliana warmed to her subject, and Celia noticed, as she noticed how Iliana absent-mindedly fingered the small gold pendant—a circle with a cross beneath—that hung on a gold chain around her neck. Let her talk it out,

Celia thought, the way we used to harangue the subject of home for months on end when we first went into exile. Let her get all of it out. Then she can walk away from it. Celia probed accordingly,

"Why more so Julian?"

"Julian was obsessed with her mother. And the death was an ugly one, long years of sickness. The death vigil itself seemed endless. I know, I was with her. But also . . . Julian was an actress and—"

"I thought you told me she was a writer."

"She is. But she was once an actress, and she—I think she needs an audience to do her best, excel herself. She needs to be watched, applauded. For much of her life, Hope was that audience."

"Then *you* became it," Celia interjected, trying to edge Iliana into her perception of what ought to be her friend's self-perception.

Iliana shrugged again. "If so, I couldn't help it. It was quite a spectacle to watch, Celia, I assure you. From the very beginning. But especially when the mother died. Julian hadn't slept for days. I never saw anyone so near to a total breakdown. After the mother was pronounced dead, she insisted on sitting alone with the body. She stayed in the room a long while. Finally she let me take her back to my flat. In the taxi going down to the Village, she was . . . translucent with an almost unearthly energy. I held her hand. She let me, but looked out the window at the morning—it was her forty-second birthday, Celia. She let me get her into a warm bath, and into bed. She wouldn't take a pill or eat anything. She was so *calm.*"

Celia shook her head sadly. "Poor *gringas.* They don't know how to mourn. They hide it all inside."

"No, not her. It was something else. She was in the grasp of— I don't know. She must have woken after only a few hours. I didn't hear her, I who always sensed the second she stirred in bed. I only know that when I woke she was in the livingroom, fully dressed, already on the telephone, making the first calls." It did not escape Celia how Iliana's face livened with recollection. "She called her mother's attorneys, she called the Jewish cemetery where her mother had bought a plot, she called the rabbi."

"Ah," Celia put in, "they are Jews."

"Julian isn't. Well, by birth, yes. But she's an agnostic. With a Catholic sensibility. She's . . . I don't know what Julian is. Perhaps she's a witch."

"A witch." Celia couldn't help herself. "This tragedy has its farcical moments, Iliana."

"Doesn't all tragedy have elements of farce? Certainly this one did. I never will forget Julian looking up at me—pale face stripped of everything but discipline—saying, 'I hadn't thought of that. The hospital says I need a funeral director. They want to know about . . . disposal of the body. How could I have overlooked that?' "

"I fail to see that particular farce," Celia muttered wryly, thinking her comment safe from Iliana's preoccupied attention. But Iliana did hear.

"Farce," she responded, "because I, of all people, could cast that part for Julian's production."

"Production?"

The waiter put down a glass in front of Iliana. She sniffed it, puzzled.

"What is this? Sherry? My *god.*"She hailed him again. "Take this away, please, it's the wrong order. I *loathe* sherry. Bring me another campari and soda? Yes, production," she continued to Celia. "A funeral is a ritual, after all, and all rituals are acts of theater. I knew that whatever Julian staged for her mother would be unique and dramatic. But even Julian had overlooked one detail: a funeral director."

"Please. Don't tell me you took on the job for her," Celia growled.

"No. But I had an old friend, from my youthful days the first time I lived in New York. She owned a funeral home; *she* was a funeral director—a woman."

"A lover?" Celia inquired, impervious to constraints of politesse in a friendship so old as this.

"Sí." Iliana stirred her new drink sheepishly. "But only a brief, light-hearted—"

"—from the old days, aha, when Ilianita was playing Cherubino to all the pretty ladies? I remember *very* well." Celia arched her eyebrows in a mute reminder to Iliana of their own period as lovers, an intermezzo of eroticism in a lifelong duet of friendship.

Iliana retorted with injured dignity, "And what good has it

done me, I ask you, to grow serious and fall so deeply in love *now?* Look what misery it brings!"

"*I* never advised you to fall into a grand passion. And with a Yankee Jewish witch! *I* never—"

Iliana gave her head a little shake, to dispel this mood and permit a return to the comfort of her reminiscences. "Anyway. As I was saying. So I remembered Jessica Maruzzo. I thought to myself, Santa María! The heavens have a patient and morbid sense of humor! Jessica was the only child of a man who owned a funeral home in New York's Little Italy. She had demanded to work in the family business—and she had inherited it. We hadn't been close for years, but being a good Italian, she always kept track of me to send Christmas cards. She and her lover—a mortician—had come to Venice once on holiday while I lived there, and stayed with me. So I rang her up. She was delighted to be of help."

Celia grinned. "Ah, *hija mia,*" she laughed, "how we do keep reappearing! And how convenient it is! You remember our old joke? That there are really only six lesbian women in the world and the rest—"

"—is done with mirrors? Yes," Iliana laughed back, lending them both a moment's respite in the pleasure of younger selves. "Well, there she was. Jessica—one of Les Six. Ready for anything—which turned out to be a macabre and humorous chain of events. I brought her together with Julian. Julian told Jess she wished to strike a balance between what might have pleased her mother on the one hand, and her own antipathy to formal religious services on the other. She said she already had found a liberal woman rabbi—"

"I didn't know they let women—"

"—and a woman cantor for the memorial service, but that the rabbi was having difficulty convincing the Orthodox Jewish cemetery that a woman could perform the burial. To compound this, Jess had never in her life arranged anything except Italian Catholic funerals. But she was game to learn."

"This could have been a movie, Iliana," Celia giggled, "a co-production between Pasolini and Jerry Lewis."

"With the women's dialogue by Von Trotta. But wait. The best is to come. Jess discovers that a special washing of the body has to take place, not by her own employees, but by Jewish women recommended by the Orthodox cemetery, women whose job it is to perform this washing as a particular religious act. The additional catch is that no Orthodox cemetery will receive a body in any way 'desecrated.' Jess pulls me aside in panic, whispering frantically, 'The eyes! What about the eyes, then?' 'What about them?' I whisper back, just as frantically and not even sure why."

"*What* about them?" Celia demanded, completely caught up now in the plot.

"Julian had donated her mother's eyes to an eye bank."

Celia made a face of disgust. "Holy saints. How barbaric."

"Well . . . that's what I thought at first, but . . . you don't understand. In any event, Jess came all unstrung. 'Dammit, Iliana, don't you understand?' she hisses at me. 'When these Orthodox women perform the washing ritual, they might see the eyes are gone! What'll I do?' I say, 'Can't you just—close the lids?' *Holá*, was she furious. '*Shit*, Iliana, don't you think I *thought* of that?' she snarls. 'It'll still *show.*' She tells me she doesn't want to go into the gory details of her job, that it always puts people off, even old lovers. That's why Jess is so happy with Muffie, I think. They can work *together*, since Muffie's a mortician cosmetologist."

"I suppose," Celia analyzed, surrendering to a totally irreverent mirth, "that they can talk shop together in the evenings. This is priceless."

"So I say to Jess, 'Well, can't Muffie come up with a solution? I mean, what do you do, stuff something under the lids or what?' Jess fixes me with the stare Mother Superior Teresa used to reserve for you and me when we were in first grade. 'Never mind,' she declares haughtily, 'I should never have mentioned it. Muffie and I will solve it. And don't tell The Daughter.' "

"Oh! Have you noticed? All funeral directors refer to the survivors as if they were archetypes. The Daughter. The Widow. The Family. *Priceless,*" Celia repeated.

"But of course I did tell The Daughter," Iliana persisted, "since I was after all The Lover of The Daughter. And The Daughter—a thespian, I tell you, as much as a mourner—was content to let Muffie and Jess solve it together. Which they must have done, because we heard no story of the ritual-washwomen running screaming out of the Little Italy mortuary, crying to the world that a sacrilegious robbing of corneas had taken place. So Jess proceeded proudly with what she called her "first full feminist funeral."

"Omigod," Celia chortled, "now we have to add in Ingmar Bergman."

"Jess had never met a woman rabbi. Julian's rabbi, just out of the rabbinate school, had never met a woman funeral director. Neither one had ever performed a ceremony in which only women were present—*and* which took place in an Orthodox cemetery, which had never experienced any of the above either. Jess was used to the elaborate caskets and dress of her Italian Catholic clients, but she managed within twenty-four hours to find the required plain pine coffin with a Star of David on top, just as she managed to locate the proper homespun cloth for the ritual shroud."

Celia wrinkled her nose. "Boring. Latins do it better."

"Don't be such a bigot. Everything was simple. Understated. We assembled, two cars filled with an all-female—they call it minyan—the minimum number of mourners, ten, by Jewish law, I learned. You can't imagine the faces of some of Julian's friends—from this publishing house she worked with—who were among the group. They got out of the car, expecting a woman rabbi perhaps but not one in pants. And surely not expecting a woman funeral director to greet them. With great solemnity, in a full cutaway."

A shadow came over Iliana's face as she pursued her memory of the scene. She stared again out the clouded café window as if seeing the cemetery on a Paris street. "Julian let me take her arm as we stepped toward the grave, but then she disengaged herself and stood alone." Iliana fell silent and Celia waited, sensitive to the change of mood. "Then, as Julian might say, good theater would have it that there comes a moment when the intermission of comic relief falls away and grief is left center-stage, alone. Julian had memorized the Kaddish. She has a low, full voice—a rich mezzo if she were a singer—and she intoned the chant together with the thinner, clear soprano of the young rabbi, a female duet in the bleak October wind. Each of us, according to Jewish ritual, then threw a handful of earth on the coffin as it was being lowered—Julian last of all, with both hands. Then she unwrapped the bundle she had with her, and out slashed against the grey autumn sky a dazzle of white lilacs, like a great pearl bird. She lifted the loose sheaf up against her breast, stepped to the edge of the open grave, and flung her arms wide so the lilacs descended, wingspread, into the earth."

Iliana paused again. Again Celia waited.

"Those were the only flowers. I wonder what her mother would have thought. I wonder if, after all, Hope would have understood. I think of all those hours of Julian speaking to Hope as she lay dying. How useless it was. How she never got through."

"How little any of us ever get through to anyone, ever." Celia contemplated her friend patiently, then murmured, "And all this time, you—?"

"I was watching. Witnessing. Waiting. The next day was the memorial service. You would have liked it, *vieja*. The music was unusual, especially for a temple, I gather: Bach's Air in G, and the English Suite No. 2—and Brahms' Lullaby."

"Eclectic for the organist," Celia observed with a smile, thinking of all her church jobs over the years, in order to survive as a keyboardist.

"What was magical was the cantor. A woman's voice gave the chants of mourning a new dimension . . . All the people attending were Julian's friends. Her mother had ended her own friendships years before her life itself closed. No, it was for Julian we all came. That day she seemed to recognize it. Dignity she had, gravity, graciousness, self-possession."

And an audience, Celia thought but did not say.

Iliana sighed. "Perhaps that was when it began. She started to distance herself from all of us, exquisitely, giving no offense. But not from *me*, I was certain. I was sure there would come a time when she would break and sob and I would hold her. It never came. Other times, yes—times of . . . rebirth. Times when she learned herself, from *me*, from my reactions to her as she began to play again, learning *how* to play. From *me*."

"It's unwise, *tonta*, to be too much the mentor. *Or* the audience," Celia ventured. She glanced at her watch. "Let's get some air, eh? We have less than an hour until rehearsal."

The other sighed and rose obediently, sliding into her coat. They wove through the clusters of small tables, paid their bill, and stepped out into the street.

"*Merde*, I *never* get used to the cold," Celia winced, slipping her arm through Iliana's and guiding her toward the Boulevard St. Michel. "Thirty years in exile and I *still* miss Managua non-winters."

Iliana stopped in front of a small building.

"Celia. This was it, no? The little hotel where all us Latin American refugees congregated? The very one?"

"*Sí, niña,* the very one. When you and I both were staying alive by giving piano lessons to bourgeois French brats. Even then, God help us, you were recovering from love."

"You have no mercy," Iliana chided. "That was after the affair with Talavera . . . and the abortion. Ach, what we put ourselves through . . . That was just before I got to study with Boulanger, may she rest in peace." Iliana cast a nostalgic look back at the building as Celia firmly led her away.

"*And* before you began to compose seriously. *And* before the first commission. And *long* before—"

"Long before the fatal commission for 'Avíos para la Eternidad'—the one that was my excuse for returning to New York for the third time. To her."

Celia hugged her friend's arm and fell into matching strides. "I always liked that piece. Jesú! A suite for synthesizer, strings, and bone percussion. When we performed it here, I thought my fingers would fall off from all those arpeggios. My dear, you may be an emotional mess but you are a fine composer."

They walked in silence for a block. Then Iliana laughed—a short, cynical sound. "You will be amused to know," she confided, "that I am not a composer. I am now a photographer."

"A what? Watch *out,* you know Paris traffic— You are now a what?"

"An art photographer. In the novel she's writing."

"Who's writing? The ghost of Nadia Boulanger?" Celia steered Iliana across the intersection, knowing all too well who "she" was. Julian, the ghost of Julian.

"In the novel Julian's writing. About this whole period."

Celia stopped short as they reached the curb, a look of outrage on her face. "She's put you in a novel? For *another* audience? That's—that's unspeakable," she sputtered.

"No, no, you don't understand." Why do I invite her attacks on Julian and then defend Julian against them, Iliana wondered, slipping her arm through Celia's this time and moving them onward. "Julian's an artist, after all. She has to use her pain, the way I've done with the requiem. Besides, what she writes is all disguised to protect—"

"Protect *her*. And she makes you a *photographer*. Taking pictures of *her*, I warrant. Still *another* audience."

"I'm beginning to regret I ever told you she was an actress," Iliana snapped.

"Don't be. It's central. She's—*used* you in every way, the bitch—"

Iliana raised her voice, oblivious to passers-by, "I won't have you talk about her like that. You have no idea—"

"An art photographer from Nicaragua. How preposterous."

"Not from Nicaragua," the other muttered into her turned-up collar, striding along now at a pace that made Celia breathless, "from Argentina."

"*Argentina!* I can't bear it. To turn you into one of those stuffy arrogant Argentinians who think that they own—"

"*No,* dammit. Stop leaping to conclusions! I know why she's doing that. She wants the reader to have instant sympathy for the character, so she made her a refugee from a right-wing dictatorship instead of—"

Celia stopped again and faced Iliana. "Instead of the truth, you mean. Which is that poor fools like us happen to be refugees from a country plagued by both right- *and* left-wing dictatorships. Poor fools like us—who fled from Somoza's hell, rushed back all dewy-eyed with hope for the so-called revolution of '79, and then, sick at the soul, found the *same* corruption, the *same* censorship, with different uniforms and slogans. Poor fools like us, *double* exiles!" Celia's eyes blazed with an old indignation. "You know how many hours I have had to spend explaining to French intellectuals why I do not return to Managua to live happily ever after in the revolution? Me, a lesbian avant-garde electronic musician? Ha!" She spat into the gutter.

"Don't you think I also have those conversations? Don't you think—"

"I'll *tell* you what *I* think," Celia yelled. A Parisian tripped past them without a glance, unruffled by two women standing on the street waving their arms and shouting in Spanish. "I think your wondrous Juliana lacks all capacity for political and aesthetic complexity. I think she has a simplistic North American mind capable only of cheap sympathy with victims of traditional despots. I think her attitude is as shallow in its own way as her country's entire Latin American foreign policy—a policy created by some creature who was a cross between a sadist and an ass! One more well-meaning tyrant and I think I go *mad!*"

Celia fell silent, glaring at Iliana. A gust of wind inspired them to move, and they began to walk again, not touching. Iliana was secretly basking in the warmth of her friend's rage on her behalf, a solace which lasted until they reached the boulevard. But as they turned onto it, she caught a glimpse of the Luxembourg Gardens, lavish even in their winter-stripped state, across the street. A perilous glimpse, because any garden, any flower, conjured up Julian in a haunting more vivid than all the miles that lay between them. Desire in the eye, in the hearing, in the memory. Julian, during a weekend in the country, returning from a dawn walk in spring rain with her arms full of wildflowers; Julian, coming like a vision of splendor back into bed, skin cool and damp with the rain's freshness, hair faintly ringleting, smelling of grass and dew, flinging blossoms all over the bed for the sheer elation of it. Julian, listening to Rachmaninoff's "Trio Élégiaque No. Two" and Messiaen's "Oiseaux Exotiques" for the first time. Julian eating an oyster, lips wrapping the fortunate creature in their fullness. Julian, diving and splashing like a berserk dolphin at the seashore. Julian, lifting from its box the gift of a white silk kimono. Julian, tipsy on champagne, lying on the sofa for three hours scowling at the ceiling and arguing aloud with God. Julian, sleeping in her arms—these arms now hugging only herself against the January wind—Julian asleep after love: small-boned body with skin finespun as gauze, limbs sprawled but never quite in abandon . . . always something maddeningly virgin about her, something withheld. Iliana reached up to her own throat, to touch the gold women's symbol Julian had given her. Julian. Juliana.

Celia glanced at Iliana surreptitiously and spotted the soundless tears. She moved closer and again linked her arm with her friend's. The gesture brought forth a cataract of words again.

"I still don't understand what *happened*, Celia. I try and try but . . . Julian always said she wished to live alone, at least for a while, to reassemble the fragments of her life. But I didn't want to believe that. We were actually *living* together, you see, and I *wanted* that: a real life. Rising together and making coffee, chatting about nothing in particular over breakfast, going off in different directions to do different tasks during the hours of the day, reconnecting at evening to prepare dinner together, to sit by candlelight, share food and talk of the day, read perhaps or play some music, enter the nighttime smoothly, through an act of love or of simple curling together, body to body in sweet weariness, in our mutual bed. I craved that proximity, that continuity. After so many years of wandering, I *wanted* that. She once turned to me and lectured me that I kept saying 'a real life.' 'Who *doesn't* live a real life?' she fumed. 'The convict, the prostitute, the Carmelite, the Bedouin nomad, the paraplegic—their lives are just as real to them. Either none of us lives a real life or all of us do.' But I meant something different, you know, Celia? Something rooted in its own sweet daily rhythms. Was it such a sin to want that, and with her?"

For answer, Celia only pressed Iliana's arm. Let her talk, she reminded herself; you're a good friend, bear with all her retrospections; don't argue, let the last of it cascade out.

"Understand me, Celia. *She* never said it was a sin. But every time I spoke of it, she reiterated her own desires—space, time, solitude, freedom. How had I ever constricted her freedom? If I could only understand . . . Then, when she began it all again—the whirl of activity—I knew it was a reach toward that freedom. And yes, then I did fight it. There was the work in untangling what shreds were left of her mother's estate. There were speeches, meetings, travels. There was her editing job, which she kept on top of everything else to put money away for her own apartment. There was her book. There was the anxiety about her husband, even though it was clear by then no reconciliation was possible. There were the world's poor and dispossessed, there were letters to write and phone calls to make . . . Yes, I became jealous, of her colleagues, her friends, her time. I fought her over time for *us.* The more I fought for that, the more she withdrew. I don't *understand.*"

Celia sighed. "You tried to possess her, *tonta.* It sounds like she wanted that and also didn't want it."

"But when all the rhetoric about loving in freedom is spent, isn't it true that at heart every lover wishes to possess the belovèd? Possess and be possessed by, utterly, eternally—no matter how unrealistic and hopelessly romantic that seems to our modern, psychologically sophisticated intellects?"

"That," Celia smiled, "is part of an unfinished discussion you and I have had many times. But however that may be, I do think perhaps North Americans are fearful about . . . commitment."

"But she *is* committed to me. Like family. Friends until we die, I know that. Maybe even periodic lovers, though not in the way I would have wanted. Yet something in me *still* believes we will one day have that—that lively, ecstatic serenity together, that—coming home to one another."

Celia debated injecting a note of realism into the delicacy of the confessional moment. What was it her friend really needed to hear, in order to heal?

"It sounds to me," she said slowly, groping for the right approach, "as if your Julian must let herself experience what she has been denied for so many years—in the childhood, in the marriage. She must go into the . . . exile of herself, you know? Perhaps she will have other lovers; perhaps other women lovers, perhaps men. It may be just as well. If she'd stayed with you she'd have coveted her freedom. Wouldn't you rather she have her freedom and covet you? You say you don't foresee her living with anyone again for some time. I wonder . . . But *you, niña.* You *must* cease the waiting."

"By ceasing the waiting one risks losing the hope." There, she had admitted it. "And Julian would neither fully claim me *nor* fully let me go. Were she a composer, Celia, she would write music redolent with hemiolia. You know? The rhythmic ambiguity—?"

"I know. That all time values are in the relationship. Are six notes of an equal time value three groups of two or two groups of three?" Celia recited, "Dunstable, Dufay, Schumann's 'Spanische Liebes-Lieder.' I know, Iliana. I *know.*"

"I didn't want the waiting to erode my love for her. I didn't want to abandon her—like her father had. That is the way of the exile. After suffering so total a severance, one goes through life protecting oneself against ever feeling too much again. *You* know that, Celia," she said gently. "But I also did not want to be like the husband, waiting *too* long—until violent expulsion seems the only pure act. I didn't want to be like the mother,

clinging, demanding, smothering—though it was in this direction the greatest danger lay. Because Julian evoked precisely
that form of loving." Iliana lifted a blasted face to the winter
sky, crying out, "What models are *left* us, we women?"

Celia found tears burning her own eyes. She didn't want
that, didn't want to feel, didn't want it all opened up again.
"We are the strong women," she heard herself say in a small
voice, "the political ones, the ones who have careers, the ones
who are feminists, the ones who dare to love women. So. You
say, I say, we all say . . . Yet the ghost of the mother rises and
walks among us, through us, between us. Maybe that is the only
love, Iliana; maybe all other loving is an imitation of that first
passion—or of the lack of it. Maybe love is just another master-
ful invention of the poets."

They fell silent again. The boulevard wind keened softly.

"I tried, Celia. I helped her look at apartments. I helped her
shop for furnishings. I surprised her with gifts she would need
to set up housekeeping—since she refused to fight the husband
over property. At first my gifts were met with delight; later
with that familiar tight-lipped expression of suffocation. I don't
understand."

Celia fought the understanding, but she understood. "Julian
felt you were equipping her with articles she wanted to choose
for herself. You were filling her longed-for space with too many
artifacts of your presence—as if you *were* going to be living
together." Not to feel this empathy, not to see life raw and
chaotic again. As devoutly as Iliana claimed she sought clarity,
so Celia claimed she sought opacity. They circled each other
and their overlapping truths, trading the wrong clues.

"But still she didn't *act*, Celia. I began to see she was waiting
to *react.* And I began to feel descend on me a role I did not—
still do not—comprehend. It was as if I had to fulfill some
promise I had no recollection of having made, honor some
unholy bargain, live up to some forgotten pledge with the
devil. So I—who wanted nothing more in the world than to
keep her close—drove her away. Not in anger. But in pressuring that she *must* decide."

The two women approached the corner of St. Germain and
the side door of the Musée de Cluny. Celia glanced at her
watch. At least she had delivered de Costa on time.

"So *you* ended it," she suggested, offering her friend the gift of dignity.

"I don't know," Iliana mumbled in bewilderment. "I don't know what *happened.* I mean, in one way, it's not ended. We see each other frequently, we have dinner at my flat or at hers, go to concerts, laugh, gossip . . . I know she'll meet me at the airport next month. I know I'll write her all about the concert in detail. The mysterious thing is that I don't know how I lost her. Or even if I have."

Obsession. Celia saw it, pitied it. Whether for a lost little nation or a mother's voice or a lover's glance or the character of a D-minor chord, it was obsession that carried and inflicted its own content. Any object of obsession was merely the excuse; it was the capacity for obsession that was the message entire. She saw it and pitied it. More. She feared it. She envied it. Iliana, ignorant of her pity and her envy, and impervious to her advice, was meanwhile putting the coda on her narrative.

"The day Julian moved from my flat, that last day at Grove Street, I'll never forget how her eyes pierced me through their tears. 'Where are you going, then, truly, my Juliana, whom I am going to lose?' I asked her. 'I don't know,' she answered, with a doleful shake of her head. 'So many dyings, so much to mourn.' Then she looked at me. 'Freedom—is it so impossible, 'Yana? Will it be the most painful dying of all? Or will it be real, a stepping off the stage at last?' I could have answered in many ways, but some peculiar power struck me dumb. 'Then is anything *ever* real, at all?' she appealed, tears running down her face. So I picked up the set of Grove Street keys I had given her, which she had discreetly put on the hall table, to leave behind—and I tossed them at her. She caught them, in surprise. I remember lifting my head high and smiling at her, with a wink, singing out as lightly as I could, 'Style, my love. Perhaps style is the only thing that ever is real.' And so she turned, still holding the keys. And so she was gone."

They stood before the museum door.

"But we have arrived," Celia announced, turning to her childhood friend. "Now. I want you to understand something, Iliana de Costa. Perhaps you did love this time in ways more profound than you ever loved before—and whatever this churlish old friend may rant, know that I respect it." She fumbled in her pocket, produced a crumpled linen handkerchief, and blew her nose loudly. "And whatever mysteries you cannot comprehend, understand this: that you are now composing in ways more profound than you ever did before. In the long and short run, exile or not, lover or not, that is what counts. That is what *lasts*."

Iliana nodded, sniffling. Celia proffered her handkerchief. "Go on, blow your frozen nose. We've shared everything else. Why stop now?" Iliana obliged and emitted a dutiful honk.

"So now we go in there to the *salle* and you take the baton and get to work, eh? This is the last rehearsal holy saints and we have a Paris premiere tomorrow. I have no more patience with these lovelorn mewlings. I have to thaw these icy fingers for your hellish tangle of notes. *You* have no more time to be The Tragic Lesbian. *You* have to cope with the unruly mixture that's waiting in there: electronic *and* acoustic musicians, *plus* chorus, *plus* three female soloists each so temperamental that together they qualify to be the Nicaraguan revolutionary junta."

Iliana broke into laughter. The two women hugged one another.

"If you are *very* good in there, I promise you a reward," Celia said, stepping back, holding Iliana at arm's length, and peering sternly into her face. "I'll treat you to supper at La Coupôle, for old times' sake."

"That would be heaven," Iliana brightened, "but only if we can take a taxi. I will coagulate with all this arctic exercise."

"Idiot. This is *Paris*, remember? You *walk* in Paris. It's not New York, where there's nothing to walk *along*. I will walk you back down St. Michel—and yes yes we can stop in the Café Luxembourg for a petit cognac if you wish—then, nicely warmed, we proceed through Montparnasse. Is it a bargain?"

"It is," Iliana vowed. "And, Celia," she added, returning the handkerchief with a straightforward look, "thank you." They walked into the museum.

Ten minutes later, Celia stood at her synthesizer, flicking dials in between chafing her stiff hands. A din of tune-up and vocalizing filled the *salle*. Then the woman in black slacks and black turtleneck mounted the podium and faced the Groupe Vocal de France and the Ensemble Electroacoustique. She glanced at Celia, raked her eyes over choir, instrumentalists, soloists. She rapped her baton for attention. The noise began to subside.

"I am waiting, mesdames et messieurs," Iliana called in a voice of authority. The room fell silent. "We begin at the top, with the Kyrie, please. *Forte, con brio.* It starts audaciously; reckless, in full passion, remember."

There was a rustle of music sheets, then stillness again. Iliana waited. All eyes were fixed on the composer-conductor. *This is home,* she thought. *This is what lasts.*

Baton in hand, Iliana de Costa raised her arms, poised for the opening *attaque.*

Julian wandered around her apartment, touching things. After all these months, the tactile existence of this new home still gave her acute pleasure. Just to caress objects that felt, still not hers, but gradually familiar, as they lived in the same place as she: these spoons, that crystal candlestick, this pottery bowl. A newspaper clipping about Laurence Millman declaring his candidacy for local Democratic district leader was propped up on the fireplace mantel—a real fireplace this time, with a log flaming and crackling cozily inside. The de Costa photograph, "Old Woman in Nursing Home," which had won the 1984 International Photography Prize, hung framed on the wall facing the fireplace. Bookcases lined the other walls and flanked the mantel. The piano smiled its perfect teeth from a corner, waiting for the one chord to be struck that would end all music. The cats—Virginia and Vita—lay curled in Yin-Yang fashion on their favorite cushion of the sofa.

She walked into her bedroom, where the afternoon light flung itself through open shutters across the bed, golden, odalisque. More bookshelves. Photographs of the major noncharacters on her bedtable. A battered Raggedy Ann doll sprawled, fearless now, on the chair.

In the study: her desk. Her own desk again, capriciously cluttered with "To Do" lists, mail, political tracts, seed catalogues for city gardeners, and galley proofs of the new book— on Thanatos as the heart of male politics and Eros as the heart of female politics—the book whose publishing advance had made possible apartment, spoons, fireplace, bed, desk, and everything else. Especially the garden she would grow upstairs on the roof in the spring. Another chance to "make the tar-paper bloom," but this time looking out over a quiet street in Greenwich Village, not far from Iliana's.

Julian had just resolved to make a cup of tea when the phone rang. Saturday, so it wouldn't be an offer of a free-lance job or a lecture—the means by which she still largely survived but which, in her newfound serenity, she had begun to resent as intrusions from the outside world.

It wasn't the outside world. It was Laurence.

"Larry! Good to hear from you! How's the Rocky Mountain Michelangelo?"

"Fine, Jule. Damn, but it's great to be back here. How're you?"

"Fine too. So how're things going these days? Is the new one finished yet?"

"Oh yeah, over a month ago. In fact, I just came back from the Midwest day before yesterday. Went out to see it installed in all formality, squack in the plaza of the Chicago Children's Museum."

"You sound happy with it."

"Very. Though I still can't get over the shock of all this happening after so long."

"Are you kidding? It's *good* news for a change. Enjoy it! Everybody's talking about Millman's marble children. That article in the New York *Times:* 'Neoclassic Vision—The Children.' Wow." Larry chuckled with pleasure. How satisfying it felt to hear him laugh again! She wanted an encore. "Laurence Millman. I can say 'I Knew Him When.' Why, if I had thousands of dollars stashed away, plus the space in which to properly house it, I'd up and commission me a Millman Child, too."

"You don't need one, Jule. They're part you, you know. From that first breakthrough one, over two years ago, straight on, they have some of your features. I mean, it's just become my own subject matter. Boy or girl, sleeping or running, leaping or breaking out through the stone, they're all part Julians."

"Well, thank god nobody's noticed but thee and me. *I* still haven't recovered from *my* shock at seeing that first one. That incredible little . . . *creature*, clawing its rough-hewn way up out of the marble, part still-born, part alive, such suffering and joy hammered together in that child-face . . ."

"It's a good piece, that one, yeah. I thought to myself as I was working on it, 'Larry, now you've gone and done it for good.

Children. How sentimental can you get. This'll be the coup de grâce to whatever's left of your career as a sculptor.' But now look."

"Well, I think they're successful *because* they have nothing to do with sentimentality. Some of them may be gaunt and starving, others sensual, others enigmatic—but not one of them is sentimental. That's what's so riveting about them— these complex states of emotion portrayed for the first time on the faces of *children.* It happens in life; it's just that nobody before you had the guts to show it in art."

"Well, thanks, Jule. So, anyway, all goes well. I've got enough bread to buy a place out here for keeps now. Been looking at land. After so many years of renting, it feels weird—but super."

"That's terrific, Lare. I'm really glad for you."

"Well. I guess that first visit back here, after— I mean, it made me lust for my roots or some such baloney. And with the pieces getting larger, and actually selling for a change . . . I need a good big work space. So I'll get me an old barn or something, right here in the Colorado mountains. A failed New Yorker, I suppose."

Julian was looking at the head he had done of her so long ago, the one she'd never let him throw away, even though he'd felt it a failed piece. The failed Julian head.

"Larry, you're not a failed anything. On the contrary."

"Well, thanks. Anyway. I just thought I'd call and say hello. Tell you your ex was about to become landed gentry and— Oh, Jule, I almost forgot. I'm sorry I didn't get that manuscript back to you yet. What with the commissions and all—"

"That's okay, Larry. Whenever you have the chance. Uh, did you ever get to read it?"

"Oh, yes, right away. You know me, I meant to write you about it, or call, but— Anyway, I think it's . . . good."

"Really? Gee, that's—"

"I, uh, I do have to say that, well, I think you're *awfully* positive on the woman lover character. And—damned unfair to the, uh, husband character. Kind of a cheap shot for feminism's sake. I mean, Christ, there's so much that's distorted, or left out entirely!"

"Yes. Well, you know, it's a *novel.* Fiction, after all."

"Oh sure, I told myself that. But even so . . . you make the woman lover a plaster saint, instead of—a home-wrecker. You make the husband—"

"I'm sorry you feel that way, Lare. Let's not dredge up . . . Look, I'll probably revise it a few thousand times more, as I always do. So—"

"Yeah, well . . . you live in a dream world, Jule. People aren't just subject matter, you know. Life's not all plots and characters and politics."

"Well. That's debatable. But when it is, then for me at least it helps make the impenetrable remotely intelligible. Anyway, I do know that life is lived a lot differently than it comes out on the page. Well, thanks for reading it, anyway. And . . . I'm glad you came through in your own work."

"I know you are, Jule. And I wish you the best."

"Sure, Larry. When you get your land, you break open some champagne and celebrate, okay?"

"Well—"

"Oh, sorry, forgot. A half glass of wine and you always fell clunk asleep, like the doormouse with his head in the teapot."

" 'Fraid so. But I'll celebrate in my own way. So . . . take care, Jule."

"You too. 'Bye, Larry."

"Yeah. 'Bye."

She hung up the phone. Goodbye, she thought, goodbye my first love and only husband. You stand now on the far side of some bridge we once claimed as our own. But may you live and breathe, may the stone sing into something beautiful under your hands.

She might have been one of his statues, standing there beside her desk, looking at the Julian head, neither of them stirring. But then she remembered she'd been on her way to make a cup of tea. She went into the kitchen and put on the kettle. Lovely kitchen, lovely table, chairs, stove, sink. Hers. Lovely leftovers in lovely refrigerator—her own chicken tarragon with Dijon mustard sauce. Lovely to cook again, just what she wished and when. Lovely fragrant tea leaves. Lovely melodic burble of the kettle coming to a boil.

That novel. She smiled and shook her head. That perpetually unfinished novel. Other books of hers would come and go, but that novel would continue to haunt her, no matter how many new rooms she moved into and through. Months had passed since the completion of what felt to her like the hundred and seventieth draft, and she still didn't know how to end it. Not for lack of an ending, but because there were too many possibilities:

Ashley lives self-sufficiently and happily-ever-after alone in her new apartment, The New Woman On Her Own. Julian wrinkled her nose in distaste. Trite. Sounds as if it had been penned by Maxine Duncan Brewer.

Leigh reconciles with Laurence and they have a child. Unrealistic. That character would never do either.

Leslie reunites with Iliana and together they journey to Nicaragua to foment an authentic revolution which embraces both feminism and art. Utopian. They'd be shot dead in a day.

Blair, finally left to her own devices, has a nervous breakdown and takes to wearing organdy pinafores and pink hairbows. Predictable. Besides, the character hates to polish her white maryjanes.

Julian sighed and poured the steaming water over her tea leaves.

Shawn falls wildly in love with an entirely new—

The doorbell rang.

"Who can *that* be?" she asked Vita, who had followed her into the kitchen and was butting against her ankles in hope of a snack. "I'm not expecting anybody, are you?"

She pressed the buzz-back and peered down the stairs. It was a familiar blue uniform.

"Hi," she called, "What are you doing about? Mail came."

"Special Delivery Express for you. From France, looks like. No rest for the weary mail deliverer."

"Sorry," she grinned, signing for the delivery and waving goodbye. It was a thick envelope. Iliana.

Julian sat down at the kitchen table and opened the letter. The familiar handwriting scrawled over many pages. She sipped her tea and read.

Only the ticking of the wall clock broke the quiet of the kitchen. Julian turned the last page. The letter lay in her lap.

The lady does have style, she smiled to herself. The lady had definitely been too impatient—and also too patient—for too long. The lady was now back in control of her own life. The lady definitely had style.

"I'll miss you," she soliloquized aloud to the scribbled pages. "I'll miss the character I drafted—"

Virginia stalked into the kitchen, Vita at her heels, both of them now loudly demanding high tea. But Julian stared at the letter, her mind elsewhere.

It's not one novel, she thought. *It's two.* She put down her teacup. *It's a novel within a novel, nested Chinese boxes, the action behind the curtain, backstage, off-camera.* Scenes began to whirl in her brain. *It's . . . all the fragments beginning to fall into place. Levels of reality . . .*

The phone rang again. But she was not about to let herself in for the remotest surreal possibility that it would be *her*, briskly accusing:

"Hello, Baby. You didn't call or come by today."

She ignored the ringing. She rose abruptly, pages fluttering from her lap. She ignored the cats. She moved to her desk like a woman in a dream, a woman possessed, a professional who's been told that she has only a half hour until showtime. She yanked a piece of paper from its nook and swiftly rolled it into her typewriter.

Never mind the drafts, the variants. Never mind the repetitions, failures, rehearsals. Nesting boxes, masks under masks. Yet each a performance. Each one an expression of love.

She began to write.

PART FIVE
October, 1983

It's me, Momma. Julian. I'm here right beside you. I'm staying with you. I won't leave you.

They say you can't hear me, Momma.

But I'll go on talking to you like this, whatever anybody says.
Because coma or no, I think you're still inside there.

Maybe some of these words might sink down to where you
are. So you'll know you're not alone. So you'll know you're
loved.

Try not to be afraid. That must be very hard. And you've had
so many hard things to do already, for so long. But you did
them all the best you could. You've always had courage. I want
you to know I know that. It's me speaking to you, Momma,
Julian. Your only child.

Try to hear me.

Try. Up through the layers, the smoke, water, distance, the
roar, the silence, whatever the space is between my voice and
where you are.

I know you're in there. You know my voice, Momma. It's me.

I'm trying to help you through this with the only tools I have:
my love for you and your love for me. And some . . . words,
Momma. And my body, too, right here. Sitting on the edge of
your bed close beside you. My touch on your body. Try to feel
me.

It's Julian. It's my hands that are touching you. One of my hands is holding both of your tight little fists. My other hand is stroking your forehead, smooth, steady . . . try to feel that. I know you may not be able to make a sign, but I want you to know I'm here.

Everything I am strains toward you at this moment. All my energy, consciousness, love.

You are my mother and your name is Hope. *Hope.* You have another name, too, Momma. You were called *Hokhmah,* which in Hebrew means wisdom. Wisdom and hope might be the same thing, Momma, so you can claim both as your own. Both are your own names.

My name is Julian, Momma. Speaking to you, reaching into you, touching your surfaces with my hands and my breath. This is your daughter's voice, these are your daughter's hands. Flesh of your flesh, bone of your bone, blood of your blood.

Can you reach back to me? Can you understand you're not alone? Try, reach up up up through all that space and silence. Grasp the me that's reaching down into you. It's Julian, Hope. It's me, Hokhmah.

Now. Let's try, you and me together. Against the whole world.

Let's try to unfist your hands.

Let's gather all our selves into . . . something like a beam of light or energy. Let's focus it directly at your hands, way way up here on your surface. Try to feel them.

Try to feel my hands on yours, flesh of your flesh caressing your flesh which is my flesh. One flesh, Momma. My hands won't force yours open, don't be afraid. They want to help you relax your hands, just a little. They want to slip a few fingers inside, so you can grasp my fingers the way a newborn baby in a crib holds on, by reflex, for comfort. It's safe with me.

Shall we try? Together.

We can do it. We can be anything we want to be, we've always known that. Can we try to hold hands and go through this together? Helping each other, not being so alone or so afraid, not hurting so much?

Trust me. Hear me. *Now.* Reach, strain up up up to meet me straining, reaching, down through the whole world to find you wherever you are in there. Try?

Open now, little Momma, open now, little hands, let yourself bud open. Think of your hands as trying to flower. It's really so easy. Let it be easy.

Yes, *easy*. Feel me, I'm here with you, *easy* to relax and let them petal by petal *yes* begin to unfold themselves, relax, open, spread, flower, *yes* you're doing it, what beautiful flowers they're becoming, petal on petal, so lovely . . . so *lovely* you are. *Yes*.

Now we're holding hands together, Hope and her baby, Hokhmah and Julian. Feel that. Take my warmth down into your chill. Take what I send down to you through these hands, this voice. Reach up up up for this love *yes*.

You did it, yes. You and me, against what they all said.

Now we can go on together and be anything we want to be.

Now, holding hands, we can do the rest of it.

* * *

So she's dying, the Vampire Mother. She hung on until something malevolent in the universe told her, as of last night, it was finally too late. So she can die in peace, safe in the knowledge that her daughter is free now from the puny male love with which that poor dumb sculptor Laurence Millman tried for two decades to win her. And in the process, lost his soul.

Hello, tape recorder, old friend and brother solipsist. You know who this is, your faithful spirit of the man who was: sculptor, never-father, longtime but nevermore now husband of Julian Travis, daughter of Hope Travis who lies dying. How many times have we sat like this, tape recorder—in my studio, alone together? You, a machine, and me, a human being trying to find out if I still had a voice? How many times have I talked to you while I was a bit drunk, waiting for her to come home?

So here I am again, still sitting at the same worktable, dawn squinting through the skylight, other members of our old circle present. Brandy bottle. Little twisted rust-metal cages all around. And monolithically mute, still waiting, still hulking massively in its corner: *It*. The untouched now-antique block of Carrara marble. It.

Except something's different. I'm not waiting for Julian. Julian's not coming home. Not tonight or ever, I think. Just about twenty-four hours ago, Laurence Millman finally drove her away. He got his point across, and without right this minute being dead or behind bars—jail bars or loony bars or liquor bars, what's the difference.

So this is the voice of a man who isn't waiting.

I'm not even waiting for Vampire Mother Hope to die. I used to wait for her to die. Not necessarily in the flesh—though I'd have settled for that—but to die in her daughter's flesh. I thought Julian and I could outwit and outlast Vampire Mother, see. Well, now I'm not even waiting to hear that Hope finally left us alone. For all I know, she's already dead. Julian called— when was that, last night? No, it was daylight. Yesterday afternoon?

Simple conversation: the dead speaking to the dead about the dying. Julian called to tell me Hope was really dying and she was at the hospital keeping the vigil. Then she asked how I was. I told her okay. I asked how she was. She said she was okay. You have to understand, tape recorder, how this all went; I mean, there were silences between each of these exchanges.

For all I know, she might've been trying to reach me for hours. But I'd left the phone off the hook in here, and forgotten about it. I wasn't in here, you see. I was lying on the floor of her study, for hours, holding on to that little foam pallet of hers that already held the indent of her body, already smelled of her sleep. I think I fell asleep myself and then I'd wake up and remember and the room would go black even though it was daylight and then I guess I'd sleep again and wake and cry and sleep, over and over.

But finally you can't sleep or cry anymore and you begin to separate out Julian from life because in the long run life is even more demanding than she is—which is really saying something. So after a point, Life demands you go to the bathroom or you'll pee all over yourself. Partly you obey from training, and partly 'cause something in you doesn't want you to pee on yourself and become more wretched than you already are. So you get up and go.

Now, that's where Life gets sneaky. Because once you're on your feet, Life has you by the balls.

Suddenly, Life says: You're hungry. Life says: A cup of fresh coffee? Life says: You're a wreck, *but* (this is in a tempting whisper) *if* you take a shower and shave and throw on fresh clothes you can go to the coffeeshop on Ninth Avenue and have coffee and scrambled eggs and hash browns and toast with butter and you won't even have to fix it yourself. Now what you *really* want to do, tape recorder, is go back into the study where the woman you loved and lived with for years used to sit and write love poems to you. What you really want to do is crawl back down on that floor and hold on to her smells and not look at the splintered doorframe and sleep again forever this time.

But Life already has you by the balls 'cause you blew it when you went to the bathroom to pee. You may not have known it at the time, but from that point on, you were stuck, you were going to have to stay alive.

So one thing leads to another which is always the hell of it. Before you know it you're back from the coffeeshop and a brief walk that you also got conned into by Life. So then you have to face the loft. At this point, see, you *still* want to go lie down on her pallet and die, but by now Life has siphoned energy into you—all that fucking food and coffee, soap, water, fresh air. So you know damned well if you lie down you won't sleep. You'll think. And that's one of the absolutely worst things Life can do to you. So you get the brandy bottle which might help but there's nothing left in it. So you look around and say to yourself, Well, before I go out again, maybe I'll clean things up a bit so I won't trip on something later when I finish the next bottle which I'll go out and get myself as a reward for cleaning things up. See? See how it works? Life, I mean? See what a conniving sneak it is?

Now at some point in this cleaning-up you discover the phone is off the hook, so you put it back on. At that moment, Life is probably sitting over in the corner next to It, laughing its ass off. Because sure enough, just a minute after you hang up the phone—it rings.

Well. You could always not answer it. But that doesn't make sense because then why did you bother to hang it back up in the first place? Maybe you should take it off the hook again. But you can't do that till it stops ringing, can you. Besides, tape recorder, there's something way down inside all this time terrified Jule's hurt or dead or crazy or runover somewhere. So you answer the phone. That's the kind of thing Life does to you.

And it's her and the conversation I already told about. And you even say, though you don't want to, "Would you like me to come up there and be with you?" And you hope to god she'll say yes and you hope to god she'll say no and there's silence. Then she says, "Thanks. But I'm okay."

So you know that Iliana or some of her women friends are with her. So you tell her to let you know if there's anything you can do. She says yes she will.

That's that.

Then it's no use anymore going out to get more brandy, because nothing you can imagine or invent would stop the pain you're feeling anyway. So you walk through the loft like you were in a slow-motion film. You look at things. Her comb. The brass bowl that was a wedding present. The first head you tried to sculpt of her, profile against the wind like a ship's figurehead. Not a good piece. But she'd never let you chuck it out. You look at everything: the floorboards the two of you sanded and finished together, the ceiling bump left where the two of you tore down a wall. The wall the two of you later built together, too. You see the old mask she claimed for her own, the mirrored kid's face with the stake in the skull, still hanging on her wall. There's nothing you don't see.

Finally, you come in here, because there's no place else to come. You look around here, too. You see the cages, the prisons, the jails you and she were in, separately and together. You see It, in all that pristine marble virginity. You pull the tarp off Its nakedness. You walk around It, just looking at the grain.

Then you realize it's night again and you look at the clock but either it or time has stopped, because years have gone by but not enough hours. So you go out for another walk and the brandy, and think tomorrow's paper should be out and maybe you'll get the paper and that'll occupy your mind for a few minutes. So you do. And you know what Life pulls on you this time, tape recorder? The date of the paper. October 7. This dawn, today, is Julian's birthday.

Yeah. That's right. We were married just before she turned twenty, though she'd thought she was going to turn nineteen that year, until she met David and he neatly hacked a year off her life. Yeah. Hope is dying on Jule's birthday. Art can't get away with stuff like that, tape recorder, you know it and I know it. But Life doesn't give a shit about realism, it makes things up as it goes along.

So at last you find yourself back here. And you get out your old friend—that's you, tape recorder—to talk with again. Because something is changing inside and tells you to get it down before it gets lost or forgotten.

I want to forgive myself.

I want to forgive everybody. Hope—she's dying, after all. I'd like to have compassion for her. God, I'd like that. But then I think how Hope managed to fix things in Jule's mind so there never would be a child with Julian's and my features together all faceted, polished, liberated, in one face. So I lose it—whatever compassion I might have had for Hope Travis. Maybe eventually I can not hate her anymore. But compassion, no. Not for Hope, who refused to free Julian, *and* me, by ever once saying "This is my belovèd daughter, in whom I am well pleased."

I'd like to not hate Iliana, too. Strange, I really liked her once. I think I half-knew even then that she was helpless in loving Julian. In some roundabout way, I understood that. Of course, understanding was easy enough when Julian was mine and not hers. Easy to be compassionate about someone who wants what you have. If they actually take it away from you, though, that cuts a wedge into the compassion-capacity, if you know what I mean, tape recorder.

I know she's a lifelong exile. I know that must be its own kind of horror, different from feeling yourself an exile in your own fucking country—like me. So. You can't go home again, what else is new. David was an exile, too, but look at the damage he managed to do. Am I supposed to feel compassion for *him?* Hell with it. I've been his whipping-boy for too many years. Far as I'm concerned, he's one of those that got away with the characteristics of the guys he got away from. There've been moments when I've wished he hadn't got away at all.

But then there wouldn't have been Julian. I guess the time'll come when I won't hate her, either. I'd even say it's already here, but I'm afraid to do that. Afraid the hate will ooze in through some back window and possess me all over again, and all I want is to be free of it, to heal.

I'd like to not hate *me* anymore. I'd like to have compassion for *me.* Not pity. Compassion.

That's a lot of work ahead, all that forgiveness and compassion for all those people. Christ. It exhausts you just to think about it. Well, I figure I have to start somewhere. So I'll start with Laurence Millman.

That's why I turned you on, tape recorder, but I didn't know it then. All I knew was that this time there'd be no hope of her eavesdropping on you, no hope of her finding messages I left behind. She's gone now, somewhere far off, head into the wind, hair flying, my proud warrior queen. I'm the only one who can say how it should go from here on in. That's how Life tricks you.

So I say that I'm not going to open this new bottle of brandy right now. That's what I say.

I say . . . I'm going to turn you up as high as you can go, tape recorder, so you can hear this. Because I'm going to get up from this table, right now . . . and I'm going over here, to get the chisel and mallet . . . and here, to get the work apron, and . . . I hope you're still picking me up, tape machine, but *God oh God I'm alive this feels good,* it doesn't even matter if my voice can't reach back to you, because *I* know what it is I'm doing, going over . . . here, to *It,* no not It, just the last *no the first* piece of marble, and I'm going to make something again with these hands. I'm going to make something beautiful, something that sings. I'm going to give birth to something. I'm going to give birth to myself. *Now.*

* * *

Now, Momma. Now that we're holding on to each other and we've rested for a little, we might be ready to do the next thing that will help. Remember it's me, Momma, Julian, talking into you, Hope and Hokhmah, *klayne libe, klayne Hokheleh.* You're not alone in there.

Let's try to release the knot in your forehead, Momma. Let's relax it very slowly so it doesn't have to worry or be scared anymore. Feel my breath on it. It doesn't have to concentrate on pain. It can remember other things. It can remember us together, laughing and planning, the two of us against the world.

Remember feeding the ducks in the park pond? The momma and her ducklings in a row behind her, looking over her back to make sure they were all safe? Remember how one little duckling always would begin to wander off, paddling to the left or to the right in the water, bumping into a lily pad or a floating leaf, and you and I would laugh at it? And how the mother duck would *Creeak* out a warning and the duckling would look so surprised at having been missed, and then would paddle quickly back toward its mother?

Remember that spring you let me make a tiny garden in our favorite corner of the park, Momma? You bought me some anemone seeds and I planted them under the Japanese maple tree so we'd know where they were. Every Sunday we'd go check to see if they came up. But they never did, and you and I tried so hard to figure out why. I wouldn't believe they still might not come up, until finally the whole spring and summer had gone by. Then I believed. Then I cried and you held me, remember, Momma? You held me the way I'm holding you now, and you said "Dry your—" You said, "Don't cry, Baby. Let them go, they're growing somewhere. It's not that easy to kill a seed. Sometimes they can lie dormant for years and then, without anybody knowing why, just sprout and grow and bud and bloom." That's what you said, Momma. "Let them go. They're growing somewhere." And you were right.

So let the knot go, let the knot bloom out into an end of pain.

I know you can do it, Momma. I saw you do it just a day ago. You looked at me, and you knew it was me, and the knot dissolved. Your whole face lit up with glory, the way you look in the photograph taken when you were seventeen in Mexico.

So I know you can do it, especially if we try together, reaching for one another through all the mist and echo, through all the memory.

Let's remember how we'd bake cookies and go window-shopping, how we'd plan our future and our fortune. No no, don't knot it tighter, Hope, let it go, release it. Don't be afraid of that memory. Don't . . . don't be afraid of having told me, "Dry your smile."

All that's forgiven, Momma. All that's finally understood.

This is Julian telling you so.

You loved me. You did whatever you knew how, to show that. You survived what David did, yes, *yes* you did *that's good release it a little more now.* You saved your baby. *Yes,* your baby is safe, sleeping, in the crib, loving you. You raised your baby, celebrated her the best you knew how, white lilacs on her birthday so she'd know how you loved her. I knew. Remember how I used to say you were the best mother in the whole world? *Yes, oh that's better, that's good,* release it a bit more now, let the knot go, let it bloom into light all over your face.

It was you I loved, you all along. In my genes, my features, my name, in the invention of me: you. In my poems, my politics, my dreams. It's you I forgive, you I'm holding now.

Forgive . . . forgive me, too? For what I've done to you and not done, meant and not meant, said and left silent. See? We can be anything we want. We can even forgive each other.

Because I do love you, Momma, *yes that's it* I always have and always will *yes let it go* and hear me say to you for all time that I know you loved me *yes*.

Thank you, Momma. You have such courage inside there where they claim you can't hear or feel a thing.

Now. I know you must be very tired. So much work for so long.

But reach, only once more, *up up up* through the darkness to where I'm reaching down through all your surfaces, telling you that you can do this one last thing, because you're not alone.

It's me here with you. We can do this together. *Come.*

*   *   *

Agnus Dei, qui tollis peccata mundi: miserere nobis.

Have mercy on her, God. Have mercy on my Juliana.

It's been twenty-seven hours now, at this death vigil. The daughter's eyes are almost as sunken in her head as the mother's. She's been at that bedside ceaselessly since we got here yesterday morning. Now it's dawn again. Santa María, it's her birthday now, and I don't think she even knows it. I don't think either remembers that one gave birth to the other on this day.

Dies irae, dies illa, Solvet saeclum in favilla . . . how long can the mother go on like this? She lies there, already more dead than living. Skin a transparent yellow like the beeswax church candles I remember as a child, her face already more skull than expression, hardly a flicker of any flame left in her. Breath rasping in heaves, sometimes stopping completely for four or five seconds. Each time, I think *there*, it is done. Then comes another whistle of agony, another inhalation. With every pause, Juliana freezes, her own breath suspended. Her body, that I would wrap in my heart for warmth, goes motionless, waiting—like my childhood saints, statues at the altar and stained-glass lenses for the light, kneeling—waiting for Judgment Day, for the world to end and the new life to begin.

Kyrie eleison, I do not believe. I left your churches and your sacraments, your priests who damned me and would damn me still for loving this small woman who hovers by her mother's dying. For loving as I do each part of her, soul, mind, and body, what gleams in her and what lies shadowed. For this they tell me I am damned. I left all that behind me, going for years now into your churches only for the art, the music, the moment's rest. *Agnus Dei,* mistake me not. This is not a return. For me there is no return to where I saw your bishops bless your generals while the festive blood martyred in my homeland flushed the gutters clean. Mistake me not. *Non credo in unum Deum,* not anymore, *Non laudemus te, Non adoramus te.*

It is her I praise, bless, adore, glorify. It is her. *Ave Maria, gratia pleni,* it is to You I turn, You who understands.

How long can she go on? How has she not collapsed? Strange sadistic miracle that keeps Julian going, driven like one possessed. No detail escapes her. She whispers into the mother's unhearing brain words she has found and studied for this moment. I have watched her these weeks, whenever I saw her, always carrying with her the books. The Kaddish. The Tibetan Book of the Dead. The Egyptian Book of the Dead. Carrying her scripts with her always for the studying. Carrying her dead with her everywhere.

She found a woman rabbi, my little atheist Juliana. She learned what Hebrew words to say, what they pray over their dying, what they do for their last confession. Yiddish words she learned, too, any words she could find in any language Hope might understand.

"Why," I would ask her, "why drive yourself this way? Hope will not know at the last. Hope will not care. Of what use is studying about a Primary Clear Light of this First Bardo in the Tibetan Book of the Dead? Juliana," I would plead, "come with me and sleep a few hours instead. Have mercy on yourself, give yourself peace."

But she would shake her head, small head so heavy with grief my breasts would ache from longing to feel its weight.

Everything had to be prepared. She arranged for the eyes to go, when the time would come, to the eye bank. "Why?" I asked her. "What is the point? Let the body rest, Juliana."

"To be of use," she would mutter. Possessed. Driven. Beyond my reach.

She had even called the father. I heard her, on my phone. At my apartment she did it. Santa María, such dignity in that voice.

"David," she said, "don't be alarmed. I want nothing of you. I want only to tell you that Hope is very ill. They say she has weeks now to live. In case you wanted to see her . . . before. I doubt she would know you, so you needn't be afraid. Nor should you misunderstand me. I am not requesting that you visit her. I merely thought you should have the option, if there was a need in you, so that afterward you would not regret . . ."

But he said no. No, she said he'd told her, in his stiff manner, thank you I see no need. Her father. My father. *Patrem omnipotentem.* And all the while, Laurence, stiff in his own suffering. How can this be, *Mater Dolorosa?* How can they permit such pain to shriek out before their eyes, such blood to rinse their gutters? How can they turn their faces always from us?

If I could make her eat something, drink something other than the containers of black coffee she asks me to bring her. If I could make her sleep, even for an hour.

"I will watch for you," I say. "I have slept. You have not. *Let* me. Let me take some of the weight. I will wake you the instant anything changes—her breathing, her color, anything."

But she shakes her head. She looks at me with eyes like her mother's. Eyes she will have plucked from her mother's sockets and set in someone else's head so someone else can see. See *what,* Juliana? The resurrection of the dead and the life of the world to come? The blood of this world, running into gutters of blindness? You must learn when to stop, I say. But she looks at me through those eyes and shakes her head.

Ave Maria, let it be finished, so we can begin again, so I can take her home—*home*—with me and teach her how to live. She's going to be with me now. *Sanctus, sanctus, hosanna in excelsis.*

I will make her laugh again, I swear it. I will feed her and stroke her head and let her sleep. I will bathe that body with my love. Mornings we will have, and noons. Slow subtle evenings and rich nights. A real life. For how long have I waited for this through how many nights alone, or alone in the arms of another? For how long, crying to the darkness *Libera me, Do-*

mine, de morte aeterna! But she has come to me at last, my Juliana. *Lux aeterna.* Mine now.

Not much longer, surely. See how she croons over the mother, strokes her, rocks slowly backward and forward, her lips whispering without pause to a woman who cannot hear. This is what we do, we daughters.

And the other lies there. Silent, distant, unhearing us, unseeing us, unknowing us, unanswering us. Having borne and forgotten us, never reclaiming us, never permitting us readmission. We seek her, we daughters, we seek her in ourselves and in each other, in the breast and the round of belly, in the line of hip and the flash of eye. We search her out where she hides from us, is hidden from us by the fathers. We search for the curve of throat, the arc of wrist, the glance, the beckoning. We strain to hear the sound of her voice, calling us home. We tug at her hands, caress her nipples, spread her, open her, enter her, *home.* This is what we do, we daughters. We exiles. *Sueño, corazón, alma.* The body of the mother. *Let me hear you,* we cry, *let me smell you, touch you, taste you. Let me come home.*

For this you have burned us alive, *Rex majestatis!* The odor of singed flesh pleases your nostrils, not that of wild honey wept from our loving. You also seek her, your sons seek her, disrobe her, rape her. But you say we, the daughters, may not seek her. For this I turn from you eternally. But to You, Mystical Rose, Tower of Ivory, to You I appeal. Hear this daughter, O body of the mother, land of birth! Hear my offering!

Take me and thrust me from You forever. Take away my faith, my art, my laughter, take even *O Mater Dolorosa no* Yes take even Juliana's love from me if you must, forever. Plunge me into darkness eternal, eternal exile. Take away my soul, let it be spent in a lifetime's care for, sacrifice for, Juliana. Take what You wish. I have nothing else to offer. But let the agony be finished. Let Juliana be free of it, free of all these deaths, all these mournings. Let her be free—*no, I can't bear it, I can't bear losing her again, no*—free—*I must offer it, it's all I have*—free of both the living and the dead *vivos et mortuos* even—*I must*—of me. Free of me.

If that is Your will. If You can accept no other offering.

But have mercy upon us. If this sacrifice must be, let me have a little time. To make Juliana whole again. To teach her how to live again. My child.

Let Juliana be born today, no seventh veil masking that beauty, no shadow blinding that smile.

Take back into Yourself the mother. *Requiem aeternam dona eis.*

And let the daughter go.

* * *

We're ready now, Hope.

It's me, still here beside you. You're not alone.

I know you're in there. You know I'm with you.

So reach up to me one last time.

One last effort now. *Up up* to where I'm reaching down for you. Hold to this voice, this link. Here is the strength to complete the journey.

Tired, yes, I know. But it isn't long now. *You can do it.* You can be anything you want to be. Hear me, hear my singing to you.

It's a lullaby. Remember? *Lullaby and goodnight, may the angels watch over you.* You can hear me. Try . . .

Yes.

These are some words for you to use, Hokhmah, *klayne libe, klayne Hokheleh.* Let them help you.

Shema Yisroel, adonai elohenu adonai achod, amen selah.

You know those words. Let them drift down through you. Let them fall like a soft rain of light drenching the darkness.

Send to this woman perfect healing, take her in love. Grant her the abundant good held in store for the righteous. All her sins and transgressions have been of love. Give her new life, replete with joy, forever.

Yis-ga-dal ve-yis-ka-dash she-may raba . . .

No more suffering now, Hokhmah, no more, not ever.

So tired . . . But you can do it, *klayne libe. Just a little more now.* You're not alone.

Don't be afraid. I'm with you. It's been me all along.

Reach *up up up* just a little more, you have the courage precise to this moment, *you have the strength, I'm sending it down to you.*

Feel me . . . *Yes.* You can hear me singing to you, *may the angels watch over you . . .*

Klayne Hokheleh, libe, can you see it now? *See the light streaming down to you,* clear and singing? It's all for you.

No more hurting, no more being tired.

Now you can let it all go, release it, petals floating through your fingers, memories falling from the flower's center, free, *it's time,* no more heaviness. *Only this lightness now,* forever. Only this *warm singing light* that you can touch, feel, hear, see. *This is what you'll always see now,* this is what you'll never stop seeing . . . Blessèd be, *meina klayne libe. This is the threshold.*

Now you can let go *yes* you can do it, you can leave all the rest behind you now *yes that's right you're letting go* isn't it *yes* radiance and music and warmth now . . . *zeit gazunt . . .*

I love you. I've always loved you.

Now you can enter the light.

* * *

God! I'm dying, God! I must be finally giving birth! The baby's finally coming, God!

Such a long labor. They never tell you it'll be like this. Got to gather my strength up through all these layers, like smoke, like water. Hurts up near the heart. I must've been carrying the baby high. They say when you carry high it's always a boy.

Got to carry it till it's born and safe. Got to clench my fists till the nails dig into my palms; then I can feel I'm doing it. Flesh of my flesh.

But it's so alone here. Dark. Cold. Afraid. *Somebody help!* I call and call but nobody hears me. *Oh God, nobody even knows I'm in here!*

Such silence. Roars like a waterfall. Beats, pounds in my head, in my wrists. Wrists like a Mayan princess, he said. Who? David? Somebody said . . .

Somebody saying something . . . like a chorus singing with no . . . words? Somebody trying to get through? *Somebody knows I'm in here!* Who's trying . . . ? *Momma? Is that you?*

It must be Momma, she'd know I'm down here. She always loved me best, more than Yetta or Essie . . . wait . . . there it is again.

Somebody's trying to help. That means there's hope, that means I—Hope's my name! That's right, I remember. If you know your name you're not so scared. That means I can do it. Maybe it's not too late to begin singing again. God-given talent pouring out of me and spilling over packed audiences. Leaping to their feet, a roar of applause . . . maybe that's what the sound is? And flowers raining down to the stage, all the petals falling . . .

That must be it! And Momma calling through the applause *Hokhmah*. Telling me I should pick up the flowers they're throwing. And curtsy. So beautiful, all the petals misting from *up up up* in the balcony, each flower . . . *open, petals spread,* floating in such . . . *lightness.*

Dizzy, I'm so dizzy. Curtsying . . . I'll fall if I don't hold on to . . . something to grab hold of, the way a baby . . . I can almost feel . . . somebody reaching down here, in . . . my crib? Somebody . . . me reaching up, somebody reaching for her baby Hokhmah. That's me! I'm *Hokhmah!* No, the baby is . . . *Julian.*

That's what I'll call the baby—Julian. Full American he'll be, strength of the peasant, elegance of the aristocrat—mine. Seize the whole world in his tiny fist. *We can do it, you and me, together against the world.* So I can *let go, open my hands* the way a flower opens, ah . . .

Not so cold anymore. Maybe I can, after all, together with . . . Who? Is that . . . you, David? Oh, don't be silly, I don't know how to waltz. Oh, well, maybe if . . . ah, how I love your touch, your surgeon's fingers on my skin like that . . . David, David, how fast you whirl me! Darling, please, ah yes, lovely giddiness but . . . have to hold on tight to you or I'll fall. *Wait* . . . somebody calling . . . hard to hear, such a loud waltz! Somebody cutting in? Now don't be jealous, David, he's an old friend, he's . . . *linda* yes yes I know that's what you always called me but hush you shouldn't have cut in like that, David's my husband, you know, and I'm carrying his son . . . oh I've missed you, too, *te amo,* so lonely it's been without you . . .

I have to go now. Momma's calling me to do the chores. She likes it when I sing around the house. We bake cookies together and sometimes we go windowshopping. We sit at the kitchen table and eat black bread. *Klayne libe,* she calls me, that's Yiddish for "little love," and *klayne Hokheleh.* My Momma loves me more than Yetta or . . .

But she's not the best mother in the whole world. *I* am. I better check the baby. Look how beautiful he is, Julian my son . . . why, he's not a boy! He's . . . it's a fine baby girl! Is she—

Is that *me* in the crib, Momma? Or is— Look! Look at the talent pouring out of her like flowers from the balcony . . . *up up way so high.* No, look here, *they're growing right out from my fingers,* my hands are earth and my fingers stems with real flowers at each . . . I knew they weren't lost! Didn't I say so, Julian? Sometimes they sleep for years and then . . . I knew it all along! You did too, didn't you Julian? This is my own baby, my belovèd daughter . . . and *you* knew it, too, didn't you, Momma? I always loved you, how silly of you not to know that, Momma! 'Course you knew that, Julian! We couldn't have done it if we hadn't followed each other, looking back to make sure none of us got lost . . . Am I lost now? I just— Sometimes I wander off and then I . . . always surprised to find out somebody's missed me, looking for me to see I'm safe in the crib . . . is the baby all right? . . . She's the daughter of a rabbi, you know, the firstborn real American, that's why I have to carry her till I can set her down safe, strong and laughing and loving, her face like a bouquet of white lilacs, like a chart full of stars, stars on the dressingroom door stars floating from the balcony worn on the sleeve to show . . . Where's everybody gone?

It's getting dark again. Like the set before they say Lights up! and I give her a last hug and wish her "Good show, Baby!" and she runs from me onto the set, always pausing for a second to look back over her shoulder with such an odd expression I guess just to be sure I'm there, that I haven't wandered off. I gesture her *Go on* I gesture *You can do it* you can be anything I want you to be, and then she turns from me and next thing you know there she is under the lights all different, somebody else, somebody who doesn't even know me, doesn't know I'm in here . . . cold again, so tired.

They all leave you alone sooner or later . . . they go off and become somebody else . . . "You have the pulse of life in you," he said, roaring in my Mayan wrists in my Klimt throat booming like the silence when the clapping stops and the house is empty . . . empty without her, the set dim now and my face slick with tears and my body slick with sweat from her, heavy jewel in the casket of my heart, and I'm still *so far* away, so far from the phone across the room high *up up up* on the table . . . *trying* to reach you. But you waltz away, lilacs in your arms, hibiscus in your hair, *te amo* you say, touching my forehead in farewell, you turn your face from me, *whore* you say, you leave me *leave me* leave me alone, you don't want to share a bedroom with me, golden girl the lucky one, you follow the weak ones the men who send flowers but never mean to stay, the brothel-keepers where your own mother puts you . . .

Wait— What? Oh *where* . . . I don't care, I don't need anybody! A whore? Then I'll be Queen of the Whores! Roomfuls of flowers sprouting right up from the dust! Fame, wealth, applause, brothel-keepers rabbis surgeons begging for my favors . . . 'cept it's so cold, see? If only . . . if I could hear the *words* to the song.

Fragments, snatches of melody, never coming together whole anymore . . . *J'y vais pour mon enfant.* Where's that from, some opera? That's why it has to be different for the baby. You don't need college, what's college? Avraham got sent all through and still wasn't half so smart as me, he never had a fortune like me and my baby will. You got to work hard to get a fortune, it's the only way out . . . and then you got to burrow it away and watch the entrances so nobody— But then, all the time your head hurts like it's knotted up, so tired . . .

Crying in here, but . . . way *up up up* there *on the surface,* no . . . Better there's no tears, better you smile and have courage. *Think about happy things.* Momma loves to hear Julian singing, David plays the piano for me every time we go to Mexico, we'll have star billing on the door of an elevator apartment . . . I'm not like everybody else, I'm not thousands of women, I'm *me!*

Shema Yisroel, adonai elohenu . . .

I know those words. Someone's *singing,* is that my voice? If only, *oh if only*—if I could speak to you. *Trying* . . . did the best I could, all I knew how. No need for her to suffer. Why should she ever learn *any*body in the world wouldn't want her, my baby, my filthy-faced muffin, my anemone, why? *No more suffering,* I thought, *klayne libe.* Why did she hate me for that, how could—

There you are again, faint echo— Who? *Julian?* Julian came home? I always knew . . . Could you, oh . . . hard to say, hardest thing ever, could you . . . *trying* to reach you, *hear me,* could you *forgive* . . . *all my transgressions have been of love,* can't you see that, Baby?

'Course you always loved me, don't be silly. Come on, dry your smile, honey, we can do this hand in hand *I feel you,* may the angels watch over you . . . *Anges radieux* . . . See, Momma? I wasn't a whore, I was the best mother in the whole world.

Yis-ga-dal ve-yis-ka-dash she-may raba . . . Oh, listen! Somebody's saying Kaddish for you, Momma, somebody's lit a candle. I can see it! Way high up, far off . . . *Momma, I love you Momma,* just like Julian loves me. Can you— Can you forgive, too?

Where are you, Momma? I can hear you now! Through the plumes of . . . of crematoria smoke, the clapping, the echo, the hooves—Momma I can hear you calling!

Help me, Momma! I want to put the burden down now. *Klayne Hokheleh*—yes, sing down to me—*klayne libe, meina tokhter.* I'm coming up to you, Momma, trying to smile, be a real American. So sleepy now. Too tired to keep climbing this staircase that spirals up and up and never seems to end. Call me again, Momma! I'm scared. Help me get there, honest I'm reaching, but it's so heavy right under the heart.

Don't be afraid, I'm with you, you have the strength, I'm sending it down to you. That's you Momma calling down *I hear you* I feel you now, touching me, warmer, better and better, yes!

I can get there, *I can do it.* See? Oh! There's the candle, getting brighter . . . lots of candles? Light— Light streaming down to me . . . Somebody singing clearer now, *lullaby and goodnight* no more hurting, *no more being alone.* The stairs wind up and up but I can get there now *I feel you with me I know you're here.*

Momma! I can see you now! Up there on the landing against the light! It glows right through you. How beautiful you look, Momma! Strong and laughing and loving, walking toward me, holding out your hands, your fingertips radiating crescent moons. What's that behind you . . . *Oh!* A door . . . what a big room! A secret sacred room filled with people, sitting, rocking, standing in groups, talking quietly. Why do they one by one turn and look at me, smiling, Momma? Why do you call to them, "This is my belovèd daughter. Take her in love"? See, Momma? They point at me, they smile, beckon, nod to me and to each other. There's Poppa and Yetta and Essie and Avraham, too. Such light in there, all golden and singing. The light *sings*.

Can I rest on the landing, Momma? Behind me . . . all those winding stairs . . . But this—it's not a landing. It's the top of the stairs . . . Momma?

Now you can let it all go. This time, *meina tokhter,* you can *release it,* set the burden down, memories falling from the flower's center. *It's time.* No more heaviness. *Only this lightness now, forever.*

Momma, is it finally true? Honest? And you always knew anyway?

Always, *klayne libe.* I always knew you'd come home. *This is the threshold.* This is what you'll always see now—this warm, singing light that you can touch, feel, hear. This is what you'll never stop seeing. Turn and look down one last time, *meina tokhter.*

Zeit gazunt hibiscus, anemone, lilac, Mario David whole world waltzing and curtsying, everyone applauding each other, everybody scared, separate and hurting, hiding, crawling for help, crying and being tired, *farewell. Zeit gazunt* suffering, smoke, bone, wealth, blood, water, fame, war, flesh, echo, dust, wisdom, hope. *Zeit gazunt.*

Yes, that's right, set the burden down, *you're letting go.* All radiance and warmth and singing light now, here and forever, yes. *I love you. I've always loved you.*

Now, Momma? Now can I come in?

Now you can enter the light.

PART SIX

June, 1986

Writing the novel failed to reassure me.

For one thing, Ashley or Leigh—or whatever I would eventually wind up naming the real-life Julian character—still didn't love herself. She had learned to like herself a bit. But in that cavernous maw of the heart, that secret desert where not all the terraced gardens of ego so shallowly rooted can conceal aridity, there she still failed to comprehend what loving herself could be. *I* had learned to love her. But then, she was my only child, my belovèd daughter in whom I was well pleased.

But here it was, already June. Completion of the novel was an alarming prospect, publishing it a terrifying one. Every woman has her own story like this. But I would be ruining my credibility by telling the truth.

I made myself another cup of tea, prudently saving the leaves to spread over the rosebush bases upstairs in the garden. "Upstairs in the Garden"—not bad for a book title, that. Sipping the tea, I wandered back toward my desk. There had to be some way to end it. Or at least to begin it.

A breeze from the open window fluttered a clipping pinned to the wall free, and it drifted to a landing on the desk. That lovely W. H. Auden quote: "In an earlier age . . . the real meant 'sacred' or 'numinous.' A real person was not a personality but someone playing a sacred role, apart from which he or she might be nobody. A real act was some sacred rite by the reenactment of which the universe and human life were sustained in being, and reborn."

Take the tea, I told myself as I would a character, and *go up to your hortus conclusus, your sanctuary.* Fortunately, I obey myself when I give me a direct order—unlike my characters, who have vexingly independent minds of their own. I shuffled toward the door, weaving through the cats—Lynn Fontanne, Katharine Cornell, and Floppy Disc.

The garden.

Not an imitation of the Laurence-and-Julian roof; not an approximation of the Iliana country weekends; not a mimicry of the childhood public park or the Sutton Place longed-for window boxes or the plants in other people's apartments. The garden.

A cloud of finches and sparrows rose in noisy dispersion, deserting their bird-feeder as a human appeared on the roof. Through their circling flutter and across the low neighboring buildings, an orange-hyacinth sunset was beginning to glow above the Hudson River. I sat down on one of the lawn chairs.

The roses were in riot. White Queen, fine as bleached linen. The palest saffron of New Dawn. Double Delight, in its spirals of carnelian and cream. And—*luxe, calme, et volupté* in perfume, shade, and texture—the Crimson Glory. Wisteria vines trailed up the overhead trellis, in places twining with burgundy clematis climbing from the far side. The silver jasmine bush was in first bloom, generously exhaling its essence on the summer air. The cascade azalea was in last bloom, dropping blossoms almost as languidly as the hanging basket of fuchsia. Trumpets of tangerine-colored hibiscus—which everyone warned me couldn't be grown in a pot on a roof—blared their final exuberance before folding themselves in for the night. Across from them, climbing the chimney, the morning glories were prepared to do the opposite—reveal their sapphire and indigo cups later, when night would melt toward dawn, then shyly tuck themselves under again in the glare of tomorrow.

Peach-brazen snapdragons exulted next to hardy petunias; the basin with gypsophila and cornflowers rallied a miniature women's suffrage garden—white, green, and purple. Strawberries, tomatoes, zucchini, watercress, sorrel, and green snapbeans promised a lush harvest. The cactus collection bristled its spines with pride. Rosemary, parsley, basil, the mints, thyme, catnip, bay leaves—I could smell the herbs' pungency green on the river breeze.

"To us, little garden," I toasted aloud with my teacup. "To this moment."

If it were possible to immerse oneself wholly in the present, tragedy couldn't exist. Tragedy requires the past and the future. Tragedy requires history.

So I offered another toast. "To Laurence. And to Iliana. And to Hope."

Goodbye, I thought, goodbye to all my loves and selves and masks and the loss of them, there, where they recede in rose-lavender light bled by the sunset. Goodbye . . .

I was not surprised to see them appear from the three other corners of the roof and slowly approach me where I sat, behind the nonexistent fourth wall of the set.

Out from behind the hibiscus, the little girl, a tattered book under her arm, her dress torn and muddy, her face grinning beneath a long scratch from under the eye to the chin.

Out from behind the jasmine, the young woman in a jade-green suit, clutching a piece of paper and carrying beige high-heeled shoes but walking in stockinged feet, hair touseled as if by a high river wind.

Out from behind the rosebush exclaiming crimson glories, the middle-aged woman clasping the Tibetan Book of the Dead in one hand and hefting a suitcase in the other, looking as if she hadn't slept much lately.

"Welcome," I said to them. "Welcome to the garden. Thank you for coming in person to say goodbye."

The child broke her formal advance and ran straight into my arms so we could burst into tears together, the blood and dirt on her small round face smudging onto mine. When she finally wriggled back to peek at me, I thought with a shock: *Why, she's shy!*

Then she smiled, and it was her own smile, one I'd never seen before. Wordlessly, she shoved her book into my lap. I looked down at the flyleaf. "For Bunker," she had scrawled, "with love, your friend, Julian Travis."

My child. My real child, hiding your loneliness, secreting your rebellions, laughing where you can, making it up as you go along. My littlest, fighting self.

When I looked up to thank her, she was gone.

But the young girl stood near now, hair parted in the middle and brushed loosely back, the way her mother had worn her hair when she too had been young. Chin tilted proudly upward, shoulders squared, feet sure-footed on the roof surface, free of their rejected shoes.

Neither of us knew quite what to do, embrace or shake hands. Then, in a gesture at once obsequious and imperious, she thrust at me the paper she was carrying. It had a city registrar's seal on it, the words Birth Certificate printed across the top. Just underneath, she had neatly lettered: "Notes for a Novel." The rest of the page was blank.

My daughter, learning as you go, seeking the phantoms and slaying the ghosts, fearing your life ahead but wanting desperately to get on with living it, already loving words on a page.

When I glanced back to thank her for her long-ago clues left so painstakingly about, she too had disappeared.

The last of the three trudged with a weary step. But even as I reached to help her with her suitcase, she moved past me unseeing, her eyes fixed on how color died along the sunset, darker amethyst now slashing the heliotrope of the lower sky. Intent on placing one foot in front of another, she didn't acknowledge me, her twin, her doppelgänger, her double, unreal as her shadow cast on a moonless night.

My . . . sister. Obsessed with discovering what is real, then preoccupied with raging against what is false, *now* are you ready? But I couldn't catch her, reach her in time to fold her in my arms before she dimmed into the river sky and vanished.

Dear Julian, dear professional, so expert at ventriloquating yourself into others' realities you have never faced your own, are *you* ready?

Dear burned-out baby star twinkling in the American dream firmament, now can you chart your splendid new constellation?

Dear coward, dear tactician, trooper, counterfeiter of the affirmations and the subterfuge, now can you concede who it was your deadliest battles were staged against?

Dear guilty sullen martyr, now can you see where you stand in the chain? What longs to be visible but is erased, what vows to survive but is converted, what yearns to hide but is displayed, what strives to contain but is broached. Hope, David,

Laurence, Iliana. What preens to disguise but is exposed. Julian. And all of us were simply children once.

With every breath, we try to endure by spilling over the borders of others. Infiltrations. Occupations. Annexations.

But I refuse to believe in borders. Borders are delusions. I affirm one planet, interdependent, unified.

Ah. *Well* then, Julian.

In the clarifying dusk, a lisianthus flower abruptly detaches itself from its stem, unfurls white organdy appliquéd wings, and flits to the Crimson Glory, then circles my head once and shimmers off. Blossom or butterfly? Artifice or art? By the eclipsing light I can barely make out the title of the book the child has given me: *Dry Your Smile.*

"Too late," I laugh aloud, and can taste in my laughter the smart of salt washing my face. "It was Kafka—in the book Momma gave me when I was only ten—who wrote 'The catastrophe we fear has already occurred.' Momma gave me. Momma. Too late, too late," I laugh.

The sun surrenders its splendor to the horizon. Unafraid of me now, the finches and sparrows return to their feeder, alighting upwinged, innocent, in victory silhouettes. A frond of wisteria, wind-detached from the trellis, waves, reaching for me unthreateningly. The dwarf Japanese maple settles into evening, dowager in her burnt-sienna lace. Each of the succulents is something else: an emerald rose, Zen pebbles; one cactus sports a bishop's mitre, another postures itself a Doric column draped in ermine. Somewhere, the chameleon who lives among the cactus pots is blatantly invisible. The begonia and the willowy freesia belie their squat bulbous origins. A first evening star winks—from the past, where it novaed long ago?

At the edge of the day, at the edge of the stage, at the edge of the grave, at the edge of the self, at the edge of the world.

Oh, exquisite theater of the universe, trickster, illusionist, there is nothing you cannot perform. Dear Blue Planet, theater in the round, dear Life, play-within-a-play. Give me to know that I am blessed by being rooted so firmly in my unreality as to now dare celebrate the self who never was and ever shall be, world without end, amen.

I know now that I need not worry how to finish it. I would go —defiant, laughing, freely celebrating what I will never understand, to build a fire in the fireplace, right in the middle of summer—and burn the manuscript, page by lying, truthful page.

If there were such pages. If a manuscript had ever existed.

I know, too, smile streaming with tears, that I need no longer worry about writing this particular book. We are free of each other, it and I, forgiven, at peace.

There is no reason now to write it at all.

The miracle we seek has already transformed us.